SWEPT AWAY

"I want to," he said raggedly. "I want to so bad, I'm dying for it. Don't ever think I don't want to. Just . . . just don't ever think that."

"OK. I won't." She nuzzled Simon's throat, kissed the sharp point of his jaw, stroked his scratchy beard stubble. "So what's the problem? You want to, I want to. No lies, promises, no illusions."

His dark eyes were tormented, full of shadows, but when she pulled his face down to hers, he didn't resist.

They both jolted at the bright shock of contact, and that was it. They were lost, swept away. El wasn't kissing him, or being kissed. The kiss held them both in its grip, had its own urgent, demanding life. It moved, ebbed and flowed like a dance of sweet, desperate abandon.

She was giddy.

BOOK YOUR PLACE ON OUR WEBSITE AND MAKE THE READING CONNECTION!

We've created a customized website just for our very special readers, where you can get the inside scoop on everything that's going on with Zebra, Pinnacle and Kensington books.

When you come online, you'll have the exciting opportunity to:

- View covers of upcoming books
- Read sample chapters
- Learn about our future publishing schedule (listed by publication month *and author*)
- Find out when your favorite authors will be visiting a city near you
- Search for and order backlist books from our online catalog
- Check out author bios and background information
- Send e-mail to your favorite authors
- Meet the Kensington staff online
- Join us in weekly chats with authors, readers and other guests
- Get writing guidelines
- AND MUCH MORE!

**Visit our website at
http://www.kensingtonbooks.com**

SHANNON McKENNA

RETURN TO ME

KENSINGTON BOOKS
KENSINGTON PUBLISHING CORP.
http://www.kensingtonbooks.com

KENSINGTON BOOKS are published by

Kensington Publishing Corp.
850 Third Avenue
New York, NY 10022

All Kensington titles, imprints and distributed lines are
available at special quantity discounts for bulk purchases for
sales promotion, premiums, fund-raising, educational or in-
stitutional use.

Special book excerpts or customized printings can also be
created to fit specific needs. For details, write or phone the
office of the Kensington Special Sales Manager: Kensington
Publishing Corp., 850 Third Avenue, New York, NY 10022.
Attn. Special Sales Department. Phone: 1-800-221-2647.

Kensington and the K logo Reg. U.S. Pat. & TM Off.

First Trade Paperback Printing: June 2004
First Mass Market Paperback Printing: March 2005
10 9 8 7 6 5 4 3 2 1

Printed in the United States of America

Chapter

1

Simon Riley cut the motor and coasted his bike to the shoulder of the road as soon as he topped the rise that led down into the LaRue River Valley. He pulled the helmet off to let the hot wind dry the sweat in his long, tangled black hair and billow out the jacket of his riding leathers. He needed a minute, or maybe ten, just to stare down at the town of LaRue, pull himself together and muster his nerve.

The cold clench in his gut was no surprise to him. Neither was the catch in his breath at how beautiful this place was. No matter how far he traveled, nothing in the world was like this green river valley in the foothills of the Cascade Mountains.

There was nothing like this feeling, either. The electric shiver of disaster in the making, like watching a baby trying to stick a fork into a light socket. Or maybe he brought the danger with him. God knows, he never meant to, but it came down around his ears every goddamn time.

The place looked so mellow, like nothing had happened here for the entire seventeen years he'd been gone. Wouldn't take long, though. Something here had it in for him. As soon as that something sniffed out Simon Riley's presence, it was going to wake right up and roll over.

A burst of laughter shook him. *Look out, LaRue. Fun's over.*

He took off his shades as he looked around. The colors and sounds and smells of this place prodded a part of his brain awake that had been buried for years under the hustle and noise of his chaotic life. The sultry aroma of peaches fermenting under a tree by the side of the road, a tangle of foliage choking a drainage ditch, the hypnotic drone of insects. The sharp-sweet tang of yarrow and balsam root, pine and fir.

A sultry, nose-tickling mélange. Home.

He knew this place so well. He'd explored every hill and gully, every canyon and rock and cave. Property lines and barbed wire fences had meant nothing to him back when he was a kid running wild.

He'd imagined himself brother to snakes and lizards, coyotes and bobcats, eagles and owls, even the occasional cougar that ventured down from the higher reaches of the Cascades. He'd imagined that they accepted him as one of their own, made a place for him in their world.

The way El had made a place for him.

He pushed the thought of El away. He was edging too close to overload already. Besides, being accepted by lizards and bobcats and one lovestruck teenage girl didn't carry much weight when you were rejected by everyone else. Though in retrospect, to give them credit, he hadn't handled their rejection that well. He'd always overreacted. Freaked out, fucked things up, made things worse.

You know you're just hurting yourself, Simon.

Those words rang in his ears seventeen years later. He'd heard them so often, from the guidance counselor, the school principal, the sheriff, the harried lady from Children's Services, just to name a few.

What the hell. He hadn't listened to them then, so why listen to them now? Simon Riley was home, and gearing up to hurt himself with all the wild abandon that was his birthright.

His eyes searched for the ravine that threaded down between McNary Ridge and Horsehead Bluff, the ragged line that led down to Gus's house. He blocked the sun with his hand and tried to breathe away the ache in his belly. It hung there, heavy and cold as a lump of lead. Too deep below the surface to be eased by any of his usual tricks.

Years back, he'd dreamed about a triumphal homecoming. In his fantasies, Gus was the way he'd been back when Simon was a little kid, before he'd crawled deep into the bottle. That Gus had opened the door for him and nodded with the silent approval Simon had felt on his skin whenever he did anything that Gus thought was praiseworthy.

Then Gus would slap together a meal of elk steaks, pan-fried potatoes and onions, biscuits, sun-ripened salted tomato slices and a beer. After they ate, he'd pull out one of those blocks of dark chocolate that he kept in the locked pantry shelf, far from thieving little-boy hands. He'd use the cleaver to hack a chunk into splinters to pick at off the cutting board. The two of them would let shards of bitter dark sweetness melt in their mouths like pure redemption as the kitchen grew dim and the time came to light the kerosene lantern.

And then, as shadows flickered and shifted on the wall, Simon would recount his adventures over the years since he'd run off. All the ways in which he had finally proven his worth.

But there would be no quiet approval or elk steak or chocolate. Gus had eaten his last meal five months ago, a .45 caliber bullet from his CPA auto. There would be no prodigal nephew's return for him. Just a silent, desolate house. The sheer, fucking, maddening *waste* of it all.

He wasn't even sure why he'd come back here at all. It was one of those blind impulses that had always gotten him neck-deep in trouble. Gus was five months gone, his body cremated. It had taken a long time for the news to make it to Afghanistan. It had shot his concentration all to hell. He'd started having the fire dream again. A roaring, ravenous circle of fire that closed in on him from all sides.

What had happened to Gus didn't square with his memories of his uncle. Nor did it square with the cryptic e-mail that Gus had sent him on the day he died. That e-mail had sounded like the ravings of a paranoid madman, yes, but not a defeated, suicidal madman.

So here he was. Financially, he could afford a break. He'd never cared much about money, but he'd managed to make a lot of it, running the risks that he did. It just sat in the bank and accumulated, since it seldom occurred to him to spend it. Returning to LaRue was an idea to approach gradually, ease into gently, so he'd flown to New York and bought the bike. Three thousand miles of highway was a bare minimum of lead-in time, and he'd spent it trying to justify the impulse.

He had to find out what had happened to Gus. Flip the finger to everyone who'd written him off as a loser. Thank the people who had been kind to him. El alone was worth a journey of twelve thousand miles. His memories of El were so bright, they shone.

Oh, shit. It was impossible not to think about El when his belly ached like this. He'd gotten deep into the habit of thinking about El to comfort himself when he felt bad. The habit was backfiring on him.

All that time on the road still hadn't braced him to give up his El fantasies and replace them with reality. There had been times when those fantasies had been his only refuge. A man had to have some safe place to go, even if it was only inside his own head. It was like not wanting to see a favorite book made into a movie for fear it would obscure his own mental images, only he knew the end of this movie would be different. And it was all just a head game anyway.

So reality would be hard. So it would hurt. Surprise, surprise.

He couldn't bully his mind into submission today. It was running wild, wherever it wanted to go, and it wanted El. His fantasy El, the only other person in all of LaRue who'd given a damn about him. Gus had cared for him, when he wasn't too drunk. He'd shown it with a gruff scrap of praise, or a dry, private joke shared between the two of them.

But El's devotion had needed no hopeful interpreting. It was there for him whenever he wanted it, like the air he breathed. Constant, and sweet, and taken completely for granted.

Since he left LaRue, he'd taken nothing else for granted.

He shaded his eyes and squinted out at the grassy hills that hemmed the valley in, baked a deep, metallic gold. The handsome house that El Kent had grown up in was visible from the highway, perched on the bluff in an oasis of lush green landscaping and forever looking down its nose at Gus's ramshackle house in the ravine below.

Kent House was a fancy hotel now. He knew that much from a random search for El's name on the Internet. It had landed him on a page on fine hoteliers in the Pacific Northwest.

> *Kent House is a gracious Bed & Breakfast perched on a hillside overlooking the LaRue River . . . paradise for sports fishermen and white-water rafters . . . breathtaking view from every room . . . two-hour drive from Portland, but worth every winding, scenic mile . . . the weekday continental breakfast is worthy of special mention for the fine pastry, to say nothing of owner and pastry chef Ellen Kent's awe-inspiring weekend buffet spread . . .*

Rave reviews from fancy critics. Damn. Not bad.

He stared down into the checkered green bowl of the valley, and reminded himself for the thousandth time that over half of her life had gone by. She would have forgotten him. She was still using her maiden name, but that meant nothing these days. She could've married a guy named Scruggs or Lipschitz, and kept her own pretty name for business purposes. She probably had a bunch of noisy kids and an SUV.

Good for her if she did. He just hoped whoever she picked deserved the kind of love she could give more than he'd deserved it.

He wondered if she dreamed of the night he'd run away

the way he still did. He'd gone to say goodbye to his friend and found himself in the arms of a lover. A storm of freaked-out passion and adrenaline.

He'd taken her virginity that night. The memory was etched in his mind. Every last, exquisite detail of it.

Wind pushed a bank of bruised-looking clouds across the sky. The cloud shadow that swept over him put an abrupt end to his speculating. Of course his return to LaRue would be heralded by a thunderstorm. It was obligatory.

He put on his shades and his helmet and accelerated towards town. The place hadn't changed much. The strip mall was longer, with monster chain stores adrift in the oceans of their gigantic parking lots. A video store had replaced the Twin Lakes Diner. A multiplex cinema had taken the place of the drive-in theater.

He glanced up the hill to where the Mitchell Stables had once stood. It hadn't been rebuilt. The country club's golf course had been extended instead, into a smooth, bland swath of green lawn that sloped gently down towards the river. Part of his brain still expected to see it a blackened ruin. The ultimate fuck-up that had drop-kicked him out of this town, and ironically, it hadn't been his fault.

The memory was all too vivid. Drinking beer with his pin-headed buddies out behind the stables until Eddie and Randy had gotten the bright idea to shoot off firecrackers. In August, for Christ's sake. The whole forest could have gone up, and the town along with it. It was sheer, dumb asshole's luck that only the stables had burned.

They hadn't even seen how or when the fire started. Simon had felt the familiar prickle of impending disaster on the back of his neck when they were already halfway down the hill, and had looked back to see the dull, ominous glow of illuminated smoke. Not one of his so-called friends had gone back with him to let the horses out. He'd done it alone. The acrid sting of smoke in his throat and the high-pitched screaming of the maddened horses had haunted his dreams for years.

He glanced up at the lowering sky. He had a couple of

minutes of grace—the time it would take to reach shelter under the awning of the Shopping Kart, where he could buy detergent and ask around for a laundromat and a hotel. Time to clean up and act normal. Not that any effort on his part had made a difference before, but hey. He could try.

Maybe he would get lucky, and no one would even recognize him.

"Did you hear the news, Ellen? Simon Riley is back in town!"

Peggy's sharp eyes watched avidly for a reaction as she swiped Ellen's eggs and paprika across the check stand's electronic scanner.

Ellen stared back at the checkout clerk. She closed her mouth and arranged her face into a mask of polite interest. "Really?"

Peggy wasn't fooled. Her mouth curled into a triumphant smile as she swiped Ellen's cream cheese and butter. "I saw him with my own eyes. He's a biker now! Big and dirty and sweaty, dressed up in black leather like a Hell's Angel. Hair all the way down to here. If I'd been your mother, I'd have heaved a big sigh of relief when that boy disappeared. He was trouble then, and he looks like bigger trouble now. After that bad business with the fire, well! He has some nerve."

"That fire was not Simon's fault," Ellen said tightly.

Peggy gave her a pitying look. "Whatever you say. That's $32.79."

Ellen handed Peggy the money with her teeth clenched. It was a mistake to let Peggy bait her. The woman had a nose like a bloodhound for people's weak points, and defending Simon was as pointless an exercise now as it ever had been.

Ellen grabbed her bags and stalked out of the Shopping Kart without so much as a polite nod of farewell. The damp from the recent thunderstorm closed around her like a smothering embrace. She looked around, lost and blank. She'd forgotten where she'd parked her pickup.

Simon Riley. Back in LaRue. Her heart thudded. Her face had gone sweaty and hot. She fumbled in her purse for her sunglasses with jittery hands. She was light-headed. Dizzy. Maybe she had sunstroke.

Duh. There was her pickup, up the block. She'd opted for the shade in front of the insurance office instead of the blazing sun of the Kart's parking lot. A sensible choice. She was a sensible woman.

She had to remember that. Hang on to that.

She hadn't thought about Simon Riley for years. Dreams didn't count, she had finally conceded, not even the feverish, erotic ones. She didn't choose them, and therefore she couldn't possibly blame herself for them. Neither did those thoughts that sneaked up whenever she wasn't keeping herself busy. Which wasn't too damned often anymore. Her life was rich and full and complete, and, of course, there was Brad, her boyfriend. No, not boyfriend. *Fiancé,* she corrected herself firmly. He was now her fiancé, as of two weeks ago Sunday, and a very nice fiancé he was, too. And in not too long a time, he would be her husband. She waited for the quiet, contented glow that reflection ought to give her.

It refused to show itself.

There had been a time when not thinking about Simon had amounted to a full-time occupation. Now she was an old pro. Now it was no big deal. She was halfway through the crosswalk before she realized that she'd walked past her own truck.

She marched the half block back to it, tight-lipped, and packed her perishables into the cooler. When Simon's uncle Gus Riley had shot himself a few months back, the shock had briefly revived old gossip. People had wondered out loud about what happened to that wild boy who'd run off so long ago. Some speculated that he'd gone to the bad and was leading a life of crime in some big, nasty city.

Not Ellen Kent. Been there, done that. She had better things to worry about. She shoved plastic ice packs around the food, sealed the cooler and climbed into the truck. She wasn't picturing Simon Riley, all big and dirty and sweaty in black riding leathers, his black hair blowing wild and loose all the way down to here. Huh uh.

She'd moved on.

The motorcycle bumped and jolted over the rutted logging road that snaked along the McNary Creek Canyon. Simon had braced himself in every way he could. He'd eaten a meal, he'd drunk strong coffee, he'd washed his clothes, he'd scrubbed himself in the waterfall's icy pool. He could think of no other excuse not to face up to Gus's house, other than the fact that the prospect made him feel sick and faint.

He cut the motor and coasted down towards the house. It was smaller and shabbier than he remembered, and it had been plenty shabby seventeen years ago. The paint had peeled away, and the house had taken on the eerie silver shade of a prairie ghost town. Everywhere he looked, time collapsed. He felt younger, angrier. Scared and confused. Fucking up every time he turned around.

He wasn't a fuckup anymore, he reminded himself. Not at his work, at least. He was a seasoned professional, excellent at what he did. He'd achieved a certain amount of fame in the journalism world for his brazen fearlessness. More balls than brains, his colleagues said, but that was what sold, and everyone knew it.

A golden eagle swooped low, checking him out. The shadow of its huge wingspan brushed over him. A swift, quiet benediction.

He took courage from that and approached the house. The rotten porch boards sagged beneath his weight. The unlocked door creaked open. The smell of dust and mold filled his nose as his eyes adjusted.

Gus had never been much of a housekeeper in the best of times, and it was evident that these had been far from the best of times. Dishes were heaped in the sink, encrusted with dried, molded food. A cast-iron skillet thick with grease sat on the filthy propane stove top. Empty bourbon bottles covered the counter, crowded the floor. The pattern of the peeling linoleum was barely visible beneath the dirt.

He walked into the kitchen. A clutter of miscellany covered the tables. Dishes, silverware, paper, and, incongruously, a laptop computer. No electric lamps or appliances. Gus must have hooked the computer to his gas generator. It was connected to a phone jack, but he saw no phone. Gus had gotten a phone line just for the Internet.

He walked slowly through the broken-down house. Dirt and junk and cobwebs. Dead flies and liquor bottles. The desolation made his throat tighten. No guilt, he reminded himself. Gus had brought his loneliness on himself. Simon would have been glad to love his uncle.

Gus had driven his nephew away with his fists.

It made him sick. He wanted to fling something against the discolored wall, just to hear it shatter. One of those bourbon bottles would do just fine. He breathed deeply and let the impulse pass.

That was the past Simon, young and dumb and full of come. He had a handle on his temper now, and he hung onto it with both hands, but it was time to get out in the open where he could breathe.

Hank's letter had said they had found Gus in front of the house. He waded out into the meadow. The grass was thick and high, a waving blaze of gold so deep the rusted cars seemed nearly drowned in it.

He couldn't say goodbye to Gus like this, with his mind shut up tight against grief and memories. He closed his eyes, unclenched his fists, and let the tension relax. He opened his mind as if he were about to take photographs. Softening, widening, until he merged with what he was observing, until he and it were one.

He reached down deep, for his best memories of Gus.

The image blindsided him the moment his guard went down. Fire roaring up, just like his dreams. Greedy, raging, consuming violence. For an instant, the waving grass seemed an inferno of licking flames.

Just as suddenly, the perception was gone. He stood in a fragrant meadow humming and buzzing with life under the blazing August sun. Doubled over and shaking, his forehead wet with cold sweat.

He pressed his hand against his belly and willed the queasiness to pass. He knew this feeling all too well. A premonition of disaster.

He knew the impulse that followed it, too. The only thing in the whole world that would make him feel better.

He had to find El.

Ellen pulled into the Kent House driveway and parked in her own spot under the maples. She ran a practiced eye over the cars of the guests in residence in the small parking lot below the house.

The Phillips family's Rover, Phil Endicott's silver Lexus, Chuck and Suzie's Jeep, bristling with sports equipment, Mr. Hempstead's massive baby blue Chrysler. Everyone here for tea today. Then her eye fell on an unfamiliar silver Volvo sedan. A new guest, she hoped. She'd had an unexpected cancellation this morning, so she had a free room. She hoped that Missy, her part-time help, had mustered up the nerve to check the new guests in. She was trying to teach the girl to be less timid, but it was uphill work.

A gust of hot wind bent back the lilacs that separated her lawn from the scrub oak and meadow grass that led down to Gus's moldering car graveyard. The Riley house had once been the carriage house of the Kent mansion. A crafty young Irishman named Seamus Riley had plied her great-grandfather Ewan with homemade white lightning until he lost his wits—and the house—in a drunken poker game back in 1918.

Seamus had settled comfortably into his new house, and married a Nez Perce woman that he'd met in Pendleton. Ellen had seen a photo of her in Gus's kitchen one day when she'd brought over some fresh bread. Simon, her great-grandson, had inherited her prominent cheekbones, her black hair and her somber, penetrating eyes.

The place had been an eyesore for as long as Ellen could remember, but Gus had been flatly unreceptive to all offers to buy him out. Perhaps Simon would be willing to sell it to her.

"Hello, there, Ellen!"

A handsome middle-aged man pushed his way through the lilacs. Ray Mitchell, Brad's father. Her future father-in-law was the very last person she expected to see stepping off of the late Gus Riley's property.

"Uh, hi, Mr. Mitchell," she said.

Ray beamed at her. "Keeping cool, honey?"

"Hardly," she murmured. Ray's hearty voice bugged her, for some reason. Hearty and Affable was one of his four settings; the other three being Solemnly Sincere, Deeply Concerned, or Indulgently Amused.

She was being unfair. Ray had never been anything but courteous to her. His social style was due to the fact that he'd been a public figure for so many years, she supposed. But Ray Mitchell's public persona seemed to have taken over the private one. She hoped that wouldn't happen to Brad if he decided to go into politics. It would drive her nuts.

"What a nice surprise," she heard herself say. "Would you like to come in for a glass of iced tea?"

Ray took the cooler from her arms. "Let me get this for you, honey. Can't stay long, but I'd be glad for a glass of your great iced tea."

He followed her into the kitchen and set the cooler on the table. Ellen stuck a tumbler under the ice maker. "Peach or lemon?"

"Lemon, please," Ray said. "Thank you. That'll just hit the spot. Hotter than the fires of hell out there, isn't it?"

He sipped his tea and murmured appreciatively. She waited to hear what he was gathering himself to say, though she had an intuition that she already knew. "You must have heard by now that Simon Riley is back in town," he began.

Bingo. She'd guessed it. A headache gathered in the back of her head, throbbing with each beat of her heart. "Yes, I did hear that."

"But you haven't seen him?" Ray's expression switched like a TV channel into Look #3, Deeply Concerned.

"I got home just now," she said. "I was in town running errands."

"So he hasn't been by here yet, then?" Ray persisted.

"Haven't seen a trace of him. What's on your mind, Mr. Mitchell?"

Ray sipped his tea and gazed out the kitchen window at the bushes that screened Gus's house. "I'm worried. Even before you got involved with Brad, I was uncomfortable with the idea of a lovely young lady living alone right next to someone so unstable as Gus Riley."

"Hardly alone," Ellen pointed out. "I never have less than six guests in the house with me at any given time."

Ray waved that inconsequential detail away. "Be that as it may, Gus had a history of mental illness. He was a land mine that could have exploded at any time. What he did to himself was a tragedy, and I'm deeply sorry for his pain, but I won't hide from you, honey—that mine has finally exploded. No one has to tiptoe around it anymore. That may sound callous to a tender-hearted young lady such as yourself, but . . ."

"Speak your mind. I can take it," she said. "I'm afraid I don't agree with you, though. Gus was always perfectly polite to me."

Sort of. Whenever she'd brought goodies to Gus's house, she'd been greeted with the sound of a shotgun being pumped. But since he'd always put the gun aside and offered her coffee, it was no big deal.

"Now there's another unexploded land mine in town," Ray said. "And it's just too close to you. Again."

"You mean Simon?" She blinked with exaggerated innocence, just to see if he'd notice her sarcasm.

He did not appear to register it. "Yes, I do mean Simon, honey. Entirely aside from that business with the fire—"

"Simon did not set that fire!" Her voice was getting shrill again.

"Ellen. Honey," Ray said. "I saw him running away from the stables with my own eyes."

"But you didn't see him set the fire!"

Ray sighed. "Be that as it may. It's been a long time, and I'm willing to forgive and forget—"

"How can you forgive someone for something they didn't do?"

Solemnly Sincere took over on Ray's face. "Let the matter of the fire be, honey. I just want you out of range. I want you to consider moving away from Kent House if Simon should decide to stay at Gus's. I doubt he'll stay long, since I'm quite sure his welcome here will be pretty darned cool, but for the time being, what do you say?"

Ellen stared at him blankly. "Mr. Mitchell, I run a business. I'm fully booked through October. Do you realize what you're suggesting?"

"I'm suggesting that you might need to re-order your priorities," Ray said earnestly. "You're welcome to stay with Diana and me until the wedding. We have plenty of room. That would be the best solution."

Ellen shook her head. "I appreciate your offer and your concern, but I just can't do that. And now I really need to get started with my teatime preparations. So if you'll excuse me . . . ?"

Ray set his glass in the sink. "Think about it," he urged. "Tell us the second you start to feel uneasy. The door is always open to you, Ellen. I promise that no one will say 'I told you so.' "

"It won't be necessary, Mr. Mitchell, but thanks very much."

She watched Ray from the window. He cast a last, lingering glance down at Gus's house before he got into the Volvo and drove away.

Another bizarre episode in an atypical day, but she couldn't really focus on it. Her mind was stuck on Simon. If he ever did come around to see her, he would find her very changed. She wasn't a lonely, puppyish kid anymore, begging for his attention.

Like she'd begged for his kiss the night he'd run away.

And oh, God, she really shouldn't think about that. She had to think about something else. Quick. Softening the butter for the scones she had to bake for teatime. Rinsing the blueberries. Anything at all.

She started putting groceries away, but it was no good. The memory reeled through her mind, unstoppable.

The night that he'd climbed up the oak to her bedroom window to tell her goodbye, she'd told him to wait. Tossed the contents of her piggy bank into her pillowcase. Run downstairs to the kitchen, thrown everything she found into the pillowcase: salami, yogurt, granola bars, trail mix.

Her legs shook, and a lump like a cannonball was in her throat. She couldn't bear for him to go. She'd never had a chance to make him see her as anything but a tagalong kid who needed help with her homework. She'd barely begun to grow boobs. She was a late bloomer, almost sixteen, but she looked about twelve. She would never know what it was like to kiss him, or dance with him, or—or anything else.

She'd found him on the lawn, shoulders shaking. His face was pressed against his knees, his long legs folded up tight against his chest, like he was trying to take up less space.

She'd dropped down to her knees next to him, and shocked them both speechless by demanding that he kiss her goodbye.

The memory still had the power to make her face go red, right there, in front of her open refrigerator, a slippery quart of half-and-half in her hand. She'd been so bold. Years later, she still had no idea where she'd found the nerve to do that. It was unimaginable.

At first he'd made fun of her, told her he didn't feel that way about her, and don't be a dingbat. Then the mocking smile faded out of his eyes, changed into a wary, waiting expression. And it happened.

Something intangible kindled between them. An ancient, prickling instinct, a swelling heat that made her skin feel too small for her body. Mysterious and powerful. Just remembering it made her shiver.

She remembered every sensual detail. Her hand splayed against his chest, his pounding heart, the damp warmth of his sweat. Her other hand against his cheek. The fine bones, the soft skin, the sharp angle of his jaw. The smell of smoke that clung to his hair.

The look in his eyes, almost scared. As if she, clueless, goofy, awkward El Kent had some mysterious power over him, to bestow or withhold something he was desperate for. It made her dizzy.

She leaned closer slowly until she felt his breath against her face, jerking in and out of his open mouth. The instant her lips touched his, the spark whooshed into flame. He'd pulled her onto his lap, wound his fingers through her hair and kissed her. Really kissed her, until her soul melted and mixed with his. Every part of her buzzed with his electricity. His lips coaxed her mouth open, ardent and eager.

She wrapped her arms around his neck, the world turning itself over and over until she was on her back, in the grass, crushing down her mother's bed of purple petunias. His body was feverishly hot. His hands slid under her nightgown, shoving it up. Touching her all over, making her shudder and gasp.

She felt so clear and bright and sure. Now was the time, and he was the one. She'd chosen him years ago, before she even understood what she was choosing him for. She wrapped herself around his wiry, shaking body and offered him everything she had, everything she was.

And he took it.

The memory made her thighs clench. Clutching his back, staring into his wide, frightened eyes. Pain that was intimate and terrible and sweet. A storm of emotion and sensation.

Collapsing into a tight, panting knot with him afterwards, both of them weeping.

Then the faraway whistle of the approaching freight train sounded, and his hot, lithe body went rigid on top of hers. He pulled away. Told her he had to make that train. Nothing could change his mind. Not even telling him she loved him.

Ellen laughed, but the laughter had a false, soggy sound. Look at her, sniveling over girlhood memories in front of a fridge that was gaping wide open in a heat wave. Serve her right if the milk went sour.

In all the lovers she'd had in her thirty-two years—not that there had been all that many—she'd never again told a man she loved him. Not even Brad. Though now that she thought of it, Brad hadn't made any declarations of love to her yet, either. Until now, she hadn't even thought of that fact in terms of an omission.

She couldn't imagine saying those words to Brad. The pain and vulnerability associated with them were light years from Brad Mitchell's high-quality universe, where things made sense. Things behaved. Whatever didn't was judged to be unworthy and promptly rejected.

Brad valued her. He appreciated her and respected her, enough to want to be her partner for life. That was love for rational grown-ups. Love wasn't ripping your heart out of your chest on a dark morning and being haunted by the smell of smoke ever since. That was juvenile stupidity. Or plain bad luck. Like a bout of food poisoning.

"Excuse me, miss. I'm looking for El Kent." The low, quiet voice came from the swinging door that led to the dining room.

Ellen spun around with a gasp. The eggs flew into the air, and splattered on the floor. No one called her El. No one except for—

The sight of him knocked her back. God. So tall. So big. All over. The long, skinny body she remembered was filled out with hard, lean muscle. His white T-shirt showed off broad shoulders, sinewy arms. Faded jeans clung with careless grace to the perfect lines of his narrow hips, his long legs. She looked up into the focused intensity of his dark eyes, and a rush of hot and cold shivered through her body.

The exotic perfection of his face was harder now. Seasoned by sun and wind and time. She drank in the details: golden skin, narrow hawk nose, hollows beneath his prominent cheekbones, the sharp angle of his jaw, shaded with a few days' growth of dark beard stubble. A silvery scar sliced through the dark slash of his left eyebrow. His gleaming hair was wet, combed straight back from his square forehead into a ponytail. Tightly leashed power hummed around him.

The hairs on her arms lifted in response.

His eyes flicked over her body. His teeth flashed white against his tan. "Damn. I'll run to the store to replace those eggs for you, miss."

Miss? He didn't even recognize her. Her face was starting to shake again. Seventeen years of worrying about him, and he just checked out her body, like he might scope any woman he saw on the street.

He waited patiently for her to respond to his apology. She peeked up at his face again. One eyebrow was tilted up in a gesture so achingly familiar, it brought tears to her eyes. She clapped her hand over her trembling lips. She would not cry. She would not.

"I'm real sorry I startled you," he tried again. "I was wondering if you could tell me where I might find—" His voice trailed off. His smile faded. He sucked in a gulp of air. "Holy shit," he whispered. "El?"

Chapter

2

The gesture tipped him off. He recognized her the instant she covered her mouth and peeked over her hand, but he had to struggle to superimpose his memories of El onto the knockout blonde in the kitchen. He remembered a skinny girl with big, startled eyes peeking up from beneath heavy bangs. A mouth too big for her bit of a face.

This woman was nothing like that awkward girl. She'd filled out, with a fine, round ass that had immediately caught his eye as she bent into the fridge. And what she had down there was nicely balanced by what she had up top. High, full tits, bouncing and soft. A tender, lavish mouthful and then some, just how he liked them.

Her hand dropped, and revealed her wide, soft mouth. Her dark eyebrows no longer met across the bridge of her nose. Spots of pink stained her delicate cheekbones. She'd grown into her eyes and mouth. Her hair was a wavy curtain of gold-streaked bronze that reached down to her ass. El Kent had turned beautiful. Mouth-falling-open, mind-going-blank beautiful. The images locked seamlessly together, and he wondered how he could've not recognized her, even for an instant. He wanted to hug her, but something buzzing in the air held him back.

The silence deepened. The air was heavy with it. She didn't exclaim, or look surprised, or pleased. In fact, she looked almost scared.

"El?" He took a hesitant step forward. "Do you recognize me?"

Her soft mouth thinned. "Of course I recognize you. You haven't changed at all. I was just, ah, surprised that you didn't recognize me."

"I didn't remember you being so pretty." The words came out before he could vet them and decide if they were stupid or rude.

Based on her reaction, he concluded that they were. She grabbed a wad of paper towels from the roll on the counter, wiped up the eggs and dropped the mess into the garbage pail. She dampened another paper towel. Her hair dangled down like a veil. She was hiding.

"What's wrong, El?" he asked cautiously. "What did I do?"

She knelt down, sponging off the floor tiles. "Nothing's wrong."

"But you won't look at me," he said.

She flung the soggy towel into the garbage. "I'm called Ellen these days. And what do you expect? You disappear for seventeen years, no letter, no phone call, not so much as a postcard to let me know you weren't dead, and expect me to run into your arms squealing for joy?"

So she hadn't forgotten him. His mood shot up, in spite of her anger. "I'm, uh, sorry I didn't write," he offered.

She turned her back on him. "I'm sorry you didn't, too." She made a show of drying some teacups.

"My life was really crazy for a while. I was scrambling just to survive. Then I joined the Marines, and they sent me all over the map for a few years while I figured out what I wanted to do with myself—"

"Which was?" Her voice was sharp and challenging.

"Photojournalist," he told her. "Freelance, at the moment. I travel all the time, mostly war zones. By the time I got things in my life more or less straightened out, I was afraid . . ." His voice trailed off.

"Yes?" Her head swiveled around. "You were afraid of what?"

"That you might have forgotten me," he said. "I didn't want to face that. I didn't want to mess with my own equilibrium. I'm sorry, El."

She turned away without replying, and began to hang teacups on hooks on the wall. His hand on her shoulder made her jump. She dropped one, which knocked the one underneath it off its hook as well.

They shattered loudly on the marble counter.

Simon hissed through his teeth and lifted his hand away. "Christ. I'm sorry. Were those priceless antiques? Please say they weren't."

"Great-grandmother Kent brought them with her from Scotland. They traveled around the Horn with her in eighteen ninety-four."

He grimaced in agony. "Shit. I hate heirlooms."

"They were part of her dowry."

"I said I was sorry," he snapped.

There was an uncomfortable silence. "Still leaving a path of chaos and destruction in your wake, I see," El said.

Anger made his defenses snap right into place. "Of course." He echoed her careless tone. "Just like always."

"Some things never change," she murmured.

"Got that right," he agreed dourly.

El edged away. "So, ah, what brings you back to LaRue?"

The chatty, let's-move-on tone in her voice set his teeth on edge. "I just got word about Gus," he said.

"Just now?" She looked puzzled. "But he died five months ago."

"It took a while for the letter to reach me," he said. "Hank Blakely wrote to me about it. My high school art teacher. Remember him?"

"Of course. I didn't know he knew where you were. Where were you, anyhow?" Her eyes were full of wary curiosity.

"Afghanistan." He offered no further explanation.

There was an awkward pause. "So he left you his property, then?"

"I have no idea," he said. "I don't particularly care."

"And you hadn't seen him since you—"

"Nope."

El tilted her head to the side and studied him thoughtfully. "Why did you come back, then?"

He made a helpless gesture. "I don't know. Gus, killing himself. I couldn't take it in. I needed to see the place. Wrap my mind around it."

"I see." Her steady, penetrating gaze made him transparent. Like he was eighteen again, scruffy and needy and underfed.

He stared right back until his cool regard made her blush and look away. "I asked around for a hotel," he said. "People told me you'd converted this place into an inn."

Her face tightened with alarm. "You want a room here?"

"I can't stay at Gus's place. There's no water, no power, and it's a foul mess. I've slept in worse places, but that one I can't take."

She twisted her slender hands together. The downy hair on her arms was pale, glittering gilt. Her nails were pink-tinged mother of pearl. He made her nervous. She didn't want him in her house. It was childish to get his feelings hurt. He knew damn well he should take pity on her and haul his ass to another hotel, but knowing it wasn't enough. The contrary bastard inside him that took after Gus wanted to goad her.

"If you're scared of me, I'll leave," he said. "I don't want you to sweat nails, El. I'll go to the hotel out on Hanson."

"Scared of you? For heaven's sake. Don't be ridiculous!"

He shook his head. "Nah. If you're uncomfortable with—"

"Why should I be uncomfortable? I'm a professional.

The motel on Hanson smells! And there are cigarette burns in the furniture!"

"God forbid," he murmured.

She glared at him. "And bugs! Do you want to share your bathtub with cockroaches? Do you want cobwebs in your window curtains?"

Bull's-eye. He got her. He lifted his hands in surrender and struggled not to grin. "Anything but that."

Her narrowed eyes said that she knew she'd been manipulated. "So I take it Missy hasn't checked you in?"

"If you're referring to the girl who was at the front desk, no," he said. "She took one look at me and ran. She seemed pretty freaked out."

El sighed. "Oh God. What am I going to do with that girl? So she didn't give you our spiel, then."

"Nope, no spiel," he confirmed.

"Very well. Follow me." She marched towards the dining room. "I'll explain our policies. Payment is in advance, cash or major credit cards. I prefer to avoid out-of-town checks. Continental breakfast is served from seven-thirty to ten on weekdays, and a full brunch on Saturdays and Sundays from nine to twelve. Early risers will find tea and coffee in the dining room from six-thirty A.M. Coffee, tea and light refreshment is served in the dining room at five—"

"Light refreshment?" he echoed. "Fancy."

"Yes, scones, or biscuits, or fresh pastry," she said, flashing a glance over her shoulder that dared him to make fun of her. "And of course, you are encouraged to join me with all the guests in the salon for a glass of sherry in the evening before retiring."

He followed her out of the kitchen, gazing at the graceful lines of her back. "A glass of sherry. Wow. Aren't we refined."

"You are also free to skulk alone in your room, if you prefer. I personally could care less." She slid behind a desk in the foyer and pulled out a credit-card machine. "The room I have available is one hundred and twenty dollars a night. Will that be cash or charge?"

"Charge, I guess," he said, bemused.

"Very well." She plucked a charge slip from a cubbyhole in the credenza and slapped it into place. "How long do you plan on staying?"

"Let's start with a week, and take it from there."

She held out her hand for his card. He fished it out of his wallet and slapped it into her palm. "Cut it out, El."

Her eyes slid away, and her professional smile slipped a notch. She fit the card into the machine. "Cut what out?"

"The professional song and dance. This is me, Simon. Remember? Hello! Anybody home in there?"

She dragged the press over his card and dialed the authorization code, fingers stabbing at the number pad. "I don't know what you're talking about. Seventeen years without a peep from you. No way of knowing if you were starving, or sick, or dead in a ditch somewhere—"

He held up his hands. "Hey, one thing at a time, OK?"

"And when you finally do get around to coming to see me, it's just because you need a place to crash. Just like old times. Good old El. So useful and convenient." The code finally appeared on the screen. She scribbled the number down and threw his card back at him. "What the hell do you want from me, Simon?"

He planted his hands on the desk, and leaned forward. "I'll tell you what I don't want. I don't want to use you. I never did. Not then, and not now. If you want me to leave, I will." He bit out each word.

She made a furious huffing sound, and wrenched a drawer open. She plucked out a long, old-fashioned key and tossed it across the desk at him. "You'll be staying in the tower room."

"Your old bedroom, huh?" He took the key. "I remember. You let me sleep there whenever Gus was too drunk for me to deal with. You brought me cookies and cocoa and leftovers.

I don't think I've ever entered that room through the door, though. I always came up the tree."

Her eyes dropped, and the pink on her cheeks deepened. She shoved the credit-card slip and a pen across the desk.

He signed it and shoved it back. "El, let me explain something."

"No. There's nothing to explain, and I've already said too much." She scrambled out from behind the desk. "I'll show you up to your room now, if you'd like. I hope Missy got around to cleaning it."

"El, let me—"

"You have your own bathroom," she said, backing towards the stairs. "I remodeled the place. All the rooms have private baths."

"Thank God," he said. "I need one. I can't face Mrs. Muriel Kent without a shower and a shave."

She cleared her throat. "My mother doesn't live here anymore. She moved down to California some years ago. I bought the house from her. So you're, um, safe."

"I see." He stared at the curve of her cheek and wondered if her skin was as soft to the touch as it looked. He tried not to look into her eyes—oh, hell. They were incredible. Hypnotic. Splashes of forest green in the midst of the sensual, liquid golden brown, and the endless black of her pupils dilated and contracted with delicate pulsations.

Sunlight slanted through the stained-glass window over the staircase, illuminating her eyes, her hair. They picked out her gilt accents: the tips of her lashes, the sun-bleached down on her arms. Her rumpled hair shimmered like an angel's halo in an ancient fresco.

She'd been dusted with gold powder.

"Simon?" she whispered. "What are you doing?"

He was so close to her. Her breasts almost grazed his chest. If he swayed forward, he could wrap his hands around her slender waist.

The memory opened up in his mind. The smoke, the dew,

the dawn. The sensual promise in El's eyes, the tight clasp of her virginal body. She'd almost convinced him to stay, but he'd known even then that whoever he got close to would end up caught in the crossfire of his bizarre bad luck. El had been the one good thing in his screwed-up life, and the kindest thing he could do for her was to stay away.

Seventeen years later, he had no reason to think that anything had changed, and yet here he was. His nose was just inches from her fragrant hair, his hands right on the verge of sliding around her waist to press that sumptuous golden softness hard against his body.

"Um, Ellen?" A light, wispy voice spoke above them.

The two of them jerked apart as though they'd been kissing.

"Yes, Missy, I'm right here." El's voice was admirably steady.

"Um, there was this guy here? And I think he wanted a room but I hadn't cleaned the tower room yet, and the bathroom was still messy, so I just cleaned it now. Maybe he went away, though." Her voice sounded hopeful as she pattered down the stairs on light, diffident feet.

"No, he didn't go away." El's voice was gentle and patient. "He's right here. Missy, meet Mr. Simon Riley."

Missy squeaked and retreated to the landing. El shook her head and heaved a tiny, silent sigh. "It's OK, Missy," she soothed. "You could've checked him in. I showed you how to use the credit-card machine, remember? You're very good at it."

Missy cowered behind the banister. She was a skinny girl in a denim jumper. Mouse-brown hair was scraped tightly back from a wan face that might have been pretty if it hadn't been so anxious.

"Hi, Missy." Simon tried to sound non-threatening.

"Hi," she whispered.

"It's excellent that you prepared the room," El encouraged. "Why don't you go rinse the blueberries? I'll show Mr. Riley to his room."

Missy nodded and scuttled past them as quickly as a mouse, eyes down. Simon gave El a questioning look.

She threw up her hands. "So? I keep hoping she'll loosen up, but it hasn't happened yet. Big deal. Things take time." She sidled past him, careful not to touch his body, and started up the stairs.

"Still trying to save the universe, I see," he said. "You always were a sucker for lost causes."

El shot a cool glance back over her shoulder. "Not at all. I'm very practical now. Not nearly as sentimental as I used to be." She took an audible breath, huffed it out, and launched into her hostess routine.

"The front bedrooms look out over the river, but your room is the only bedroom that also has a good view of Mount Hood . . ." Her voice was brisk and practiced. He let his attention drift, his gaze wandering down her heavy cascade of wavy, sun-streaked bronze hair. The curling wisps that kissed the top of her ass were bleached to silver-gilt.

"—and this is the library, as you can see. Lots of books and magazines for browsing, but we ask, as a courtesy to other guests, that this be a quiet room. If you wish to converse, there's the sunroom, the salon, the dining room, the parlor, and the porch."

"It's going to feel strange to put my feet up and read a newspaper in Frank Kent's inner sanctum," Simon remarked.

El paused at the door that led up to the tower room. "I'm sure he wouldn't begrudge you the pleasure," she said. "He died six years ago."

Simon cursed himself silently. "Sorry."

"It's all right," she said. "Up these stairs is the—"

"I've been here before, remember? Please, El, would you relax?"

She continued as if he hadn't spoken, her voice tightly controlled. "Here is the tower room. I'm afraid that the room wasn't large enough for a queen-sized bed—" she unlocked the door and pushed it open, "—so I hope a full size will do." She gestured for him to enter.

Simon looked around, disoriented. Gone was the twin bed with the ruffled pink-and-white spread, the white vanity piled high with books, the poster of the sultry-eyed maiden riding a unicorn.

Now the room was pretty, tasteful, neutral. An old-fashioned four-poster was covered by a colorful quilt. The wallpaper was a delicate, understated floral pattern. There was a washstand, a cheval mirror, a wooden bureau, a braided rag rug.

He felt bereft. "It's not you anymore."

"I took the master bedroom suite for myself when I remodeled."

"I see." He stared forlornly out the window at the oak tree. At least that was more or less the same. Just bigger.

"The bathroom is right at the foot of the stairs," she informed him. "I'll make sure that Missy left you fresh towels and washcloths, and—"

"Stop it!" His voice came out harsher than he'd intended, and she flinched. He stopped, and sought to put his lost, groping feeling into words. "We were friends," he said helplessly. "Don't freeze me out. Can't we pick up where we left off?"

El let her hair fall forward to veil her face. "Do you remember where we were when we left off, Simon?"

Hell, yeah. Fire and smoke. Adrenaline racing through his body, screams of terrified horses echoing in his head. The slender girl twining herself around him, the bewildering flare of heat and need. Like he could ever forget. He cleared his throat carefully. "I remember."

El backed towards the door. "Then you understand why we can't pick up, just like that. Look, it's almost teatime, and I have to—"

"El, please don't," he persisted.

"—to get things organized. Missy can't manage alone. If you like, you can join us all for coffee, tea and scones in a half hour in the dining room." She hesitated, her eyes brimming with emotion, and shook her head, dismissing it, and him. Her hair swirled as she spun around.

The door clicked shut. Light footsteps tapped down the stairs, pausing to make sure that his bathroom had towels and washcloths. Ever the perfect hostess. Her quick, light footsteps faded.

Simon wrenched off his boots and flung himself onto the bed. He bounced on the orthopedic mattress. Just like the Kents. Nothing but the best. He'd surprised himself as much as her by the impulse to stay here. For the first time, he realized that the harm he could do here in LaRue might not only be to himself. And he was unprepared for how outrageously pretty she was. That was unfair. A dirty, nasty trick.

El had been so good to him. He'd launched himself into the world with nothing but her pillowcase of food and money to sustain him. She'd become a symbol of home and safety in his mind, but it wasn't fair to think of El that way. She'd just been a needy, affectionate kid.

A total sweetheart. And he'd taken advantage of that sweetness. He'd nailed her the night that he left, right in her mother's flowerbed.

He'd had lots of sex since then, but even the very hottest of it—and some of it had been very, very hot—hadn't come close to the emotional intensity of that fumbling explosion in the flowers with El.

Simon closed his eyes, and rolled onto his belly. He was an opportunistic prick, in the privacy of his own dirty mind. He had no business in the Kent mansion, having erotic fantasies about the golden princess. Domestic bliss looked warm and cuddly from the outside, but it was beyond his reach. He knew exactly how that script would play.

It started out small, breaking eggs and smashing teacups. It got progressively worse from there. Once El figured out that he was more trouble than he was worth, he'd be out on his ass.

He preferred to spare himself that humiliation from the get-go.

He was always up front with the women he slept with that commitment was not part of the deal. He tried to make it up to them by satisfying them sexually. That, at least, was something he could be generous with. It was an art, to please a woman in bed, and he'd dedicated himself to it with all of his considerable intensity.

But a woman like El would never be satisfied until a man was on his knees in front of her, promising her the moon.

Dealing with what had happened to Gus was going to hurt like hell. It wouldn't be right to use El to comfort and distract himself knowing he was just going to leave again. He'd wronged her that way once already, and she was still pissed about it.

Women like her weren't for men like him. Guaranteed disaster.

Ironic. It made him laugh, but the sound was dry and bitter. He was so out of place in this prim room. This was a room for old-fashioned, well-bred, proper sex. Not that he'd ever actually had any sex like that, but his dirty mind was up to anything. Four-poster bed, fine linen sheets, big puffy pillows, classy woman? He could see it.

He'd be on top of her, of course. Missionary position. Lights off, moonlight streaming through the window. Their bodies would be discreetly draped by the quilt as he moved inside her. Embracing her tenderly. Gazing respectfully into her eyes. Dignified, proper, decorous.

Whoops. Oh, man. The joke was on him. His dick was so hard, he had to roll onto his side to give it some space. He knew exactly how her slender body would feel naked beneath him, taking him inside her, deep and slick and yielding. He would kiss her as he fucked her, deep, hungry kisses. He would suckle her breasts while she struggled towards pleasure against his body. Giving herself to him, like she had that night years ago when he'd tasted how wild her girlish passion could be.

So much for respectful, well-bred sex. His fantasy went right off the rails, and before he knew it, the pillows got knocked off the bed, the fancy quilt flung to the floor, the sheets torn off the mattress. Lights flipped on so he could see every pink and gold detail, so he could run his tongue over her smooth skin, lick up every salty bead of sweat.

He wanted to turn her body every which way till he figured out what made her shudder and sob with pleasure. He wanted to put it to her deep and hard. Ride her all the way to the end of the line.

He was sliding his hands into his jeans to give himself some relief when something small and round rolled off the pillow, hit the top of his head and lodged itself in the crook of his neck. He fished it out and started to laugh. A chocolate, wrapped in gold foil. Trust El to bonk him over the head with a chocolate the minute he started getting ideas.

He unwrapped it. Bittersweet, dark as midnight, like the kind Gus used to love. He sat up, stuck the chocolate in his mouth and buried his face in his hands. El's face glowed a hazy gold on the insides of his closed eyes as the taste of rich chocolate lingered in his mouth.

You know you're just hurting yourself, Simon.

Talk about famous last words.

Chapter

3

So Simon had been all over the world. Yay for him. Ellen felt very provincial. Domestic, garden-variety, boring. She'd never had a real adventure in her life. She had no tales to tell.

The thought was supremely depressing.

And Simon was in one of her bathrooms at this moment. Naked in the shower. Soapsuds running down his body. She wanted to turn herself into vapor, slide under his bathroom door and watch him shave.

The thought made her face go hotter and damper than it already was. She was disgusted with herself. Ranting at him like a fishwife. For years, she'd pictured meeting him again, but not dressed in cut-offs and a limp, sweaty blouse. Not with her hair all frizzy, clinging to her sweaty neck and forehead. Frowsy, frumpy. Mystery quotient, less than zero.

She was gratified to see a large pot of coffee already perking in the kitchen, sending its heady fragrance into the room. She was filling the creamers with half and half when Missy let out an agonized squeak.

"There's broken cups behind the drainboard! They weren't broken when I washed up the cups this morning, I swear they weren't!"

Ellen hastened to reassure her. "No, Missy, that was my fault. I broke them earlier and forgot to clean them up. Why don't you carry the coffee tray into the dining room while I take care of it?"

Missy seized the tray and scurried out, her face pathetically relieved. Ellen gazed after her and sighed. Missy had been working for her for over a month, but she was as skittish as the day she started.

Ellen was sympathetic of the girl's anxiety. She of all people knew how it felt to be speechless and shy, but it bugged her today. Everything bugged her. She had to calm down before Brad came to get her. They were supposed to pick out her ring this afternoon.

Her fiancé. All of a sudden, that sounded so strange and far from her. Her stomach cramped painfully.

Engagement jitters, she told herself. Marriage was a huge step. It was normal to be nervous. It would be stupid not to be.

When she'd accepted Brad's proposal, she'd accepted reality over fantasy. About time, too. Smoky passion in the flowers belonged to the fantasies of the past. Brad was the real, concrete future.

Concrete. Yes. That was the perfect metaphor for Brad. Solid for sure, but such a heavy, inflexible material to work with.

Simon was startled to find the room completely full of people. There was an elderly guy with a bow tie and striped suspenders. A sunburned, athletic-looking couple, tenderly feeding each other bites of buttered scone. A harried lady, who had to be the mother of the two boys of about eight and ten who were chasing each other around the table. A middle-aged man with gingery hair. El presided over everything, gracefully pouring coffee into delicate porcelain cups. Baskets of pastry steamed on the table, breathing out a buttery, mouth-watering scent.

The old guy's eyes lit up when he saw Simon. "Hey, it's the motorcycle man! You all have to check out that BMW he's got!"

"Coffee, tea, iced coffee, iced tea or lemonade?" El asked him.

Simon's heart sank when he saw those fragile teacups. "Got any Styrofoam?"

Her lips twitched. "These aren't Great-grandmother Kent's teacups. These I bought for ten bucks apiece at the Hood River Antique Show. If you break one, I'll just bill you."

"Great," he said, relieved. "Coffee, then."

"Everybody, this is Simon Riley, who just checked into the tower room. Simon, this is Phil Endicott, Lionel Hempstead, Mary Ann Phillips and her two boys Alex and Boyd. Down at the end are Chuck and Suzie Simms, our honeymooners." El passed a basket of pastries to him and pushed a lazy Susan loaded with butter, honey, and jam after it.

"Do you really have a motorcycle?" Boyd asked, wide-eyed.

"Sure do." Simon slathered butter on a scone. He took a big bite and almost moaned. Wow. Oh, yeah.

"Will you give us a ride on it?" Alex chimed in.

"Alex, that's rude!" his mother protested.

"It's OK," Simon offered. He broke off a corner of scone and heaped it with two different kinds of jam. "I'd be glad to."

The boys shrieked with delight, but the horror on Mary Ann's face dismayed him. Shit. Score: LaRue, one. Simon, zero.

Phil Endicott hastened to cover the awkward pause. "So, uh . . . what line of work are you in?"

"Photojournalist," Simon said.

Phil's eyes widened. "Oh really? How did you get into that?"

He'd answered that question often enough to anticipate it. "I just answered a want ad. A documentary filmmaker needed an assistant who was willing to travel. He taught me the trade."

"Been anyplace interesting?" Chuck asked.

"Depends on what you'd call interesting, I guess." Simon snagged another couple of scones from the basket and piled them on his napkin, for safety's sake. "I just came back from Afghanistan. Before that I was in Iraq. I go to wherever the action is with my team, get the story and the pictures, and sell it to the big news agencies."

He regaled them with a few of his tamer adventures. El played it cool, pretending not to listen, but he knew she was catching every word.

"So what brings you to this neck of the woods, Mr. Riley?" Mary Ann asked. "Nothing newsworthy happens around here."

"Call me Simon." He seized his fourth scone. "I'm here to see El."

"You mean Ellen? You mean, you two know each other?" Mary Ann's curious eyes darted from him to El, then back again.

"Simon grew up in the house next door," El hastened to explain. "We knew each other when we were kids."

"She baked great cookies even then," Simon said. "My God, these things are good. Pass me the basket, please. She hasn't lost her touch."

Lionel winked at him. "Better work fast, Riley, if you like them scones so much. You got yourself some competition, boy!"

"Lionel!" El hissed. "Do you mind?"

"I'm a believer in telling it like it is, young lady." Lionel's voice had a self-righteous ring.

Simon stopped chewing. His mouth had gone dry. Of course a woman like El wouldn't have stayed single. Of course not. He swallowed with difficulty and washed the crumbs down with a gulp of coffee.

He turned to El. "So?"

"So what?" El poured coffee into Phil's cup and avoided his gaze.

"Who is he?" he demanded.

"Simon, this is hardly the time or place to—"

"Spit it out." His voice was steely.

She set the coffeepot on the trivet with a thud. "Brad Mitchell."

The room went dead silent. The grandfather clock on the mantel ticked loudly. The other guests exchanged nervous glances.

Simon finally found his voice. "Brad Mitchell?" The name almost strangled him. "You're kidding, right? Tell me you're kidding."

There was a chorus of thuds and squeaks as many chairs were shoved back from the table all at once.

"Boyd, Alex, come along." Mary Ann hustled her offspring out the door and looked back with a pained smile. "Bye-bye, folks!"

"We're, uh, going to go, ah, hiking," Chuck mumbled, as he and Suzie scurried out the kitchen entrance. "See you guys around."

"Good luck, young fella!" Lionel called, as Phil Endicott nudged him firmly out the door. "My vote's for you!"

El stared down at the table. "Gracefully done, Simon. You cleared the room in less than ten seconds."

"Brad Mitchell?" he repeated stupidly.

"Yes. I fail to see why that is so hard to believe."

"Hard to believe? It's impossible to believe! I know the guy, El! He's a snake!"

She bristled. "I'm sure he's changed. Brad is a very nice man."

Simon shook his head, speechless. A woman like El, so bright and sweet and generous, wasted on that sneaky, self-important bastard. It was criminal. "El, let me tell you a couple of things about Brad—"

"No, Simon." Her voice was resolute. "I don't want to

hear it. I believe in seeing the best in people. And I never listen to cruel gossip."

She was right. It wasn't his place to tell her. She would have to figure it out for herself, but it made him sick to think of it.

He set down the teacup and stuck his clenched hands into his lap where they couldn't do any damage. "He won't stand by you, El," he said tightly. "Not like you deserve."

She made a sharp, angry gesture. "So? Who gets what they deserve in this world? Besides, I don't expect anyone to stand by me. No one has so far."

Simon stared at the crumbs on the tablecloth. "I'm sorry I let you down. I didn't have a choice. At least that's how I saw it at the time."

El covered her face with her hands. "I cannot believe I said that," she whispered. "I'm sorry, Simon. It wasn't right. You don't owe me a thing. I don't even know you. I don't know anything about you."

"That's not true. You know me better than anyone."

El's hands dropped away from wet eyes. "Oh, please! Get real! We were just kids!" She dabbed her nose with a napkin.

"Weren't you listening? I tried to fill you in," he protested.

"In front of a whole roomful of people!"

"It's just as well there are people around," Simon said.

El took a careful sip of coffee. "What do you mean by that?"

Ah, what the hell. He never could keep his big mouth shut to save his life. "You know what I mean," he said. "The thing between us. It hasn't gone anywhere."

El set her cup down and rose to her feet. His dismissal was written all over her face. "Maybe it hasn't gone anywhere, but we have," she said quietly. "So if you'll excuse me—"

"Have dinner with me." He sprang to his feet and moved to block her exit. Her retreat made him feel panicked and furious.

El backed up. "Simon, I—"

"Just dinner. Please. It's been so long, El. I missed you. I want to know every single thing that's happened to you since I left."

The nervous tremor that shook her could have been laughter or tears. "Wouldn't take long. We'd run out of conversation by the time we finished the appetizers."

"Like hell we would. We never ran out of conversation before. I never met such a chatterbox as you in my life."

Her smile was tight. "Things change."

"Yeah, right, whatever. If you run out of things to tell me, which I doubt, then I can tell you everything that's happened to me."

She laughed softly. "Oh, yeah? Over the past sixteen years, eleven months and thirteen days?"

Her words startled and moved him. He stared at her downcast eyes and willed her to look up at him. "You didn't forget me, then?"

She shook her head. He took a strand of her hair between his thumb and forefinger. It glittered with its own light against his brown hand. If she just looked up, if she just met his eyes, he would have her.

"Look at me, El," he commanded softly.

She shook her head again. She was no fool. She was on to him.

"Have dinner with me," he begged.

El blew out a sharp breath and shook her head hard, like she was shaking herself awake. "I can't, Simon. I didn't forget you, but I had to assume that you'd forgotten me. Brad's picking me up in a little while. We're going to Sigmund's Jewelry to pick out a ring."

Simon turned and stared out the window until he was sure he could control his voice. "That serious already?"

"We've been seeing each other for a while."

He didn't want to go to the next place his mind was taking him, but it was a one-way street. Brad Mitchell was her lover. It was Brad who was having decorous, old-fashioned sex with El in her fancy four-poster.

And those fancy teacups would make a real loud, satisfying noise when they smashed against the fine wood paneling.

He pushed that impulse right back down into the depths from which it had arisen. "So? When's the happy day?"

She started gathering teacups from the table into her arms. "We haven't set an official date yet, but we're thinking about September."

"Congratulations," he said. "Excuse me if I was out of line."

"Please, don't worry about it," she assured him.

El flinched as a car horn blatted outside. She looked out the window. "Oh. There's Brad now."

Simon joined her at the window and peered out at the car that waited for El beneath the maple. A Porsche. Of course. Brad Mitchell would settle for nothing less than top of the line, being the crown prince of the known universe.

El looked flustered and guilty. "Um . . . please excuse me."

"Oh, don't mind me," Simon said as she scurried out the door.

Brad beeped again. The sound jarred her, and she steadied herself against the maple. Her heart hammered, her face was red, her eyes watered like she'd been chopping onions. She couldn't get into Brad's car in this condition. Let him beep all he liked.

She gritted her teeth as Brad's horn let out a loud, impatient bray. She'd tried to break him of that rude habit. It didn't seem so much to ask for him to come to the door, but Brad had told her not to be silly. What was the sense? Coming to the door was an inefficient use of his time and energy. Assuming, of course, that she was punctual.

Brad was very, very good at getting the last word.

She wiped her eyes, counted slowly down from ten and walked down to where the Porsche waited, motor humming.

The chilly blast of air-conditioning made goose bumps

prickle on her arms. Brad pulled her face to his and gave her a quick kiss.

"We're late, honey," he said. "You're flushed. You feeling OK?"

"Yes," she said. Her back flattened into the seat as the car surged forward. She fastened her seat belt.

"Mom's put an engagement announcement in the *Chronicle.*"

Ellen was startled. "Already? But I thought that we—"

"I heard her talking to your mom on the phone this morning," he said. "They're already arguing about caterers and florists."

She opened her mouth, but no sound came out.

"Moms," Brad said philosophically. "Can't live with 'em, can't shoot 'em. Dwight Collier will do our engagement photos."

"Dwight Collier? But he hasn't changed his style since the seventies!"

"Yes, I know," Brad said impatiently. "But he's a golfing—"

"Golfing buddy of your dad's, yes, of course," she muttered.

Brad frowned. "I would appreciate it if you made an effort to be more positive about this. Our wedding will be a community event. Of course our friends want to be involved. Mom said to tell you our appointment with Dwight is Saturday at nine A.M."

"But I can't make that appointment!" Ellen protested. "I serve a full breakfast until noon for my guests on weekends, and I have a full house! That's nine people to cook for!"

Brad swooped around a curve with enough centrifugal force to fling her against the seat belt. "Get someone else to do it for one morning, for God's sake. This just points out the fact that you're going to have to rearrange your priorities once we're married."

Ellen braced herself against the dashboard and the door

as Brad executed another sharp curve. "She might have asked my schedule," she said. "Two hours later would have been fine."

"Mom takes some getting used to," Brad said. "My advice is to pick your battles carefully, or you'll just exhaust yourself. But this brunch issue brings me to another thing I've been meaning to discuss with you. Your business."

Ellen chomped down on her tongue as they bumped over a cattle crossing guard. "Brad, could you please slow down?"

"Relax, Ellen. I know what I'm doing. Now, it's great that you've got this hotel thing going—"

" 'Bed and Breakfast' is the term," she said tightly.

"Whatever. The point is, it's a nice little business, and you've done an excellent job. One of the reasons I proposed to you is because I admire your initiative. You're a self-starter. I respect that."

"Uh, thanks." Ellen shot him a nervous glance. "I sense a 'but.' "

"But you can't run a hotel forever," Brad said. "We have to have to set up housekeeping somewhere, right? You can't possibly expect me to live in a hotel with strangers underfoot."

"Uh, I guess not," she faltered. She actually hadn't thought that far ahead. A glaring oversight if there ever was one.

"You must turn a nice profit these days, but you work long, hard hours for it, right?"

"I guess so," she admitted. "But I don't mind. I enjoy the work."

"I'll need some of that quality time for myself, once we're married," Brad said. "And it's not like money's going to be a problem for us."

"I, uh, hadn't really thought about it that way," Ellen said. "Brad! Look out for that cow!"

Brad braked. They skidded to a stop just inches from the placid cow. Brad honked. She ambled off the road, taking her own sweet time.

"Stupid animals," he muttered.

"Brad, would you please, please slow down?" Ellen pleaded.

"Don't worry," he snapped. "Everything is under control." He took off with a roar. The Porsche bounced down the hill. "Where was I? Oh, yeah. You've been playing house for a bunch of strangers, Ellen. It's time to grow up and do the real thing. So?"

"Um, so what?" she hedged.

Brad's jaw tightened. "Weren't you even listening?"

Ellen twirled a lock of her hair. "Let me see if I've got this straight," she said. "You want me to give up my business."

Brad frowned. "I'm not asking you not to work. I'm asking you to shift your focus, and work with me, on our own household and our own future. You've got to think about the family."

"What family? Yours?"

Brad looked hurt. "Ours. I assume you want one. The pitter-patter of little feet, and all that? I thought that was a priority for you."

"Yes," Ellen said. "I do want that."

"Well, then? You can keep your baking business for the time being, as long as it's not too time-consuming, and we'll set up Kent House for the two of us. Mom can't wait to help you redecorate."

Ellen stared straight ahead. "Oh. How nice of her to take such an interest," she said woodenly. "A seven-bedroom house for two people?"

Brad's hand tangled possessively in her hair. "Like I said, it won't always be just us," he pointed out. "It's a great piece of property. A real showplace. Wasted as a hotel. You're lucky to have it."

"Luck has nothing to do with it," Ellen said. "I'll be paying twelve hundred dollars a month on it for the next twenty-four years."

Brad was silent as the car bumped over the railroad crossing. "I was under the impression that your mother had given you the house."

"Nope," Ellen said. "She gave me as good a deal as she could, but it's a valuable property. Expensive to maintain, too."

"You should have told me."

"I'm telling you now," she said shortly. "It never occurred to me that you might assume that I owned Kent House free and clear."

They drove in utter silence for a couple of minutes. Ellen stared out the window at the storefronts. Brad had hit the nail on the head when he said she was "playing house." Making a welcoming, beautiful home, even if it was just for strangers, had given her more satisfaction than any other work she'd tried since college.

Her dream had always been to fill that house with people, laughter, cooking smells, but there was a hollowness to her "playing house" that all her hard work couldn't fill. She felt it most keenly at night in her bed. The only thing that could really fill that house was a family. Not like her own when she was a kid. She'd rattled around all alone in that huge house. Her mother had been busy with her volunteer work for charity foundations. Her distant father had been absorbed with his business. She'd been a shy kid, lost in her books and dreams.

Her strongest connection had been with Simon. The fantasy of making a home with him had sustained her throughout the loneliness of her adolescence. But she could not have Simon. She'd accepted that. If she wanted to fill that house, she had to look elsewhere.

Brad had offered her a family. A way to fill that hollow space and give it meaning. And he was correct when he guessed that she would value family over work. All of this was true, right, and reasonable.

So why did she feel so frightened?

She looked over at Brad's grim profile. When he wasn't scowling, he was a very handsome man. Tall, powerfully built, his catlike green eyes striking against his tan. The bulge of his biceps stretched out the sleeves of his polo shirt. "Our kids will be great-looking, whether they take after you or me," he'd once remarked.

Ellen tried to imagine making kids with Brad, but her brain couldn't quite encompass the idea. They hadn't gotten around to becoming lovers yet. Once they were married, she was hopeful that—no, she was absolutely confident that these details would iron themselves out. After all, Brad was very attractive. Women sighed over him. He was ambitious, smart, shrewd. Princeton educated. A successful lawyer. Rich, too. Not that she cared, but there it was.

Brad slid his hand underneath her hair and rubbed her neck. "Don't pout, Ellen."

Ellen shook her head. "Just thinking."

"Stop thinking, then, if it puts that sour look on your face." Brad pulled up in front of the sparkling window display of Sigmund's Jewelry. "Diamonds ought to make you feel better."

A half hour later, her head was throbbing as she stared at the array of diamond rings. They all looked very much the same. Cold, glittering stones, clutched in ruthless prongs like fleshless golden claws.

"I still think the white gold one with the tiny sapphires on either side is the prettiest," she insisted wearily.

Brad exchanged a speaking glance with Bob Sigmund. "Ellen," he said with exaggerated patience. "That's the most inexpensive ring we've looked at so far. Get it through your head that it's not just yourself you have to consider. The ring you choose reflects on me, as well."

"Check out this beauty, Ellen." Bob Sigmund waved a huge diamond under her nose. "Two carats, pure white, and not a single flaw. Just look at the clarity of this baby. Very impressive."

"It doesn't feel right on my hand," Ellen protested. "It's just too—"

The bell dinged, the door flew open. Brad's mother, Diana

Mitchell, swept in. She was a tall, attractive woman, elegantly dressed in flowing white pants and a long, filmy pastel shirt. Her pale blonde hair was swept up into pouffy curls. "Ah! How are you, Ellen?"

"Wonderful, thanks." Ellen smiled and did the air-kiss thing.

"Hi, Mom. Glad you could make it," Brad said.

"Wouldn't miss it! When Bradley told me that you two were getting the ring today, I just couldn't resist! I thought that you could use a woman's advice! Am I right?" She paused expectantly.

Ellen gathered her strength for a cheerful affirmative, but Brad broke in before she could speak. "I'm glad you're here, Mom. I've been trying to convince Ellen to think a little bigger. She keeps saying she wants this one." Brad held up the offending ring to his mother.

Diana peered through her bifocals and dismissed it with a wave of her hand. "Oh, for heaven's sake. You can't get that one. People will call my son stingy. A pretty girl like you deserves a beautiful ring, like this one Bob's showing you. Now, *that's* a proper engagement ring!"

The flashing brilliance of the stone sent a needle of pain through Ellen's throbbing head. She looked at Diana Mitchell's expectant smile. She looked at Brad's annoyed frown. She wondered if it was actually worth all this resistance. After all, it was just a ring.

The big, protruding diamond was beautiful, too, in its own garish way. She would learn to like it. The same way she would have to learn to like a lot of things. Like her future mother-in-law, for instance.

"OK," she said.

"Excellent choice!" Diana beamed.

Brad grabbed her hand, slid the ring onto the appropriate finger and kissed her hand. "Good girl," he murmured.

Arf, arf, she restrained herself from saying.

Diana Mitchell gave Ellen a stiff hug and kissed the air beside her ear. "Congratulations! You'll be a lovely bride, sweetheart. Your mother and I think the third Saturday in September would be perfect. It won't be quite so hot anymore, but the weather should still be holding. I've already reserved the country club. Won't that be nice?"

"Oh. Ah . . . yes." Ellen followed them out onto the sidewalk.

"Time's a' wasting, my dear! Speaking of time, be bright and early for your engagement portrait at Dwight's studio Saturday!"

"Actually, Mrs. Mitchell—"

"Bring at least five or six changes of clothing. We'll do casual, formal, and everything in between." Diana gave her a critical once-over. "We should aim for the old-fashioned look, with all that hair of yours. Better yet, maybe I should schedule a hair appointment before the session, at eight o'clock. Maybe a layered cut. Oh, you'll be adorable. I'll call Marilee, my stylist, and tell her exactly what we need."

"Mrs. Mitchell, what I was trying to say is that Saturday morning isn't good for me. I'm in the middle of serving brunch to my guests."

Diana looked shocked. "You'll just have to arrange something, Ellen! That's the earliest appointment Dwight could give me! We need to get moving! It takes time to organize these things!"

"But I—"

"And speaking of your guests, what's this I hear about Simon Riley actually staying at your house?"

"What?" Brad spun around and stared at her.

Diana folded her arms over her ample bosom. "I assumed that Bea Campbell had gotten her facts wrong. I never believe gossip."

Ellen cleared her throat. "Uh, well, actually, it's . . . true."

The silence that followed her words made her feel as cold and transparent as one of those diamonds, caught in a relentless golden prong. "He arrived right before teatime," she said, with false bravado. "A room opened up this morning, so I, uh, checked him in." She sneaked a glance at Brad's face. A vein pulsed visibly in his temple.

Diana cleared her throat. "Well. All the more reason for you to be done with this hotel business. What was your mother thinking?"

"Mother has nothing to do with it," Ellen snapped. "I am an adult, and I have a living to make."

"And if she knew you let trash like that into her family home?"

Brad opened the passenger door and made a curt gesture towards Ellen. "Get in. We need to talk."

Ellen clutched the seat as they swooped around the curves of the twisting road over the bluffs. Brad pulled into the over-flow parking lot below Kent House, but as she reached for the door handle, the automatic locks slammed down with a menacing *thunk*.

"Hold it," Brad said. "You need to explain yourself to me."

"Simon happens to be my friend," she said quietly.

Brad's eyes narrowed. "Oh? Just how good a 'friend' is he?"

Ellen rubbed her pounding temples. "I haven't seen him for years, Brad. Don't start."

"Don't play dumb with me. It's not possible for you to be my fiancée and Simon Riley's 'friend' at the same time. He leaves. Today. Is that clear?"

"No. It is not clear." Ellen's chin lifted. "I will not throw him out."

Brad unlocked his door and got out. "I'm going to come in and have a talk with your 'friend.'"

"He's not here." She slammed the car door shut. Gravel crunched beneath her feet as she headed to the steps. "He went out."

"Where did he go?"

"How should I know? To a restaurant, I expect."

She was all the way up the steps before she noticed that Brad was no longer following her.

"I meant every word I said, Ellen," he warned. "Riley leaves."

She spun around. The pressure that had been building inside her all day suddenly broke its bounds. "That is enough!"

Brad stared at her, blank with astonishment.

"I have been pushed around enough for one evening!" she yelled.

"I'm not pushing you around." Brad's self-righteous tone grated her raw nerves. "If you would calm down, you would understand—"

"I don't want to understand!" she bellowed. "I have a headache!"

Brad looked as horrified as if she had sprouted a physical deformity. "God, Ellen! What's wrong with you? You are screaming!"

She stopped herself, clenched her shaking hands and tried to breathe. "I know," she said. "I'm sorry. I'm going to go lie down for a while. Have a nice evening. Thanks for the ring."

"Oh, you're so welcome," he muttered.

His door slammed. The car slewed around in the gravel and roared away. Ellen gasped and coughed in the choking cloud of dust.

Chapter

4

Simon stared down at his half-eaten steak. It was tender and flavorful, but it didn't tempt him. He was being about as entertaining as a bump on a log for his old friend Cora. He'd run into her today while washing his clothes at her laundromat, and had mistakenly thought that having company tonight might cheer him up. Big mistake.

He took a swallow of his beer. "Sorry, Cor. I'm not very good company tonight."

Cora rested her chin on her cupped hands. "That's OK," she said gently. "You're hung up on Ellen, aren't you?"

"Nah, she's just an old friend. It's not like that."

The people at the next table were staring at him. He recognized Willard Blair, and his wife Mae Ann. They were giving him a fishy look.

A vague memory took form in Simon's mind. An illicit tractor race on Willard's property that had ended badly. Considerable property damage had been involved. The devil in him gave them a big, cheeky grin. He toasted them, lifting his beer mug high.

Willard and his wife broke eye contact quickly.

"Just a friend, huh?" Cora's voice was ironic. "So it's no big deal to you, then, that she's engaged to Brad Mitchell?"

"Don't remind me," he muttered. "She deserves better."

"Right." Cora stole one of his French fries and dipped it into his ketchup. "And the fact that she's got tons of curly blonde hair, big, brown eyes, perfect tits, legs to die for? All that's irrelevant to you?"

"Come on, Cora," he said sourly. "There's more to it than that."

Her dimples flashed. "Then you're not like most men I know."

"That's probably true," he said. "Unfortunately."

Cora's sharp eyes made him uncomfortable. He gazed out into the restaurant at the other diners. His breath froze in his lungs as he recognized Eddie Webber, his best friend from high school.

Eddie had never been the sharpest knife in the drawer, but he'd been willing to hang out with Simon when not many others would, and Simon had been grateful for his friendship. At least he had been until that fateful night seventeen years ago.

It was Eddie who had been the source of all those firecrackers the group of guys had shot off at the Mitchell Stables. Before they all ran off and left him alone to take the blame for a fire he didn't start.

Eddie was eating barbecued ribs. He'd gained a lot of weight, and his red hair was thinning on top. He stopped chewing as he recognized Simon. His eyes slid away.

Simon looked down into his plate, feeling even bleaker. "It makes me sick that she's engaged to Brad Mitchell. Ruins my appetite."

Cora had been reaching out for another French fry. Her hand stopped in midair. "Yeah," she said heavily. "That Brad. He's a pisser."

Her strained tone made him take notice. "Sorry, Cor. I forgot. Didn't you used to be his girlfriend? I questioned your taste even then."

"Yeah, I was crazy for him for a while. It ended badly." She took a sip of her frozen margarita and tried to smile. "I've put it behind me, but you know what's funny? My bad judgment in men has endured the test of time. That's why I'm still single."

"You're better off without Brad Mitchell," he told her.

"I suppose," she murmured. "You know, Simon, you're made of stern stuff if you have the guts to be seen in public with me. Even your reputation might suffer, bozo, and that's really saying something."

He stared at her blankly. "Come again?"

"Didn't you know?" Cora's grin was impish. "I'm the scarlet woman of LaRue. It started the summer you ran off. The first rumor was that you and slutty gold-digger me had a hot, nasty affair while I was trying to trap Brad into a white trash marriage—"

"No way!" He was aghast.

"Uh huh. No joke. Then the word was that you'd gotten me pregnant, and that I sneaked off and aborted our secret love child. Since then, man, anything goes. You would not believe the shit some people say I'll do for fifty bucks, or a line of coke."

"But that's such bullshit! What idiot would have believed that?"

Cora tried to laugh, but the effort was hollow. "Brad believed it."

"So that was why he started pounding me that summer," Simon said. "He thought that we—"

"Yup." Cora took a gulp of her margarita. "Let's let it go, though. If I think about it, I'm liable to drink too much."

"OK," he agreed readily. "If it's so bad, why are you still here?"

"I did leave for a while. I lived up in Seattle for a few years, but big cities aren't my thing. I felt rootless. Then Grandma died and left me her double-wide. So I held my nose, came back, and opened up the Wash-n-Shop. It's a good business. Not what I dreamed of, and I work like a bastard, but it's mine. Nobody can yell at me or order me around."

"Amen," Simon said. "I try to run my life like that, too.

Except when I pull an idiot stunt like coming back to LaRue. It's like begging to get bashed in the head. Ellen and Brad? Jesus. The ultimate insult."

Cora nodded. "Ellen's a sweet girl. That's why it's a bad match. He's going to shove her around, and she'll try to please him and accommodate his flaming bitch of a mother, and end up getting squished like a bug. It's gonna be ugly."

Simon covered his face with his hands. "Gee, thanks, Cor, for making that picture so vivid in my mind—"

"Brad should marry a woman who can kick his arrogant ass on an hourly basis," Cora said grimly. "But I'm not good enough friends with Ellen to tell her that. Maybe you could."

"I already tried," he said. "She doesn't want to hear it from me."

Cora's hand jerked, sloshing her margarita over the table-cloth. "Oh, crap. Speak of the devil. Too late to run for the ladies' room."

Simon turned his head. Sure enough. Brad peered through the restaurant window. His gaze locked with Simon's, glittering with rage.

"Oh, crap, crap, crap," Cora moaned, as the restaurant door swung open. "This is going to seriously screw with my digestion."

He was big. Simon ticked off details with a detached professional eye. Bigger than he'd been in high school, but it was pumped-up gym bulk, not streamlined fighting muscle. Big, clenched fists, muscles twitching in his jaw, neck muscles contracted.

An inconvenience, but not a problem, the well-honed data processor in Simon's head concluded. Unless he pulled out a gun, which was unlikely. "Hi, Brad," Simon said. "Been a while."

Brad's eyes slid to Cora. "Well, well. Look at this. Didn't waste any time, did you, Cor?"

She gave him a dazzling smile. "Oh, I never, ever do, Brad. You know me. Seize the moment, that's my motto."

His eyes flicked back to Simon. "I heard about you slinking around town today."

"What constitutes slinking?" Simon asked.

"You should have stayed away," Brad said. "Nobody wants you here, Riley. Burning property makes enemies."

Simon sawed off a hunk of steak, put it in his mouth, chewed it.

Brad's face tightened. "Listen to me. Get out of Ellen's house. Then get out of town. I don't want you near her. I will go to any lengths necessary to make you leave. Do we understand each other?"

Simon chomped a wedge of garlic bread. The restaurant was silent but for the sound of his bread crunching.

"Answer me when I speak to you!" Brad snarled.

Simon took a leisurely swallow of beer.

Brad's mouth tightened. "OK, fine." His voice was menacing. "You brought this on yourself, just like you did back in high school."

Simon slid out of his chair as Brad grabbed his arm. He seized the flesh between Brad's thumb and forefinger and flipped his wrist over, torquing it in one sinuous move. He applied pressure to the twisted tendons until Brad doubled over, gasping. "Let's take this outside."

"Let go of me, you worthless piece of shit," Brad hissed.

Simon applied more pressure. Brad sucked air as Simon herded him around the tables of diners. Cora ran ahead, and yanked the door open. Her eyes were big and worried. Simon let Brad pitch forward.

Brad sprawled over the hood of his Porsche and scrambled to his feet. He cradled his wrist. "If you've broken my wrist, I'm suing!"

"I didn't break anything," Simon assured him. "Put ice on it."

"Besides, you started it," Cora said. "I saw you. Big bully."

Brad's eyes swept over the skin-tight jeans, the cleavage, the dangling earrings. "Who's going to believe the town tramp?"

Simon feinted towards him, and Brad stumbled back. "Don't speak to her that way, or I really will give you something to sue me for."

"Keep away from Ellen, or I will ruin your life," Brad snarled.

"I'm shaking," Simon remarked. "Absolutely terrified."

Brad shot Cora a final, contemptuous glance and climbed into his car. The tires squealed as he took off.

Simon started to shake with leftover adrenaline. It was no surprise how unwelcome he was in this town, but that didn't make it easier to bear. He realized that Cora was speaking, and yanked his attention back to her. "Sorry, Cor, what did you say?"

"I said thanks for sticking up for me."

"Same to you," he said.

She stuck her hands with some difficulty into the pockets of her tight jeans. "Where'd you learn to do that kind of thing?"

"What kind of thing?"

"The way you handled him. That fighting stuff. Very cool."

"Oh, here and there. I learned some in the service, and some on my own. Kung fu, aikido and karate, mixed together." He met Cora's heavily made-up eyes, and felt a rush of affection for her. Cora was a nice woman, good-humored and honest. She didn't deserve the grief this place had given her. She deserved it far less than he did.

"I'm sorry Brad was ugly," he said. "I wish you hadn't heard that."

Her smile was pinched. "I'm used to it. I wish I could say that I don't care, but it would be a big fat lie." She tilted her head to the side and studied him. "Why couldn't I have gotten hung up on you instead of Brad? You're just as good-looking. Maybe even better looking, in a totally different way. And you're a much sweeter person."

Her words gave Simon a nervous twinge, but Cora's eyes were guileless and direct, not flirtatious. "Actually, I'm not," he said. "Sweet, I mean. I'm not much of a prize. More trouble than I'm worth."

"Bullshit," she said. "You're holding out for a curly haired blonde with long legs and big brown eyes, right? I'm on to you, dude."

A wave of misery came over him. He looked down at the sidewalk.

Cora put her hand on his shoulder. "Sorry. I didn't mean to dig. You know, this is like that Shakespeare play we studied in English, remember? The two couples who get lost in the woods, and the fairy screws up and puts the magic flower juice on the wrong people's eyelids so everybody falls in love with the wrong person?"

"*A Midsummer Night's Dream*," he said. "You're right."

"What a godawful mess," she said. "I should get my head shrunk."

"He's the one who needs it, not you, Cor," Simon protested. "He treats you like—"

"I know, I know. But he was the first guy I ever slept with. He made a big impression. I've had nicer guys, but they fizzled. But hey. My dad was a jerk, too. So I'm attracted to men who treat me badly. How kinky is that? I should be on *Jerry Springer*."

Her forced attempt at humor was painful to watch. "You deserve better," he told her. "You deserve the best, Cor."

"Don't worry about it. I'll work it out." She smiled at him, a little too brightly. "How about we call it a night? Give me a ride home, OK?"

"OK," he agreed gratefully.

He paid for their unfinished meals.

Cora slid off the bike when he braked in front of her double-wide at Twin Lakes. She slapped him hard on the back. "Good luck."

Simon lifted an eyebrow. "For what?"

"Figure it out, Einstein."

When Ellen finally heard the rumble of the motor, she jumped out of bed so fast she almost tripped over her own feet. Her heart thudded as she shucked the summer nightdress, yanked on her cut-offs and a T-shirt, slipped into her thongs. She had to cross paths with him before he went upstairs. Their last interchange had been awful. This sick feeling in her belly wasn't going to let her sleep. She was halfway down the stairs when she realized that she'd forgotten her bra.

Oops. It wasn't as if she had massive bazongas that had to be forcibly restrained. She was smallish-to-medium, but they did tend to bounce and sway enthusiastically when left to their own devices.

She had to make a split-second decision. Either she faced him like this, tits to the wind, or she risked letting him see her scurry up the stairs like a rabbit. Dignity won out over panicked impulse. She shook her hair forward so that it covered her chest just as the door opened.

She ambled down the steps, and smiled at him. Just a woman wandering around her house. Minding her own business. Getting something cold to drink. The picture of casual nonchalance.

"Hey," she said. "You're back early."

"Is it early?" His dark eyes had an inscrutable gleam. He held his helmet under his arm. His black hair was rumpled, straggling out of his thick ponytail and dangling around the chiseled line of his jaw.

"Only eleven-thirty," she said.

His eyes brushed over her. His gaze was like a physical touch against her skin. "Were you figuring I'd be out all night?"

She shrugged, and regretted it when his eyes flicked to her chest. "I didn't figure anything," she said. "Why should I?"

He pushed his hair back off his forehead. "Well, I'm back."

She descended the stairs as smoothly as she could, trying hard not to bounce. She checked to make sure that her tight, tingling nipples were hidden by her hair and walked by him towards the kitchen. "You don't have to explain yourself to me. It's none of my business."

"So you're not interested?"

The hard note in his voice made her turn. "You know very well that you interest me, Simon," she said quietly. "You're my friend."

"Your friend," he repeated.

"Yes." She pushed open the swinging door to the kitchen. "Would you like a glass of iced tea?"

"The perfect hostess, huh?" His voice had a bitter edge.

"Stop being difficult," she snapped. "I came downstairs for a cold drink. Don't feel obligated, if you'd rather be alone. It's not like I—"

"Yeah, I'll have some of that iced tea."

She floundered for a moment, and blushed. "Well?" She beckoned to him. "Come on, then."

He followed her into the kitchen and watched as she pulled a pitcher of iced tea out of the fridge. "This is mint-flavored green tea. No caffeine. It won't keep you awake," she assured him.

His short, dry laugh annoyed her. She whirled around and glared at him. "What? What's that about? The mighty Simon Riley isn't affected by caffeine? Is that it? Am I silly to concern myself?"

He shook his head. "Nah. I'm just not sleeping lately. Caffeine, no caffeine, it makes no difference. Nice of you to worry, though."

She dropped a handful of ice into his tumbler, poured the tea and handed it to him. "There you go. It's good for you. Full of antioxidants."

They stared at each other for a long, awkward moment. Ellen nodded towards the kitchen table. "Do you want to sit down?"

"There's a full moon tonight," he said. "Have you seen it?"

"No. I suppose we could sit out on the back porch and look at it, if you prefer." Something inside her was waving its hands in frantic negation as the words came out of her mouth. Simon plus moonlight equaled incredible danger to her emotional equilibrium. Such as it was.

"Yeah, I prefer," he said.

It's just a glass of iced tea, you big sissy, so act like a freaking grown-up. She pushed the screen door open. They took their places on the top of the steps, a decorous couple of feet of space between them.

The moon floated high and brilliant in the sky. Gus's roof was a square of reflected moonlight lost in a sea of moving leaves. Crickets chirped. The wind rustled and sighed. Ice cubes rattled. The butterflies in her belly fluttered so desperately, she could feel the frantic roar of their wings in her chest, her legs, her face.

Simon gestured towards Gus's house. "Hank Blakely told me in his letter that you found him after . . ." He trailed off.

"Yes. I was heading over with a loaf of banana bread," she said. "I brought him goodies every week or so. I got halfway through the meadow, and . . . saw him."

"Christ," he muttered. "I'm sorry that happened, El."

"I kept my cool," she said. "I just turned around, went home and called the police. They told me later he'd been dead for almost a week by then. He was lying in the meadow, about ten feet from the house."

The wind had picked up, tossing and bending the branches.

"Thanks for doing that," Simon said.

"For what?" she asked. "For calling the police?"

"For the goodies," he said. "For being nice to him."

"I'm surprised that you would feel grateful on his behalf."

He shrugged. "And I'm surprised that you would bring him banana bread."

Ellen set her glass down and hugged her knees. "I felt sorry for him. He was so alone. He was always polite, but I wouldn't say we were friends. I could never be friends with anyone who had ever hit you."

Simon let out a sharp sigh, and hunched down between his shoulder blades. "Whatever," he said wearily. "I'm still glad that you were nice to him. I don't know why."

"Probably because you loved him," El said.

Simon made a sharp gesture with his hand. "I don't feel any need to analyze it."

His curt tone silenced her for a moment, but curiosity prodded her on. "Were you in touch with him after you left?"

"Not until a couple of months ago. I got this weird e-mail. Out of the blue. He'd sent it care of a news magazine that had run some of my photo spreads. It got forwarded all over the place until it found my inbox."

"What did it say?" she asked.

Simon stared out into the moonlit night. He took a final swallow of his iced tea, drained the glass and set it down on the step. He pulled his wallet out of the back pocket of his jeans.

He fished a slip of folded paper out of it, and handed it to her.

Ellen unfolded it. Simon had torn off the unused half of the page with all the forwarding e-mail addresses. She held it up to catch the light that shone through the window in the kitchen door.

Not a word, not a keystroke wasted. She could hear Gus's laconic, whiskey-roughened voice in her mind as she read the terse message.

To: whom it may concern:
From: augustus riley

pls forward this private email from a close family member 2 any address u may have in yr files for Mr. Simon Riley, Photojournalist.

Simon
i send u this c/o the mag where i saw yr photos. will be brief.

today i got proof that i am not crazy. now i can tell the truth 2 everyone, including u.

can't say more as this forum is not private.

pls contact me at above address. will tell u the story if u want 2 hear.

if something happens 2 me, yr mother guards proof.

am sorry i was not a better uncle 2 u.

have seen yr fine work in magazines.

yr mother would be proud.

i am 2.

yr uncle, augustus riley

The letters blurred. She bent forward so her hair would screen her face. Her throat ached for everything the battered scrap of paper revealed about both men. Simon carried it in his wallet, like a precious artifact. The paper was limp, the creases soft from having been unfolded and refolded so often. Where most people would have photographs of family to treasure, Simon had only this cryptic note from a dead man.

Nothing and no one else in the world.

The knot in her throat swelled. Simon's stoic loneliness and Gus's tragic solitude spoke to her own. She ached with it, amplified it like a resonating chamber. The wind in the trees was mournful. The crickets' song said *too late, all gone, never again.* It broke her heart that Gus had condemned himself to loneliness when love was there for the taking. But he had found no way past his anger and fear. He had lost himself.

It made her sick and sad. Even the moon sailing across the sky looked solitary and remote. And she was working herself into a state. She had to cut it out this second, or she would start blubbering. Simon would not appreciate that. God forbid he think that she pitied him.

She blotted her runny eyes on a hank of her hair and sniffled very quietly. She refolded the piece of paper and handed it back to him. She didn't trust herself to speak for several minutes.

Simon was in no hurry, either. He tucked the piece of paper back into his wallet and stared up at the moon.

When she could count on her voice not to shake, she tried again. "Do you have any idea what he was talking about in the e-mail?"

Simon shook his head. The wind ruffled the hair that dangled around his jaw. "Not a clue," he said. "No idea what story he wanted to tell me. No idea what the proof might be, or how my mother could possibly guard it, being as how she's been dead for twenty-eight years. The timing is so strange. Why send me that, after all these years, and then stick a gun in his mouth? It doesn't make sense."

"No, it doesn't," she agreed.

"I'm so damn curious, you know?" He laughed softly. "It's like a kind of torture. Gus used to love to tease me like that. Dangle the bait, make me beg for the punch line. But as contrary as he was, he wouldn't kill himself without telling me the story just to spite me."

"Good Lord," she murmured. "I should think not!"

"I've racked my brains about what the damn story could be about. There was him getting shot up in Vietnam, but I don't know the details. And something bad happened to him when I was small. I remember my mother being upset. Then she died, and I stopped noticing anything. There's a big blank spot in my memory right about then."

Ellen had been only six, but she remembered the day Simon's mother had died in that fire. Sparks from her wood-burning stove, it was said. Every kid's worst nightmare, and for Simon, it had come true.

From then on, he'd been set apart from the rest of them. He knew a terrible secret that none of them wanted to know.

"I learned not to ask questions about certain things after I went to live with Gus," Simon said. "I asked once to see the pictures he took in Vietnam. He freaked. I never asked again. Same thing happened whenever I talked about my mother, so I learned not to mention her."

"Is there anyone else who might know?"

He shook his head. "There's no family left to ask. He had no friends that I knew of. Sometimes, when he was drunk, he would harangue an imaginary enemy. Stuff like, 'you're going to burn, I'll see you writhe in the flames of hell,' yada yada. I figured it was memories from 'Nam plus what happened to my mother. Plus bourbon."

"I see." She wanted so badly to scoot close to him, take his hand, or put her arm over his shoulder. She didn't dare give in to the impulse.

"When Gus started to talk to the burning guy, that was my cue to get the hell out of there and sleep in the woods." He shot her a sideways glance. "Or in your room," he added. "That was even better. Warm and soft, and it smelled good. You were so sweet to me. All those cookies and chocolate milk and leftovers. My Tupperware angel."

The caressing tone in his voice made her shiver. "Don't make fun of me," she whispered. "I had to make sure you ate something. You never ate anything at Gus's house."

"Oh, that's not strictly true. I did OK in the mornings," Simon said. "It was the evenings that were rough. By then he was drunk, and he never wanted to eat when he was drunk. It spoiled his buzz. Besides, evenings were when he started in on 'what evil lurks in the hearts of men,' which was a huge downer. I tried to avoid that particular rant."

His casual, ironic tone made the lump swell up in her throat again. Even now, he pretended it was no big deal.

"Maybe the e-mail was just paranoid alcoholic rambling." He sounded like he was trying to convince himself. "Guess I'll never know."

"Did you ever try to reply to his e-mail?" she asked.

"God, yes. Over and over, but he never got back to me. Then I got Hank's letter, and finally understood why." He buried his face in his hands. "I was deep into this intense project in

Afghanistan. If I'd known . . . but it wouldn't have made any difference. His e-mail is dated the estimated day of his death. I just wish . . . ah, fuck it. If wishes were horses, beggars would ride. My mother used to say that."

Crickets sang, wind rustled and sighed. Ellen pressed her fists against her shaking mouth and silently ached for him.

"Did you know that some of Gus's Vietnam pictures won journalism prizes?" he asked.

"No," she replied softly. "I didn't know that."

"He was talented. Before he got wounded, anyhow. That's when his troubles began. But he was really, really good. One of the best."

"Like you," she said. "He was proud of you."

Simon lifted his shoulders, let them drop. "Hmph."

"So am I," she insisted.

"You've never even seen my work." He sounded quietly amused. "How would you know?"

"I just know."

They stared at each other. The shadows of the night wrapped them in hushed secrecy. The butterflies in her belly dipped and whirled.

Simon reached out and gently pushed her hair back over her shoulders. "Don't hide behind your hair. That's a bad habit. A sixteen-year-old can get away with it. A gorgeous woman has no excuse."

She was intensely conscious of her nipples pressing against the thin cloth. "And you, embarrassing me and putting me on the spot? That's a bad habit of yours. And you have even less excuse than me."

"I didn't mean to embarrass you." He brushed the tip of his forefinger across her cheek. Her breath caught at the sweet, tingling shock of contact. "How'd you get to be so fucking beautiful, El?" he asked. "How could you do that to me?"

"Simon." She forced the word out in a shaky whisper. "Don't."

His hand dropped.

She turned away, wrapped her arms tightly around her knees. "So . . . where did you go for dinner?"

"Claire's," he said. "I went with Cora."

She stared at him. "Oh. Good steaks," she said finally.

"The best," he agreed. "Cora seems to be doing well."

"So did you guys, um, catch up on old times, then?"

He laid his warm hand on her knee. She jerked, and he lifted it quickly away. "Cora's great, but you're the one I want to catch up with."

Ellen twisted her fingers together. "Isn't that what we're doing? So, um, what did you eat?"

"I had the fries, she had the salad. I had a beer, she had a frozen margarita." Amusement softened his low voice. "We talked. Afterwards, I took her home. Then I went for a ride up on Horsehead Bluff to watch the moon rise. Otherwise, I would've been back before nine."

"Oh." She was ridiculously pleased. "Must be beautiful up there."

"The moon's so bright, it puts out almost all the stars in the sky. The valley is filled with moonlight." His voice was spellbinding. "A single star is dangling under the moon like a diamond earring. Look."

She looked at it. His soft words vibrated through her body.

"Want to go up on the ridge and see it?" he offered. "I'll show you."

She was taken aback. "Uh . . ."

"Do you have a helmet?" he demanded.

"Hell, no. I've never been on a motorcycle in my life."

Simon's head whipped around. "Never?" He sounded shocked. "Holy shit, El, and you're what, thirty-two years old?"

"Don't scold me," she snapped. "I'm a wuss about stuff like that. And I didn't have the right kind of boyfriends."

He reached for her hand and plucked his helmet off the steps. "Let's go, El. You've got to try it. I want to break the spell."

"But I—" She gasped as he pulled her onto her feet.

"Put this on." He stuck his helmet on her head.

"But what about you? Don't you need a—"

"Don't worry. We won't go fast," he assured her. "No one will see us. I'll take you up the back way to the lookout on Horsehead Bluff. Never rode a motorcycle, my ass. Jesus! It's just not right!"

He sounded so outraged that she had to laugh, but her laughter broke off abruptly when he grabbed her hand and pulled her across the lawn. His hand was so big and warm, rough calluses scraping her soft skin. It sent a delicious rush of energy and quivering heat through her body. "Simon, I don't know if this is such a good—"

"Shh," he soothed. "Just a ride on my bike. It's so minor, El."

He swung his leg over the bike and waited for her. His patient stillness was a challenge in itself. Just like old times. Simon twiddling his thumbs while scaredy-cat El gathered her nerve.

But if she thought a glass of iced tea on her porch was dangerous, how much more perilous might a moonlit motorcycle ride be?

It occurred to her that motorcycle rides by moonlight would not be part of her future as Brad Mitchell's wife. It was now or never.

She shoved the thought away. She couldn't handle the concept of *never* tonight. Never was just too sad, too final. Too awful.

This was just a secret little side trip to nowhere. It meant nothing, changed nothing, and Brad would never know. She climbed on.

Simon reached back, grasped her hands, and wrapped them around his waist, pulling until she was flush against him, her breasts pressed against his back, her nose buried in his satiny hair.

He uncurled her cold, clenched fingers and splayed them against his hard belly. He gave them a reassuring pat. Oh, he felt good. Hot and firm and vibrant. His big body practically thrummed under her hands.

A gorgeous male animal.

"Hang on," he advised her. The motorcycle surged forward.

Chapter

5

He was so high. His blood raced with wild euphoria. It pulsed through his body, fizzed in his brain. El clung to him, her fingers tightening on him every time they swooped around a curve. He wondered if she were torturing him on purpose by leaving off the bra. It didn't seem her style, but after all this time, it was unlikely that she could still be that naive about her effect on men.

But then again, El had always been a case apart.

The other question in his mind burned even hotter. When she threw on her T-shirt and cut-offs, did she leave her panties off too? Was her ass completely bare in those low-slung shorts? He wanted to wrap those cool, trembling fingers of hers around his dumb handle. He guaranteed it would hold firm. Solid as a goddamn rock.

Yeah, it was sleazy, but he had his limits, and he'd zoomed right past them a long while back. She was so beautiful, and the moon was full, and he felt raw and naked after showing her the e-mail, spilling his guts about Gus. El saw right through his bravado. Always had.

She was wasted on Brad. The arrogant prick would flaunt her beauty like a trophy and never even know the real treasure that he had in his grasp. He wondered what their sex was like, and shoved the thought away too late. Red rage coiled inside him, ready to strike.

Let it go. Don't think of it. He had a part of El that Brad would never know. He had their childhood bond. He had her virginity, and she had his. Their night in the flowers. A secret treasure. This ride in the moonlight was his, too. Life was short, and pain was long, and to hell with the future. If she took him to her bed tonight, he was going for it.

The motorcycle climbed steadily up the Horsehead Bluff mountain service road, switching back in long, lazy zigzags. The landscape widened below them as they climbed. He topped the rise and they bumped along the gravel road that followed the crest of the ridge.

A moonlit panorama fell away on either side of them. Hills segued into jagged mountains on one side of them, and the broad sweep of the river valley spread out on the other. LaRue was a glittering triangle below them. The moon blazed over them in an immense expanse of sky.

Wind lifted their hair. He killed the motor at the highest point and coasted to a stop. "This is my favorite spot," he told her. "You can see everything. All the big volcanoes, every town for forty miles."

"Even the moon looks different, with so much sky around it," she said. "I've never been up here at night. It's another world."

He turned to look at her. "There's a lot of things you've never done, aren't there?"

She stiffened, and pulled her soft warmth away from his back. "Just what is that supposed to mean?" she snapped.

He held her gaze and let his silence answer her.

She scrambled off the bike and pulled off the helmet as she backed away. "Maybe I haven't traveled the world, and dodged bullets and laughed in the face of death, but that doesn't mean I'm a coward!"

"I never said you were a coward," he said. "You're brave and honorable and kind. You defended me even when I didn't deserve it."

"Of course you deserved it! Don't be silly." She backed into the middle of the road and spun around, arms wide, helmet dangling from one hand. Drunk on the moonlight, just like him. "This is the first time in so long that I've looked up into the sky and seen infinity," she said. "Usually I'm looking at the inside of a blue glass bowl."

Inexplicable tension gripped him. "It's dangerous outside that glass bowl."

She laughed at him. "Are you trying to scare me? Weren't you the one who just implied that there are too many things that I've never done? Make up your mind, Simon. You can't have it both ways."

He shook his head. "I just don't want you to get hurt."

"Oh, come on. Who wants to hurt me?" She lifted her arms to the sky, supplicating the moon. "How could I get hurt?"

He himself was the obvious answer that leaped to mind. Brad was a close second. The list stretched out from there, endless and ugly. He'd seen so many ways that people could get hurt. It was his trade.

"I hope you never know," he said.

She made a disgusted sound. "Oh, don't even!"

"Don't what?"

"Get all remote and mysterious on me. That tone in your voice says, oh, wise Simon with his vast experience of the world must protect poor clueless Ellen who doesn't know her ass from her elbow. Spare me, please. I *hate* being condescended to. Hate it, hate it, hate it."

He laughed. Her words freed him, and his mood floated up. "You're finally loosening up, thank God. Now you sound like the El I used to know. Always scolding me. Bursting my bubbles."

"Was I such a snot?" Her voice was uncertain.

"I loved it," he told her. "That was how I knew you cared."

The silence grew thick again.

El turned away, and gazed out at the mountains. "So, ah . . . where did you go when you left LaRue?"

Simon sighed inwardly. She'd panicked again. There was the tense, chatty, hostess-with-the-mostess voice. Back to square one.

"I hitchhiked south as the weather got too cold for my clothes," he told her. "I finally ended up in San Diego."

"How did you live?"

"Odd jobs. I painted houses, worked road crews, picked oranges. Anything I could find. I got a job in a photo lab once. That was a break. The owner was so happy when he found out I knew what I was doing."

"And the Marines?"

He shrugged. "Got an itch to travel. I was in the first Gulf War as a soldier. The second as a journalist."

She wandered to the side of the road and brushed her hand over the waist-high mountain grass that rippled in the wind. "I had a dream once, that you were there, during that war. I saw you in a dusty desert place with a gun in your hands."

"Don't step off the road, El," he warned. "It's rattlesnake season."

"I don't worry about rattlers when I'm with you. Remember that time I stepped too close to a snake, and whoosh, you threw your knife and cut it in half before it could strike? Just like that."

He laughed. "You bet I remember that."

"Why are you laughing?" she asked. "I was so impressed."

"I'll tell you a secret. That was sheer, blind beginner's luck. I made out like it was no big deal just to impress you."

She started to giggle. "No way! You big liar!"

"Sorry to ruin the myth. All I can say is that I got right to work and learned to throw that knife for real, just in case I ever had to save you from another snake. I had to live up to my new macho image."

"So, could you—"

"Yeah," he said. "I could. I'm very good with a knife, and I've got you and that snake to thank for it. I'll show you sometime."

"Well," she said. "That's good. Reality is better than fantasy."

"Reality usually hurts like hell," he said.

She stopped laughing, and looked away. "True." Her voice was subdued. "It usually does. I have to get up at the crack of dawn to make coffee and get breakfast together, so I should probably, um . . ."

"I'll take you back," he muttered.

He kicked himself. He should've said something slick about fulfilling fantasies, but no. He had to bring up painful reality.

She put the helmet on and climbed behind him. He could hardly believe how innocent and trusting she was. She'd grown up, but the essence of her was the same; that bright core of ineffable El, sharp wits and laughter and sweet, tender warmth. She seemed to have no clue of the danger she was in, alone in the moonlight with him and his hard-on. He could stop this bike anytime, turn around and . . . whoa.

But he didn't. He savored her soft warmth against his back, her small hands clutching him. Her trust was the sweetest thing of all.

At the top of the driveway, she patted his shoulder. He braked.

"Let me grab my mail," she said. "I was so rattled today after my errands, I forgot." She collected envelopes from her mailbox.

He scooted back as she made to climb on behind. "Get on in front," he directed.

She hesitated. "But I don't know how to—"

"You won't. We'll just coast down the driveway," he coaxed.

She clambered on in front of him. Her rib cage jerked in a soundless gasp as he pulled her back against his chest. They rolled the bike silently down the driveway and into the shadow of the maples.

The big house was dark and silent. The rustling leaves made a shifting, fluttering dance of moonlight and shadow.

She tried to slip off the bike, but he wrapped his arm around her slim waist and held her against him. "Just a second, El."

Her body stiffened. "What?" Her voice was a nervous wisp.

He lifted the helmet off her head and hung it on the handlebars. He brushed her hair gently back off her face. "I want something in return for showing you the ridge in the moonlight."

He actually heard her gulp. "Um, Simon. I can't—"

"Please." He scooped her hair away from her cheek on one side and leaned closer. "I ask so little. Just tell me one thing."

"What thing?" she demanded.

"Remember the night I left? When I came to say goodbye?"

"Of course. How could I forget that?"

"You were stark naked underneath that nightgown when I stripped that thing off and laid you down in the flowers. Remember?"

The mail slid and tumbled from her hands, falling to the ground on either side of the motorcycle. "Petunias," she whispered.

"What's that, sweetheart?" He was so close, his lips almost touched the fragrant hollow beneath her jaw.

"They were petunias," she clarified. "The flowers."

"Petunias. So that's what they're called. Just the sight of them makes me hard," he said. "When you threw your clothes on tonight, you left off your bra." He stroked her shoulders, the soft contours of her back, the whole graceful, sweeping curve of her spine, right down to the loose cut-offs. His finger slid under the denim waistband. "Did you leave your panties off tonight, too? Like you did that night I left?"

She hesitated an instant too long. "Certainly not."

"Liar." He let his breath caress her throat. "I've always been able to tell when you're lying."

"Think what you like," she said. "But you should keep your thoughts on other things."

"I tried," he said.

She sagged against him. "Me, too," she whispered.

He put his hand against the outrageous softness of her cheek. She vibrated against him, a fine, rapid tremor. He touched the lustrous warmth of her hair, the delicate bones of her shoulders, the curve of her waist. He let his hand slide beneath the fabric of her T-shirt and splayed it against the warmth of her soft belly.

The top button of her cut-offs popped open without a struggle. Her only protest was a shuddering exhalation as his hand slid beneath the heavy cloth. Lower and lower, by degrees measurable only in soft caresses, in sighing gasps. His fingertips reached her curly tangle of pubic hair. "Nope. No panties," he murmured. "Just like I thought."

She squirmed against him, and whimpered as his fingertips teased over the silky whorl of hair. Her legs already straddled the bike's seat, so he just pulled her back against him to give his hand the space to slide down . . . and his fingertips found a hot, slick paradise. She was so wet and ready. She shook at the light, glancing touch, and arched back into a bow of shuddering tension.

"I want to touch you, El," he murmured against her ear. "I want to make you feel good. You're so beautiful." He waited, nuzzling her.

She moved against his caressing fingers and made a mewling sound. He'd give her every opportunity to wrench his hand away and tell him to stop. She hadn't done it, hadn't said it. She was all his.

Her head fell back against his shoulder, her face turned to his. He finally did what he'd been dying to do since the moment he saw her in the kitchen. His lips brushed over the trembling softness of her mouth, savoring the full, sensual shape, the silky texture, the sweet flavor. He drank her in, caressed her mouth with his lips and tongue while his fingers slid lower, teasing their way inside the moist, hot recesses of her body. Petting and caressing the moist folds.

He thrust his tongue into her mouth at the same moment that he slid one long finger deep inside her. The invasion made her cry out, the small muscles inside her clenching around him. He made coaxing sounds, soothing her with kisses, and caressed the quivering bud of her clit with his thumb. She was so responsive, so open to him. He let his senses widen into a deep, intangible awareness of her pleasure, made up of fierce attention and empathy and passion.

He massaged her tight, moist sheath while his thumb tenderly circled her clit. So delicate and small. Hugging his finger with every tiny muscle inside herself. Being inside her was going to feel amazing.

He set up a gentle rhythm, careful not to scare her, and gave her just enough space to move with him; a slow, intuitive dance between his delving hand and the hidden secrets of her body. He let his other hand creep up the way the first had crept down, brushing over the dip of her navel, exploring the shelf of her rib cage and the swell of those breasts. She'd still been budding when she was sixteen, and now she'd bloomed into lush perfection. His fingertips brushed over her soft skin, her warm curves, her small, taut nipples with awe. He held her tight as she squirmed against his hand, and muffled the sobbing sounds she made against his mouth, deepening the kiss for the sake of her modesty.

He would make her come right here, and then carry her upstairs and lay her out on whatever bed was closest. Peel off her clothes and show her how much he'd learned about giving pleasure since that crazy night seventeen years ago. He pressed his erection against her bottom as his fingers wrought pleasure on her writhing body.

She panicked and fought it, but it was too late to retreat. He needed it now as much as she did. He insisted, pushed her straight into it and held on tight as the spasms of her pleasure tore through her. He thrust his finger deep inside her so that he could feel the rhythmic pulses gripping him. He rocked her in his arms until the ripples subsided, kissing her throat, her cheek and murmuring approving words; how beautiful she was, how sweet, how hot.

He slowly withdrew his slick fingers, and shoved her cut-offs down so that her bottom was half bare. He caressed her perfect ass cheeks and traced the shadowy cleft, seeking the same well of heat from behind that he had just caressed from the front. If it weren't for those shorts, he could bend her over right now. Just open up his jeans and ease his cock into that tight, supple pussy. Work himself in and out with slow, lazy thrusts while he reached around and caressed her clit.

He licked the slick fluid off his fingers. Her lube was so warm, so sweet tasting. "I want to devour you, El," he said. "Lick you up like melting ice cream. All night long. Let's go upstairs."

A shiver racked her body. Her slim shoulders shook, as if she were laughing, or . . . oh, Christ, no. He pushed her hair aside. "El? Jesus, what is it? Did I hurt you? What did I do?"

She shook her head and turned her crumpled face away from him. She pried his hand off her hip and then held it tightly in both of hers for a moment, as if she didn't know what to do with it. She brought it to her lips and kissed his knuckle. "Let me go, please."

His exultant triumph deflated. He had always hated to see El cry.

He moved back and gave her space. She clambered off the bike and buttoned up her cut-offs. She knelt and gathered up the envelopes scattered on the ground. She kept wiping her face and sniffling.

"I didn't mean to make you cry," he said helplessly. "I just wanted to make you feel good. I'm sorry."

"I'm the one that's sorry. I can't do this. I made a promise, and I can't blow it off for . . . for a quick roll in the hay with an old flame." Her voice was a shaking rush. "I can't believe I let it go so far."

Her words infuriated him. He grabbed her wrist and pulled her back. "A roll in the hay with me wouldn't be quick," he said. "It would be the longest, hardest roll in the hay you ever had."

"Don't. This is not the kind of person I am. I'm sorry. I . . . I led you on. I shouldn't have come downstairs, I shouldn't have gone out onto the porch. I shouldn't have gone for that motorcycle ride—"

"You shouldn't have checked me into your hotel."

Her silence was assent. "I'm sorry," she whispered again.

He let go of her arm. "Don't be. I was a dickhead to push you." He yanked the helmet off the handlebars, put it on, and revved the engine.

"Where are you going?"

"What do you care? Your bed's full, babe."

She flinched at his knife-sharp tone. "Simon—"

"You've moved on," he said. "I get the message. I don't blame you. Don't sweat it, El. Chalk it up to the full moon."

He turned the bike, accelerated up the driveway and hit the highway. He felt like shit for jerking El around like that. Making her miserable and confused. Making her cry. What a self-serving asshole.

He hadn't even had "the talk," the one he gave to all the women he wanted to have sex with. He knew how she would react. She would tell him to take his no-commitment rule and shove it right up his ass. She would phrase it in a classier way, but that would be the gist of it.

It's starting already, an unsurprised voice in the back of his head commented. He'd gotten into a fight and made El cry, and he'd only been here for six hours. Trouble had dogged him all his life. His mother had always jokingly said that he was a bad penny, before her house burned to the ground with her in it. That had been his first clue.

Gus had never let him forget it, either. Put him in a room with something breakable, it would break whether or not he came near it. Put him near a clock, it would inexplicably stop. Things exploded, cars crashed, fires started when he was around, even when he kept his head down. When a nearby volcano had blown up and covered three states with a choking cloud of ash, he'd been convinced it was his fault.

And when Gus's drunken rages had intensified, he hadn't been surprised. Desperate and miserable yes, but not surprised.

After he left LaRue, he'd figured that the more chaotic and anonymous the place, the less likely people would notice the shadow that followed him. So he gravitated towards cities. Then he joined the Marines, and that was even better. They sent him to places that were in such bad trouble, his own shadow was barely noticeable. He landed in the perfect profession, pursuing wars, coups and natural disasters so aggressively, they never had a chance to pursue him back. Disaster was a crop that never failed, if you had the stomach to harvest it.

He'd never stuck around any place long enough to catch the blame for ruining someone's property, or heart, or life. As long as he chased danger and disaster, danger and disaster never caught up with him.

He'd found his own weird equilibrium. He had the tiger by the tail, but if he let go, the tiger would turn on him and rip him to pieces. And the second he'd seen El in the kitchen, his blood had rushed from his brain into his lower body, and that tiger's tail slipped out of his grasp.

Now it was only a matter of time.

Ray's heart thundered with hot anticipation. Everyone was dead except for him and the two wounded Vietcong sprawled at his feet; an old man and a young girl. Everything was burning. Flames, smoke, stink.

The asshole helo pilot had run his rotor right into a coconut tree, disintegrating the sucker. It had landed on the hooch and exploded, killing Ray's men and roasting the VC inside. All except for these two.

The door gunner had taken a bullet to the throat. The radioman was buried in the rubble, just his broken, splintered hand sticking out. When the time came he would be all broken up about his men. He had the routine down cold. He could even sob on command.

But nobody was looking today. No need to pretend.

He took the gas he'd siphoned out of the fifty-gallon drum that had been meant to refuel the burning helo. He poured it

*over his prisoners. They struggled and screamed. He'd killed
more than he could count since he'd arrived at this jungle
slaughterhouse, but fire was special. The lizards and cats
he'd burned when he was little had taught him that. No one
had ever known. He'd been so careful, so patient, waiting for
his chance. He smiled at them, waved his hand bye-bye. He
lit the match—*

The vibration of his cell phone from the pocket inside his
pajamas dragged Ray out of his dream, if one could call it a
dream. It was more like a vision. He'd done some reading on
post-traumatic stress syndrome. Flashbacks were common,
particularly in times of stress. And enjoyable as it had been,
blowing a hole in Gus Riley's head had definitely qualified
as stressful.

He checked the display. It indicated that he had to drag
himself out of his bed to rendezvous with one of his employ-
ees. Scotty and Bebop couldn't wipe their own asses without
detailed instructions.

He leaned back and idly stroked his lingering erection.
The dream was coming too often, affecting his sleep. Both
sleeplessness and sleeping aids diminished his ability to
keep his mask well fortified.

And each carefully planned time that he indulged in his
secret hobby, it was harder to reestablish his mask. Sometimes he felt it buckling under the internal pressure. Hairline
cracks, dust falling, a rumbling sound. The power was overwhelming now. It had forced him to retire from his position
as district attorney, which he regretted bitterly, but just too
many people were asking him if he was OK. Too many times
he'd found himself blank and confused. No idea what look
had been on his face, what words had just come from his
mouth.

Killing Gus had eroded his mask. He wondered if finding
the proof Gus had dared to taunt him with would give him
"closure," as Diana put it when she was talking about emo-

tions. Usually her own. He looked at Diana's sleeping form on the bed next to him. She was the most self-absorbed woman he'd ever known, and he was glad of it. That quality gave him privacy. Controlling Diana was easy; a thoughtless mix of coaxing, cajoling and flattery. He was widely known to be a saint of a husband, deeply in thrall to his domineering wife.

His reputation privately amused him.

Brad had been the dangerous one, back when he'd been a curious, persistent child. But Ray had taught his young son not to intrude upon his privacy. Brad kept a wary distance from his father, and had for many years. Brad was a smart boy. Ray was proud of him.

Ray pulled on his bathrobe and slipped on his loafers. He paused to look up at the full moon, and strolled across the grass.

A hoarse whisper issued from the shadows of the gazebo. "Boss?"

"Good evening, Bebop," Ray said. "Anything to report?"

"Yeah. And how. Looks like your future daughter-in-law is screwing Riley. Ellen the Angel ain't quite so angelic after all. No surprise to me. Women are all the same. Dirty sluts."

The shock of that unpleasant news reverberated through him. Ellen Kent had been the exquisite crowning touch to his perfect family, and Riley had soiled her on his first day home. Stressing his mask. Hairline cracks, expanding into a webwork. Rumbling. Falling dust.

" . . . going on? You OK, Boss?" Bebop's voice sounded frightened.

Ray bent over for a moment to let blood run back to his head. "I'm fine." He forced his voice to stay even. "No problem. Thank you."

"You was making weird sounds, like you was hyperventilating—"

"I'm *fine,*" Ray bit out. "What exactly did you see?"

"Well, she comes out onto the porch with him, and they talk. Then she gets on his bike with him, and they take off.

Then they come back and stop under the trees. Couldn't see 'em in the dark, but I didn't have to, if you know what I mean. Man, was she ever lovin' it—"

"That'll do," Ray said sharply. "The details don't interest me."

"Want us to keep watching?" Bebop's voice was eager.

"Yes," he said. "But I would like for you to do more than watch. I want you to arrange for an unpleasant incident. I want Riley to feel very unwelcome here. I do not want Ellen injured, but I do want her to think very hard about spending time with him. Are you and Scotty up for it?"

Bebop thought about it. "Can I call a couple of extra guys?"

"If you can do so without telling them anything they don't need to know," Ray said. "An envelope with the extra money will be in the usual place tomorrow. It is important that you be anonymous. Understand? Riley must not find out who you are."

"How soon you want us to do it?"

"As soon as the perfect occasion presents itself," Ray said. "I trust you to handle the details."

"No problem," Bebop said. "We'll mop the floor with the bastard."

"Then I leave it in your capable hands. Good night, Bebop."

It took Bebop a moment to figure out that he'd been dismissed. He finally took himself off and swaggered away into the dark.

Chapter

6

Ellen pulled a pan full of fragrant apple cinnamon muffins out of the oven. It was nine, breakfast was almost over, and Simon still hadn't come downstairs. The motorcycle was parked beneath the maple when she got up that morning, though. She'd checked. First thing.

Mary Ann poked her head into the kitchen. "Ellen, is there some more milk? Boyd just used it up on his cereal."

"Of course. Just a second." A flash of motion out the window caught her eye as she opened the fridge. Simon was coming out of Gus's house. She stood on tiptoe to see what he was doing.

"Uh, Ellen? The milk?" Mary Ann prompted.

"Sorry." Ellen passed her the carton, flustered.

Mary Ann went back to the dining room, her face discreetly curious. Ellen turned back to the window. So Simon had gotten up early and gone over to Gus's place even before she'd started preparing breakfast at six. All morning, she'd been picturing his long body sprawled out naked in a tangle of sheets. She'd imagined him rolling over, giving her a sleepy, unguarded smile.

She was going to start crying again if she went down that mental track, and she'd been crying all night. When she wasn't having erotic dreams, that is. Which meant, of course, that this morning she both looked and felt like one of the living dead.

Simon was avoiding her. She didn't blame him. Last night had been so embarrassing. She would avoid her, too, if she were him. But then again, whatever discomfort he might be feeling was no reason for him to miss breakfast. She knew he liked her muffins. He'd liked them fine seventeen years ago, and they were a hell of a lot better now than they had been then. And he'd paid for the food already. Breakfast was included in the price of the room. It was his right.

Ellen dug out a plastic tray. Grabbed a strawberry yogurt from the stash in the dining room. Heaped a cereal dish full of blueberries. Searched the shelves until she found a plastic traveling mug, a relic from her college days. She filled it with coffee and a generous slosh of half and half, having noticed how he took his coffee the day before. It was embarrassing, to have studied him so minutely, but it was attention to detail that counted in a Bed and Breakfast. What made it special was the hostess's willingness to go the extra mile.

Yeah, like that detour up Horsehead Bluff last night, a derisive voice in her head piped up. That had been taking hospitality a smidge too far. And she'd been a hair's breadth away from taking it all the way. On her lawn right in front of a house full of guests. Bent over the handlebars of his motorcycle. Spread out on the hood of Lionel's Chrysler. On Great-grandmother Kent's hand-braided rug. She'd run the whole gamut of possibilities in her dreams last night.

If she'd had any idea how scary and confusing it would be to see Simon again, maybe she wouldn't have wished for it so fervently. She felt like a bomb had exploded inside her.

She pried four muffins out of the pan, sliced off their tops and slathered them with butter and apricot jam. She hesitated, slathered another two and added them to the plate. She stared at the overflowing tray with a twinge of shame. This was so much like the old, childish El. So needy. Eager for approval as a bouncing puppy. It made her wince.

This was different, she argued to herself. He had paid for this service. It was her professional duty to feed him. And she knew he was hungry. She'd never known anyone who ate as much as he did. He had a metabolism like a raging grass-fire, devouring everything in its path.

I want to devour you, El. Just lick you up like melting ice cream.

The memory of his soft words made her feel faint.

Simon caught sight of her as soon as she left her kitchen door. His eyes followed her as she crossed her lawn, pushed the tray carefully through the lilacs, and headed down the grassy hillside.

She didn't dare to meet his eyes, which left her gaze free to skitter madly over the rest of his body. He'd opened his blue work shirt and rolled up the sleeves above his el-bows. His forearms were thick and sinewy. The shirt flapped in the hot breeze, revealing his powerfully mus-cled chest, a taut, sculpted belly. A vortex of gleaming dark chest hair decorated the hollow between his pecs, and arrowed down in a thin, silky black trail to the waist-band of his jeans.

His hair was pulled back into a loose, messy ponytail. In the sunlight, the sheen of highlights in his hair were red. Glints of deep ruby in the gleaming black. A hint of his Irish forebears.

Oh, Lord. She'd thought that moonlight was dangerous. Blazing sunlight was ten times worse. The sun showed up what an outrageously gorgeous man he was, in intimate, merciless detail. She couldn't handle it. She felt blurry and stupid and red in the face.

"You were about to miss breakfast." She proffered the tray to him.

He took it, and stared down at it as if no one had ever of-fered him food before. "Uh . . . thanks. You didn't have to do that." He laid the tray down on a crate that appeared to be full of empty liquor bottles.

"I know I didn't," Ellen assured him. "I just wanted to."

But she suddenly saw the heaping breakfast tray through his eyes, and was ashamed of how much it revealed about her.

How pathetic. She wanted to run away and hide under a rock.

"You don't have to feel sorry for me anymore, you know," he said. "I can take care of myself these days."

"Sorry for you?" Ellen stepped back, and tripped over a rusty box spring. She flailed her arms to steady herself. "I don't feel sorry for you! You're entitled to breakfast, and I was seeing to it that you got some!"

"El—"

"I'm not sorry for you! Far from it! If you don't want it, throw it out. I promise, I will never embarrass you or myself again by trying to be nice to you, because you don't deserve it!" She spun around.

"El, please." His pleading tone stopped her. "I'm sorry I said that. It was stupid. I just . . . wasn't ready to see you yet."

"I'll leave, if you want." Her voice was small and tight.

"No! Please, don't be mad, El. It was sweet of you to bring me breakfast. I appreciate it. Really. I promise. OK?"

She turned back around. "OK," she said warily. "Maybe."

Simon dragged a box over and made a courtly gesture towards it before sinking down cross-legged into the meadow grass. "Have a seat. You should be safe on that. It's full of old *National Geographics.*"

She sat carefully down. "Thank you."

He picked up a muffin and consumed half of it in one huge bite. The tension in his face softened as he chewed. Something inside her relaxed slightly. At least he had good food to eat this morning. She could offer him that much, however insignificant a gift it might be.

He washed it down with a swallow of coffee, and sighed with appreciation. "The muffins are great," he said, tearing the foil off a yogurt container. "I love it when they're hot and the butter melts and oozes all through them. I didn't know how hungry I was. Want one?"

"No, I already ate. They're all for you."

He dumped the yogurt over the berries. "Good," he said.

He focused on the food for a while, which gave Ellen several precious moments to observe him without being observed. She studied him as he ate, trying to pinpoint the changes.

He'd become sharp-edged, battle-hardened. The grooves carved around his mouth, the lines around his eyes, the crackling hum of live-wire energy all hinted at past adventures. A wealth of stories to tell. A life so far removed from her own tranquil life, they barely overlapped.

They'd sure overlapped last night under the maple trees. The thought made her face heat up.

He inhaled every crumb of food with such appetite, she regretted not having brought him more. "I thought that you'd slept late," she said. "Then I saw you out of the kitchen window over here."

He took a big gulp of his coffee. "I'm an early riser, no matter what time I go to bed. Thought I'd get going on this mess."

Ellen looked around at the piles of junk. "You can use my truck, if you need to haul stuff to the dump," she offered.

He shoved his hair back off his sweaty forehead and nodded. "Thanks. I'll probably take you up on that."

"Looks like quite a job," Ellen offered.

"It will be. It's bad in there." Simon's eyes looked haunted.

"Are you looking for the proof Gus talked about in the e-mail?"

He looked embarrassed. "I guess so. Can't seem to let it go. Would you come into the kitchen for a minute? I want to show you something. Watch yourself on those porch boards. They're just about to go."

She followed him over the rotten, sagging porch and into the squalid kitchen. The air inside was stale and bitter. "I've been in here, when I brought him sweets," she said. "He always offered me coffee."

Simon picked up a handful of paper that lay on top of a

laptop computer on the table and held it out to her. "Take a look at this."

She stared down at them. "I thought he didn't have electricity."

"He had a gas generator," Simon said. "I fired it up this morning."

El took the sheaf of paper from his hand and looked through it. Computer language, mixed with a list of names and numbers. She looked up at him, puzzled. "What is this? I can't make anything of it."

"It's a transcript of a failed log-in attempt," he said. "Gus had the security auditing enabled. Someone tried to break Gus's password and get into his encrypted system. Two weeks after he died."

Ellen looked into Simon's fathomless eyes. "Oh. Wow."

"Yeah. Weird, huh? Who would have cared what was on there, except for maybe me?"

She looked more closely at the pages. "There's your name," she said. "And . . . is that your mother's name? Judith?"

"Yeah. Middle names, too. My date of birth. The date of my mother's death. A bunch of women's names that I don't recognize. A date in 1973 that I don't know the significance of. Some Vietnamese names. This was someone who knew Gus well enough to make a stab at his password, but not quite well enough to guess it."

A shiver went through her, a chill wind from the grave. "Simon," she whispered. "That is so creepy."

"Yeah," he agreed. "This guy knew more about Gus than I do."

"So he didn't guess the password then? Or she? It could be a woman," Ellen said.

"No," Simon said. "Not in this attempt, at least. This person isn't much of a cryptographer or hacker. This was just somebody screwing around, trying to get lucky."

"That doesn't narrow it down much," Ellen said. "LaRue isn't overflowing with cryptographers. Did you get into the computer?"

"Sure," he said absently. "Piece of cake."

"Stop being so nonchalant and just tell me how!" she demanded.

Her sharp tone seemed to startle him. "It was no big deal. I know the way Gus's mind works. When I came here to live, Gus used to leave me notes in code to puzzle out when I got home from school, to develop my reasoning skills. The rule was, if I cracked the code before he came back from work at the aluminum plant, we had chocolate after dinner."

"And if you didn't?"

He shrugged. "No chocolate. So I started out simple, my mother's name in large case letters, and mine in small. I scrambled them into various patterns. I hit the jackpot on the fifth try. Start with the last letter of Judith, H. Then the last letter of mine, N. Then the first letter of her name, J, the first of mine, S. Then the second to last of hers, and so forth. It comes out to this." He scribbled on the back of the paper and held it up. *HnJsToUiImD.* "Bingo," he said.

She shook her head. "I would never have figured out a bizarre, convoluted thing like that," she told him. "Not in a gazillion years."

Simon grinned. "Ah, but you never lived with Gus Riley."

"So?" she demanded. "What's in there? Find anything?"

His smile vanished. "Not much. Looks like he mostly surfed with it. His Web site favorites are the news magazines that printed my work." He hesitated. "I think he bought this thing to follow my career."

The dingy kitchen suddenly seemed more desolate.

"He had a file of my stuff up on this shelf," Simon said. "I found this, too." He pulled a box file down. "Correspondence with a detective agency in Seattle. Letters, invoices. It took them three years to find me."

So much emotion was hidden behind his words, she was almost afraid to reply. She tried to make light of it. "What, were you in hiding?"

"Might as well have been. I worked under the table. Lived in group houses where no one even knew whose name was on the lease. I didn't have a car or a credit card or a bank account. I didn't show up on the radar at all until I joined the Marines."

She put her hand on top of his. "He needed to be sure that you were OK," she said. "I'm glad he did. I'm glad you know that he cared."

He stared down at her hand against his. The energy between them charged itself instantly. She snatched her hand away.

He put the dusty file back up on the shelf. "A lot of good it does me now," he said. "I missed my chance to fix things between us. All I've got now is a bunch of questions that bite my ass. And a depressing mess to sort through." He looked around himself. "By the end, I'll be tempted to douse the place with kerosene and toss a match on it."

"Oh, God, don't do that!" Ellen gasped.

Simon's mouth tightened. "I was kidding."

"Don't kid about burning buildings in this town," she said. "Nobody will laugh."

"Do you really think I would do a thing like that?" he demanded. "That I leave a path of blackened devastation wherever I go?"

"Of course I don't think that," she snapped. "But you did have a tendency to, ah, make messes."

"That was only because you knew me during the time in my life when my arms and legs were suddenly ten inches longer than I reasonably expected them to be," he said sourly. "I've grown up since then, El. I'm actually pretty coordinated. You'd be surprised."

Oh, no, I wouldn't be, the voice inside her crooned.

She gathered up her dignity and her wits. "Please don't take everything so personally. I just had a knee-jerk reaction to the idea of the carriage house burning down, that's all."

"Carriage house?" His eyes narrowed. "This is the Riley house."

"And I've been meaning to talk to you about that." Ellen

seized onto the change in subject eagerly. "The house. I was wondering if you would be interested in selling it to me."

"Selling it?"

"I tried to convince Gus to sell to me, but he was so stubborn. And since you live so far away . . ." She let her voice trail off, daunted by the chill emanating from him. "My mother would help me out if you were interested in—"

"I'm not interested."

"But you don't—I mean, what use is it to you if you don't—"

"I'm not interested." His voice was stony.

Ellen bit her lip. "I seem to have offended you again. I didn't mean to. It was just a business proposition."

His cold stare made her shiver. "I know how eager you must be, along with the rest of LaRue, for me to get the hell out of here. Can't wait to tidy things up, right? Wipe the unfortunate Riley era away and slap a coat of fresh paint over it."

Her mouth fell open. "How *dare* you say that to me? I have always been your friend, Simon! You broke my heart when you ran away!"

He turned away. "I'm sorry," he said quietly. "Something about this place makes me furious. I don't mean to take it out on you. It was nice of you to bring me breakfast."

He looked so sad and lonely, it made her heart hurt. "Simon?"

He looked at her, his eyes wary. "Yeah?"

"I didn't want you to go," she said. "I did everything I could think of to make you stay. Don't you remember?"

He gave her a swift, jerky nod.

Ellen blinked away hot tears. "I don't know what it's worth, but I want you to remember that." She started for the door.

Strong arms caught her from behind. "It's worth a lot to me, El." His low voice shook. "It's worth everything."

She wiped her eyes on her sleeve. "Simon, don't."

"Don't what?" He turned her to face him. A lock of hair had escaped from her loose braid. He tucked the sun-bleached wisp gently into place. His fingertips sparked fire on her skin.

"Don't touch me," she begged. "Don't talk to me like this. It mixes me up. It makes me crazy."

"I can't talk to you any other way, El." His eyes were somber. "I didn't want to believe it."

"Believe what?" she demanded.

He pulled her closer. "You put a spell on me, when we made love that night. I always suspected it. Then I saw you, and I knew."

The light shining in from the half-open door dazzled her. The meadowlark's song outside the house was a sweet, liquid warble. Insects hummed a drone of sultry enchantment. The wind rushed and sighed around the house, whipping the grass into undulating waves.

"You got it backwards, Simon," she whispered.

"Same thing. Same spell." His arm slid around her waist.

She splayed her hands against his chest, but could not bring herself to push him away. She felt scattered, lost, undone. "I shouldn't be saying this," she said. "I shouldn't have told you that."

"It doesn't matter. I already knew."

Her chin went up. "Am I so obvious?"

"I'm not condescending to you," he said quietly. "I just know you, El. I know you inside out."

"I've lived more than half my life since you left, and now you come waltzing back out of the blue and say you know me! You are arrogant!"

"Bring me up to date, then," he challenged her. "What mysteries do you have to disclose? The suspense is killing me."

The mockery in his voice hurt. "Don't," she whispered. "I don't like being made fun of now any more than I did back then. Maybe I'm boring and obvious, but I still have feelings."

"Oh, shit." Simon rested his forehead against hers. "I'm fucking up every time I open my mouth today. There's nothing boring about you. Nothing obvious, except for how gorgeous you are. How sweet and kind. That shines out of you, El. That's very obvious."

A flower of bright violet light glowed and pulsed at the point of contact between their foreheads. "Ellen," she said in a tiny voice. "People call me Ellen these days. Not El."

He stroked her cheek. "Nah. You'll always be El to me."

"But it makes me feel sixteen again."

He studied her face. "I feel like a teenager with you, too," he admitted. "But it's different." He stroked the curve of her cheek.

"Different how?" she breathed.

He leaned closer. "Stronger."

There was a loud knock on the screen door. She sprang away.

Simon cursed under his breath and strode to the door. "Yes?"

"Mr. Riley?" The voice was a nasal, inquisitive tenor.

Simon paused warily. "Who wants to know?"

"I'm Marshall Plimpton, of Zeigler, Wickham & Plimpton. I heard that you were back in town, so I decided to take this opportunity to—"

"What's your business, Mr. Plimpton?"

"Your late uncle's will." Plimpton sounded huffy and self-rightous. "I assumed you'd be interested . . . ?"

Simon did not reply, just looked him over. Plimpton stuck his face close to the ripped screen to peer inside.

Ellen resisted the urge to shrink back into the shadows. The man's fleshy face split into a knowing grin. "Oh! Am I interrupting anything—er . . . oh. Aren't you engaged to Ray Mitchell's son?"

Ellen forced herself to smile. "Yes. I'm Ellen Kent. I live next door."

Plimpton's eyes darted from her back to Simon, bright with avid speculation. "I came to tell you about your uncle's will. I had no way to get in touch with you, otherwise I would have already—"

"So tell me," Simon said.

Plimpton's smile faltered, then stretched wider. "May I come in?"

Simon hesitated for a moment, and cracked open the screen door.

Plimpton stepped into the kitchen and looked around with fascinated eyes. "My. Just look at this place."

"Actually, I'd rather you didn't." Simon leaned against the wall and crossed his arms over his chest. "So what do you have to tell me?"

Plimpton glanced at Ellen, and quirked his eyebrow at Simon.

"You can say anything in front of her," Simon said.

"Oh? Is that a fact." Plimpton's eyes flicked over her hungrily. She was terribly conscious of her flushed face, her tousled hair.

The wariness in Simon's eyes turned to flinty anger. "Get on with it," he said abruptly. "I have a lot to do around here. As you can see."

"Ah, yes. Of course." Plimpton's eyes flickered at Simon's tone. He looked for a place to lay his briefcase. Finding none, he gingerly set his case on the floor and unlatched it, pulling out a sheaf of papers. "I don't know how up to date you were about your uncle's financial status—"

"I assumed that he was destitute," Simon said.

"Ah." Plimpton's grin showed all his teeth and a good portion of gums. "Augustus Riley named you as the sole beneficiary of his will. You inherit all his worldly goods, including this property and its contents, as well as an insurance policy for one hundred thousand dollars. Which is null and void in the case of suicide, of course."

"Of course," Simon said with equanimity.

"And then there is . . . this." Plimpton pulled out another sheaf of papers with a flourish. "His other assets."

"Other assets?" Simon frowned. "What other assets?"

"You truly had no idea?" Plimpton was enjoying himself.

Simon jerked his hand impatiently for the man to continue.

"Your uncle must have been a very, ah . . ." Plimpton's eyes swept the wretched room, ". . . frugal man. When he died, the total value of his investments exceeded eight hundred thousand dollars."

The stunned silence was finally broken by Plimpton's chuckle.

"Did you say . . ." Simon broke off, his face blank.

"I did, Mr. Riley. I did say. You are the sole beneficiary of eight hundred and twenty-two thousand, four hundred dollars."

"But how did he . . ." Simon swallowed. "Where did it come from?"

"It's my understanding that he invested the claim money from your mother's life insurance policy twenty-six years ago. Never touched the principal. Reinvested all the dividends. He was a shrewd investor, your uncle. It took a beating in the market downturns, otherwise it would have been well over a million. But it held up quite well, all in all."

Simon looked around the wretched, dingy kitchen. His face tightened. "Jesus," he murmured. "Why?"

The sympathetic expression Plimpton pasted on his face was not a very good fit. "Perhaps he wanted to surprise you. He certainly—"

"It was a rhetorical question," Simon said. "Not an invitation to speculate on my uncle's motives, thanks."

Plimpton's chest puffed out. "I didn't mean to—"

"Thank you for informing me. Leave those papers with me, and I'll look them over at my leisure."

Plimpton's face reddened. "Actually, I wanted to draw your attention to certain details—"

"Leave me your card." Simon plucked the papers from Plimpton's hand. "We'll discuss the details in your office. When it's convenient."

Plimpton's eyes glittered. "I'm so sorry to have *inconve-*

nienced you so profoundly, Mr. Riley, by taking the time to come all the way out here to personally inform you of this. Most people would be overjoyed to find out they had inherited a sum of money like that."

Simon let an audible breath hiss between his teeth. "My uncle ate a bullet. These days, I'm not particularly overjoyed about anything."

"I didn't mean to imply—"

"Your card, please," Simon repeated. "I need to think about all this. Have a good day. Goodbye."

Plimpton yanked out his card and flung it onto the cluttered table. He turned his eyes on Ellen. "I'd be careful if I were you, miss," he spat out. "You shouldn't be here. And I think you know it."

Ellen flinched as he slammed the screen door behind himself. They both waited until they heard Plimpton's car pull away.

"Well," Ellen said briskly. "That was a lot more unpleasant than it needed to be. You didn't have to be so . . . Simon? Are you all right?"

Simon's back was turned to her. His broad shoulders were rigid. The papers Plimpton had left him were crumpled in his clenched fist.

His arm whipped out, a vicious backhand swipe that sent several liquor bottles flying off the counter to shatter on the floor. "Fuck you, Gus. You stubborn, crazy old *bastard*." He grabbed another bottle.

"Simon, stop it!" she said sharply. "Right now!"

He stopped. The bottle dropped from his hand to the floor. He hunched over and put his hand over his face.

She wanted to go to him so badly, but the barely restrained violence quivering in his body held her back. "You need to, um, calm down," she faltered. "I'd better get back to my—"

"Stay."

The hard edge in his voice jolted her more than the shattering glass. He started towards her, boots crunching on broken glass.

She shrank back against the screen door. He stopped suddenly.

"Do not be afraid of me," he commanded.

She almost laughed at the irony of it. "Yeah, right! You're throwing a tantrum! I don't approve, and I don't want to watch!"

He stared at her for a moment, and pulled a rickety kitchen chair from under the desk. He put it in the middle of the floor facing her.

He sat down, slowly and deliberately. "So I'll stop. See? I know how to stop. I'm sorry. Don't be afraid of me. Please."

She sensed that he was trying to make himself less threatening, but it wasn't working. The magnetic force of his eyes terrified her.

"You came over here to nurture me." His voice was soft, hypnotic. "You love to comfort me, El. I know you do."

She tried to swallow. Her throat was too dry. She pressed herself back against the screen and fought the pull of his intense charisma.

"So comfort me," he said. "Get over here . . . and comfort me."

Her throat tightened. "You know that I can't—"

"I need it, El. I need it bad. Please. Come here to me. Now."

"Plimpton was right," she said. "Most people wouldn't need any comforting after news like that."

"I'm not most people," Simon said.

She took a step towards him. "I know," she whispered.

His eyes were hollow with grief and sleeplessness, but still he glowed with raw power. He held out his hand. So sure of himself.

She stared down at his long, graceful brown hand. Time flowed by, unmeasured, unnoticed. His hand did not drop.

Simon had never been afraid of silence, never bored with

waiting. It was one of the otherworldly qualities about him that had always fascinated her. He'd once waited in the branches of the oak tree outside her window for three hours one night, waiting for her light to flip on.

Her feet carried her across the room. Her hand reached out, and was engulfed in his big, strong one. His warm fingers curled around hers, tugging her closer until she stood right between his thighs. He lifted her hand to his lips and kissed it. "Thank you."

"For what?" she demanded. "I haven't even comforted you yet."

"Yes, you have," he said. "All your life." His face contracted, and he hid it against her breasts.

She couldn't breathe. She didn't know where to touch him, what to do with her hands. The top of his head was tucked beneath her chin, his powerful frame shook against her, his arms were wrapped around her waist, his thighs gripped her hips. Her breasts felt hot and swollen pressed against his face. Intensely sensitive at every point of contact.

He knew her so well. He was exploiting her weak points, the seductive bastard, but she couldn't keep herself from stroking his back. Trying to soothe the rigid tension that gripped his body.

He nuzzled her breasts. "Remember how you used to pet my hair when I slept on the floor in your room?"

She froze. "But . . . I only did that when you were asleep! And I barely touched you! You couldn't have felt that!"

"I never went to sleep before you," he confessed. "I faked falling asleep so that you would pet me. I liked it."

"You big fake," she said. "So all that time, you knew . . ." She stopped. Her throat was starting to shake. ". . . how I felt about you."

"Yeah, I knew," he said. "It was so great. So sweet. I came to your room mostly for that. No one else treated me like that."

"So if you knew, why didn't you ever do anything with me?" she demanded. "Why didn't you ever touch me or kiss me until the night you left? I know I was no raving beauty, but I—"

"I didn't dare mess with my one good thing," he said simply. "You were my safe place. I couldn't tempt the gods to wreck that for me, too." He let the papers that Plimpton had given him fall onto the dirty floor. "Touch my hair like you used to, El."

She shook her head.

He lifted her hand to his lips, then to his cheek. He pressed her palm against the side of his head, stroking it down over the shining mass of his hair. Willing her to obey him. She felt the silent imperative. A hidden current to drag a foolish swimmer into deep, wild water.

Strength drained from her legs. He sensed it and pulled her down into his lap—and matters were suddenly worse. He pressed her hands against his hair in silent pleading. His body was so lithe and strong. His hair was so shiny, gliding through her fingers. Not sticky and snarled with pine pitch as it had been from all his forest rambling as a boy.

She could concede him this much. Just a brief, gentle caress, if it would make him happy, and then she would step away and be strong.

Yeah. Right. Every tiny, stupid choice she made pulled her deeper into his trap. It was up to her to get up and walk away, but she knew that if she pulled away, his arms would close jealously tight around her and he would coax and plead and trick her into taking one more step, then another, until she was in so deep, there would be no retreat.

And then he would have her. He could take anything he wanted, and she would have no one to blame but herself. The thought made her ache with a longing so deep and fearful, it felt like madness.

She gave in to the moment. She petted his hair until the rumpled locks were perfectly smooth, and each slow caress pulled her deeper into his crazy spell where time had no meaning and thoughts dissolved before she could think them. All the reasons why she couldn't, she shouldn't, melted into white noise, faded into wallpaper. She pulled out the elastic tie that held back his ponytail and smoothed his hair over his shoulders, stroking it away from his starkly beautiful face. His eyes closed, and he sighed with pleasure as heavy skeins of black silk slid between her fingers. This was not comfort. No soothing caress.

This was for her own hungry hands, her own famished heart.

Their faces were scant inches apart. She smelled the coffee she had brought him on his breath. The soap he'd used, the rosemary mint shower gel that she stocked her guest bathrooms with.

He lifted her up. She flailed for a moment, before he snagged her leg with his ankle, swung it around his legs and pulled her back down onto his lap, straddling him. He clasped his hands around her waist, holding her right where he wanted her.

Any pretense about comfort and soothing evaporated. This position was raw sex, with nothing but thin layers of cloth to separate the bulge of his erection from the soft ache of yearning between her legs. The steely strength of his grip made her feel as helpless and pinned as if she were naked and he were actually penetrating her.

She tried to struggle away from him, but his arms tightened.

"Shhh," he soothed. "Just a hug. I want to wrap you all around me and feel how sweet and soft you are. I want to drink you up like a cat lapping cream. I won't do anything you don't want me to do."

Ah, he was sneaky. She muscled herself a couple of inches away from his hot, naked chest. "This is not just a hug! Stop it!"

A teasing, sexy grin transformed the lean planes and angles of his face. "So let's make it a hug and a kiss," he suggested.

She swatted his shoulder. "That's worse, not better!"

"Try it. We'll see how much worse it gets."

Unasked questions vibrated between them. They were both afraid to hear the answers. Unwilling to let go of the moment.

Simon seized her hand and rubbed it against his cheek. "I love it when you touch my hair. Pet me like that again. Please, El."

She seized big handfuls of his hair and yanked on it. "Don't do this to me," she pleaded. "It's cruel!"

"It's you who did it to me!" he protested. "I was minding my own business, trying to be a good boy, and here you come, bringing me delicious things to eat. You're gorgeous and sexy and sweet. You say nice things to me, and pet my hair, and then expect me not to kiss you? Not to touch you? Get real! I'm human!"

"Yeah, sure," she snapped. "You may be human, but I'm eng—"

He cut her words off with a savage kiss.

He coaxed her mouth open and thrust his tongue into her mouth. She wrapped her arms around his neck and met his ravishing intensity with her own. Their bodies wound into one desperate, writhing entity. This kiss was not a lead-in to sex. This kiss *was* sex.

When she lifted her face to gasp for breath, she discovered that he'd undone the buttons on her blouse. He caught her fumbling hands in his when she sought to whip her blouse closed and stared at her heaving bosom, framed in the front-clasp ivory satin demi-bra. He undid the clasp with one deft, single-handed flick. It fell open.

Simon's breath rushed out. "Oh, God, El." The low words sounded strangled. He pressed his hot face to her naked breasts.

It was impossible not to put her arms around him and cradle his head against her bosom. Time warped and stretched, wrapped them in a secret, magical cocoon. She could have stayed tangled with him forever, but Simon lifted his face and began to caress her breasts.

"You're so soft," he said. "You know when a brand-new

leaf uncurls? How tender and perfect it is? That's what your breasts are like. Fucking perfect. You blow my mind."

He lowered his head and began to make love to her breasts with his hot mouth. He licked every curve and contour, suckled her nipples, ravished her breasts with passionate skill. His mouth demanded and pleaded in equal measure. She couldn't breathe, couldn't speak. She arched back and clung to him, eyes closed, head flung back.

What he demanded was far beyond comfort. The feelings in her heart were melting into hot, liquid softness and pouring out before him, and he lapped them up eagerly with his ravenous mouth, his swirling tongue. He drew them from her with a fierce hunger, but in taking he gave such lavish pleasure, she couldn't tell who gave, who took.

She stared down at his face at her breasts. A whimper of pleasure jerked from her mouth at each wet, dragging stroke of his mouth, each swirling pull of sensual suction. Her breasts were wet from his mouth, her nipples tight. Every caress sent shivers along the surface of her body and deepened the pulsing ache inside her. She was a glowing cloud, she was liquid, she was air, she was fire, she was everything, merging entirely with this tender giving, this hungry taking.

She writhed in his possessive grip as tension rose. The unbearable sweetness crested and broke, and rippled endlessly through her body. She sagged against him. He rocked her in his arms.

"God, Simon," she whispered. "What are you doing to me?"

"Making you come." His voice brushed over her, velvety soft. "And now I'm going to lay you down and do it again."

She lifted her head, and blinked down into his face. Her naked chest was pressed against his, her crotch grinding against his rock-hard erection. Panic clutched at her belly. "We'd better, um, cool it."

His face tightened with frustration. "Oh, Christ, no." He dragged her closer to him. "Not again. You're torturing me, El."

"Me? Torturing you? Hah!" She scrambled out of his arms and struggled to re-fasten her bra over her breasts. "You lured me into this, and I let you lure me. Comfort, my ass. What, am I stupid? I don't know what it is about you. I don't even know myself when you're around me."

"Let me tell you how it would be if you let me lure you."

Ellen knew damn well that his caressing voice had the power to muddle and enchant her. She slapped the screen door open and ran.

Chapter

7

It was stupid to chase her, but he was beyond reason, beyond anything but this clawing need to pull El down into the long grass, rip off her clothes and do to her once again what he'd dreamed of doing for the last sixteen years, eleven months and fourteen days. Only this time, he'd do it right. He'd make it last, make her melt and sob with pleasure.

He caught her in the meadow beneath her lilac bushes. She stumbled and fell to her knees in the deep grass. He followed her down and pinned her with his body. "I'm not done, El. Let me tell you how it would be. I would make it so good for you."

She struggled beneath him. "Don't do this to me!"

"Don't be afraid," he begged. "Please, El. I would never hurt you. I would never force you. Don't shake like that. Relax."

"Then let . . . me . . . *go!*"

He put his mouth close to her ear. "Just let me finish telling you, and I swear, I'll let you walk away."

"Stop!" She heaved under his weight. "We're out in the open!"

"I just want to please you." He shoved her hair away from her flushed, tear-stained profile. "El?"

She dabbed at her nose, sniffing. "OK. Tell me," she whispered. "Go ahead. Drive me crazy. You have the power. You could seduce me if you wanted. I wouldn't be able to stop you. And then?"

"Huh?" His body thrummed with lust and anticipation. He could barely follow her words. "What?"

"After all those orgasms," she said. "What happens then?"

He opened his mouth to reply. Nothing came out. She pushed him off. He rolled away without protest. They were both breathing hard.

"Bang! Bang!" yelled a childish voice.

Alex's freckled face popped out of the lilac bushes. He leveled a green plastic water rifle at Simon and squeezed off a spray that hit him dead in the face. "Don't hurt Ellen, or I'll shoot you again!"

Boyd clawed his way through the bushes and swept them with a ten-year-old's world-weary cynicism. "He's not hurting her, stupid," he told Alex. "He was trying to kiss her. Yuck. Grown-ups are gross."

El adjusted her blouse and smoothed down her hair. Her mouth was a flat, colorless line. "Why don't you boys go play somewhere else?"

"I thought you were engaged to that guy with the Porsche," Boyd said. "You're supposed to kiss him, not Simon."

"Get lost, you two." El's voice was unusually sharp.

Boyd and Alex shrugged at each other and crawled back through the bushes. Their gunfight continued as if nothing had interrupted it.

"Shit." Simon wiped the water off his face with his sleeve and fell down onto his back. He stared up at the sky. He wanted to howl with frustration. "Let's go discuss this somewhere private."

He regretted the words as soon as they left his mouth.

"Discuss?" El's voice shook. "Discuss is the same as comfort, right? All my guests will know what happened out here, probably at teatime over biscuits and jam. That's if they haven't already seen it with their own eyes out the window!"

She closed her eyes, put her hands over her red cheeks. "In any case, Boyd is absolutely right. I'm not supposed to be kissing you. I'm engaged to someone else."

He jerked up out of the grass. "You can't be serious about marrying that asshole! You can't go through with it!"

El struggled unsteadily to her feet, mopping her eyes. "I'm tired of pointless dreaming," she said. "I can't wait around for my wildest fantasies to come true. I want a husband. I want children. Three or four of them, if possible. I want a family, Simon, and I don't have much more time to waste. It's time to grow up and get on with it."

"But he's wrong for you!" he yelled.

She looked him in the eye. "Have you got a better suggestion?"

Panic stabbed at him. Here it was. She wanted him, he wanted her. It should be so simple, but it wasn't. The moldering hulk of misery that was Gus's house reminded him. The Mitchell barn in flames, the screams of the terrified horses. The blackened ruin of his mother's house. Violence and brutality and loss on every side.

He could never stay out of range. He just didn't know how.

Years in the field had left him cynical and hard. He couldn't change the world, any more than he could shake off his own shadow, and anyone close to him had to run the same risk. He would protect her if he could, but he'd never been able to protect anyone. Least of all himself. His voice locked in his throat. He stared at her, paralyzed.

El waited. The glow of cautious hope in her eyes faded. Her gaze dropped. "I didn't think you did," she said, with simple dignity.

"El, I—"

"Don't. It's all right. I appreciate your honesty, if nothing else. You never tried to lead me on, or . . . oh, never mind. Let's forget it. This never happened, OK? I've got to go and clean up the breakfast things."

She pushed through the lilac bushes and marched across

her lawn, her back very straight. She disappeared into her kitchen.

Simon rolled onto his stomach and hid his hot face in a tangle of grass for several minutes. When he got up, he went back down to Gus's house and dragged a wooden cabinet out of the junk pile. He pulled it out onto the grass and proceeded to methodically kick the shit out of it until it was no more than a tangle of bent nails and raw splinters.

Cora slowed way down when she saw Bebop Webber's black Ford truck ahead of her on the road. Interacting with Bebop would ruin her day, and she wasn't having such a great one to begin with. She was taking a break from the Wash-n-Shop to deliver Ellen Kent's linens. Usually she hired someone else to do deliveries, but Cliff was laid up with a torn rotator cuff, so she was cloning herself and doing it all.

She also meant to sit down, have a glass of iced tea and shoot the breeze with Ellen. Cora had been distant with Ellen lately, and she was feeling guilty about it. It wasn't Ellen's fault that Brad was a pig and a snake. She was a sweetie, and didn't deserve to be snubbed.

She rounded the curve at the top of the bluff, and saw the ass of Bebop's truck, jacked up on oversized wheels, bouncing onto the abandoned logging road that led up the McNary Creek Canyon.

Strange. That road led to nowhere, winding up into empty hills until it faded to nothing. No one lived up there. It was private property, too. Riley property, to be precise.

Bebop. The thought of him left a sour taste in her mouth. A little discreet investigation on her part had led her to discover that it was Bebop and his brother Scotty Webber who had been responsible for spreading the word that she "did" stag parties. The fee schedule they quoted was four hundred for six guys, a hundred a head for any guy over six to a maximum of ten, oral included in the price, anal extra.

She'd gotten phone calls from the scum of the earth for months afterwards, even after she'd gotten her number changed.

She'd been tempted to poison the Webber boys to death with toxic cleaning solvent, but a murder rap would be the finishing touch for her rep. She had to content herself with shattering sleazy assholes' eardrums with her police whistle whenever they called. That was fun.

And she tried hard to think good thoughts. Her late grandma who had raised her, for instance, the sweetest old lady who'd ever lived. Her sunflowers. The cherry tomatoes that were coming in. Wind ruffling the meadow grass. Why ruin a beautiful summer day thinking about those snaggle-toothed, scum-sucking, lie-spreading—oops.

Wrong line of thought. Down she went. Wheee, sliding right down the slippery slope into a real bad attitude.

She pulled over at the turn-off to the logging road and switched off the engine. It was probably a bad idea, but she was curious as hell, and if she saw Bebop doing something sinister, it could come in useful.

She got out of her truck and slunk up the road, darting from the cover of one huge pine tree to the next. Yikes, he wasn't alone. Scotty was with him. Double slime action.

Bebop had parked behind a stand of pines that hid his truck from the two houses that were visible from here: Kent House perched up on the bluff on the other side of the ravine, and the Riley house below. He and Scotty were standing on the edge of the road, staring up at Kent House. Bebop had a pair of big black binoculars. He lit up a cigarette. He stuck his hand in his sweatpants and massaged his crotch. Ick. He said something to Scotty, passed him the binoculars. Scotty trained the binoculars down towards the Riley house.

Huh. Well. Didn't get much weirder than that. Maybe the Webber boys had a crush on Ellen. God knows they weren't the only ones. Ellen never even noticed the guys who fell to the ground in her wake with their tongues lolling out. Her cluelessness was an endearing quality.

It also made Ellen completely wrong for Brad, but Cora

was not going to think about that today. That was bad-attitude thinking.

Bebop turned around and flopped his thingie out to take a piss. Cora shrank behind the tree. She couldn't risk being spotted by those two. Alone in the woods with Bebop and Scotty would be a bad scene.

It made her feel very uneasy. She ran back to her truck and headed on up to Kent House, pulling up close to the house. The canvas bags of folded sheets and towels were wickedly heavy, but she worked out hard and had awesome bi's and tri's and deltoids. She hoisted one of them up in each arm and loped towards the kitchen.

"Yo! Ellen!" she called. "Get the door for me! I'm loaded to the gills!" The screen door opened, and she was about to spout off a cheerful greeting and launch right into the creepy weirdness of seeing the Webber boys lurking in the woods.

One look at Ellen's face drove it right out of her mind.

Ellen looked terrible. Which was to say that she still looked gorgeous, but it wasn't her usual gorgeous. Today she looked tragically gorgeous; like the chick in the famous opera who dies of consumption in the hero's arms while belting out a high C. Waiflike. Pale under her tan, eyes shadowed and bruised looking, lips bluish.

She gave Cora a wan smile. "Hi, Cora."

Cora suppressed a cynical grunt. When she, Cora, looked like shit, she never looked like beautiful, tragic, operatic shit. She just looked like plain old regular shit. Oh, well. To each her gifts.

"What's up, Ellen? Are you OK?" she asked.

"That bad, huh?" Ellen tried to laugh. She reached out to take the bags of sheets, but Cora clucked her tongue and frowned. Ellen looked like she'd collapse like a dry twig under that much weight.

"I got it for you, honey," she said. "Just open the doors for me and I'll carry them into the laundry room for you."

Ellen smiled her thanks and led the way. Cora studied her from behind as she followed her through the house. Ellen had braided her hair into two braids and wound them up over her head. Pale, curling wisps straggled down her neck and around her ears. The fresh-off-the-boat-from-Bulgaria look. A hairdo which should be forbidden by law for beautiful blonde waifs. It made her look vulnerable. And when it came to looking vulnerable, Ellen Kent didn't need any help.

"You look a little under the weather," Cora attempted.

Ellen made a dismissive gesture with her hand and smiled back over her shoulder. "It's a stressful time. Getting ready for the wedding and all. You know how it is."

Damned if I do, Cora thought. No wedding plans on the horizon for this chickie. She was as free as a bird. "Is Brad giving you a hard time about Simon being here?"

Ellen spun around so quickly, Cora almost ran into her. "How did you know about that?"

Cora pushed past her into the laundry room and set the bags on the floor. "Brad ran into us at Claire's last night. Simon had to use his kung fu moves to make him back down."

Ellen's eyes went all big and horrified. "Good God. Simon didn't say anything about that to me."

"I figured Brad's hurt pride would make him pissy with you afterwards," Cora said. "Knowing him."

"Ah," Ellen said. "Do you? Know him, I mean?"

Woo hoo. Dangerous ground. "Pretty well," Cora said cagily. "Not as well as you, I expect."

An odd look flickered across Ellen's face. Just as quickly, it was gone, and Ellen was smiling her usual serene, lovely smile.

Cora tried to joke her way over the bumpy moment. "I'm sure you can jolly him out of it. Men are simple creatures. Doesn't take much."

Ellen's eyes dropped, her mouth tightened, and Cora felt like she'd just said something crude and inappropriate. Crap. She was striking out big-time today.

Ellen tried to smile, but her face was so tense, it looked like a grimace. "I guess I'll learn how soon enough."

Cora stared at her for a second, openmouthed. She grabbed

Ellen's wrist, pulled her into the laundry room and shut the door.

"Hold on," she said. "Do you mean what I think you mean? You're engaged to Brad Mitchell, and you haven't even slept with him yet?"

The question flustered Ellen. She blushed, and began to stammer. "W-we, um, haven't been engaged for very long."

Cora stared into her eyes. "Scared?"

"No!" Ellen's shoulders went back. "Brad hasn't ever brought it up, and I'm comfortable waiting, so I never did either. I guess we're just, uh, savoring the anticipation. What, Cora, do you think I'm abnormal?"

"Nah," Cora lied. "Not at all. Savor away. I doubt you'll have any complaints when the time comes. A word of advice, though? Give him a test drive. He's intense. Turbo-charged. Not for everybody."

The delicate pink blush became a deep crimson one.

"You're not a virgin, are you?" Cora demanded suspiciously.

Ellen rolled her eyes. "Of course not. So, uh, you and Brad . . . ?"

"Yeah," Cora said. "In high school. You were a couple of years behind us. I guess that's why you never heard all the sordid details."

"I would really rather not hear them now," Ellen said.

"Don't worry. I don't want to go there either," Cora assured her. "It just took me by surprise, that he's not . . . that you're not—"

"It's very private," Ellen said tightly. "I'd rather not discuss it."

"No problem. It's like we never said anything." Cora forced a grin. "I'm out of here. Got to scoot." She paused for a second as a sudden suspicion took root in her mind. She had to test her theory.

"Say, do you know if Simon's around?" she asked.

Sure enough. A flawless, perfect, utterly false smile took over Ellen's face. It was almost eerie. "Down at Gus's house,

I think," Ellen said brightly. "Go on and drop by. I'm sure he'd love to see you."

Cora scurried for her truck. She felt like shit. Here she'd been making this big effort to mend fences and act like a grown-up, and all she'd accomplished was to make both Ellen and herself more miserable than they had been before. Which was really saying something.

Unreal. Ellen and Brad and the Miraculous Immaculate Engagement. What were they thinking?

Or maybe that was the problem. They were thinking too much. Brad was one of those guys who did too much thinking and not enough feeling. The convoluted, complicated bastard thought himself into knots. Always had. That was probably why he'd become a lawyer.

It was bizarre, though. She knew for a fact that he loved sex.

If she were engaged to Brad Mitchell—in a parallel universe in which he were not an asshole, of course—she wouldn't be able to keep her hands off his big, yummy bod. She'd handcuff him to the bedpost and gag him with one of his expensive silk ties so he couldn't say anything rude. Then she'd have at him like a wild hell-witch until he was totally spent and whimpering for mercy. Limp as a cooked noodle.

With Brad, that was more of a challenge than it sounded.

Oh, well. Who knew what Brad's screwed-up motives were for this uncharacteristic celibacy. Ellen's were clear as crystal. She wasn't going to bed with Brad because she didn't want Brad. She wanted Simon.

What a freaking, godawful, depressing mess.

She was back at the Wash-n-Shop before it occurred to her that she'd forgotten to mention Bebop and Scotty's weird surveillance.

Oh, whatever. She could only ask so much of herself at a time.

* * *

One of the many downsides of giving in to the urge to throw a tantrum was having to clean up the shit he broke. Simon was grimly thorough about it, sweeping the broken bourbon bottles into a small mountain in the middle of the kitchen floor along with decades' worth of dirt. He kept his eyes fixed on the warped broom moving over the floor, but all he saw was El's face, pinched with hurt and disappointment.

He attacked the dining room with the broom just to keep moving. He wouldn't even have seen the crumpled newspaper if the packing tape attached to it hadn't stuck itself onto the broom fibers. He leaned down to pry it off, and noticed the newsprint. Foreign. He spread it out.

It was a page of the *Saigon Giai Phong,* a Communist daily from Ho Chi Minh City. He'd seen it on his travels through Vietnam. The packing tape stuck to it had ripped the edges of several foreign stamps off whatever package it had been on. That was strange.

A pounding on the kitchen door jarred his attention away.

"Hey. Anybody home? Riley, you in there?"

Simon's shoulders tensed. That voice was all too familiar. He walked back into the kitchen as the screen door squeaked open.

Wes Hamilton, the patrolman who had hauled him into the station on so many unpleasant occasions, had taken the liberty of letting himself in. If there was one thing he had learned from this man, it was to keep his mouth shut and pick his battles. "Afternoon, Officer."

Wes Hamilton folded his thick arms over his chest and looked him over. "It's Lieutenant these days. So. It's really you."

"It's really me," Simon said. "Lieutenant."

Wes shook his head. "I could hardly believe that you have the balls to come back here, after the shit you pulled."

"I do, in fact, have the balls," Simon said evenly.

Wes's eyes slitted. "I see you're still a smart-ass."

"Sometimes," Simon said. "I try to stay mellow."

Wes grunted. "What the hell are you doing back here, Riley?"

"Putting Gus's stuff in order," Simon told him. "Actually, I was going to come into the station to talk to you guys."

"Oh, yeah?" Wes snorted. "That'd be a sight to see. What about?"

"Gus," Simon said.

Wes looked around the dingy room. "Not much to tell," he said. "It was all routine. I was the first one to arrive after Ellen Kent called us. I secured the scene. The forensics guys came, did their thing. They took him away and autopsied him. The reports were turned over to the district attorney. He ruled it a suicide. We took the crime-scene tape down. He was cremated. End of story. Any questions?"

"Yes," Simon said. "Who's the district attorney these days?"

Wes grinned. The effect was strange, coupled with the freezing glare in his eyes. "Ray Mitchell." His tone was gleeful. "He just retired. Ruling Gus a suicide was one of the last things he did."

Simon tried to play it cool, but Wes caught the expression in his eyes and started to chuckle. "Yeah, ain't that ironic? Your old pal. I don't recommend paying him a social call. He's still pissed about you torching his stables. Three hundred thousand dollars' worth of damage, they say. Good thing the guy has more money than God."

Simon shook his head and let it go. There was no point in starting in on the stable fire with Wes. It was a waste of his energy.

"I got a question for you, Riley," Wes said. "Exactly how long do you plan on staying around here?"

Simon gave him a thin smile. "No idea."

"I'll give you a friendly suggestion then," Wes said. "I don't think LaRue is a healthy place for you. I think you'd better get onto that big motorcycle of yours and get going. Real soon."

"That suggestion doesn't sound too friendly to me," Simon said.

Wes shrugged his massive shoulders. "Friendlier than you deserve."

Simon fought back the perverse impulse to laugh. Wes was trying to stare him down. Jesus. He'd mastered this trick in middle school.

Wes let out a snort and rolled his eyes, as if bored with the game. He looked down at the pile in the middle of the kitchen and nudged it with his boot, scattering dirt across the floor. "Cleaning this place up?"

"Trying to," Simon said.

"Don't envy you," Wes said. "The guy lived like an animal."

No way would he rise to such obvious bait. Simon grunted, folded his arms, and waited.

"I imagine he must have had a lot of pictures lying around, huh?"

"Imagine so," Simon said. "Haven't gone through them yet."

"What are you going to do with all them pictures, anyway?"

The question struck him as odd. "Don't know."

Wes rocked from one foot to the other. "Huh. Well," he muttered. "A place is always better once you get rid of the garbage."

Simon counted down from ten. "I'd better get back to work."

"Yeah, you get to it. Think about my advice. A man's got to look out for his health. It's all he's got, in the end, you know?"

"It's real nice of you to take an interest," Simon said.

Wes's eyes slitted at the sarcasm, but he turned to go.

"Lieutenant?" Simon called. "One more question."

Wes swiveled his head back on his thick neck. "What?"

"Did you serve in Vietnam?"

Puzzlement flickered in Wes's eyes. "Yeah. Nha Be, in '68. Why?"

He hesitated. "Gus was there," he said. "Just wondering if you'd ever run into him."

Wes shook his head. "Heard he got shot up. Not serving his country, though. Just risking his worthless ass for some pictures. They say that's your trade now, too. Figures, don't it? Just out for yourself."

"I've served my country, too," Simon said quietly. "The Marines. I was in the Gulf War. And Bosnia."

"Hmph." Wes's eyes narrowed to puffy slits. "Is that a fact."

Simon wondered briefly at the stupid impulse that had prompted him to say that as he waited for the guy to leave.

Wes stomped out. "Think about what I said."

Simon listened to the car pull away, and let the tension in his shoulders out in a long sigh. Newspaper crinkled, and he looked down at his clenched hand. He'd almost forgotten the Vietnamese newspaper.

He was glad to have something to think about other than Wes Hamilton's pointless hostility. His puzzlement prompted him to crouch down and sift through the heap of crap with his fingers. Grocery receipts, wood chips, cigarette butts. One empty plastic film canister.

He got down on his knees and peered under the furniture. A scrap of airmail paper under the bureau caught his eye. He fished it out.

The writing was small and neat, a feminine hand.

To Mr. Augustus Riley, or Heirs of Mr. Riley. I write on behalf of my father Dat Trong Nguyen, who was interpreter and guide to Mr. Riley in 1973. He is very ill now, and request me to inform you that he has not forget your brave and selfless action. His great regret is that he could not help you when you were wounded and did not come forward to return the camera which you entrusted to him on that day as he feared for his life. I enclose this camera with my father's apologies

and his best wishes for your prosperity and health, to
which I add

The rest was torn off. No address. Simon stared at the
dusty film canister, and at the old Leica camera that had
been part of the clutter on the kitchen table. A shudder of excitement ran down his back.

Photos. Gus's proof had to be photos.

Chapter

8

Coffee. Simon needed it, now. He'd been sorting through Gus's photo files since five-thirty A.M., after an endless night of tossing and turning. He had to put something into the gnawing hole in his stomach. Maybe he could slink into the Kent House dining room and get some coffee and a piece of bread without being noticed by anyone.

He emerged from the lilac bushes just as the kitchen door burst open. A big, hard-faced lady with a bouffant hairdo came out and marched down the path with implacable purpose.

Missy scurried after her. "Mrs. Wilkes, please! You can't just leave! Brunch is about to start, and we're supposed to do the egg thing and the herb potatoes parmesan and the baked pears, and I can't—"

"So fry 'em up some eggs real simple. Any fool can cook an egg."

"But Ellen said you'd do it!" Missy wailed.

"What's the problem here?" Simon asked cautiously.

Mrs. Wilkes looked him coldly up and down. "Oh. You're that Riley boy, right? I heard you were back in town causing trouble."

"Yes, ma'am, that's me," he said. "What's going on?"

"She's leaving! She's supposed to do brunch because Ellen had to get her picture taken!" Missy's face was a mask of unspeakable woe.

"My daughter-in-law just went into labor. I'm going to the hospital," Mrs. Wilkes said. "Good luck, Missy. Keep the flame low." She climbed into a big pickup truck and took off.

Simon looked at Missy's heaving shoulders. He felt helpless and threatened. "Hey. Don't cry, Missy. It's not the end of the world."

Missy twisted her thin hands together. "I just know I'll screw it up," she moaned. "I'm scared!"

"You don't have to be," he told her.

Missy blinked at him, bewildered. "Huh?"

He chose his words carefully. "The trick is to pretend that you're not," he said. "Concentrate on that, and after a while, you almost convince yourself. Then one day you wake up and whatever it is just doesn't scare you any more." He thought of El. "Some things still do, though," he amended grimly.

Missy's face fell. "So I have to wait a really long time before I don't feel scared anymore, then, right?"

He felt a sharp pang of sympathy for her. "No way. You can start practicing right now."

"Oh, yeah. Right. By cooking a fancy brunch for eight people?" Missy's face crumpled again.

"I'll help you," he heard himself say. He couldn't let the poor girl face this alone, no matter the risk to himself. It would be ungallant.

Hope dawned on Missy's tear-splotched face. "Can you cook?"

Simon hesitated. "Did El write down what to do?"

"Yes," Missy said eagerly.

"If it's written down, there should be nothing to it, right? We both can read. Come on, let's go for it."

Missy trotted after him into the kitchen, dabbing her nose on her sleeve. "Ellen left the recipes right here. The ingredients and stuff are on the counter, and she said we could cut the herbs right before we put 'em in 'cause they're better fresh," she babbled.

Simon examined the recipes. His heart sank. "What's Hollandaise sauce?"

"It's yellow," Missy offered. "I think it's got egg in it. Or maybe it's butter. Or lemon. They're all yellow."

He read on. "Do you know the difference between basil, sage and parsley?" he asked apprehensively.

Missy bit her lip. "Ellen always gets 'em. They're out by the path, but I'm not sure which is which."

His dread deepened by increments. "Uh, what does 'season to taste' mean? A lot, or a little?"

Missy shook her head slowly.

They stared at each other in a moment of mutual terror.

Simon forced out a laugh. "What's the worst that can happen? It's an opportunity to practice not being afraid, right?"

"Right!" Missy straightened her scrawny shoulders gamely.

"Don't worry," he told her. "When all else fails, improvise!"

Chuck and Suzie stared down at the greenish, runny "Simon's Emergency Special Omelet." They gave each other a speaking glance.

"I don't believe I've ever tasted an omelet flavored with mint and jalapeño peppers before," Mary Ann said dubiously. "It's a little odd."

Simon forced himself to grin. He'd been hoping that the aromatic leaves he had sprinked over the eggs were basil. "It's an acquired taste."

"Mom, I want some of Ellen's muffins!" Boyd whined.

"Me, too! This egg thing is gross," Alex said crabbily.

"Don't be rude, boys," Mary Ann remonstrated.

"It's OK," Simon said with stoic calm. "We'll do another round of English muffins, and you can eat them with jam, OK?"

"Don't burn 'em again," Boyd grumbled.

"Missy, throw in another batch of English muffins!" he yelled. "And watch them this time, OK? The toaster's not popping up!"

"OK!" she yelled back.

Missy was having a great time being his partner in disaster. He was glad that somebody was having fun. It had been a hellish two hours. Active duty subduing ruthless terrorists was relaxing in comparison. At least there he'd had a gun. But you couldn't make an omelet by shooting eggs.

"Could you put these potatoes into the microwave?" Lionel asked sympathetically. "They're a tad crunchy for an old geezer like me."

"Sure thing, Mr. Hempstead," he said, just as Missy burst through the door holding up a smoking pan.

He felt a sense of doom. "What happened?"

Tears welled up Missy's eyes. "The baked pears! We forgot 'em!"

Simon stared into the pan. The pears were pitifully shriveled beneath their blackened coating of brown sugar and butter.

"Did you taste them?" he asked. "They might still be edible."

"Gross!" Alex commented disdainfully.

"Gag!" Boyd corroborated.

Phil Endicott looked apprehensive. "Is Ellen cooking tomorrow?"

"Far as I know," Simon said.

"Thank God." He turned to leave.

"Stick around," Simon called after him. "You can fill up on English muffins!" He and Missy looked at each other in horror.

"The muffins!" they cried out in unison, lunging for the kitchen.

It wasn't clear who bumped into who, but as they burst through the door, the glass baking pan flew out of Missy's uncertain grip. It sailed through the air and crashed into the tiles of the kitchen floor. The pan broke, the pears flew. Flakes of blackened sugar flew everywhere, syrup spattered the cupboards and dribbled down the woodwork. The curtains over the toaster simultaneously burst into flames.

At that moment, El walked in the kitchen door.

Simon was almost grateful for the task of putting out the fire. He yanked the curtains down, tearing the curtain rod off the wall in the process, and flung the flaming mass into the sink, cursing as he singed himself. He turned on the water. The curtains hissed as they extinguished themselves. Steam rose up in smelly, billowing clouds.

He turned to face El's horrified gaze. His mouth dropped open.

El was unrecognizable. Her hair was tortured into a billowing mass of ringlets. Her luminous blush and freckles were gone, hidden under a layer of matte beige pancake makeup. Her eyelashes were crusty and black. A new lipline was painted outside her own natural lips with dark pencil and filled in with pink gloss. A shout of nervous laughter burst out of him. She looked like a cartoon character.

A very, very angry cartoon character, he realized belatedly. "Uh, sorry," he mumbled. "Your face, uh, took me by surprise."

Ellen walked into the kitchen and looked around herself. Simon followed her gaze and saw it through her eyes. Puddles and spatters and pathetic remnants of failed culinary experiments overflowed every counter. More than one egg had ended up on the floor, but in the heat of battle neither he nor Missy had dared to stop and mop them up. A pall of steam and smoke fogged the air. The place looked like hell.

"Where's Connie?" El's voice was not her own.

"Her daughter-in-law was having a baby, so she left," Missy whispered, lips trembling. She scuttled through the puddle of pear syrup and fled, leaving a trail of sticky footprints behind herself.

Simon choked on another bark of hysterical laughter. El turned to him. "Is something funny, Simon?"

"No way." He schooled his features to blandness. "Not at all."

"I come back from the most humiliating four hours of my life, having these stupid engagement pictures taken. I find my kitchen destroyed and my house on fire, and you have the nerve to laugh at me?" El's voice rose dangerously in pitch and volume.

Simon tried to look contrite. "I swear, I'm not! I'm sorry about the kitchen. I was only trying to help."

"Help?" She turned around in a full circle. "You call this help?"

Simon felt a sensation that he used to get a lot when he was a teenager, like his guts were tying themselves in knots. Another futile exercise in bad judgment. El would be better off if he were back in Gaza, or Chechnya, or Kabul.

The screen door creaked. An immaculate vision in a white linen pantsuit stepped gracefully inside. Muriel Kent, El's mother.

Muriel sniffed the air in the kitchen with distaste. Her eyes fell upon El, and widened. "Good heavens, Ellen! What in God's name have you done to your face and hair?"

El looked from Simon, to her mother, to the smoking mass in the sink. Her cartoon face crumpled. She fled the room without a word.

Muriel watched her go, one carefully plucked eyebrow arched in puzzlement. Her eyes fixed on Simon, and narrowed in recognition.

"You," she said in a flat voice. "Diana called me yesterday to tell me you'd been sighted."

Simon looked down at himself. Singed hands, smeared and spattered shirt and jeans, sweat rolling off the tip of his nose. He felt like a dog caught on the furniture. "Uh, hello, Mrs. Kent."

"I had a feeling we hadn't seen the last of you, young man." Muriel started to put down her handbag on the counter. Her eye swept the room, looking for a clean surface. Her mouth pursed, and she draped the handbag back over her shoulder.

Simon stared at her. Muriel Kent had always reduced him to a brainless, tongue-tied state. Here he was, almost thirty-five years old, and she still had the same effect on him.

"I take it Ellen has you to thank for this mess," she said.

Simon suppressed the urge to grovel. "I was, uh, filling in. Missy, the girl who works for El, didn't want to do breakfast alone, so—"

"Please, don't explain," Muriel said. "A picture paints a thousand words." She peered into the sink at the smoking remains of the curtains. "I see you have no vocation for the kitchen."

"I'm pretty good with a propane camp stove and a survival knife." He instantly regretted his cheeky tone. His hands embarrassed him, just hanging at his sides, so he tried to shove them into his pockets.

They were so crusty and sticky, they wouldn't slide in.

Muriel Kent's eyebrow climbed. "I had a feeling things were getting out of hand. It looks like I didn't come back a moment too soon."

"Yes, ma'am. I mean, uh, no, ma'am," he said inanely. "Can I offer you a cup of coffee? I think there's still some in the carafe—"

"Don't presume to welcome me into my own family home, Simon."

"I thought the house was Ellen's," he heard himself say.

Muriel's acrobatic eyebrow climbed even higher. "Technically, I suppose it is." Her keen eyes raked him up and down. She let out a sharp sigh. "Maybe I'll have some of that coffee after all. Come along with me, Simon. I want to have a word with you."

She picked her way across the sticky kitchen floor. He followed her reluctantly into the messy, deserted dining room. She poured herself coffee, stirred in a pack of Sweet'n Low and sat down.

Her calculating eyes were fixed on him over the rim of her cup as she sipped it. "Do you have any idea why my daughter is so upset? Other than the state of her kitchen, that is?"

Simon shrugged. "I imagine it has something to do with spending four hours with the Mitchells," he said. "Engagement photos."

"Ah." She took another dainty sip, holding out her pinkie like a goddamn duchess. "So you know that Ellen is engaged to Brad."

He grunted affirmatively.

Muriel crossed one snowy white linen-clad leg over the other. "I was so happy to hear that my daughter had finally decided to take that step into the next phase of life. She'll be such a good wife for a settled sort of man. A wonderful mother, too."

The danger gauge on the back of his neck had never failed him, and it was telling him that this woman was gearing up to rip him to pieces. His mind raced, examining and rejecting various ways of excusing himself from her presence without being rude.

Fuck it. He would just be rude, if worse came to worst.

"I certainly hope that nothing happens to throw a wrench into those plans," Muriel added.

"Can't imagine why it would."

Her mouth thinned. "Do not play dumb with me, Simon. The very fact that you're staying in this house with my unmarried daughter is enough to throw a wrench in those plans. It's incredibly irresponsible of you to park yourself here. Of all places."

He would not lose his temper with this woman. "It's an inn," he said. "I'm paying a hundred and twenty dollars a night for the privilege."

She harrumphed. "And you can afford that?"

"Easily," he said with rigid calm.

Her face was speculative. "Hmm. I imagine Ellen was thrilled to see you again. She was so attached to you when she was a girl."

A sense of impending doom gathered inside him, like a drum roll. "Uh, yeah. It's great to see her again."

"She's such a sweet girl, my Ellen. Wants to mother everyone, feed everyone, rescue everyone. Sometimes I worry about her."

Simon's jaw clenched. "Meaning?"

Muriel smiled sweetly. "I just hope you're not planning on taking advantage of that nurturing quality, that's all. Ellen deserves some happiness. I would hate to see her life upset."

Simon's hands clenched. "El is an adult."

"Ah. So she is. So she is," Muriel murmured. "And so are you, Simon. I imagine you must have come back to deal with Gus's estate?"

He nodded.

"Well, then. I'm sure you'll be more reasonable than Gus about selling us the carriage house. It belongs back in the family."

Simon cleared his throat. "My great-grandfather Seamus Riley won it fair and square from Ewan Kent. It belongs in the Riley family."

Her lip curled delicately. "What Riley family? You're the only one left that I know about, and you're not about to found a dynasty with your propane camp stove and your survival knife."

Simon forced himself to unclench his fists. "I'm not selling."

"Oh, don't be stubborn and ridiculous. What good is that old house to you? We'll give you an excellent price."

He was opening his mouth to to say something he would almost certainly regret when El quietly entered the room. Her hair was wet, and smoothed behind her ears. Her face was scrubbed, and she looked damp and luscious in her jeans and a snug yellow T-shirt. He smelled the warm, tangy scent of her shampoo all the way across the room.

"Hello, Mother." She leaned over to kiss Muriel's cheek. "Sorry about that. You caught me at a bad moment."

"Don't mention it, honey. Bridal nerves." Muriel patted El's jaw. "You missed a spot."

El winced. "I'll make another pass at it later with the cold cream. I tried to say no, but she just ran right over me. I'm lucky I got out of there with my hair still on my head. She wanted to have me layered."

"Diana Mitchell is an insufferably bossy woman," Muriel said. "That's one of the reasons I'm here. To give you moral support. Heaven knows, I'm almost as bossy as she is."

El's smile was wan. "I'm very glad to see you, but you should have given me advance notice! I have a completely full house!"

"It's impossible for me to imagine that there might not be room for me in this enormous house," Muriel said stubbornly.

El sagged down into a chair. "OK. You can have my room," she said wearily. "I'll get a cot out of the storeroom, and set it up in the—"

"No need," Simon said. "She can have my room."

El looked alarmed. "But where will you stay?"

He shook his head. "Don't worry about it."

El began to protest, but Muriel cut her off. "Thank you very much, Simon. That's extremely gallant of you."

"I'll, uh, go get my stuff out of your way."

His feet dragged wretchedly as he climbed the stairs. It was the right thing, the only thing to do. Better for everyone if he removed himself from temptation so the wedding plans could run smoothly.

Since he had no right to impede them.

Missy was perched on the flight of stairs that led to the tower room. She looked up, wiping tears from her reddened eyes. "Ellen threw you out, right? And it's all my fault." She pressed her face against the knobby knees that poked out from her jumper. "It's always my fault."

"No, it wasn't," he said gently. "When it comes to getting thrown out, I don't need any help from anybody. I do it all on my own."

Missy rubbed her nose. "What are you going to do?"

"I'll think of something," he assured her. "I can always camp out."

The misery on her face impelled him to crouch down and

pat her shoulder. She felt as fragile as a baby bird. "Don't feel bad," he urged. "Even if we crashed and burned, the important thing is that we tried."

"Yeah, try to tell Ellen that," she said soggily.

Good point, he privately conceded. "Never mind that. It doesn't matter. You put yourself out there on the line, and that's good. It was the right thing to do. You get points for that, even if you fuck up."

Missy's waterlogged eyelashes fluttered. "From who?"

Missy was too literal minded. "I don't know," he said helplessly. "In general. If nobody gives you points, just give them to yourself."

She looked doubtful, but intrigued.

"Really," he urged. "I mean it. Repeat after me. If nobody gives me points for putting myself out there and giving it my best shot, then I'll just give them to myself. Go on. Say it. It's good practice."

Missy swallowed, blinking rapidly. "If nobody, um, gives me points for, um, giving it my best shot, then I'll just, like, give 'em to myself."

"Great." He patted her shoulder again. "You're catching on. And you know what? Ellen needs your help. That kitchen is a mess."

Missy leaped up, vibrating with alarm. "Oh, God. I better hurry."

"Chill," he suggested. "Take it easy. Just take a deep breath, go down there, and calmly do your job." He gave her an encouraging pat.

"Um, Simon?" she said timidly.

He glanced back. "Yeah?"

Missy's swollen eyes were big and solemn. "Thanks for being nice to me. And trying to help me. You get points, too. From me, anyhow."

He tried to smile, and trudged on up into the bedroom. His stomach ached as he gathered his things into the duffel. It didn't take long. He packed light, needed very little. This fancy room did not belong in his life. Neither did El Kent.

He was economy style, she was the deluxe model. Best to swallow that down. No more head games or self-indulgence in the moonlight. No more sweet, tender comforting.

He was zipping his duffel shut when he heard the tentative knock. He froze. It sounded again, a timid tap-tap. Muriel Kent would never knock on a door like that. She would pound like a drill sergeant.

He yanked the door open. El stood there with her heart in her eyes. He wanted to grab her so badly, every cell in his body ached with it. "What do you want, El?" He made his voice deliberately hard.

Her luminous eyes were brimming with tears. "I don't want you to go again." Her voice sounded like a little girl. "Not yet. You just came back." Her face crumpled. "You were gone for such a long time."

A lump formed in his throat. He gathered her into his arms. The soft weight of her head against his shoulder felt so sweet, so right.

"I won't be far," he said. "I'll pitch a tent behind Gus's house."

"A tent?" She mopped at her eyes with the back of her hand.

"Yeah, I've got one packed onto the bike. There's earwigs in the grass, but I've slept with worse. And there's the creek for washing up."

"So you're not leaving for good?"

"Not yet," he said gently. "Soon, though. You know I can't stay."

Her arms slid around his waist. The look in her eyes terrified him.

"Don't look at me like that," he begged. "We've been through this. I'll just hurt you if I stick around. I don't want to break your heart."

"So don't," she said. "Just don't break it. It's so simple."

It wasn't simple at all, but he was helpless to explain. El followed him into the room as he backed away. "Don't do this to me," he protested. "I'm not a good guy. You know what I want. If you offer it to me, I'll grab it and take as much as I can get. And you'll get hurt."

"Just don't go," she repeated. "I can't bear it. Not yet."

"I'm nothing but bad news for you." His voice shook. "Do us both a favor. Tell me I don't deserve for you to look at me like that. Tell me to fuck off, El. Wash your hands of me before it's too late."

El laid her hand on his chest. "I can't," she whispered. "I can't."

Simon stared down at the slender hand splayed against his egg-spotted T-shirt. Her sweet scent made him feel dazed and stupid.

"Don't hate me, El," he begged.

"Never," she said.

He wasn't sure how they got to the bed, but next thing he knew, he was on top of her, all over her, winding his hands into the wet silk of her hair, tasting her soft lips in a famished kiss. His body crushed her into the bed, his aching hardness was cradled between her legs. She wrapped herself around him and moved as if he were inside her.

She had done that to him that night seventeen years ago, moving beneath him with that innocent sexual allure that had blown his mind wide open and given him his first hint of what passion really meant.

Leaving him to search the world for it ever since.

This was it, the whole thing, revealed in all its danger and glory. He rolled over, dragging her on top of him, pressing that exquisite softness against his body, dragging his mouth across her lips, her jaw.

He unbuttoned the top button of her jeans and slid his hand under the waistband. Thrust his hand underneath her T-shirt to caress the velvety softness of her breasts cupped tenderly in the satin bra.

"Ellen? Are you up there?"

Muriel Kent's suspicious voice cut through their delirious passion like a knife. Ellen jerked away from him and leaped to her feet. She'd barely finished buttoning her jeans when the door burst open.

"There you are!" Muriel's brow furrowed. "What on earth, honey?"

"I was just, ah, helping Simon carry his things down," Ellen said.

Muriel's gaze rested on El's flushed face and tousled hair. It swept over Simon's duffel, on the rumpled bed. "I see. Well, then. Once you've helped Simon carry down his single, solitary bag, perhaps Simon might make himself useful and carry my suitcases up."

Chapter

9

Ellen picked listlessly at her apple caramel tart and looked around the candlelit table. Her eyes lit upon her future father-in-law. Ray was acting strange tonight. Usually he was full of jokes and hearty, back-slapping good cheer. Tonight, he was silent and distracted. Deeply Concerned was stamped on his face as he listened to Muriel and Diana's chatter, but the relative merits of white chiffon and cream-colored taffeta didn't warrant Deeply Concerned. He should have dusted off Indulgently Amused for the occasion. He wasn't paying attention.

Not that she had any right to judge. She hadn't thought of a thing to say for herself all evening long. Her eyes slid to Brad, across the table from her. Brad wasn't wearing any mask tonight. His eyes were fixed on her, glittering with intensity. His fork moved back and forth to his mouth, but his gaze never shifted. Ellen fidgeted in her chair.

"You haven't eaten a bite of that apple tart, sweetheart, and it's the specialty of the house." Her mother's brow crinkled in concern.

"It's very good." Ellen took a hasty bite. "I'm just so full. The filet mignon was delicious."

"You didn't eat that either," Brad said. "You haven't eaten at all."

"Worried about fitting into your wedding dress? Don't worry. Brides always shrink a bit." Diana forked up a bite of chocolate mousse. "Thank goodness you've put a stop to that Riley person staying in your home, Muriel." She flashed a triumphant glance in Ellen's direction.

A frown flashed over Muriel's face. She dabbed her mouth with a napkin. "It was very gentlemanly of Simon to give up his room for me."

Brad snorted. "Gentlemanly? Not. He hasn't changed. Out for himself and to hell with the rest. A lying, cheating, no-good sack of—"

"Brad!" his mother exclaimed.

"Garbage," he amended, "even before he burned down our—"

"He did not!" Ellen's fork clattered loudly to her plate.

"Ellen, calm yourself," Muriel snapped.

"I am sick of hearing Simon put down! He is my friend, and he never burned down a goddamned thing!"

A loud guffaw broke the shocked silence that followed her words. Ray's shoulders began to shake. "Folks, don't you think we sh-should stay away from c-c-certain incendiary topics?" His face was going red. "Let's not get all w-w-worked up, now, OK?"

The silence grew even more strained as Ray's laughter subsided to chuckles, then to intermittent snorts. No one at the table wanted to meet anyone else's eyes. The restaurant was quiet, all eyes on them.

Diana sniffed haughtily. "It doesn't strike me as that amusing."

"Sorry, honey," Ray said meekly. "Just got the better of me."

"But to get back to what we were saying, you should use that pretty head of yours for something other than holding up your hair, Ellen," Diana said. "Ray saw Simon running away from the barn, which subsequently burned to the ground. After which, he disappeared. You do the math. The formula is not difficult."

Ellen stared into her dessert plate. "He had other reasons for leaving."

"And what might those be?" Diana blinked expectantly. "Do tell."

Ellen shook her head. Simon's problems were none of the Mitchells' business, but their accusations drove her crazy. She ached to defend him. And to make matters worse, inappropriate thoughts were constantly popping into her mind. Like the realization that she disliked Diana Mitchell. She would never learn to like that woman. She could not bully or cheerlead herself into it. No point in trying. Lost cause.

A sobering thought, and she'd been plenty sober to begin with.

Brad pushed himself away from the table. "Let's take a break from talking about a certain person, folks. I'm sick of the subject."

"I think Brad is right," Muriel said decisively.

Diana's spoon tinkled as she stirred her coffee. A pout marred her carefully made-up face.

Ray leaned over and patted Diana's hand. "Let's be nice, honey," he wheedled. "Let bygones be bygones. Water under the bridge, hmm?"

Brad tossed his napkin on the table. "Would you all mind if I whisked Ellen away for a little quiet time? There's been so much confusion lately, we haven't had a moment to ourselves." He smiled winningly at Muriel, and turned his intense gaze back on Ellen.

She shivered. There was raw possessiveness in his eyes, but no warmth. She wondered how she could have not noticed that before. Maybe this chill from him was new. Maybe he was just angry.

Or maybe she was simply seeing him with new eyes. Comparing him to Simon, just as she had compared every man who had ever gotten near her to Simon. Which had made her love life, the barren wasteland that it was, she reflected with a sinking heart.

"Of course. Run along and have fun," Muriel said.

Diana gave them a sour smile. Ray chuckled and patted her hand. Indulgently Amused had finally made an appearance.

They went through the requisite round of kisses, and Ellen followed Brad out of the Overlook Lodge and through the parking lot.

Brad opened the car door for her. "Want to go get a drink?"

Ellen shook her head. "I'm pretty tired. I'd like to go home."

"Fine." He got into the car and shoved the key into the ignition.

Ellen cast around for something to say, and thought of Ray's bizarre laughing fits. "Brad, is your father OK? He seemed odd tonight."

Brad grunted. "Who the hell knows. He's been odd ever since he retired. But then again, he's always been odd."

"I can't seem to get a sense of him," she said. "He's so—"

"Don't try." Brad's voice was hard. "Dad's a mystery, and he doesn't appreciate anybody trying to solve it. Just smile and nod and give him a wide berth, and you should be OK. For the most part."

Ellen subsided into a chastened silence. "I, uh, had no idea you had problems with him," she finally ventured.

"I don't," Brad enunciated the words with bitter clarity. "I don't have anything with him. Anything at all."

"And that's, um . . . not a problem?"

Brad braked violently at the red light. "Let it go, OK?"

She stared down into her lap and twisted the strap of her purse around her fingers. "I didn't mean to make you angry."

Brad made a frustrated sound. "I'm not. But you can only agonize about a person for so long, and then you just have to say to hell with it, and move on. Otherwise, that person becomes the focus of your life."

"I know exactly what you mean," Ellen said quietly.

"So the deal with me and my dad is this. I'm all done wondering about him. We are polite to each other, and it ends there. I don't care what's going on inside his head. No curiosity whatsoever. Understand?"

"Yes," she said. "I'm sorry, Brad. I just never knew that—"

"Can we please change the subject?"

"Of course," she murmured.

Ellen racked her brains for something to change the subject to. She tried to remember what they usually conversed about. The realization that dawned on her was an unpleasant one. She'd never really conversed with Brad at all. She'd listened to him talk about his successes, his prospects, his plans, while she made approving noises. Or else he held forth about how she should run her business, in which case she smiled and nodded and was appreciative of his interest.

The few, rare times she had shared things about herself, thoughts and feelings and opinions, he'd seemed politely bored. Which hadn't really surprised her, since she had always secretly suspected that she was a somewhat boring person. Nice and kind, yes, and she knew she wasn't stupid. She just wasn't particularly exciting. Which was no crime, but still. It had seemed safer to let him talk about himself.

Simon never made her feel boring. She'd never struggled for things to talk about with him. There was never enough time to say it all.

And so? That thought was so supremely irrelevant, it made her furious. Here she went with stupid, meaningless comparisons again. Simon did not want to marry her, father her children, grow old with her. Simon had a different agenda. Simon was another issue, entirely apart.

With Brad so grim and silent, they had nothing to say to each other. At least nothing that she had the courage to say.

It was a long, tense, uncomfortable drive home. When they pulled up in front of Kent House, she half hoped that Brad would give her his usual quick kiss and leave her to wrestle with her feelings.

Not tonight. He turned the car off and got out.

"We need to talk," he said. "Let's go inside."

Her belly leaped up, twirled and plummeted down. It was a reasonable request. He was still officially her fiancé, and God knew she had to find the courage and the nerve to deal with this awfulness.

She couldn't go on like this. They had to have it out.

He followed her into the house. She looked around, hoping Mary Ann or Lionel would be around to take the edge off the tension.

Not a soul was in sight. Everyone was still out to dinner.

Brad looked around. "Let's go up to your room. I don't feel like meeting any of your hotel guests this evening."

Also perfectly reasonable, Ellen reminded herself, but his footsteps behind her on the stairs made her feel pursued.

Brad followed her into her suite, which was a small living room with a connected private bath, and a small alcove for her bed. He looked around. "I've never seen your room," he commented.

"I suppose not," Ellen said nervously.

"Don't you think that's strange?" He wandered around the room, examining knickknacks, peering at her pictures. "Since we're engaged."

"Um, I wouldn't know. I've never been engaged before." She put down her purse and tried to think of something more intimate, more honest, to say. Her mind was clenched like a fist, in defensive mode.

"We've got to talk," he said again.

Amen to that. "Go right ahead," she retorted. "I'm listening."

He flung his jacket on her couch. "There are a lot of things we've never talked about, Ellen. I thought we were on the same wavelength, but I was wrong. We're not communicating as well as we should be."

"Um, probably not," she agreed.

"For instance, I decided that we should wait to have sex until we were married," Brad said.

She opened her mouth. Nothing came out. She closed it again.

"I thought it was more romantic to wait, since we weren't planning on a long engagement." He reached up and loosened his tie. "You seemed like a restrained, dignified woman. I admire that. I believe that strict rules should govern personal relationships as well as society as a whole. Otherwise it just becomes a sordid mess. I've been there, and done that, and I don't want to go back. That's why I chose a woman like you to marry. I want an orderly life."

"Orderly? Me?" She thought of yesterday in Gus's kitchen, twined around Simon's body, her blouse opened to his hot, ravenous mouth. She blushed. "I'm probably a lot less orderly than you think I am."

Brad's eyes moved down over her body, a slow, assessing gaze.

She shivered. She'd been so grateful for the fact that Brad had seemed content to wait to explore the physical side of their relationship. She'd thought that his delicacy was a good sign. That he would be a considerate husband in that regard. He advanced towards her.

She took a nervous step back.

"It occurs to me that you may have taken my waiting as a sign that I'm not interested," Brad said. "I am. Very interested."

"In, um . . . in what?"

He sighed impatiently. "Interested in sex, Ellen. With you. You're a beautiful woman. I would never have chosen you to be my wife if I weren't physically attracted to you."

His eyes were so cold. His voice so calculated. It seemed surreal, with the memory of Simon's delirious passion so fresh in her mind.

"Ah . . . thank you. I think," she faltered.

Brad put his hands on her shoulders, and brushed them over her arms. "I think we should take our relationship to another level."

He pulled her close and kissed her. A cool, curious part of

her mind monitored her reaction to his embrace, to his warm, skillful lips moving over hers. No rush of glowing heat. No soft unfurling in her chest. No ache of longing, no rising hunger or sweet sense of fulfillment.

Just a painful sense of wrongness deep in her belly that grew and swelled until it became a powerful urge to shove him away. She'd never fantasized about sex with Brad. She'd just hopefully assumed that as their intimacy grew, it would unfold naturally.

It wasn't going to happen.

She put her hands against Brad's chest and pushed him gently away from her. "No," she said.

He let go, stepped back. His eyes questioned her.

She shook her head. "I don't want to have sex with you."

Brad's face reddened. "Not now, or not ever?"

"Not ever," Ellen said. "I don't love you. I'm very sorry that it took me this long to figure that out."

She barely recognized her own voice. It was so clear, so decisive. She had never been honest with Brad before. In fact, it had been a long time since she had been honest with herself. She'd forgotten how it felt.

Brad looked away. His throat bobbed.

Ellen slipped off the ring and handed it to him. He stared down at it. "This is about Simon, right?"

"Simon has nothing to do with this." Ellen savored the ring of honesty in her voice. "Absolutely nothing. This is between you and me."

He shoved the ring into his pocket and grabbed his jacket off the couch. "After he uses you and dumps you, don't bother crawling back to me," he said. "I don't take used goods."

She blinked at him. Well. The nastier he was, the less guilty she had to feel about jilting him.

"I won't," she said. "Get out, Brad."

Simon shoved the file cabinet closed. Someone had searched these cabinets. Gus had been obsessive about keeping his photos in order. Simon remembered his uncle's complex, idiosyncratic filing system, and this was not it. These files had been shoved into the drawers in no particular order at all.

He pulled out his pocketknife and used the screwdriver to pry open the boards that covered the secret closet that Great-grandfather Seamus had built in the twenties to hide his moonshine. The Rileys were sneaky to the bone. He peered into the black cavity with his flashlight, and sighed. More dusty boxes of photos. God help him.

He dragged one out and riffled through it. These files, at least, were still organized according to Gus's system. The intruder hadn't gotten into Gus's secret closet. Simon pulled one out at random, blew off the grit, and held up his flashlight to supplement the glow of the kerosene lantern. Another beautiful woman, this one a juicy blonde in various sexy poses; blowing a kiss, looking over her shoulder like Betty Grable, splashing at the McNary Creek waterfall. Her light, tilted eyes seemed familiar somehow, but he couldn't put his finger on why.

She was part of a whole collection of pretty women. Gus's camera had loved them all up with passionate skill and a brilliant eye for composition. His uncle had been a kick-ass portrait artist. The girls in the photos looked radiant, adoring, dazzled. Sexually satisfied.

It made him itch to take El up to the waterfall with that old Leica. See if he could capture her rare, luminous beauty on film. The artist in him salivated at the thought of playing with dappled light and shadow on her body. Nude, if he could coax her into it. Black and white, so he could develop the film himself in Gus's darkroom, and—oh, Christ.

As if he needed a photographic record of the havoc he would wreak here to torture himself after he left.

He wondered if Gus had tortured himself with these pictures. Simon didn't remember any women in his uncle's life after he came to live here, but clearly there had been a time when Gus had loved their company. Something big must have happened to drive him so deeply inward. If he could just figure out what it was.

Maybe it had to do with this *"brave and selfless action"* that Nguyen had witnessed. Something about photos. Something about Vietnam. Something about his mother. But what connection could his mother have with Vietnam?

He'd found many photos of his mother. Beautiful ones that stirred memories in the deepest part of his mind. Plenty of opportunities to bash himself in the head with needless pain in these file folders, but nothing that looked like proof. But maybe the intruder had already found what he was looking for, and taken it away.

The batteries in his flashlight were running low, but he had to concentrate on something or he'd start surfing the alternating waves of lust and self-loathing again. The condoms he'd bought at the vending machine down at the tavern were burning a hole in his jeans. He had decided on the new game rules. He wouldn't seek her out, or pressure her in any way. But if she came to him, oh man.

He was so fucking ready, he was about to explode.

But he would give her the exact same talk that he gave to all the other women he slept with. No illusions, no promises, just hot, juicy sex, as good as he knew how to make it. She could decide for herself if she wanted him on those terms, and his conscience would be clear.

Theoretically, that was how it worked, but he couldn't get his restless body to calm down and agree to it. What if she called his bluff and told him to get lost? He would spontaneously combust.

He tucked the blonde back into her folder, and saw Gus's bold, square handwriting on a folder that poked out of the box.

WES HAMILTON AUG. '87. The month that Simon had run away.

What the hell? He pulled it out, and a sheaf of photos fell into his lap. A man getting out of a car with a woman who was wearing a very short skirt. Going into a motel room. The photo was careful to frame the motel sign. The man and woman coming out, laughing. A kiss. The man's hands on her ass. The camera focused mercilessly in on the man's face, leaving the rest of the picture a blur.

A younger, slimmer Wes Hamilton, the way he'd looked back in the bad old days when it had been his personal mission in life to make Simon's life hell. And the woman was most definitely not Wes's wife, the tight-lipped and narrow-hipped Mary Lou Hamilton. Who also happened to be the daughter of Wes's boss at the time, LaRue's chief of police.

Holy shit. Gus had been blackmailing the guy. Simon shuffled through the series, and started to laugh. Even Gus's blackmail photos were dynamic and compositionally perfect. Ever the finicky artist.

He heard the rumble of an engine. He blew out the lamp and jumped to his feet. After Wes's visit, he didn't care to be blindsided.

Brad Mitchell's Porsche was pulled up in front of Kent House. Brad and Ellen were back from dinner. The two of them got out, exchanged words. Brad followed Ellen into the house.

The photos of Wes scattered over the kitchen floor.

This he was not prepared for. The light switched on in her bedroom. Adrenaline surged through his body, the urge to run over there, burst in on them, and—

No. He clenched his fists. Her choice. Brad had offered to marry her. Brad had more right than Simon to kiss her and touch her. To slide between those cool sheets and cover her slender body with his.

He wanted to vomit. He couldn't stand here and stare at her bedroom window while this was happening. The scene played out in his mind's eye, horribly vivid and detailed. Complete with sound effects.

He had to turn away. Go inside. Swallow the bile. Move. Turn, asshole. Stop staring at that window. Turn around. He couldn't. He was rooted to the ground. Minutes crawled by. Three. Five. Eight. Ten.

The front door slammed. Brad stomped out to his car. Slam went the car door, too. The car squealed away.

The stars came into focus. The song of the crickets and the frogs swelled to a joyful crescendo. The waning moon hung low and fat and butter-yellow on the horizon. The wind off the river was perfumed with sap and flowers, the mountains full of shadowy allure. Life was sweet, full of possibilities. All because El was alone in her room.

The next cognitive leap wasn't much of a challenge, though. Whatever had made Brad so angry probably had to do with Simon Riley, professional troublemaker. He stared up at her window. Her silhouette flickered across the shade. He wondered if Brad had upset her.

He should check on her, make sure she was OK. If she spat in his eye, he'd walk down to the tavern at the railroad yard and get blind drunk. It wasn't his preferred coping mechanism, but what the hell. It was a time-honored family tradition, and it would do in a pinch.

He slipped through Gus's meadow, through the screen of lilac bushes, across the yard. He closed the kitchen door behind himself without a sound, and listened. The house was completely silent.

He crept up the stairs, down the corridor. He stopped in front of the master bedroom door and lifted his hand to knock. His hand froze.

What an idiot, chasing her like a lovestruck puppy. He had nothing to offer her.

The door opened, and his mouth went dry.

El was illuminated from behind by the rosy light of a silk-shaded lamp. Her hair was haloed by the light, loose and soft and flowing. She was wearing a silky, cream-colored thing that he supposed could be construed as an evening dress, though to him it looked like lingerie.

She stood in the door, waiting for him to say something. He swallowed, cleared his throat. "How did you know I was out here?"

"I felt you," she said simply.

He stared at the faint shadow of cleavage at the modest neckline of her dress. "I saw Brad leave," he said.

Heavy waves of hair redistributed themselves as she nodded. Her face looked different. Soft, radiant. Unguarded. Her sweet smile made him want to fall to his knees and beg for mercy.

"He seemed mad," he managed.

"Oh, he was. Very," she said in a husky voice.

Simon stared at the way the soft fabric molded itself to her hips, the soft curve of her belly. "I don't mean to intrude," he said, backing away. "I just wanted to make sure you were all right. When I saw your fiancé take off like that, I figured maybe he—"

"He's not," El said.

"Huh?"

"He's not my fiancé anymore."

Simon's world was whirling, shifting into a new shape. Until it settled, he had no place to put his feet. No ground upon which to stand.

El took his hand in hers and backed into her room. "Come in, Simon." She tugged him gently after her.

Cora had almost finished her clean-up routine, and was thinking hard about a nice bowl of pasta salad, leftover roast beef and a glass of chilled white wine in front of the boob tube as she dumped the contents of the lint filters. She saw the headlights pull up outside the Wash-n-Shop and peered out into the dark. The back of her neck prickled.

She'd had enough trouble in her life that by now she knew to pay sharp attention to what those short hairs told her. Sucky bad timing that her last customer had left less than five minutes ago. She ambled casually to her office nook in the back, where she kept her stash of detergent, fabric softener, quarters, and her handy-dandy baseball bat.

It was Brad Mitchell who shoved open the door.

Brad's green cat-eyes flicked over her, full of cool speculation. The way a guy would look at a car he was thinking of buying.

Don't panic. Brad Mitchell might be an asshole, but he wasn't in the same flea-bitten category as Bebop and Scotty. The danger he presented was only to her peace of mind, not to her physical person.

But her peace of mind didn't have a baseball bat to defend itself with. When it came to Brad, her peace of mind was monumentally undefended. She couldn't control her reaction to him, no matter how it humiliated her. The sick, hopeless anger and frustration. Worst of all, the stupid thrill of hope that this time it might be different.

And it never, ever was.

"We're closed." It was all she could think of to say.

Brad's eyes swept her laundromat with the lofty air of a guy who had never done an honest load of laundry in his life.

"I'm not here to wash clothes," he said.

"Oh, excuse me. Of course not," she replied. "I'm sure your mama has an army of servants to wash them for you."

He lifted a bottle of whiskey to his lips and then gestured with it towards the baseball bat. "Ever have to use that thing?"

"I've waved it around a few times, but I've never smacked anybody with it," she replied. Check him out, wearing a suit in this heat. Looking good in it, too. Vain, arrogant clown. "Not yet, anyhow," she amended.

He set the bottle down on the folding table and gave her his patented X-ray stare. That look unnerved her. She could never tell what he was thinking behind it, which had led her into all kinds of trouble. Since she, in her ingenuous stupidity, had projected silly, girlish dreams onto it, and then found that behind it was a big fat nothing. No trust, no faith. No love. Nada.

"So, Brad?" she demanded. "If you don't want to wash anything, then what the hell are you doing here?"

He shrugged his jacket off, draping it over the table next to the whiskey. Bad sign. She didn't want him getting too comfortable here.

"Tell me something, Cor," he said. "Why do you dress like that?"

"Dress like what?" She looked down at her black bike shorts, her lemon-yellow halter top. Or sports bra, depending on her mood.

"Like a tramp," he said.

She wondered how much of that whiskey he'd already drunk. "Brad, it's a hundred degrees in the shade," she said. "The real question you should be asking yourself is why the hell are you wearing a suit?"

"And in January, you wear skin-tight fleece. Answer the question."

She put her hands on her hips. "All right, then. I'll be honest, even though you don't deserve an explanation," she said. "I've got a beautiful body. I work real hard to keep it that way." She spun around on her tiptoes, arching her back. Smoothed her hands over her chest, brushed them over her naked midriff and the curves of her hips. "It's nice, huh? I like to show it off. If you've got it, flaunt it."

"I imagine that's another one of your favorite mottoes?"

Cora stretched her arms up over her head, tossed up her hair, hiked up her bosom. "You bet it is, bozo."

"So it's true," he said. "Just like I thought. You provocative bitch. You do it just to piss me off."

Her arms dropped, and she laughed out loud. "Like hell! Don't flatter yourself! You never entered my mind. And you still haven't told me what the hell you're doing here in my laundromat, wasting my time."

"I just had a really weird evening," he said.

"And why is that my problem?" She tossed the bat into her office and leaned against the dryer, crossing her arms beneath her breasts. She squeezed her arms up to accentuate her cleavage. His eyes fell to her chest. *Eat your heart out, dickhead,* she thought.

"I can't imagine why you would want to confide in me about your weird evening, but I'd like to have some dinner and put my feet up," she said. "So spit it out. Get it the hell off your chest, so I can go home."

"Actually, I thought it was something you ought to know," he said. "Since your latest lover is cheating on you."

Latest lover? She blinked at him for a second, disoriented. "My latest who?" She hadn't had a lover in almost a year.

"Simon Riley," he said impatiently. "He's been fucking my fiancée. What a flash of déjà vu, huh?"

She closed her mouth. "Oh. Wow. That was, uh, quick."

"I wonder, if I picked another woman right now, if Simon would dump Ellen and go right for my new woman instead." Brad's musing voice sounded cool, almost amused. "If this hypothetical woman belonged to me, she'd automatically be irresistible to him. You figure?"

"No," she said. "I don't figure. Simon wouldn't do that, because he really wants Ellen. And besides, I never belonged to you."

"No?" He took a step towards her. The hot glitter of anger in his eyes sparked a shiver of fear mixed with a delicious tangle of erotic memories. Brad had always been sexually intense when he was angry. Probably because he rarely expressed his anger any other way.

"Simon and I have never, ever been lovers," she said. "As I have told you before. Simon is just my friend."

"Funny. That's exactly what Ellen said. Her friend." Brad took a step towards her. "Just a friend," he repeated. "What does 'friend' mean these days? What does friendship entail? Want to be my friend tonight, Cor? Because I'm feeling really . . . really . . . *friendly.*"

"No. I'll tell you what friendship entails. Respect, kindness, trust, caring. Things that you don't know shit about, Brad Mitchell. I don't want to be your goddamn friend, since you don't know how to be mine. And I think you'd better go. Right now."

Brad did not reply. The glow of fury in his eyes was the

scariest thing she'd ever seen, and the street outside was completely dark and deserted. Maybe she should have hung onto that baseball bat after all.

She pointed towards the door. "So? Out you go, Brad. Thanks for the heads-up about Simon and Ellen, but since Simon is not now, nor has he ever been my lover, it is irrelevant to me. I don't care who he sleeps with. I just hope he's happy. And if you want somebody to hold your hand because Ellen dumped you, well, hah! It ain't me, babe."

"It's not my hand I want you to hold," he said.

His gall still had the power to stupify her. "You arrogant pig," she whispered. "How dare you come on to me? After what you did?"

"Why not?" he said. He pulled a diamond ring out of his pocket and tossed it up. It twinkled and spun. He stuck it back into his pocket. "Everyone else comes on to you. Can't I take a turn? I'm not engaged anymore. I'm a free man. I can be friendly with anyone I want."

"*You* want?" The bitter explosion of laughter hurt her chest. "Since you, of course, are the hub of the world? What about what I want? Did it ever occur to you that I—"

"I know exactly what you want, Cor."

She reached deep inside herself for the oomph to tell him to fuck off, like he deserved. The impulse petered out to a breathless nothing.

It was true. Brad did know what she wanted. It was as if he were specifically made to turn her on. He was built like a bull, to start with, which was a nice bonus, though by no means essential. But it was the essense of him, the smoldering wildness hidden behind that cool facade that did it for her. He'd gone at her with a relentless intensity that had always driven her clawing, screaming crazy with excitement.

And his shell was so smooth. Honor society, football team, debate club, valedictorian, clean-cut and handsome and bound for law school. Mr. Goddamn Perfect. She'd loved being the only one who knew the secret. That in bed, he was a wild animal who could never get enough.

She'd had lovers since then with more finesse and technique, but for brute staying power, no one measured up to Brad. She'd stumbled out of hotel rooms the morning after, barely able to walk.

He saw it flash across her face; the memories, the hunger. His eyes gleamed with triumph. He leaned closer. "Let's go to the motel on Route Six. Celebrate the end of my engagement with me, Cor."

She hauled off and slapped his handsome, smirking face as hard as she could, which was pretty damn hard, with all the iron she pumped and all the laundry she slung around. "Fuck you, Brad!"

Brad put his hand over the angry mark on his face. He stared at her, flushed and panting. Damn. Hitting him had turned him on.

Contrary, kinky, screwed-up bastard that he was.

"Is that how you want it?" he asked. "Fine with me. More than fine. Suits my mood right down to the ground."

"No." She stuck her face close to his. "Your God complex is making you stupid, Brad. That was a no. A big, fat, nonnegotiable no. If you ever want to enjoy the pleasure of my company again, you would have to beg on your knees for the privilege. You would have to heap flowers in front of me and kiss my feet and plead for my forgiveness for being so mean. And you would have to mean every goddamn word of it."

"Oh, that's ironic," he said. "Kiss your feet, huh? On my knees, in front of Lush Lips MacComber, the undisputed queen of the blow job. There's a kinky thought. Who the hell do you think you are, Cor?"

She advanced so aggressively, he took a step back. "I know who I am! I'm Cora Jean MacComber, business owner, goddess in progress. I run a laundromat. I make dirty things clean, but I don't think I could do much with you. Professional secrets will only get you so far."

He rolled his eyes. "I wasn't asking for your résumé—"

"I know exactly who I am," she yelled. "I grow great tomatoes. I make fabulous enchiladas. My smoked salmon cannot be beat. I'm a lapsed Catholic who still prays to the Virgin Mary because I think she's cool. I grow beautiful sunflowers. I'm trained as a lifeguard. I know how to do CPR. I don't tell lies. I know and like and respect myself!"

"Do not preach to me," he growled.

"I'll preach if I want! This is my turf! You have no right to come here and insult me! Who the hell do you think you are, Brad? Do you even know? Have you ever even asked yourself that question?"

He didn't answer. His Adam's apple bobbed. His face was a hard, expressionless mask, but she knew him well enough to read it in his eyes. Furious desolation, hidden behind a six-foot wall of glacial ice.

Oh, no. No way. She refused to let herself feel sorry for him. She would not fall into that trap. He didn't deserve her compassion.

"You haven't, have you?" she taunted. "You just swallowed what Mama and Daddy told you. You're just a Mr. Perfect Shell, but there's nobody home in there." She knocked on his chest as if she were knocking on a door. "Yoo hoo. Anybody in there? No? Didn't think so."

A muscle was twitching in his jaw, the one sign of emotion that he could never hide. She leaned forward and moved in for the kill.

"What a shame," she murmured. "And he looks so good on paper, too." She clucked her tongue. "Ellen's lucky she figured it out in time."

She felt it, the instant she went too far. She knew she was in for it, she and her big, fat mouth. He shoved her back against the dryer and kissed her. A hard, punishing kiss, but the sensual, whiskey-flavored invasion of his tongue detonated an explosion of lust and anger inside her. Sex had always been a duel between them, a sweaty struggle for ascendancy that left them both exhausted.

His hand slid down over her belly and between her legs, pressing against her clit through the stretchy fabric of her bike shorts.

He stepped back and let her go, and she wasn't quick enough to pull herself back together and do the hard-bitten, tough broad act before he saw it all written on her face. How easily he could bring her low. Eyes brimming with tears. Mouth trembling like an adolescent girl.

A cruel, satisfied smile curved his mouth. Bull's-eye. He'd gotten her. He grabbed her hand, and pressed it over the bulge at his crotch.

"One thing I do know about myself," he said. "I want to fuck you. For hours. Just how you like it." He pulled his business card out of his pocket, and tucked it into the valley of her cleavage. "Give me a call when you change your mind. We'll set something up."

When hell freezes, when pigs fly, shove it up your ass, they all jostled for position in her mind and missed the comeback beat. She covered her face with her hands. She was speechless with humiliation.

Brad wrenched the door open. "I'll be thinking of your beautiful body tonight while I jerk myself off," he said. "Sweet dreams, Cor."

Chapter

10

Ellen gripped Simon's wrist and pulled him into her room before he could change his mind. If this was all she could have of him, she was grabbing it. She had the rest of her life to snivel and whine and repent of her folly. She closed the door behind him. "I want you," she said.

The hunger in his eyes sent a primal thrill through her body.

"You know what I am," he said. "I won't tell you pretty lies."

"Why should you? And yes, I know what you are, Simon." She placed her fingertips against his hot cheek. "I know you so well."

He flinched. "Don't. I came up here to make sure you were OK, not to seduce you. I'm trying to do the right thing, and if you—"

"This is the right thing," she said.

He wound his fingers into her hair and tilted her head back. "You were about to get married. I came along, and it went up in flames."

"You're being silly. You told me that Brad was a mistake, and you were right." She petted his face. "It would have ended anyway. Better sooner than later. All you did is remind me of how it feels to really want someone. And that's a good thing. Painful and scary, but good."

He grasped her wrist and pulled her hand away from his face. "Maybe you were better off before you remembered."

She shook her head. "I'd forgotten what real feelings were like, but I won't be able to forget again. There's no going back."

His eyes were full of doubt. "El, I can't make any promises—"

She laid her finger over his lips. "I know you can't," she said softly. "I don't need promises. It's OK. Really. I'm OK with that."

"No love words," he said. "Just sex. That's all it'll be."

She stroked his hair off his forehead. "I don't need to hear you say love words. I know you so well, Simon. I know everything I need to know about you. You don't have to say a single thing."

"Oh, God." He closed his eyes, shook his head. "What the fuck am I doing here? I never wanted to ruin your life."

She wanted to laugh, but his face was so grim, she knew it would be a mistake. "If you're going to ruin my life, you should at least do it properly. As it is, I've got all the frustration and none of the perks."

"What perks?" He scowled.

She pulled him deeper into her room. "I'm teasing you, Simon," she said gravely. "I'm trying to make you loosen up. Maybe even smile."

"Forget it," he snapped. "I've got no sense of humor tonight."

She slid her arms around his waist and kissed the hollow of his throat. "Every woman should have her life ruined by a man like you."

"A man like me?" He scowled at her. "What kind of man am I?"

She tried not to smile, and failed. "Undomesticated."

He looked aggrieved. "What, so I need to be house-trained? Jesus, El, is it that bad? Am I such a mess?"

Laughter bubbled up, nervous giggles that could betray her and turn into tears at any moment. She fought them down. "Don't be so sensitive. I meant untamed, not untrained. It's very different."

"I don't see the difference," he growled.

She pulled one of his hands up and rubbed the back of his knuckles against her face. "It's the difference between a puppy and a timber wolf," she said demurely. "You come riding up on a motorcycle, dressed in leather, hair blowing in the wind. You're so sexy and smart, and gorgeous. You drive me crazy every time you put your hands on me." She kissed his hand. "You're magic. What can I do but grab you?"

He still looked wary. "So I'm the archetypal wolf, then, right? And every woman should try one before she settles down with Mr. Right?"

"Oh, hush up. You're going to be huffy and defensive no matter what I say. You're not an archetypal anything. I want you because you're Simon Patrick Riley. Period."

He caught her in his arms as she pulled away. "I'm just scared, El. That's why I'm freaking out."

She closed her eyes, and forced herself to say it. "You don't have to, you know. If you don't want . . . if this is so upsetting to you—"

"Fuck, no!"

The violence in his voice startled her, but he held her against him so tightly, she couldn't pull away or even look up at his face.

"I want to," he said raggedly. "I want to so bad, I'm dying for it. Don't ever think I don't want to. Just . . . just don't ever think that."

"OK. I won't." She nuzzled his throat, kissed the sharp point of his jaw, stroked his scratchy beard stubble. "So what's the problem? You want to, I want to. No lies, no promises, no illusions."

His dark eyes were tormented, full of shadows, but when she pulled his face down to hers, he didn't resist.

They both jolted at the bright shock of contact, and that

was it. They were lost, swept away. She wasn't kissing him, or being kissed. The kiss held them both in its grip, had its own urgent, demanding life. It moved, ebbed and flowed like a dance of sweet, desperate abandon.

She was giddy. If he hadn't held her so tightly, she would have floated right up out of his grip. His hands slid over the back of her dress, looking for the opening. "There isn't one," she told him.

"Huh?" He kissed her throat, her shoulder. Sweet pleasure rippled over the surface of her back.

"No zipper," she explained. "It's stretchy. Just peel it off."

He took the shoulder straps delicately in his hands and slid them down over her shoulders. The dress caught on her strapless bra.

He stepped back, letting his arms drop. "Take off your clothes for me," he said. "I want to watch you do it."

Ellen's arm crept up instinctively to keep her bodice from falling. She'd just thought she would fall into his thrall like she had the other times, and he would make all the moves. Challenge gleamed in Simon's eyes. He wanted her, but he wasn't going to make it that easy.

"I won't bully you like I did at Gus's house," he said quietly.

"You didn't bully me." Her breasts tingled as she thought of exactly what he had done to them yesterday at Gus's house. "I knew what I was doing. I may have been confused, but I'm not stupid."

"I know you're not. But I knew what I was doing, too. I won't trick you tonight. Tonight we'll know exactly where we stand. No bullshit."

She crossed her arms over her chest, shivering. "Simon, I—"

"Indulge me, sweetheart." His voice was low and softly seductive. "Strip for me. Offer yourself to me. And I promise, I'll take you."

Well. She'd asked for this. She had to screw up her courage and go through with it, no matter how embarrassing.

She tried to be sensual and provocative in her movements, but she was too self-conscious. Her cheeks reddened, her hands shook, and she could hear herself breathing in the silent room as she tugged the dress down to her waist and over her hips. It settled around her feet. She stood before him in her strapless bra and panties and thigh-high nylon stockings. Her hair fell forward to hide her blush.

"Don't hide behind your hair," he said.

She flung her hair back over her shoulders, proud and shy.

He stared at her, fascinated. "Take the rest of it off."

She unfastened her bra, let it drop to the floor. She pulled her panties down, let them fall. She bent over and peeled the stockings down slowly. She glanced up and saw herself reflected in the beveled mirror. Her face was flushed, her eyes dilated with excitement.

She understood now why he had demanded this striptease. He was reaching into her secret depths to coax her into opening herself to him. A ritual of seduction, to disarm and arouse her from within.

"Turn around." His deep, soft voice made her shiver.

She spun around for him, lifting her arms and inviting him silently closer with her eyes. Finally, he reached for her.

He touched her gently with his fingertips, as if she were made of fragile crystal. His breath was hot against her chest, the delicate rasp of his calluses against her skin made her shiver and moan. He cupped her breast, slid his hand down tenderly over her belly, and then between her legs. She clutched his shoulders, panting.

"Widen your legs, baby," he whispered.

She did as he asked. He caressed her between them with butterfly softness, teasing the length of the sensitive cleft with his fingertips.

"How do you want this to go, El?" he asked.

"What?" Her fingers dug into the thick muscles of his shoulders. "I-I don't know. Whatever you were just doing was fine. It's all fine. Everything you've ever done. You've never made a wrong move."

"No requests, then?" His voice was soft with amusement.

"You're trying to fluster me, aren't you?" she accused him. "Maybe you should tell me what's on the menu before I order."

His teeth flashed in a quick, appreciative grin. "Did you like it when I sucked on your breasts yesterday?" He bent over her chest and circled her nipple with his tongue, tugging on it delicately with his teeth. "You liked the way I petted you on the motorcycle?"

"All of it," she said unsteadily. "I love it. I want more. I want it all."

He sank to his knees, trailing kisses down her belly, and grasped her hips. He buried his face in the lush thatch of dark blonde curls between her legs, his hot breath tickling her thighs.

Her legs started to shake and buckle. "Simon!"

"Something wrong?" He stroked his face softly against the fine-textured skin of her hip, insinuating his hand between her trembling thighs. One finger delicately probed the soft flesh hidden there. She stared down, transfixed, as he deepened the caress, seeking the silky wetness of her arousal hidden in her inner folds. Opening her up.

"Not wrong," she quavered. "I'm just . . . I'm melting."

"I'll tell you what I want," he said. "To spread your legs wide open and put my mouth to you." He urged her legs wider and pushed his face against her mound. He slid his tongue delicately into the cleft of her labia, and the sweet caress racked her body with spasms of pleasure. "I want to lick up your lube until you melt into a lake of hot, yummy girl juice. I want to dive into it and wallow in it all night long. My face between your legs. My tongue shoved into your pussy."

She clutched his head, shuddering. "Stop," she gasped.

He looked up. "Scared?" he asked. "Chickening out?"

She shook her head violently.

"That's good, because it's too late to stop," he said.

She steadied herself on his broad shoulders. "I'm going to fall down," she admitted. "I can't stand up if you do that to me."

He rose to his feet and led her to the sofa. He slanted her a doubtful look. "Don't tell me this thing is one of Great-grandma Kent's goddamn antique heirlooms from Scotland."

"Um, actually, it is," she admitted.

"Oh, fuck me." He stared at the portrait of the stiff blonde lady in a black high-collared dress that hung over it. "Don't tell me, let me guess. This would be Great-grandma herself, right?"

"Uh . . . yes," she said. "Why do you ask?"

He blew the painting a mocking kiss. "Look down your nose all you want. She's mine tonight. Grab us a towel, babe."

She gave him a blank look. "A towel?"

"For the couch," he said patiently. "I want to go down on you, right here, on your sainted great-grandma's fancy couch. You're going to get wet. You'll need a towel under you."

She fled into the bathroom and came out with a fluffy bath towel clutched against her cherry-red face.

Simon pried it away, and flung it over the faded upholstery. "Damage control." He pressed her gently down until she sat on the edge of the couch, and sank to his knees in front of her.

"Why don't you take off your clothes, too?" she asked.

He stripped off his T-shirt and flung it away. "Better?"

She made an involuntary sound of delight. All that lean, exquisitely defined muscle moving beneath gleaming golden brown skin, the breadth of his chest and shoulders, the sinewy grace of his arms. Amazing. Excessive. Nobody needed to look that good.

She ran her hands over his shoulders, hungry to explore every detail, but Simon was focused on his own agenda. He leaned forward, kissing the tops of her thighs, and Ellen pulled out the elastic tie that held his hair. She spread it all over his muscular back and stroked it.

He peered up impatiently through the tangled dark veil and shoved it behind his ears. "El, give me my hair thing back," he complained. "Oral sex is tough to do with your hair all over the place."

She threw the hair tie across the room. "Cope," she said. "I like the way you look with your hair down. It turns me on."

"Oh. Well, in that case, fine. I'll deal with it." He stared down at her naked body, running his hands over her hips. "I never did get a good look at you naked that night in the dark. I always regretted that."

"Me, too," she said. "I always wished that we'd had more time."

"Open up," he asked her. "Let me see you now. Open your legs."

A tension she'd never known she carried released in a long, shuddering sigh as she yielded to his tender demands.

"Oh, God," he whispered. "Look at you." He slid his hands up the insides of her thighs, opening her still wider, and caressed the slick, moist crevice of her labia. "I figured you for pale pink." His voice was soft and dreamy. "To go with your freckles and your blonde hair. I figured pale pink nipples, and a pale pink pussy with golden curls around it. But look at you. You're pearly pink here—" he caressed her outer lips, and parted them tenderly with his fingers. ". . . but in here, when you're turned on, you're deep crimson. El's secret, hidden fire. Raspberry red. Sweet and delicious. You're so beautiful, baby."

He thrust his finger inside her and withdrew it, gleaming with moisture. "I love the way your pussy clings to me like it can't bear to let me go." He thrust deeper. She cried out, squirming around the invasion.

He bent down and began licking her with long, wet, greedy strokes. He folded her thighs back and held her writhing body in place while he suckled her clitoris, lapped every fold, caressed every crevice. He thrust his tongue into her sheath, ravenous for her female essence.

She sagged against the stiff cushions of the couch, thighs folded up and totally exposed to the tender, merciless lash of his tongue. The wave inside her loomed so huge, she wasn't sure she could survive if it crashed over her, but Simon ignored her whimpering protests. He followed the rising arc of sensation with single-minded intensity and held her as the climax racked her, his mouth still fastened over her sex.

He scooped her into his arms as soon as her eyes fluttered open and carried her to the shadowy alcove that held her bed. He laid her on the rosebud quilt. The dark silhouette of his powerful body stood out in sharp relief against the light in the living room as he bent to unlace and kick off his boots. He fished into the pocket of his jeans and tossed a couple of foil packets between her pillows.

He stretched out on the bed beside her. "Got them at the tavern."

She touched his shadowed face, amazed at how feverishly hot he was. "Thanks for remembering," she said. "I didn't think of it at all."

He kissed her fingers and pushed her onto her back, gently urging her legs apart. His long, sensitive finger slid inside her, moving in sensuous circles, massaging and opening her until she was moving against him in a jerky, involuntary motion. She was wet, slick, soft and desperate. She clutched his head in her hands.

"Simon, please. Make love to me now. I want to feel you inside me. I've been dreaming about it for—"

"Not yet." His soft voice was implacable.

She almost screamed with frustration. "Why not? Don't torture me! I can't take being teased right now. I feel—"

"You wait." He slid lower and pushed her legs wide, and went at her again, suckling and lapping her. Teasing and tormenting.

Tension tightened to the point of pain, and she arched up off the bed, sobs of ecstasy jerking through her.

The bed creaked as Simon gathered her into his arms and rained tender kisses over her cheeks, her jaw, her lips. She smelled her own sexual scent on his face. "You liked that?" he asked.

She pressed her face against his hard chest and nodded. His silky chest hair tickled her nose. She inhaled his spicy, unique scent, dragging as much of him into her lungs as she could. He tangled his hands in her hair, kissing and cuddling her until the tremors subsided.

"OK. Now," she said. "Do it, Simon. I've waited long enough."

"You'll wait a little longer." He slid his finger inside her again, and her sensitive body clenched around him tightly. "You're not ready."

"What, are you crazy? Why aren't I ready?" she pleaded. "I've never been so ready in my life. Why are you doing this to me?"

He slid two fingers inside her. She stiffened and gasped.

"Because you're small," he said flatly. "And I'm not."

She struggled up and reached for his belt buckle. "I'll be the judge of that, thank you very much. Let me see you. Get these off."

He caught her hands, and pried them off his belt. "You've seen me naked before." His voice was soft with laughter.

"Oh, hardly!" she snapped. "At four in the morning, with my eyes full of tears? I wasn't exactly detail oriented at the time!"

He rolled over on top of her, blocking all the light with the dark silhouette of his head and shoulders. "Did I hurt you that night?"

She hesitated. She'd never been able to lie to him. He knew her too well. "Um . . . well, yes," she admitted. "But I was a—"

"A virgin, yeah. I know. It was obvious," he said. "And I didn't know what the hell I was doing. I was too rough on you."

She wrapped her arms around his neck. "So what if you were? What does it matter now? I'm not a virgin anymore."

"I've wished ever since that I could do it over properly,

and tonight, I'm by God going to do it right. So don't even bother rushing me, El. You're ready when I say you're ready. Not before."

His sharp tone startled her. "Excuse me for having an opinion!"

"Have all the opinions you want. Won't change a thing." He brushed his fingertips over her hips, caressed the crease between her mound and her thigh, toyed with the wet curls of hair, and kissed her throat. "Want to know a secret, El? I was a virgin that night, too."

Her heavy-lidded eyes popped open. "No way!"

"Way." He tickled the wet vortex of hair that hid her clitoris.

"But the girls in school went on and on about what a hot kisser—"

"Sure, I did lots of kissing. Petting, too. But I never did the nasty until that fateful night. Don't you remember my lack of technique?"

"No, I do not remember that," she snapped. "You're obsessed with technique. I don't give a good goddamn about your stupid technique."

"Oh, it's not stupid now. Don't knock it till you've tried it."

"Oh, goody. I can hardly wait," she grumbled. "If it happens before I die of old age, that is—"

He cut her off with a pleading kiss. "Have mercy, El. I'm not doing this to piss you off. This is important to me. I'm so jacked up tonight. I don't want to lose control and fuck it up."

"Why would you?" She kissed his forehead, his sharp cheekbones. "Listen to how calm it is. Nothing but wind in the trees, frogs croaking and crickets singing. No burning buildings for miles around."

He jumped as if she'd pinched him. "Don't jinx me!"

She petted his hair. "Don't be silly," she soothed.

"Please, El," he begged. "Don't joke about that. I can't take it."

She wrapped her arms around his neck. "I won't. I won't," she crooned. "It's going to be fine."

He rolled onto his back, clutching her on top of him. His lungs heaved. And she used his moment of weakness to her own advantage, reaching down to unbuckle his belt.

"Hey. I felt that," he growled.

"Just let me see." She ripped open his jeans. "It's only fair."

He sighed, and shoved his jeans down over his hips. He flung them away and sat up on her bed. The lean, beautiful lines of his waist, his hips, his flanks, were lit from one side by the light from the living room, painted with the dusky shadows of the alcove on the other.

His erection jutted out before him. He was right, she conceded privately. He was big. Heavy and long, the heart-shaped head broad and swollen, gleaming with moisture. Far bigger than any of the other men she'd been intimate with. Though the list was admittedly a short one.

She reached out a tentative hand and wrapped her fingers around his penis. He was so hard, so hot, his skin exquisitely soft and smooth. She stroked him gently, and his body quivered in response.

He covered her hand with his and dragged it along his hot, velvety length in a tight grip that made her squirm with excitement. He pried her hand away. "That's it. No more. I'm too turned on," he said. "One more stroke and I'll come all over your quilt. I'd rather come inside you."

She groped among the pillows until she found one of the condoms. She ripped it open and handed it to him.

He sheathed himself and pushed her down onto her back. His thick, silky hair tickled her face and shoulders as he caressed her with the blunt tip of his shaft, making himself wet with her slick moisture.

He started to push inside, and blew out a sharp, hissing breath. "You're tiny," he said. "Has it been a long time?"

"About, oh . . . five years," she admitted.

His body went motionless. "Five . . . *years?* But . . . Brad? Didn't you guys—"

"No," she said softly. "Never. We were waiting."

"Good." His voice was savage. "I hated the idea of you with him." He pushed deeper, and the pressure intensified.

She arched and shifted, seeking a more comfortable angle.

"Why?" he demanded. "Why five years? You're so beautiful and sexy. Every man who saw you must have wanted you."

The apprehension in his voice told her that he already knew the answer. "I measured everyone against you," she said simply. "No one ever excited me one tenth as much, so I figured it couldn't be real. And then I would just start feeling sad and cold and empty, which tended to be a big turn-off for the men involved. Poor guys. Wasn't their fault."

"Oh, El." His voice was rough with dismay. "Oh, Christ."

"And then, after a while, I stopped even wanting to try. Until now. I want it now." He began to pull away, and she yanked him closer. "Don't," she said desperately. "Please. If you stop now, I think I'll die."

His hands tightened painfully on her shoulders. "But you were only sixteen when I left!"

"So you think I'm stupid?" she said wildly. "You're right! I'm a total idiot! But it's not like I had any choice! It just happened!"

"El—"

"This is not your fault, Simon! I'm not asking for your pity and I'm not begging for your love. I'm thirty-two years old, and I know better. But please, just give me this one thing!"

He kissed her jaw soothingly. "I couldn't stop now even if I wanted to, which I don't, so calm down, OK?"

"OK." She shivered as he pushed himself deeper.

He pressed his hot face against her neck. "Relax," he pleaded.

"You, too." She hugged him, vibrating with shaky laughter.

He rotated his thumb around her clitoris, sliding deeper

inside her with each slow, gentle push. "El?" His voice was choked with effort.

She moved against him, clenched around him, and kissed his face. "It's OK. I love the way it feels. I'm fine."

"I don't want you to feel fine. I want you to feel wonderful."

She laughed. "You ask so much of yourself."

"Wrap your legs around me," he instructed.

She clasped herself around him and dug her fingers into the thick, sinewy muscles of his shoulder. She felt stretched, invaded to the utmost. He was so much more intense than her dreams and fantasies. So big and powerful, the weight of his hard body pinning her down, his thick shaft penetrating her more deeply than she knew was possible.

She wanted to drink in his mysterious power and vitality. He transformed everything he touched. Before he came back, she'd felt like a wax doll. Now she was so alive to feeling, she ached and burned with it. The force of it cracked her open, turned her into something new, unknown. A molten sea of emotion, accepting his body inside her own. Melting and moving around him in helpless, passionate surrender.

The heat in her chest expanded into something so deep and wide and huge, it burst its bounds and flung her into sweet oblivion.

Simon fought back his orgasm so he could watch hers. He didn't want to miss a second of this beautiful woman convulsing around him.

Her cunt contracted around him, tight pulses that milked and pulled him deeper. He wanted to bind her to him in every way possible; body and soul, a gold ring, a baby. Anything, everything.

He wanted to claim all that beauty for himself.

He felt huge and heavy on top of her slender body. He nuzzled her face, and tasted tears. "You OK?" he asked hesitantly. "Did I hurt you?"

Her arms and legs tightened. "Let me cry if I damn well want to."

"Uh, OK," he said meekly. "Is this routine?"

"Is what routine?" she snapped.

"Crying when you come. Let me know. So I can brace myself."

She sniffled, and dabbed at her nose with the back of her hand. "I don't know," she said defensively. "Could be. Can't say. Big sissy."

"I am not a sissy!" he protested. He reached out to flip on the bedside light. It cast a reddish glow. He scooped up her trembling legs below the knee and folded her up so he could see all the details: his cock lodged tightly inside her body. The tender inner folds of her labia distended around him, the tight clutch and pull as he pulled himself out, the delicious resistance as he forged back in.

She gasped, clutching his arms. "Oh, God."

"I get deeper inside you when I fold you over like that. Is it OK?"

She nodded. "It's amazing," she whispered.

"I want more," he told her. "Can you take more?"

Her eyes were so soft with love, they sent a stab of fear through him. "I can take anything you can dish out," she said.

He drove himself inside her, harder than he meant to. "Do not challenge me, El," he warned her. "That's not a good vibe for us."

She braced herself, digging her fingernails into his biceps. "You don't scare me one bit, so don't even try. Just don't bother."

"You're not scared of anything? Lucky you, babe."

He let go. Took her at her word and gave in to instinct. He pumped himself inside her deep and hard and selfishly. He expected her to cry out, to make him stop, make him say he was sorry.

He was completely unprepared for what actually happened.

It was like being shoved off a cliff. He tumbled in freefall, and found himself in her arms, shaking violently, wound around her, covering her tear-stained face with wild, frantic kisses. Her mouth opened to accept the thrust of his tongue the same way she took in his pounding cock. Emotion shot up through his chest. A geyser of heat, of light. A volcanic explosion rose, and broke. Obliterating him.

Her soft hands against his hair pulled him back from the floating, timeless nothingness. She petted him so gently, smoothing his damp, tangled hair against his sweaty shoulders. He could feel her total acceptance of everything he'd done. Everything he was.

His throat closed up. He lifted himself off of her body and rolled away, off the bed. He stalked into the bathroom to get rid of the condom. His throat was wound up tight. He took his time washing up in El's bathroom, staring into the mirror as he let the sweat dry.

His fantasies hadn't come close to how red hot, how sweet she was. And he'd never dreamed of the depths of her feelings for him.

The damage he could do here was catastrophic.

El knelt on the bed, waiting for him when he walked out. Her eyes were filled with a terrible acceptance. "What's wrong?" she asked.

He lifted his hands, let them drop. Shook his head.

"Did I do something wrong?"

"It's not you," he told her. "You're perfect, El."

"No, I'm not perfect," she said. "I'm far from perfect."

He shook his head. "I keep looking over my shoulder. Someone's going to come along any minute and kick me out on my ass. Get lost, Riley. Who the fuck let you into paradise?"

Her shoulders shook, with laughter or tears or some combination of the two. "It's all in your head," she said. "No one wants to throw you out. You're not stealing from anyone. It's all in your head, Simon."

"I know that," he said. "But that's not good news. What's in a man's head is all he's got. That's his reality."

She slid off the bed and wrapped her arms around him. His body reacted to the silky contact. His cock stiffened against her thigh.

"It's not all you've got anymore," she said. "You're not all alone in your head anymore. You've got me. And I love you."

His ears started to roar. "Don't, El," he said sharply. "You promised."

"No love words, I know. I said that I wouldn't expect them from you, but I never promised not to give them to you myself. And I love—"

"Stop." He covered her mouth with his hand. "If you want more sex, I'll give you more sex. That's all."

She seized his hand, kissed his palm and pried it open. Her eyes never dropped. "I'll take what I can get."

"You deserve more," he said.

"I deserve *you.*" She pressed herself against his body. "I want more. The full dosage. I want to swallow you up. I want to crawl inside you and wander around. I want to read your mind. All of it. Even the ugly stuff. I'm not afraid of you. So stop being afraid of yourself!"

She was so beautiful like this, lit up with anger. She dazzled him.

"You don't even know what you're saying," he said. "You've got some romantic fantasy idea built up, and it's not me. I'm—"

"So you think that the great and terrible Simon will blow all my circuits? That I can't handle you? Hah. Arrogant jerk. Think again."

His blood boiled at the look on her face, his cock was rock-hard, as if he hadn't just had the most explosive orgasm in his entire life. "You're provoking me," he said. "Is that what excites you?"

Her chin went up. "Everything about you excites me."

"OK. You want all of it, you get all of it."

He spun her around and pushed her facedown onto the bed.

* * *

She was afraid to look into his face. "Simon?"

"Give me that other condom," he said.

She rummaged around beneath the pillow until she found it, and twisted to pass it back. He shoved her back down as soon as he took it, his hand between her shoulder blades.

He paused to put it on, and shoved her thighs apart. He slid his hand between them. His toying fingers made a soft liquid sound inside her body. He grasped her wrists, trapping them behind her back.

"Open your legs," he said. "As wide as you can."

She felt silly to hesitate. She'd been begging him to have his wicked way with her, but she hadn't realized how helpless and exposed she would feel if he did. She parted her legs slowly. He shifted on the bed till he knelt behind her, and shoved them even wider.

"Bend your knees. Arch your back and raise your ass in the air."

She tried bargaining with him. "Let go of my arms, and I'll—"

"No. I want you like this. Head down, face pressed into the sheets, legs spread out, back arched, that perfect ass in the air—perfect."

She panted into the sheets, her face so hot it felt feverish. She felt twisted, arched into a bow. Muscles strained and taut. The secret places of her body wide open for him to look at, to touch, to penetrate. She tried to relax, but the tremors that shook her came from someplace so deep inside that she couldn't dream of controlling them.

His hand tightened around her wrists, stretching them exactly as far as he could without hurting her. "You're trembling," he said.

She nodded against the sheet.

"Are you afraid of me?" he asked. "I'll stop if you want me to."

She shook her head. She couldn't bear to speak.

"So it excites you." He circled his fingertips delicately over her bottom and trailed them gently down the cleft between her buttocks, a teasing, feather-light caress. She jerked violently.

"Don't worry," he soothed. "I'm just admiring the beautiful details." His voice brushed over her, dark and warm and velvet soft. "Your ass is gorgeous. There's this pretty pink flower bud here . . ." he circled his finger tenderly around her anus, ". . . and then you swell open into this tender scarlet flower . . . here. It pulls me. Wow." His hand slid lower. She shuddered at each light, glancing touch.

"And your ass cheeks," he said. "Your skin is so smooth, and the swell of your hip is so sexy. These strong, sleek muscles underneath. The perfect female body. There's nothing so beautiful in the world."

He let go of her arms and shifted on the bed. She let out a moan of shocked pleasure as he began to kiss her there; warm, wet caressing strokes. His mouth moved against her, his tongue delving into her sheath from behind, licking and lapping and dragging over her sensitive flesh. Each sensual stroke rocketed sensation through her nerves, making her shudder and weep. "Your cunt is so tender. And your lube is so sweet. I could eat you all night." His voice resonated through her sensitive flesh like another caress. "You're wet all the way down to your knees. You're shaking like you want to come again right now."

She whimpered in wordless assent, her hips jerking against his hand as he delved inside her with his hand, seeking that pulsing glow of awareness deep inside her body that she'd never known existed. Caressing it until the long, delicious wave of helpless pleasure throbbed through her.

She was so dazed, she could barely make out the words, until she heard him repeating her name. "What?" she gasped.

"Did you ever think about me when you touched yourself?"

She started to laugh. God, had she ever.

"What's so funny?" he said suspiciously.

"What a stupid, obvious question," she choked out.

"What was I like in your fantasies? Did I lick you like . . . this?"

"Simon, please." She was going to shatter, explode, go crazy if he went on with this torture. He made the most intimate parts of her body his own personal territory with his relentless, sensual exploration.

"Anything you want, babe," he crooned. "You want my hands, my tongue, my cock? Tell me what you want."

"I want you inside me again," she said. "Please."

He seized her hips, and dragged them back until she was up on her hands and knees; head down, hair pooling below her face onto the tangled sheet. He probed her tender opening with the swollen bulb of his penis, pushing hard against her resistance. Nudging inside.

"It's so good," he groaned. "Am I different from your fantasies?"

She'd fantasized about him, ached for him, longed for him, but the reality of him was almost more intense than she could bear. His penis felt huge sliding into her. "Yes," she whispered. "Very different."

"How?" His breath caught with pleasure as he slowly withdrew, and lunged deep inside her once again.

"You're . . . you're bigger," she said unsteadily.

"What, you mean my cock?"

Tremors of laughter made her already shaking body feel like it would dissolve into mush. "Oh, please. I mean everything about you. You're all over my body, all over my life. You crowd out everything else."

"Is that a good thing or a bad thing?"

She tried to look back at him, but he thrust his hips against her, and she had to brace herself and redistribute her weight.

"It's not good and it's not bad. It just is," she whispered.

He gripped her hips harder and slowly pumped himself in and out. "How else am I different from your fantasies?" he demanded.

"You're a hell of a lot more talkative," she snapped.

He laughed, a free, delighted sound without bitterness. "I love it that you thought of me when you touched yourself. That turns me on."

"It was the only way I could make myself come," she admitted.

Tension gripped him. She'd miscalculated. She'd thought the confession would please him, but he retreated instantly to a remote, icy distance even while his body penetrated and overwhelmed hers.

"Christ, El. Don't do this to me," he muttered.

"I can't help it," she said. "I'm just telling you the truth. I love you, Simon. I always have. I love—"

"Don't. I'm giving you everything I can. Don't ask for more."

"I'm not asking for anything. I can't help the way I feel—"

"Shh. I don't want to hear it." He leaned over her body, pressed his hot mouth against her back. His dark hair tickled her damp skin. He held her hips in his long fingers, his grip verging on painful, his shaft pulsing inside her. "I want to fuck you hard, El."

His harsh tone seemed to tell her, not ask her, but still he waited for her response. His big body thrummed with hot, volatile energy.

She let out a long, shaky breath. "I might fall to pieces," she said.

"I'll hold you together," he said. "You can take me."

And she did. He took what he wanted, no love words, no tenderness, just his hands holding her body in place as he ruthlessly proved his point. He didn't want her to love him, but it was too late.

He was so fierce and strong, but her body was primed to welcome him, and every deep, sliding intrusion of his throbbing shaft drove her higher. No matter how angry and remote he was, this was Simon, and she couldn't help but nourish herself with his wild energy.

At first, she just braced herself against his powerful thrusts, but soon she was shoving herself back against him for more, sobbing and gasping and demanding everything he had. He collapsed on top of her and drove his hips against hers in a series of short, stabbing thrusts. He went rigid, let out a strangled sound. The explosive energy of his climax pulsed inside her. She lay on her belly and tried to breathe.

He lifted himself off. She turned her back to him and rolled herself into a tight ball, arms around her knees, hair over her wet face.

He'd made his point. She'd gotten the message. She couldn't look at him or speak to him without showing how much she loved him, and she couldn't bear to be punished for it, even if he punished her with pleasure. It was too hurtful, too shameful to have her love shoved away.

Simon got up, went into the bathroom. The water ran.

He stood by the bed and stared down at her for several minutes. Then he pulled his clothes on and left.

Chapter

11

Simon crept down the stairs, his boots in his hands. The pressure in his chest had built up to the critical point. He was about to yell obscenities, throw furniture out the window. He had to get outside, where there was space around him, so he couldn't hurt anything.

The sense of impending disaster kept getting stronger, and he'd gone against all his instincts, indulged himself and fucked her anyway.

He'd been so cruel and cold. He wanted to race back up the stairs and beg her to forgive him and love him and pet him again.

He tiptoed onto the porch. The rattle of ice cubes in a glass startled him. He dropped his boots and whirled, sinking into a defensive crouch. Moonlight illuminated Muriel Kent's face as she rocked gently in the porch swing. She saluted him with a glass, and took a sip.

"Well, well, well. What have we here," she said dryly. "Stand up straight, Simon. I'm not going to attack you, whatever you might think."

He straightened, willing his heart to slow down. "You scared me."

"I suffer from insomnia ever since my husband died," she said.

"I'm sorry," he offered.

Muriel's eyes gleamed in the moonlight over the rim of her glass. "Can I mix you a whiskey sour, Simon? That's what I'm drinking."

"No, thanks," he said. "I'm not much of a drinker."

She studied his face in the moonlight. "I suppose you wouldn't be, considering."

He kept warily silent and waited for her next move.

"I have a feeling the wedding is off," Muriel said. "I saw it in Ellen's face at the restaurant. And I have you to thank for it. Right?"

No need to reply to that. His silence was answer enough.

"You're not what I had in mind for Ellen," she said.

Simon crouched to pick up his boots. "Brad Mitchell may be rich and connected, but he's a stuck-up bastard. El deserves better."

"And you think you're better?"

Her scornful tone stung, but when it came to cold bastards, he could give Brad Mitchell a run for his money. He deserved every insult she could throw at him.

The ice cubes rattled as she sipped her drink. "I would have hoped my daughter would pick a man who would stay the whole night with her and be there for coffee in the morning. But look at you, Simon. Slinking away by cover of darkness. Some things never change."

It occurred to Simon that the whiskey sour she was drinking was probably not her first. He might be unlucky enough to learn more about what Muriel Kent was thinking than he had ever wanted to know.

"Ah, well. My poor baby has to take her chances, like we all do," she murmured. "But if you run from her, you are a coward, and I have no sympathy for you at all."

The judgment in her voice pissed him off. He sat down on the steps with his back to her and yanked one of his boots on. "I'm used to acting like a thief in the night when it comes to El," he said. "You didn't want me anywhere near her when we were kids. What do you expect?"

"I expect you not to act like a kid," she said. "I always knew you were going to be trouble. From the very day you came to live with Gus I knew it. I took one look at you, and I saw it all happening."

"Oh, please. I was nine," Simon said dryly. "Give me a break."

Muriel clucked her tongue. "Why should I? It's the truth. It was inevitable that any motherless boy raised by a misfit like Gus Riley was bound to turn into an angry, troubled young man. It was also very obvious, even then, that you were going to be far too good looking, for your own safety or anyone else's. And I knew that combination was going to be an irresistible lure for a sweet, selfless girl like my Ellen. Moth to the flame and all that nonsense, eh?"

He pulled the other boot on with a sigh. "Mrs. Kent, you're—"

"And all my knowing didn't do a damn bit of good, did it? Nothing has changed." She raised her glass to him, and took a deep swallow. "Fate," she said. "You just can't shake it. What will be will be."

A chill shivered through him. He thought of El, curled up in bed with her back to him, silently crying. He rubbed his face, and tugged his bootlaces tight. "I won't be here long," he told her. "There's a limited amount of damage I can—"

"Bullshit. Don't insult my intelligence."

He gulped back the rest of what he was going to say.

"Exactly how much time do you plan to take to toy with my daughter's affections before you run off to some miserable place full of exploding bombs again, Simon? Tell me, so I can prepare myself."

He got to his feet, and forced himself to answer her question at face value. "I have to clean up Gus's place. Get things in order. I came back here mostly to ask questions. I want to understand . . . why."

"Why he shot himself?" She shook her head. "I wish you luck. You won't find many people who can tell you about Gus. He cut all ties. He didn't even do his shopping in town after you left. He was furious with everyone after the fire. He bought his groceries over in Wheaton."

"I don't blame him," Simon said. "I remember how it was. Everyone looked down on us and judged us. So did you, Mrs. Kent."

Her laughter had an ironic edge. "Oh, it goes both ways, young man. Gus judged us, too, you know. He was merciless."

He was so startled, he could think of no reply.

"I went to school with your mother, you know," Muriel went on. "Judith was such an intelligent, beautiful girl. Very gifted. We were friends. Gus was a few years older, but I was acquainted with him."

"I see." He didn't have the nerve to ask her how that was relevant.

"We lost touch when she went off to college," Muriel mused. "I got married. Our paths diverged, and she went the counterculture route. But I was so terribly sorry when I heard that she had died."

He waited, still groping for the thru-line.

"I saw her in town once with you when you were maybe four. She was so proud of you. She thought you were some kind of genius."

He tried to speak, but his mouth was too dry. He swallowed, and tried again. "Shows how much she knew."

"Don't be flip," Muriel snapped. "It's childish and disrespectful."

"Sorry," he said.

"Anyway, to get back to my point, Gus judged everybody, Simon. He judged LaRue for being backwards and provincial, but what did he expect of a small town? It's like judging an orange for being round. He judged my husband for being a successful businessman. Frank was a good bit older than me, so Gus judged me for marrying money. As far as he was concerned, we were bourgeois, money-grubbing clones who would sell our souls for a new kitchen appliance."

Simon was dumbfounded. "Oh. I, uh, see."

"When he got back from Vietnam, he was even worse. He was furious with the whole world. He grew his beard down to his navel, and stomped around glowering, and then he judged people when they got nervous. He was a piece of work, that Gus. Arrogant as they come."

Simon struggled to fit that information with his memories. "Was he arrogant and judgmental enough that someone might have blown him away and set it up to look like a suicide?"

Muriel was shocked into silence. The porch swing ceased to squeak, the ice cubes ceased to rattle in her glass.

"My goodness, Simon," she murmured finally. "What a question."

Simon hesitated for a moment. "Once when I was little, he got word that some guy he'd known in 'Nam had killed himself," he said. "He was so upset, I stayed outside for two days."

"Oh, dear." Muriel sounded uneasy.

"Anyhow, Gus went on about how Gary had taken the coward's way out, and no matter what, he would never do that. He made me promise I would never do it either. I was only ten, maybe, but I knew what death was. I knew I didn't want to be dead. So I promised. We promised each other. And Gus always kept his promises."

Muriel put down her drink and brushed at the corner of her eye, a quick, embarrassed gesture. "I'm sorry, Simon."

Simon looked away from her. "He was drunk, of course. But he was . . . well, he promised. And he sounded like he meant it."

"Life can change your mind about things." Muriel's voice sounded older, devoid of its usual crisp tone. "Regret and loneliness and pain. Aging. It might have just worn him down."

Gus had been about as easy to wear down as a steel

girder, but Simon shrugged. "Might have, I guess," he said politely.

She was quiet for so long, he started to wonder if that was his cue that the odd conversation was over and it was time to fade away. But the second he started retreating into the dark, her voice stopped him.

"Offhand, Simon, I can't think of anyone who might have had a grudge that severe. People disliked him, but he never got in anyone's way. He did spend some time in the mental hospital, but that was—"

"Mental hospital?" He stiffened. "I never knew that! What for?"

"A long time back," she said. "I'm not quite sure. I think he had a breakdown after he came back from Vietnam. The effects of his head injury. Stress flashbacks or some such thing. It was all very tragic, but I never quite got the details straight. There were conflicting stories."

today i got proof that i am not crazy. now i can tell the truth 2 everyone, including u. A strange, cold thrill ran up Simon's spine.

"Your mother died while he was in the hospital, if I'm not mistaken," Muriel said. "Awful. Must have been a terrible time for him."

"Uh, yeah," he muttered. "Pretty much sucked for me, too."

She gave him a quelling look. "Simon. That goes without saying."

He let out a sour grunt in lieu of apology.

"There were certainly a lot of women who were crazy about him back then, I'll tell you that much. He was the bad-boy heartthrob of LaRue. Those flashing eyes. Those cheekbones. That mouth."

That didn't square with the bearded mountain man that he remembered, but it did with the photographs. "Gus? A heartthrob?"

"It's true," she assured him. "Not to flatter you, young man, but he looked quite a bit like you do now, in those days. When I was in school he was running around with . . . let's see, oh, lots of different girls. Frieda Ginestra. Sue Ann O'Donnell. Diana Archer, too."

Frieda, Sue Ann, Diana, had all been on the list of password attempts. "I don't know who those women are," he said.

"You know Diana. Brad Mitchell's mother," Muriel said.

"Her?" His mouth fell open as the beautiful, cat-eyed blonde in the bikini photo slipped into focus in his mind. "And Gus? Holy shit!"

Muriel chuckled. "Wild youth. Diana was one of the beauties of the county. Hard to imagine? But we all have our moment."

The swing creaked softly in the silence for a moment. "But I can't imagine some middle-aged LaRue matron killing Gus in a fit of mad passion thirty years after the fact," she went on thoughtfully. "Though I have had some hot flashes where I definitely felt capable of—oh, dear. I'm sorry, Simon. It's really not a joking matter at all."

"It's OK," he said. "Gus would've appreciated that. Gallows humor was the only kind of humor that he had."

Muriel chuckled again. "You know what? I'm going to tell you a little secret, Simon. Something I've never told anyone."

Apprehension gripped him. He felt an urge to flee. "Uh . . . what?"

"There was a time, back when you were teenagers, when I was convinced that Ellen had an eating disorder."

Simon was disoriented by the abrupt change of subject. "Huh?"

"I would make a big meatloaf, or a roast, or lasagna, and put the leftovers into the fridge. The next morning, poof, they were gone. I was really quite worried for a while. I even took her to a psychologist."

"I remember," he said slowly. "She told me about that."

"The psychologist told me there was nothing wrong with Ellen, which was a relief. But that didn't solve the mystery.

So one night, I did a little investigating to see what happened to that food."

"Oh. I see," Simon said guardedly.

She sipped her drink. "After that, I started cooking more food."

Ice cubes rattled as she drained her glass. She rose to her feet before he could think of any sort of a reply.

"I'm not quite the ogre that you think I am, young man," she said. "I'll toddle off to bed. See if I can get some sleep. Good night, Simon."

"Good night," he echoed faintly.

He stared blankly at the empty porch for several minutes before it occurred to him that he had nowhere to go. He'd forgotten to pitch the tent. The meadow grass was crawling with ants, earwigs and snakes, and there was no rest to be had at Gus's house. Too many ghosts.

He kept picturing how it would have been to fall asleep in El's arms, her hands moving on his hair. It made his throat ache.

Fuck it. If he had no place to sleep, he might as well get to work.

"Ellen, you can't huddle in your room for the Peach Festival right after jilting your fiancé," Muriel Kent insisted. "You promised Bea you would do the pie table, and you've got to face the gossip. Otherwise it looks like you're in the wrong."

Ellen sifted flour into the bowl, and cut in the shortening. "People can think what they please. And besides, I am in the wrong." She stood on tiptoe to see if the U-Haul was still parked outside Gus's house.

It had been coming and going all morning. Evidently Simon had decided not to take her up on her offer of the use of her truck. Nor was he interested in any other favors from her: neither seeing her, nor speaking with her, nor having anything whatsoever to do with her.

She bit her lip, looked away from the U-Haul, and carefully poured cold water into the pastry mixture. Keeping busy was the trick.

"You're just going to have to find the strength, Ellen, because I won't have my daughter slinking around as if she were ashamed!"

"It's not up to you, Mother!" Ellen slammed the sifter down. A cloud of flour wafted into the air.

Muriel took a startled step backwards. "Good Lord, Ellen!"

"I'm tired of being bossed around!" Ellen grabbed a handful of pastry out of the bowl. "My whole life I've been a good little girl, and what has it gotten me? Nothing! From now on, I'm going to do exactly as I please, and I do not feel like going to the stupid Peach Festival and smiling and chitchatting and pretending everything's just great!" She wadded the pastry into balls and slapped them down onto the marble pastry slab. "Missy and Bea can handle it without me, and if they can't, well, tough titties. The good citizens of LaRue won't die if they don't get a piece of my pie this year. They may suffer, but they won't die."

A smile slowly curved Muriel's mouth. "Well, I'll be. It looks like my little girl might have finally found her backbone. I assume you were doing exactly as you pleased last night before Simon sneaked out the front door at three in the morning, hmm?"

"Mother!" She attacked a pastry ball with the rolling pin.

"Why not just go to the Peach Festival with your Simon?" Muriel suggested. "Make a statement. Make a splash. Be scandalous, honey."

Ellen winced. "He's not 'my Simon.' "

Muriel blinked. "Ah. I see. Just what is he, then?"

"That's nobody's business," she said in a clipped voice.

Muriel examined her daughter with worried eyes. "Lighten up on that pastry, dear, or you'll toughen it."

"I know what I'm doing," she snapped. "At least with pies." She peeled a piecrust delicately off the board and draped it over a pie tin.

"I know this probably isn't the best moment to say this—"

"So please, please, don't," Ellen begged.

Muriel barged on. "You've been pining for that boy for most of your life, and God knows, he's ruined your other prospects—"

"Mother!"

"So use some of that new backbone of yours, and fight for what you want!" Muriel announced. "You have to try a little harder."

"I did try!" Ellen's voice edged on hysteria. "I tried everything! I was brave to the point of idiocy! I dumped my fiancé, I offered him my body, I told him that I loved him! I left no stone unturned!"

"Calm yourself, Ellen," Muriel murmured.

"Hah! Calm myself how? I tried begging and pleading! I tried comfort! I tried pastry! I tried sex!"

"For goodness' sake. Spare me." Her mother fluttered her fingers and shuddered delicately. "I don't need the gory details."

"Don't ask if you don't want to know! And don't tell me to try any harder, because I'm at my wits' end. Do you understand, Mother? I take one more step at trying harder, and I'll go right over the edge!"

Muriel stared at her, blinking like an owl. "My goodness, honey. How dramatic. I had no idea you were so . . . passionate."

"Neither did I." Ellen stopped, sniffed violently, and looked at her goopy white hands. She pressed her forearms against her leaky eyes. "I'm only this way when it comes to Simon."

Muriel pulled a Kleenex out of some magical invisible stash and pressed it against Ellen's nose. "Go on, honey. Blow your nose."

Ellen laughed soggily and snuffled into the Kleenex. "Thanks."

"In a case like this, all one can do is look on the bright side of the situation," Muriel said briskly.

Ellen let out a derisive snort. "Oh yes? And that would be?"

Muriel's smile was sly. "No matter what happens, you no longer have to face the grim specter of having that monstrous bitch Diana Mitchell for your mother-in-law. Isn't that something to be grateful for?"

Ellen's face started to shake. "Don't make me laugh, Mother, or I'll just start crying, I'm warning you."

"Honey, we can weep for gratitude together."

That cracked them up. They finished Muriel's whole packet of Kleenex between the two of them.

Simon pulled onto the road that led to the dump. Hard work was supposed to clear the mind. Based on that principle, he'd put aside the photographs and launched into the phase of junk elimination. Box after box, bag after bag. Junked furniture, magazines that were decades old, warped shoes, towels so ragged they were almost unrecognizable as towels. Rusted car parts, corroded objects he couldn't identify.

And liquor bottles. So goddamn many liquor bottles.

The further he delved into the wretched house, the deeper he dug into Gus's desolation. The more the past pressed down on him.

And it didn't matter how hard he worked. Wild thoughts kept racing through his mind, like sneaking up to her room tonight, apologizing for being a mean, cowardly dog and vowing to love her for the rest of his life. Just so he could lose himself in her body again, and again. For as long as fate would allow him.

He was a real glutton for punishment today.

He pulled up at the dump, expecting to see Max Webber, but the guy who came to the door of the cottage wasn't Max. It was Eddie, Max's son. Simon's ex-best friend and companion in adventure, who had refused to look him in the eye the other night.

Sweat broke out on Eddie's sunburned, balding brow.

"Hey, Eddie," Simon said. "It's been a while."

"Uh, yeah. Hi, Simon," Eddie's eyes shifted away. They landed on a big metal shelf piled high with fireworks. Eddie's father had always done the fireworks for the town holidays. It made them both think of those Roman candles and sky-rockets on that long-ago July night. Eddie's face turned even redder. He shoved his hands in his pockets.

Shit. As if he needed anything else to bring him down today. "Still doing fireworks, I see," Simon said.

"Uh, yeah. My dad and I are doing the Peach Festival."

"Good for you." Simon studied the burly guy shifting from one leg to the other. "Have you heard from Rick, or Mike or Steve or Randy?" he asked, naming the boys who had been with them that night.

Eddie cleared his throat. "Uh, Rick works for the railroad. Mike sells cars in Vancouver . . . Randy lives over in Pasco. Think he's a gym teacher now. Don't know about Steve. Haven't seen 'em in years."

"Ah." Simon nodded. "Well, whatever. Just curious."

"Yeah. It's, uh, g-g-good to see you, man," Eddie stammered.

Simon grunted. "I need to dump some stuff, Eddie."

"Sure, sure, whatever you want," Eddie said hastily.

"I need to make a bunch of trips, so prepare youself. You'll be seeing a lot of me," Simon said. "And hey. Eddie?"

"Huh?" Eddie looked anxious.

"Relax. Don't sweat it. It was a long time ago," Simon said quietly.

When he pulled out to get another load, Eddie was staring after him thoughtfully. His eyes didn't slide away this time. He gave Simon a tentative wave. Simon waved back. What the hell.

Chapter

12

The kitchen was hot and fragrant with the rich smell of pastry and baking fruit by afternoon. Ellen pulled the last of the pies for the festival out of the oven to cool, and positioned the kitchen stool in front of the screen door where she had the best view of Gus's house.

She fidgeted on the stool, finger-combing her sweat-dampened hair back. She was sore between her legs. Every time she thought of the night before, excitement surged through her and transformed her body into an ache of yearning. She dropped her red face into her hands. Sulking all alone in the hopes that he would feel guilty and come to his senses was clearly ineffective. She was going to have to make the next move. Again.

Anger simmered inside her. He had used her body last night and then walked away from her without a word. He was ignoring her today as if nothing had happened. At least she should tell him what she thought of him and his bad manners. She had nothing left to lose, not even pride. That had gone up in flames last night.

She felt naked and terribly vulnerable without it.

She crossed the lawn, pushed through the lilacs and the

deep meadow grass. She climbed up onto the porch. Her stomach fluttered wildly. Backbone, she told herself. She lifted her hand to knock.

The door opened before she had a chance. "Hi," she said.

Simon nodded in response. His loose, open shirt was streaked with dust and dirt. He stared at her silently. He did not invite her in.

Ellen clenched her teeth. Coming here had clearly been a mistake, but she would just have to tough it out somehow. "Looks like you've made progress." She tried to keep her voice light.

"I've been back and forth to the dump all day," he said.

Ellen glanced back at the U-Haul that was parked in the yard outside. "I noticed that you decided not to use my truck."

"I didn't want to bug you."

That stung. "And you thought it wouldn't bug me that you vanished last night without saying a word? And avoided me all day?"

Simon's eyes slid away from hers.

Ellen sighed. "Are you going to invite me in, Simon?"

He stepped back into the room, and gestured for her to enter.

Ellen walked in. The kitchen looked twice as big, with most of the junk cleared away. The floor was swept, but cobwebs still festooned the rafters. A heavy, charged silence lengthened between them, making her breathless. She searched for something to say. "What's in the boxes?"

Simon looked relieved at the change of subject. "Gus's personal stuff. I've been sifting through the trash for it. Those are his cameras."

Ellen lifted an old camera out of an open box. "I remember this one. You used to take pictures with it when we were kids."

"Yeah," he said. "Gus taught me the tricks."

"I didn't know he taught you photography."

"He was pretty good to me, when he was in his right mind." Simon took the camera from her and turned it over in his hands. "I've been thinking about Gus all day. I thought I hated him, after I ran away. Then when I found out he was dead, I realized that I didn't. I never really had. What happened here wasn't his fault."

"What do you mean, not his fault?" She bristled. "He was the adult, and you were the kid! Whose fault was it, if not his?"

"What I mean is, he was depressed and sick, and it got the better of him," Simon said. "But he did the best he could."

"The best he could?" Ellen's face turned red with old anger. "I saw how you looked after he'd been at you! You call that the best he could?"

He sighed. "You're deliberately not getting the point."

"Oh, I get it! You used to do this when we were kids. Pretend it doesn't hurt. Pretend it's no big deal. Remember when you and Eddie bet who could hold a cigarette to their arm the longest? And you won."

"Ten bucks," he said wryly.

"You said it didn't hurt, and then it got infected. Remember that? You've still got the scar." She grabbed his wrist and shoved up his sleeve, uncovering the puckered, shiny scar on his forearm. "See?"

Simon looked uncomfortable. "El—"

"Now here you are again, saying it doesn't hurt! It's nobody's fault! He was doing the best he could! It's no big deal! You didn't come over today because you didn't want to *bug* me!"

Simon's face hardened. "What do you want from me, El? We all have to cope with our lives somehow. This is my style. Yours is different. I try to act like it's no big deal, and that usually works for me."

"Was last night no big deal for you, then?" she demanded.

He stepped back, startled. "Whoa! I didn't know we were talking about that!"

"Just tell me quick, and don't try to soften the blow."

Simon put the old camera gently back into the box. "No, El," he said quietly. "It was a very big deal for me."

Ellen fought to keep her mouth from trembling. "I forced you into a corner, and made you say that, and I'm sorry," she said. "But I can't be as compassionate as you about Gus. I'll never forgive him for driving you away from me." She headed for the door.

"El, can I show you something?"

She stopped, and turned. "Show me what?"

He pulled several large, heavy albums out of one of the boxes, and laid the stack on the table. "I found these earlier this morning."

Ellen walked over to the table and opened the first album. A birth certificate. Black-and-white baby pictures. Simon as a toddler, held in the arms of a beautiful smiling woman with long, shining dark hair and high cheekbones. "Is that your mother?"

He nodded.

She turned page after page. More photos. A small, grinning Simon in front of a Christmas tree. Simon on a pony. Childish attempts at art, things made with paste and glitter. School pictures, starting with kindergarten. The album was packed, without an inch to spare.

"My mother must have started it, and left it here for some reason. Nothing survived the fire at her house. I never knew it existed." Simon opened the second album. "And Gus continued it. This is my third-grade picture. I came here to live in third grade. He put in everything. Report cards, art projects, even some of my English themes. I didn't even know he bothered to look at this stuff, let alone memorialize it."

Ellen leafed through the pages, and stopped on a series of striking black-and-white landscape photos. A newspaper article entitled LARUE YOUTH WINS ART SCHOLARSHIP was taped beneath them.

"I remember these," she said. "The year you won the

scholarship for the summer art program, but you couldn't go because—"

"Because I was on probation. Yeah, I remember." He looked embarrassed. "My art teacher wanted to kill me."

"Was that the tractor race where one of the tractors ended up nose down in Willard Blair's stock pond? Or was that the time that you and Eddie borrowed the mayor's wife's convertible for a drag race?"

"Do we have to dwell on it?" His voice was sour.

"Sorry." Ellen hid a smile and turned the page. Blue ribbons from student art exhibitions, charcoal sketches, pen and ink drawings. His senior year school picture. She stared at it, her heart full. It was the same one she had hidden deep in her wallet, battered around the edges from having been pulled out and stared at so often.

The pages went suddenly blank.

Ellen closed the album. "He was so proud of you," she said. "This makes me like him better. I could almost forgive him now."

"I think he hoped I would find this someday," he said. "A sort of backhanded apology. He was such a devious bastard. He liked to say things indirectly. Leave himself a built-in escape route."

Ellen laid her hand on top of his.

Simon stared down at her hand. "It'll have to be enough."

She looked away quickly to keep from choking up, and her eyes fell on a pile of files. "And these?"

"My photo spreads," he said. "He collected them, too."

She opened the file. Simon moved up behind her and looked over her shoulder. "That was the Palestinian refugee camp," he told her.

Simon's graceful, eerily beautiful photographic images told a stark, eloquent story of suffering. She looked through them slowly, and opened another file. Simon peered over her shoulder again.

"This is the war in Afghanistan," he said hesitantly. "Maybe

Zebra Contemporary Romance

To start your membership, simply complete and return the Free Book Certificate. You'll receive your Introductory Shipment of FREE Zebra Contemporary Romances, you only pay $1.99 for shipping and handling. Then, each month you will receive the 4 newest Zebra Contemporary Romances. Each shipment will be yours to examine FREE for 10 days. If you decide to keep the books, you'll pay the preferred subscriber price (a savings of up to 30% off the cover price), plus shipping and handling. If you want us to stop sending books, just say the word… it's that simple.

FREE BOOK CERTIFICATE

Yes! Please send me FREE Zebra Contemporary romance novels. I only pay $1.99 for shipping and handling. I understand that each month thereafter I will be able to preview 4 brand-new Contemporary Romances FREE for 10 days. Then, if I should decide to keep them, I will pay the money-saving preferred subscriber's price (that's a savings of up to 30% off the retail price), plus shipping and handling. I understand I am under no obligation to purchase any books, as explained on this card.

Name _____

Address _____ Apt. _____

City _____ State _____ Zip _____

Telephone (___) _____

Signature _____

(If under 18, parent or guardian must sign)

Offer limited to one per household and not to current subscribers. Terms, offer and prices subject to change. Orders subject to acceptance by Zebra Contemporary Book Club. Offer Valid in the U.S. only.

Thank You!

CN035A

ll..l..ll...lll..ll.l.l.ll.l.l.l..ll.l..l.l..lll..l

Zebra Contemporary Romance Book Club

Zebra Home Subscription Service, Inc.

P.O. Box 5214

Clifton , NJ 07015-5214

you shouldn't, uh . . . there are some really gruesome ones in this batch."

She thumbed slowly through the clippings. A shiver racked her, to think of the man she loved in such proximity to violence and death. She looked up over her shoulder into his face. "You don't have to be so protective of me," she said gently. "Your photographs are incredible."

He looked uncomfortable. "Statistics. I threw away hundreds of shots to get those images."

"Don't bother," she said. "You can't downplay this. You can't say it's no big deal. Incredible is incredible, no matter how you did it."

He stared into her eyes. "Thank you," he said.

Her eyes fell on the dusty, irregularly shaped winged object that lay on the table next to the box of cameras. It was made out of unfired clay. A dirty string protruded from one end.

She picked it up. "What on earth?"

He took it from her, looking embarrassed, and turned it over in his hands. "A present I was making for my mother. We'd just seen this nature film about homing pigeons. I wondered how that must feel, to always know your way home. I figured maybe it was like an invisible string, always pulling them. My mom traveled a lot, to the galleries that sold her sculptures. So I made her a homing pigeon with a string on it. So she would always find her way home to me."

She studied the little bird. "Now I see it," she said. "This end is the head, with a pointy beak, and this is the tail. How old were you?"

"Eight," he said. "I never got to give it to her. That was the day they came and told me about the fire."

She put the bird gently down on the table, turned around and stared out the window until she could trust herself not to cry.

When she turned back to him, Simon placed the lopsided

bird in her hands. The gesture seemed almost ceremonial. "For you," he said.

She cradled it in her hands. "But I've never had the least bit of trouble finding my way home," she said. "I almost never stir from it."

"You are home, El," he said simply. "My only home."

She dragged in a sobbing breath and reached up, placing her hand against his cheek. Simon closed his eyes and covered her hand with his. He kissed her palm. The heat of his soft lips made her quiver.

"I'm sorry I wasn't more welcoming when you knocked," he said. "I felt bad."

She put the clay bird down and held her arms out.

Simon didn't hesitate. He grabbed her and held her so tightly, he squeezed the breath out of her lungs, but she didn't care. She didn't need air. She had Simon. At least in this sweet, perfect moment, she had him. She buried her nose in his hair. He smelled of dust and sweat.

He let go abruptly. "I'm sorry. I'm filthy, and I smell. I shouldn't—"

"I don't care," she said. "Grab me again. I loved it."

He wiped his forehead with his sleeve and grinned ruefully as he showed her the gritty streak that remained on the cloth. "I was about to head up to the waterfall with some soap and fresh clothes. Before I came looking for you. At which point I planned to get down on my knees and kiss every part of you I could reach until you forgave me."

"Forgave you for what?" she asked. "You never lied to me."

"Oh, stop it," he grumbled. "You just make it harder when you say stuff like that. You deserve a Prince Charming, and I'm not him."

"I don't want some stupid old Prince Charming," she said. "What a big bore. I want my confused, undomesticated, screwed-up Simon. Call me crazy, but get your butt back over here. Now."

A reluctant, appreciative smile tugged up the corners of

his somber mouth. "I love it when you're stern, but I would rather smell good when I touch you. Want to go up to the waterfall with me?"

All the sensual possibilities of the waterfall spun dizzily through her head. Simon, naked and wet and laughing. "Ah . . ."

He saw it in her eyes. His smile widened to a grin. "Yeah?"

"OK," she agreed. "We can take my truck. I'll go get some towels. And my bathing suit. I'll be back out in a minute."

"Don't forget this." He put the small bird sculpture in her hands. "Keep it safe for me, El."

She cradled the precious thing in her hands as she hurried back to the house and up the stairs and laid it in a place of honor next to the old photograph of Great-grandmother and Great-grandfather Kent. She liked the way the two objects looked together. Two faces of the same shining coin. Longing for love and home and family. Respect for the past, and hope for the future. The glue that held the universe together.

She tugged on her bathing suit and threw her clothes on over it. Her heart pounded as she grabbed the wool picnic blanket out of the laundry room and piled towels on top of it. She set up for an absentee tea with feverish speed, leaving three pies, a pile of dessert dishes and spoons, and an apologetic note to her guests. "An unexpected emergency" was how she phrased it. This feeling definitely qualified as an emergency. Her heart was hanging on a thread over the abyss.

Simon was waiting by her truck with a battered knapsack, a watermelon tucked under his arm and a smile that made her blush.

She started up the truck, and pulled onto the bumpy, untended road that connected with the McNary Canyon logging road. They were both silent as they bumped along the narrow road. She concentrated on her driving in an effort to ignore the tremor in her hands, her pounding heart, her hot cheeks. A smile that she couldn't seem to control.

"How long has it been since you went swimming up here?" he asked.

"Years," she said. "Gus put up signs in the woods that said TRESPASSERS WILL BE SHOT ON SIGHT. Look, there's one of them right there. See that tree?"

"Stop here, at the wide spot," Simon said. "This is the best place to hike down to the stream."

She pulled over and threw the clutch into park. He reached for the towels and blankets on the seat, but Ellen put her hand out. "Wait. Remember when you told me you'd gotten really good with your knife?"

"Sure," he said. "Do you want your demonstration now?"

"Yes," she said demurely. She pointed to Gus's sign, about fifteen yards away. "Can you hit that sign from here?"

He looked at the sign, and his eyes gleamed as he looked back at her. "Which letter of the sign would you like me to hit?"

She sniffed. "Oh, puh-leeze. You big show-off."

"Really," he urged. "Pick a letter." He climbed out of the truck.

She followed him out, admiring what that radiant grin did to his gorgeous face. "Fine. Hit the 'o' in shot, then, if you're such a stud."

Simon crouched down and pulled a wicked-looking black knife out of his boot. He lifted it with a careless gesture. Let it fly.

Thunk. It speared the "o" dead center and quivered there.

"Ah." She gazed at it. "Well. I guess you weren't exaggerating."

"Never do, sweetheart." He loped over to the sign, retrieved his knife and sheathed it in one graceful movement.

"I guess you can save me from the snakes, then," she said.

He looked down at her sandals and her bare tanned legs. "Boots and jeans would be better."

"I didn't think of it," she confessed. "I was flustered."

He kissed the tip of her nose, grinning, and grabbed the melon, blanket and towels from the cab of the truck. She followed him down the rugged hillside to the creek, keeping her eyes on her feet as she picked her way carefully over the big, tumbled boulders.

"Here we are," he said. "Earthly paradise."

She looked up, and gasped. "Oh, wow. I forgot how beautiful it is."

The canyon was narrow at this point, and dense with pine and fir. The waterfall was about ten feet high, dumping water down a smooth, mossy sluice. It rushed over the lip of stone, pounding and churning the center of the pool into bubbles and foam, rippling out into a wide basin of crystalline water that glowed a deep blue-green.

Simon tugged off his boots while Ellen pulled off her T-shirt and cut-offs. He looked at her modest one-piece, and started to laugh.

"After what we did last night, you still need a bathing suit, babe?"

"We're outdoors," she snapped. "Anybody could come along."

"We're miles from the main road, on private property," he pointed out. "If anybody intrudes on our privacy, I'll break both his legs."

She frowned. "That's not a very neighborly attitude."

"I'm not a very neighborly guy." His eyes raked her body. "I'd be severly pissed if anybody else saw you naked, sweetheart. But I want to see you naked in this waterfall. I want it bad."

She caught her breath as he stripped off his shirt and flung it away. He was so incredibly beautiful. Every detail of his lean, muscular body, his golden skin, his striking face. He looked like a god.

"Just so you know. I do not have any intention whatsoever of having sex outdoors," she told him. "You should know that right up front. I'm a locked-door, clean-sheets, lights-off kind of girl."

His slow, wolfish grin made her knees wobble. "You don't even know what kind of girl you are yet, sweetheart."

"I know what kind I am better than you do," she said sharply. "So don't presume to tell me."

"And we're arguing over a non-issue," he soothed. "How about you just come into the water with me and let all those unimportant details sort themselves out as we go along?"

His voice was the soul of sweet reason, but she knew the gleam in his eye. She shook her finger at him. "Don't even. I'm not falling for it."

He reached back and pulled the hair tie out of his hair with seductive slowness, muscles flexing and stretching. He shook the thick, heavy mane out over his shoulder, and just stood there, grinning.

"Don't preen," she said breathlessly.

He put his arms behind his head, rolled his neck and his muscular shoulders, flaunting himself at her. "Why not?"

"You know perfectly well that you're gorgeous," she said. "And conceited, too. You're showing off like a peacock fanning its tail. Trying to impress me. It's a silly trick and I see right through it. So stop it."

He looked fascinated. "How should I interpret this? A subtle cue that you want to see my tail?" He unbuckled his belt and shoved down his jeans. His erection sprang out, bobbing heavily before him. He turned around, legs wide, and lifted his arms. "Do you like my ass?"

It was only the most muscular, tempting, touchable, bitable ass she'd ever seen, in person or in film or photos. "Stop it, Simon!"

He looked around and examined her flushed face. "But it's working," he said. "Why should I stop something that's working?"

She turned her back on his teasing laughter and busied herself by spreading out the picnic blanket on a soft carpet of pine needles and small, feathery ferns. She heard a huge splash, and turned just in time to see his torso explode out of the pool in a shower of glittering drops.

He laughed in delight and flung his hair back off his face.

"It's incredible, El," he called. "Come on in. You have to feel this."

She tiptoed over the sliding pebbles to the pool and stuck in her toe. She gasped. "It's freezing! You must be nuts!"

"No excuses, babe." He swam across the pool, vaulted out and started towards her. Wet, naked and grinning, his eyes full of purpose.

She backed up, shaking her head. "Don't you dare, Simon Riley. Don't even get near me with that look in your eye. I'm not—no!"

He scooped her into his arms. She shrieked and struggled as he carried her to the water, but the shock of cold water when he tossed her in was a blinding delight to every nerve ending. She came up spluttering and giggling. She wiped the water out of her eyes and looked at him.

Their laughter died away.

The waterfall roared behind them, the deep water trembled and rippled. Gusts of cool spray wafted around them. She barely noticed.

His stark male beauty dazzled her. The golden brown skin, the sculptured lines and angles of his forehead and cheekbones and jaw, the expressive grooves around his eyes and mouth, the beads of moisture that clung to his skin. His flat brown nipples were tight with cold. His dripping hair was slicked back from his forehead, clinging to his neck and shoulders like black paint. Water trickled lovingly down every cut and curve and contour of his body, exalting every detail. She wanted to touch him everywhere. Lick every single drop of water away.

His eyes were so somber. Infinitely deep. She could lose herself in the dark enchantment of his eyes and never find her way back.

He drifted closer. "You're so fucking beautiful, El. It's unreal."

She wiped the water off her face. "So are you."

"Pull your bathing suit down and show me what the cold water does to your nipples."

She glanced down at the tight nubs pressing against her bathing suit. "You can see it perfectly well through the cloth," she said.

"I showed you mine," he coaxed. "Now show me yours."

"I never asked you to show me yours!" she said. "Do not pressure me, Simon. I'm not comfortable with—"

"—much of anything, right?" he finished. "Skinny-dipping must be on that long list of things you've never done, huh?"

She bristled. "I'm sorry if I'm too prissy for your tastes, but I—"

"It's so sad." He shook his head in mock regret. "You just can't let yourself go."

"You're manipulating me and making fun of me, and it's not fair!"

He smiled. "Look around, baby." He waved his arm around in a big circle. "No one's here. No one will see you but me. Pull that suit down. Feel the wind and the water and the spray against your bare skin. I want to see that tan fading down to ivory on your breasts. And those little raspberry nipples, puckered up all tight and rosy. Drops of water trickling around them. My gorgeous water nymph. If I saw you that way, I could die happy. Just do it for me, and I'll stop pushing you."

"Oh, no you won't," she whispered. "You big liar. You won't stop."

He swam around her in slow circles, weaving a spell with his eyes, his smile, his caressing voice. "Please. I'm asking so nicely. I'm being such a good boy. Show me that you're not afraid."

He was doing it again. As playful and seductive as he was, she felt the power he wielded like a throbbing force field all around her. He knew just how to position her, how to push her into wanting what he wanted. The water pounded in her ears. Every nerve ending in her body tingled with the cold, but she didn't feel cold any longer. She was red hot. The water felt pleasantly cool against her feverish flesh.

This time she would play her cards better. She wouldn't ruin it by talking of love. She would seize the moment, use him for pleasure like he used her, and keep her tender, unwanted feelings to herself. She would take everything she could get of him. No shame, no regrets.

She felt around with her feet until she found a smooth boulder that was the right height to stand on. She rose out of the water so that the water line kissed her navel, seized the straps of the suit, and tugged them down. She peeled the wet fabric slowly over her breasts, let it cling, deliciously suspended on her taut nipples, and finally pop over.

She folded it down to her waist, lifted her arms and spun around, displaying herself to him. "Happy now?"

His eyes devoured her. "Ecstatic."

The spell he was weaving deepened, tightened. Her breath was sharp and ragged. The drops of water on her skin should be hissing off into pure steam, her face felt so hot. Her naked skin took in so much more sensory information naked, as if she had eyes and ears all over her. Every inch of her skin was wide awake and deliciously sensitive.

"You just love persuading me to take my clothes off, right?" she said breathlessly. "That really turns you on, doesn't it, Simon?"

"Would you rather I ripped them off you by force and leaped on you like a starving wolf? That could be arranged, babe."

His predatory smile made her press her trembling thighs together. "Um, no, actually. I'm not the starving-wolf type."

"I know you're not," he murmured. "You're the golden goddess type. Shy and prim. Never gone skinny-dipping in your whole sheltered life." He reached for her hand, and kissed her fingertips, one by one. "I have to prepare you carefully before I make any sudden moves. I'll wait until you're so ready, you're screaming and yelling and calling me names. And then, oh, God, the payoff. You are white-hot. Explosive."

She tried to laugh. "So it's just a calculated seduction technique?"

He swam closer, clasping her waist. "There's nothing calculated about the way you make me feel," he said. "I'm riding the rapids with no paddle, El. Just trying to stay afloat." He rose up out of the water and drew the taut tip of her breast into his hot mouth.

The intense sweetness of the caress made her cry out. Her head dropped back. So hot and wet. His greedy tongue swirling, licking, hungry for her pleasure. She clutched his head to her chest and clung to him as shock waves of bright sensation jolted through her.

He slid his hand between her legs, pressing his fingers gently against her mound through the fabric of her suit, moving in expert, tender circles. She clenched her thighs around his hand. He pulled her hand down and wrapped her fingers around his hard, hot penis.

"Touch my cock," he demanded. "Touch me while I touch you."

She lifted her face for his kiss, desperate for more contact, and they kissed and caressed each other, rising and falling on waves of delirious pleasure. She was gasping against his mouth, poised on the brink of an explosive climax—and he suddenly let go.

He pried her hand away from his hard, hot penis and floated a short distance away from her. She felt dazed and adrift without him.

"I've got a condom in my jeans pocket," he said. "What do you say, El? Have you changed your mind about outdoor sex?"

She shook with excitement and frustration. He'd outmaneuvered her again, and she was so hungry for him, she almost didn't care.

She swam to the edge of the pool and clambered out. Her legs almost buckled when she stood on them. She peeled her bathing suit down, stepped out of it and tossed it over a sunny rock.

She turned to face him, naked in the dappled sunlight.

Chapter

13

Simon swam to the edge of the pond. He was weak with relief, after that awful moment when he thought he'd pushed her too hard. That he'd be walking home alone with his tail between his legs.

His dick would never have forgiven him.

He forced himself to move slowly as he climbed out. She was excited, but still skittish and nervous, after the mess he'd made of last night. Hyper-aware of how vulnerable she was with him. So was he.

He had to compensate for being bigger and stronger by hanging on to his control somehow. Damn near impossible, the way he felt.

He had to distract himself. Do something, anything else, until the roaring in his ears abated. He scooped up the watermelon, pulled his knife out of his boot sheath and sat down on the plaid wool blanket, willing his hard-on to relax to half mast. "Want some?"

She looked down at him, puzzled. "I thought you wanted . . ."

"You thought right, but there's no hurry." He stabbed the rind, dragged the knife around, then pried it open. Ah, good. Juicy and crimson. "You have to taste this. Come here. Sit down. I'm starving." She sank down onto the blanket, curling her legs daintily beneath her.

"You haven't eaten?" She looked worried. "Why didn't you say something?"

"Who cares? I'll eat some of this melon, and then I'll lick up some delicious girl juice, and I'll be in hog heaven."

She covered her face with her hands. "Oh, God."

"Is that not OK with you?" He feigned puzzlement. "You seemed to really go for it last night."

She peeked through her fingers. "Don't tease me, Simon."

"Then don't egg me on." He sliced out a big, crimson chunk of melon and flicked the seeds away with the point of his knife. He held it up to her lips. "Take the first bite, angel."

She lowered her hands from her very pink face. She looked soft and deliciously wet, her gold-tipped lashes still dark from the water, hair still dripping onto the blanket. She opened her mouth and accepted the fruit. Her lashes swept down, and she made a low, husky murmur of approval as she savored it. "Delicious."

He cut a long wedge. "This is how I like it," he told her. "Not icy cold out of a fridge. It has to be warm from the sun on one side and cool from the earth on the other. Torn open with a knife that's a little too small, so that the flesh is jagged. Red mountains and pink lakes of sweet juice. A wet, sticky, sexy mess. Yum."

She laughed at him as he devoured the chunk of fruit. "Is everything about seduction with you?"

He smiled at her and held up another piece of melon in answer to her question. "Open your mouth."

She leaned forward and ate the fruit from his hands. The clasp of her soft lips closing around his finger made his cock jerk and swell.

"Feed me a piece now," he commanded.

She held out her hand. "Give me your knife."

"Just rip it out with your fingers," he urged. "Let the juice drip down your arm. I'll lick you clean if you get sticky. Don't worry."

Her eyes were bright with excitement, her breath jerked unsteadily between soft, parted lips that had flushed deep, raspberry red. The glow of desire on her cheeks made his body throb with eagerness. She scooped out a choice piece and lifted it to his lips.

He hung on to the slender hand that fed him, licking each delicate finger, tracing every pink rivulet of liquid that trailed down the pale, soft skin of her inner arm. The game blossomed from there into a sensual pagan ritual that grew hungrier and more frenzied, punctuated by laughter and kisses. The juice dribbled down her chin, onto her breasts. He licked and kissed the juice away, wallowing in the petal-fine softness of her skin. Exploring her lush, tempting beauty with his tongue.

Finally he shoved her down onto her back and held the hollowed-out cup of melon rind over her body. He tipped it and let a thread of warm, sweet juice spill out over her breasts, her belly, her pussy.

She giggled and struggled, but he held her down. "I'm so hungry, El," he coaxed. "Starving. I need this. Let me lick you all up. Please."

She collapsed onto her back with a sobbing moan and let him have his way. He went for it full-out, and licked up all the juice he'd spilled over her with lashing strokes of his warm, strong tongue.

He coaxed her legs open and buried his face between them. She tangled her fingers into his wet hair and moved against his mouth as he slid his tongue into the secret well of liquid pleasure inside her. He spread her wide and studied every tender pink detail, all the different textures: the plump outer lips covered with tight blonde ringlets, the soft suede tenderness of her flushed, crimson inner lips, the sweet, slick flesh deep inside. He put his mouth to her and tried every technique he knew to find out what made her writhe and buck against his face.

The hunger inside him felt almost savage. He wanted her to come for him, wanted that bright burst of energy right against his face, his tongue shoved deep inside her. He persisted until she yielded it up to him. She cried out as her beautiful orgasm throbbed against his mouth.

He raised himself up, wiped her warm sex juice from his face, and stared down at her. She was panting and rosy red, eyes closed. Tears trickled down the sides of her face into her wet, tangled hair. So trusting and open. So goddamn vulnerable, it made him afraid for her.

And furious with himself, for making a simple thing complicated.

She sensed the conflict inside him. Her eyes opened. "Simon?"

He shook his head. She reached out to him. He flinched as she touched his hand.

"Don't you want me anymore?" she asked.

The soft uncertainty in her voice infuriated him even more. "Of course I fucking want you!" he snapped. "Just look at me."

She struggled up onto her elbow and wrapped her cool fingers around his stiff, aching cock.

"I want you, too," she said. "So why are you upset?"

"I don't know." He shrugged helplessly. "It just keeps happening to me. I swear, I'm not usually weird about sex. You lie there with that look on your face. Your eyes full of tears, for Christ's sake. The beautiful virgin sacrifice. I don't know. It makes me nuts."

She hastily wiped the tears off her face. "I'm sorry. I can't help it," she said. "I didn't know it was such a turn-off."

"It's *not* a turn-off," he snarled. "It's the opposite of a turn-off."

She drew her legs up to her chest, and hid her face against her knees. "I'm confused," she whispered. "I don't know what you want. I'm trying so hard not to ruin it, but it just keeps happening anyway."

He felt like an idiot and a jerk. He reached out to stroke her hair.

"Baby," he said gently. "You didn't ruin anything. Last night was amazing. I've never had sex like that in my entire life."

She looked up into his eyes. "Then why did you run away?"

He hesitated. "Overload," he said. "Last night I worshipped at the shrine of your beauty. You bestowed your trust upon me like a goddamn starry crown. Simon Riley, in bed with the golden goddess. I had to get out of there before you figured out what the hell you'd done."

"Goddamn it, Simon! That's not fair!" She slapped his hand away from her hair and launched herself at him.

He caught her flailing hands just before she could smack him. "I never said I was fair," he said. "That's another of my many defects."

She struggled in his grip. "I am *sick* of your lame excuses! If you don't want me, just say so! I'll never bother you again!"

He jerked her into his arms, and held her, his face inches from hers. "I do want you," he said roughly. "But I don't want a lofty goddess. I want to fuck you left, right and sideways. I want you to suck on my cock. I want to come in your mouth. I want to make you scream and beg for mercy. I want you in every way that there is."

She blinked, and shook with a rush of silent laughter. "Uh . . . that sounds pretty great to me, Simon," she said huskily. "I don't see what the problem is. I never asked for you to treat me like a goddess."

They stared at each other. The waterfall thundered behind them.

El leaned forward and kissed him all over his face. Small, hot, moist kisses. "I love it when you talk sexy to me like that," she whispered. "When you tell me what you want. It makes me so wet. I'm no golden goddess, Simon. Let go of my wrists. I want to touch you."

He did as she asked, his fingers loosening. She promptly reached down and grasped his hot, aching cock in both hands.

"I'm not a plastic doll," she said. "I'll do anything you want."

He shuddered in her grip. "Anything?" he muttered. "That's a broad, sweeping statement. Watch it with your big promises, babe."

She smiled, and milked him boldly. "Big bad Simon," she mocked. "Stop trying to scare me. You just make me laugh."

"Great. I'm so glad I amuse you," he said shakily.

She gave him one last, teasing kiss on the tip of his nose, bent down and drew his cock into her mouth.

It was a challenge. There was so much of him, Ellen didn't quite know what to do with all of it, but she was so titillated, she was more than willing to figure something out. She decided to lick him the exact same hungry, extravagant way that he had licked her. Slow, dragging strokes, circling around his swollen glans and then licking up the salty, glistening drops that wept from the small slit at the tip. He was salty and delicious. She ran her tongue up and down the broad stalk, tracing the distended veins. He was velvety smooth. Hot and hard to bursting. Every stroke, every touch made him tremble and groan.

It was his turn to be helpless and in her thrall, and she loved it.

She drew the head of his penis tenderly into her mouth, which was as much as she could possibly fit, and pumped the rest of his thick length with her hands, swirling her tongue around him. She tried sucking him deeper inside, but he gently pushed her face away.

She wiped her mouth and looked up. "Don't you like it?" she asked anxiously. "I thought you wanted—"

"I love it," he said abruptly. "Sure I want it. It's amazing. But right now, I want to fuck you. We can play around with that later."

At least he was talking about a "later." That was promising.

Simon pulled a condom out of his jeans, ripped it open and handed it to her. "Put this on me."

Her clumsy, sticky fingers struggled with the lubricated latex for a moment. She finally managed, with some difficulty, to roll it over his penis. He leaned his forehead against hers, panting. His body jerked and trembled with every clumsy attempt she made.

She expected him to push her onto her back, but he pulled her onto his lap instead, arranging her legs so that she was astride him. "Lift yourself up and let me . . . just take me in. Like that. Sink down. Slowly, now . . . oh, God, that's good. Oh, sweetheart."

He gripped her hips and forced her body down over him. The thick club of his shaft forged slowly inside her. She sucked in a breath.

He stopped, his face worried. "Am I hurting you?"

She sank down, wedging him deeper. "A little, but it's worth it."

"If you're sore, we don't have to—"

"Don't even *think* about driving me out of my mind and leaving me hanging!" she snarled. "Just shut up and . . . and fuck me, already!"

He grinned, delighted. "Whoa!"

"Right now! Or I'll . . ." She flailed around for a suitable threat.

"You'll what?" His eyes gleamed with hot fascination.

"I'll punch you in the eye!" she announced.

He leaned back, arranging them so that he rested on his elbows, his legs stretched out. "Yes, exalted mistress," he said meekly. "I am at your command. Ride me, fuck me, take me. Do with me as you will."

"Don't you dare make fun of me, Simon Riley!"

"Never," he said hastily. "I meant every word. I swear."

She moved over him, awkwardly at first, rising up and sinking slowly down onto his thick shaft until her body moistened his and the movement found its own sliding, surging momentum.

Simon seized her hips, and drove his powerful body up from beneath her, grinding inside her and stirring her to her depths. She writhed, wailing as he brought her to a deep, sweet, wrenching climax.

He rolled her onto her back and rose up onto his knees, spreading her wide. He rode her hard, until his own explosive pleasure coursed through his body and echoed through hers.

His shout of triumph echoed through the canyon.

They collapsed in each other's arms. The sun had abandoned them, dropping below the wall of the canyon. Ellen stirred and opened her eyes when she felt him tracing the line of her jaw with his fingertip.

"It's no good," he said. "It just keeps on happening, no matter what I do."

Alarmed jolted her out of her lethargy. "What keeps happening?"

His face was full of shadows again. "It doesn't matter how hard I try to drag you down to earth. I just end up worshipping you anyway."

She kissed his hand. "That's OK," she said. "I worship you, too."

He pulled away, and turned his back. "Christ. Please. Don't."

He pulled off the condom, and shoved it into a plastic bag that he pulled out of his knapsack. He knotted the bag with an angry tug.

He stalked back to the pool and dove in without looking at her.

She blinked back tears. It was silly to feel hurt and abandoned. He was always like this after sex. She should just get used to it.

She ran her hands over her body. She was sticky from melon juice and sex. She stumbled down to the pool and jumped into the water with a gasp. The water felt far colder, now that the sun was gone and Simon's rigid back was turned to her. She rinsed herself quickly, and hastened to dry off and pull her clothes back on.

Simon was lacing up his boots, still carefully avoiding her gaze, when they heard the pop and shatter of broken glass from the road above. Simon jerked to his feet. Ellen's belly clenched into an icy knot.

Crash, tinkle, twice . . . a third time . . . a fourth time. A muffled, snickering burst of male laughter followed the last crash.

They listened, still as statues. Simon's eyes swept over her. "Get your sandals on quick, babe."

She hurried to comply. She started gathering up the towels with shaking hands, but Simon shook his head. "Leave the stuff. We'll come back for it another time. Stay close behind me. When I signal, I'm going ahead to check it out. Do not speak or follow me until I call for you."

"But I—"

He seized her shoulders. "Promise me you'll do as I say."

She knew better than to argue with that tone. She nodded mutely, and tried to copy his smooth, silent stride as they picked their way over the boulders and up the hillside. She was very conscious of the knife that glinted in his hand. When they got closer to the road, he shoved her gently behind a grove of firs and put his finger to his lips.

She twisted her hands together in the silent, agonizing period that followed. It was probably less than two minutes. It felt like hours.

"Come on up, El." His voice was grim and quiet. "All clear."

He reached down and gave her a hand as she scrambled up over the shoulder of the road. She stared at her truck.

All of the windows were smashed. All four tires were flat. Words were scrawled on the door in big, crude letters written with a felt-tipped marking pen. FUCK OFF FIREBUG was on the door. She walked around the truck. The other side read WE SAW YOU DOIN IT SLUT.

She looked up and down the deserted road. "This, uh, would be the reason that I generally prefer not to have sex outdoors."

Simon's face was a grim mask of tension. "I'm sorry, El."

"It's not your fault. I said yes. You didn't force me." She

pressed her hand over her mouth to subdue her nervous laughter. "It's funny. How statistically improbable is this? The one time in my life that I cut loose and do something naughty, whammo. I get slammed. They're not big on spelling or punctuation, are they? Missed a few commas."

Simon stared down the canyon road. "You don't happen to have a cell phone on you, do you, babe?"

She shook her head. "Not with me. Why?"

He shook his head. "This isn't random. These aren't assholes who just happened by. This road leads out to nowhere. They know who I am, who you are. They followed us here, which means they were watching us before we left. And now they know we're on foot, in a narrow canyon with them between us and any kind of help. And it's going to get dark soon." He met her eyes. "I hate it," he added flatly.

She shivered, in spite of the balmy warmth, and wrapped her arms across her chest. "Should we try and get home some other way?"

Simon looked up at the striated basalt cliffs above them, and his eyes flicked over her bare legs and sandals. "I've done it. But the quickest way is still a dangerous climb, with sheer rock faces, and thick scrub, and poison oak. It would take hours. We don't have enough daylight, and it's rattlesnake season. Your legs would get cut to ribbons."

She shivered. She wished he would hug her, but he looked so grim, she didn't have the nerve to ask. She took a deep breath. "Well, Simon?" she said. "I'm game. Either way. The road or the cliffs. You call it, and I'll trust your judgment. You're the one who knows kung fu."

He stared down the canyon road for a long, thoughtful moment. "I say we take the road," he said. "I'm betting that they've run away, since this," he indicated the truck, "is a coward's trick. And if they fuck with us . . ." He tossed the knife up, caught it between his fingertips and crouched down to slide it back into its boot sheath, "God help them."

By tacit agreement, they didn't speak for the entire long walk. She scurried to keep up with his long strides. Shadows deepened in the canyon as the eastern sky darkened. Pink clouds gathered over the westward hills. A single, faint star came out above them.

They angled sharply downward into the woods that grew along the creek. She stumbled over a rut in the mud. Simon caught her arm.

"Sorry," she whispered. "I'm just so—"

"Shhh," he hissed. He shoved her towards the dry ditch on the side of the road. She stumbled and fetched up against the bank.

A dark shadow hurtled out of nowhere. Simon spun to meet it.

Simon parried the clumsy punch easily, and slammed one of his own into the guy's solar plexus while he assessed the threat.

Four big guys. Black nylon stockings over their faces made their faces look grotesquely squashed. The tallest of them flung himself onto Simon from the side. Simon noted the guy's fetid body odor as he slid aside and sent him hurtling like a battering ram straight into the guy with black furry hair on his fists. Both guys went down, skidding in the dirt.

The other two launched themselves. Simon blocked an uppercut and stabbed two stiff fingers up under the guy's sweaty, slimy jaw. Slimy reeled back, choking and flailing. A vicious side kick to the ribs sent the fourth guy stumbling heavily onto his ass with a grunt of agony. He was a fatter guy, with a big, overhanging gut.

"Fuckin' shit!" Slimy hissed as he struggled to his feet. "You guys never said this guy was a fuckin' professional!"

Simon rammed his elbow into Slimy's nose before anyone had a chance to reply. Slimy cried out hoarsely, and reeled. Simon kneed him in the groin, and that took the guy whimpering to the ground just in time to spin around and deal with Stinky and Furry Hands again, who were dancing warily back to ransom their bruised pride.

Simon scanned for El as he sank down into guard. She was on her hands and knees by the side of the road, the only heart-in-the-throat variable in this fight. These clowns hadn't pulled weapons. They had no training to speak of, no tricks up their sleeves, no surprises for him. No need for knife-work. This was just exercise, some unloading of his aggressive tendencies. Creative anger management.

Annihilating these dickheads would be fun, but he didn't want El to watch the process. "Run!" he shouted. "Get clear!"

She dragged something up off the ground, but he didn't see what because Furry Hands lunged at him, roaring, while Stinky threw a punch from the other side. Simon blocked the punch, chopped down on Stinky's neck and found himself in Furry Hands's sweaty embrace.

Simon tripped him, flung him to the ground and kicked the side of his knee. Tendons ripped and gave. Furry Hands shrieked.

Simon spun around. Big Gut hurtled towards him, and El darted after, a big, heavy tree branch in her hand. She whipped it down at Big Gut's meaty shoulder with admirable force. He howled, spun around and grabbed the branch, but El would not let go of it. She shrieked a challenge and shoved it back at him.

Big Gut stumbled back a step. "Fucking bitch!" he snarled.

Big Gut lunged at her. Simon dove to stop him, but Stinky barreled into him from the side, knocking him to the ground.

Pure fear, having to take his eyes off El. Dealing with Stinky was quick and dirty; a fist slammed up under the guy's rib cage, a finger stabbed through the nylon mask into his eye, and Stinky was fucked.

Simon bounded onto his feet. El was poised on the river-bank. Big Gut shoved the branch against her chest. The rocks under her feet gave way. She clutched at the branch for balance. Big Gut let go of it.

El cried out sharply as she tumbled and slid out of his sight.

Big Gut took one look at Simon, and took off running. The other three followed, stumbling and limping after him like whipped dogs.

Simon barely noticed. His combat Zen-calm had vanished. His heart almost exploded with panic as he bounded and slid over the unstable boulders to where El sat, hunched in the rushing water of the creek. "El?" he demanded. "Are you OK? Say something!"

She looked up, dazed. "I'm OK. Just banged up a little." She bent her legs up out of the water and hissed as she touched her knees.

"You sure?" He sank down next to her into the icy creek and wrapped his arms around her. "Oh, Christ. You scared me so bad."

She leaned into his embrace. "Did they run away?"

They just barely heard the roar of an engine over the sound of the murmuring water. The sound quickly receded. "Gone." His arms tightened. "I'm sorry. I called it wrong. We should have gone into the—"

"Oh, shut up. You handled it fine. They're gone, right? Kiss me."

He obliged her, but lifted his head a moment later. "Are you sure you're OK?" he asked. "Your legs? Did you break anything?"

"Let's get out of the creek, and we'll see," she said.

She grabbed his hand. He pulled her up and set her carefully on her feet. He knelt in front of her in the knee-deep water, and ran his hands gently over her legs. They were badly scraped, rivulets of blood welling and trickling down, diluted with the creek water.

She stroked his tangled, dust-caked hair. "Don't worry," she said. "I'm just jittery, and I'll have some scabs and bruises. That's all."

He snorted. "Now who's being macho and saying it's no big deal? Let's get you home. You sure you can walk? I could carry—"

"Don't be absolutely ridiculous."

He hovered anxiously as they clambered up the rockslide. She refused to let him carry her, so he contented himself with putting an arm around her waist and cuddling her against him as they walked.

He stopped when they reached the meadow. "Let's get off this road and cut through to the woods," he suggested. "If we go through that stand of firs up over the rise, we'll be able to see your house."

They pushed into the waist-high meadow grass hip to hip, as close together as he could hold her to him and still keep moving.

"You never had to use your knife," she said. "Thank goodness."

"Those four I could've handled with my hands tied behind my back. If I'd been alone." He slanted her a reproachful glance. "You should have run when I told you to. I could have hauled them in."

"Oh, yeah. Like I could run off and leave you while four big guys are attacking you." She rolled her eyes. "Please. Spare me."

"You're very brave, and I appreciate you trying to help, but you trashed my concentration and put yourself in danger."

"All right. I'm sorry. If we're ever ambushed by thugs on a dark road again, I'll try to do as you say. But I won't make any promises."

El stopped. The tension that seized her body made him snap instantly into fight mode. "What is it?" he demanded.

"Look!" El's voice was soft. "What on earth?"

Simon's eyes followed her pointing hand. Memories welled up inside him, a rush of feeling that gave him a moment of vertigo. The grove was filled with animal statues, eerie and stately in the gloom.

"Oh, wow," he whispered. "My mother's sculptures. This is all the stuff that was in her studio when she died. Gus put it out here in the woods. A memorial sculpture garden for her."

"It's magic," El said softly.

"I thought so, too," he told her. "I used to sneak out here to sleep with a blanket and a tarp. I felt like her animals were guarding me."

The pines and firs that towered over them created a dim, vaulted hush, like a vast cathedral. Animal sentinels surrounded them.

Coyotes, eagles, cougars and deer were mixed with mythical animals: gryphons and sphinxes, centaurs and unicorns, and with stranger, even more surreal things, animals out of a fever dream. Their original color had given way to a mottled gray, splotched with random patterns of lichen in every shade of brilliant orange and yellow.

"It's true," El said in a hushed voice. "It's so calm here. The animals guard the space. It makes me feel safer, too."

He crooked his arm around her waist and pulled her briskly along. "That's great, sweetheart, but I'll feel safe when you're all washed up and covered with Band-Aids, tucked up in your nice, clean bed."

"With you?" She stopped in her tracks.

He tugged her back into movement. "We'll see," he hedged. "I need to see what I can find out about those assholes who—"

"I want you in my bed with me tonight." She dug in her heels and forced him to stop again. "Not wandering around in the dark God knows where, getting into God knows what kind of trouble. No way, Simon."

"We'll discuss it later," he said.

"We'll report this to the police, and let them handle it."

Simon let out an ironic grunt. "Yeah, and that experience will just put the crowning touch on my day. Can you pick up the pace, sweetheart? Just through that meadow, and we're home free."

Perfect timing, for his purposes, that Muriel Kent's white Taurus pulled up just as they were limping across the lawn. Her arrival was quickly followed by Chuck and Suzie's Jeep. The hubbub that followed provided the perfect cover to slip

away. He looked back, right before he pushed through the
lilac barrier, and then wished that he hadn't.

El was looking straight at him, her eyes full of silent re-
proach.

Chapter

14

"So let me get this straight, Riley." Wes was enjoying himself. "You have the dispatcher beep me away from a relaxing dinner with my family because I'm the only one in the world you say you can possibly talk to. I haul my ass down here, and this is all you have to say?"

Simon swallowed back his frustration. "It's serious," he said grimly. "El could've been hurt."

"Indeed she could have, and you should think long and hard about that," Wes said. "So let's run through this one more time. You and Ellen Kent were carrying on at the waterfall up McNary Creek—"

"I said swimming," Simon repeated.

"Oh. Excuse me. Swimming." Wes leaned back in his chair. His eyes moved slowly over Simon's dirt-caked clothes. "After which you went back to the road and found Ellen's truck covered with graffiti."

"Vandalized. We found it vandalized," Simon specified wearily. "Tires slashed, windows broken, rude graffiti."

"Rude graffiti," Wes repeated. He looked down at his notes. FUCK OFF FIREBUG, and WE SAW YOU DOIN IT SLUT. Guess those bad vandals must have gotten a real good look at you two . . . *swimming.* Hmm?"

Simon smiled thinly. "Must have."

"Must have been quite a sight, to get them so excited. Almost wish I'd been there myself. So. You and Ellen walked back on the canyon road, where you were attacked by four masked assailants, all of whom you miraculously defeated. But you didn't get a good enough look at them to iden-tify—"

"One of them shoved El off the creek bank," Simon re-peated. "I forgot them and went after her. They were big, muscular, in good shape. One was heavy in the gut. They wore jeans, T-shirts, work boots."

"Like every other guy in this town," Wes said.

"And nylons over their heads. They smelled bad. Does that help?"

"I'll tell you what doesn't help," Wes said. "You being a smart-ass doesn't help one little bit."

Simon let out a silent sigh. "I'm not trying to waste your time, Lieutenant. I'm just trying to do the right thing. I as-sume the guys who vandalized the truck are the ones who jumped us, so you should—"

"The last thing I need is you, jerk-off, telling me how to do my job. You got me, Riley?"

Simon bit his tongue. "I'm just worried about El," he said.

"That's real good of you," Wes said. "I told you this place wasn't good for your health. Look at you, Riley. You look like shit."

He gritted his teeth. "Lieutenant—"

"And it looks like you're not much good for Ellen Kent's health, either. Just yesterday, she was a fine-looking, respectable young lady running her pretty hotel, engaged to the richest guy in town. Now she's got a smashed-up truck, she's been knocked around, and a bunch of assholes have seen her . . . *swimming*. With the likes of you, right out in the open. Christ, Riley, what were you thinking? What's the moral of this story? I know you're kinda slow. Do I have to spell it out for you?"

Simon waited for a moment to answer. "The moral of the story is that you should find out who did it," he said quietly.

Wes grunted. "I need Ellen to come in and make a statement," he said. "We need her fingerprints so we can rule hers out when we dust the truck. Yours, we've already got on file."

Simon nodded.

"Why didn't she come with you?" Wes looked suspicious.

"She had freaked-out hotel guests to deal with," Simon said. "Plus, she was upset and scraped up. I'll tell her to come in."

"OK, Riley," Wes said. "That's all I need from you, but I still don't understand why you had to drag me away from my dinner. You could have told all this to any of the—"

"I wanted to talk to you personally because of this," Simon said. He pulled the stained manila folder out of his canvas tote bag.

"What have you got there?" Wes's eyes narrowed.

"I was hoping you'd tell me." Simon flung the file on Wes's desk.

The older man's face turned a purplish shade. He stared at the folder, but made no move to open it. Finally he reached out with one finger, lifted the edge of the folder and peeked inside. He let it drop.

"Fucking shit," he muttered.

There was a tense silence. Wes took a handkerchief out of his desk drawer and mopped his brow. He would not meet Simon's eyes.

"What's it about?" Simon asked.

Wes snorted. "What do you think? It's about you, bonehead. It's about your asshole uncle, covering up for his asshole nephew."

"Me?" Simon was baffled. "How the hell is this about me?"

Wes leaned over his desk, thrusting his face forward. "You'd just turned eighteen when you burned down those stables.

Gus didn't want us to hunt you down and slam your ass in jail with the big boys. You were all out of sympathy points, Riley. You were at the end of the line."

"I see," Simon said quietly.

"So this was Gus's brilliant solution. Fucking ironic. He decided that it had to be my job to convince everybody to just let it all go. Just let you disappear and become somebody else's problem."

Simon blew out a long, whistling sigh. "Jesus, Wes. It must have been really hard for you to put in a good word for me."

"Practically choked on it," Wes said.

Simon examined the older man's face intently. "Did you search Gus's house for these photos?"

Wes's chest puffed out. "I did not violate the integrity of a crime scene, if that's what you're asking," he said stiffly. "I know my job."

Simon searched his face, but he sensed no shifting or twitching. No sense of concealment. Just anger and embarrassment. "Somebody's been through Gus's stuff," he said. "Somebody who was interested in photographs. You don't have any clue who else might have done that?"

"Why the fuck should I care about Gus's stuff? That house has been abandoned for months. Could have been anyone. I didn't go looking for those goddamn pictures because I figured, what the hell, after all this time? The guy's dead, right? I figured it was over."

Wes wasn't lying. He hated Simon's guts, but he wasn't hiding anything. Another futile stab at solving this riddle, another dead end, and all he'd had to show for it was another dose of abuse.

Lucky for him he had a thick skin. He got up and turned to go.

"Hey. Riley. Hold it right there. What are you planning to do with those pictures?"

He'd almost forgotten about the photos, his mind had

ranged so far ahead. "Keep them," he offered. "They're no use to me. And I've got the negatives. I'd be glad to run off copies if you need any."

"Smart-mouth son-of-a-bitch. Are you threatening me?"

Simon focused on the vein throbbing in Wes's temple. His anger and sarcasm drained away, leaving a dull emptiness in its place. He shook his head. "I don't do things just to hurt people. I've got better ways to spend my time."

"Then get lost. Spend your goddamn time out of my sight."

Simon thought of something at the doorway, and turned. "One more thing, Lieutenant."

Wes glared at him. "Yeah?"

"When Ellen comes in here to talk to you about what happened today? I suggest you be real careful with her feelings. Real polite and respectful, you get me? The soul of courtesy and professionalism. I would appreciate that very much. Do we understand each other?"

"Get out of here. Goddamn punk."

Simon hastened to oblige.

He poured gasoline over his prisoners, soaking them. They struggled and screamed. No one watching, and these two were all his. He smiled down at them, waved his hand bye-bye. He lit the match, let it drop, and stepped back to watch the show. Yes. He laughed at the liberation. The wild euphoria, the energy released. The hot, sexual rush.

A hoarse yelling from behind him jerked his head around. It was Gus, that smart-ass pothead photographer from his hometown, always underfoot with his goddamn camera. He wasn't supposed to be here. No one was supposed to be here. Gus ran out of the mangrove jungle, hair flying, eyes bugging, mouth wide open yelling "no."

Ray lifted his pistol. Took aim—

". . . going on? What's so funny? Uh, Mr. Mitchell?"

Wes Hamilton's voice cut through his vision. For one disjointed moment, he saw the image of his writhing, flaming prisoners superimposed over the scarred wooden tabletop at Tracey's Pub.

The candle had triggered the flashback. He knew better than to let himself stare into an open flame. He was getting sloppy.

He swallowed back the laughter that still shook him. "Excuse me, Wes. I was just thinking about something someone said to me today."

Wes blinked at him. He had that worried, wary look on his face that Ray had come to hate. He'd been seeing it all too often lately.

Ray sipped his whiskey. "So? You were saying? Riley came crying to you because he got roughed up in McNary Canyon?"

"Uh . . . he claims that he fought off the attackers, sir. Evidently they, ah, saw him and Ellen. Together. If you know what I mean."

"You don't have to be so uncomfortable, Wes," Ray said meditatively. "She's no longer engaged to my son. She can spread her legs for anyone she wants. Relax."

Wes's eyes dropped. "Uh, yeah. Well, anyhow. That's all Riley told me. So I'll, er, be heading home." He took a final swig of beer.

Ray nodded. "Thank you for the call, Wes. I appreciate the courtesy."

"Hey, no one wants to keep a closer eye on that lowlife slime than I do," Wes said fervently. "So you, uh, take it easy, sir. See you around."

Ray thought of Ellen as his eyes followed Wes out of the pub. So pretty and demure and shy, but he knew the truth about her. She was soiled. A dirty slut. Unworthy. She should be punished.

Ellen had disappointed him. So had Brad, who should have seen it coming and handled it better, but Brad was soft. He didn't look it, but he was soft inside, where it counted. He tried hard and put on a brave face, but not even the harshest discipline had managed to purge that secret softness out of his boy. And Ray had tried. Oh, had he tried.

Ray avoided looking at the candle flames as he finished his drink. He had no soft spot. He had found his perfect balance of forces. The secret fire he held inside himself, and the iron mask that contained it.

The tension between those two forces was an exquisite torture.

It was raining outside. Ellen huddled on her couch with her chamomile tea, but the teacup shook so violently, she kept spilling on herself. The tapping on the window made her heart swell, hot and soft and eager. She put the cup in its saucer and peeked out the curtain.

Simon grinned at her from the maple branches outside.

She opened the window and the screen. "Simon?"

He swung himself inside gracefully feet first, and perched on her windowsill, dripping with rain. "Hey, babe."

"Simon, what are you—"

He yanked her close and cut off her words with a passionate kiss.

She forgot her question with his warm, ardent lips moving over her face, his arms gripping her. His face was cool and wet with rain.

She finally leaned her head back, gasping for some air. "I missed you," she told him. "Where did you run off to?"

He nibbled her throat, then licked it with a long, hot swipe of his tongue. "I went to talk to the police, like a good little boy. Wes Hamilton told me you need to go in and make a statement tomorrow."

"OK," she said. "I will."

His body was practically vibrating under his damp, muddy clothing. His eyes had a wild glitter. "Are you OK?" she asked timidly.

"I'm just jacked way up on adrenaline and I can't seem to come down," he said. "That's all. It's routine."

"Is that why you climbed up to my window? To blow off steam? Tarzan of the jungle. You are so silly, Simon."

He wrapped his legs around her and squeezed her inside his tight, powerful embrace. "Stay close to me, El," he muttered. "Let me touch you all over. So I can be sure you're OK."

She stroked his snarled, filthy hair, his big shoulders. "I'm just fine," she assured him. "One of these days, you have to start acting like you have a right to be here. You sneak around like Zorro."

"I didn't want to see anybody but you," he said. "And the maple is a joke, compared to the oak tree. I could do the maple blindfolded."

"Who says you have to see anyone?" she said. "Just come in the door, come up the stairs, and—"

He put a finger over her lips. "Shhh. Two reasons I came in the window. The first is that the parlor is full of people sucking down cognac and chattering about what happened tonight with your mama. It looks like a goddamn cocktail party in there. I didn't feel like seeing all eyes on filthy, muddy me while I slink upstairs to your bed."

"Simon, you're the hero of the day," she protested. "Everybody knows why you're muddy, and nobody would dream of—"

"The other reason I climbed up the tree is because I knew it would make you smile," he said softly. "God, I love making you smile."

She was so charmed and flustered, she forgot what she was saying, and let him yank her right back into his fierce, hungry kiss.

He finally lifted his head, nuzzling her cheek. "How do you feel, sweetheart?" he asked. "Did your mama get you all patched up?"

"I'm great," she assured him. "Just a couple of scrapes and—"

"Let me see." He wrenched the bathrobe down over her shoulders.

She stumbled back, laughing, and twitched it shut. "Not next to an open window with the light on! I've learned my lesson today!"

He jumped down from the window, pulled the screen closed and yanked the curtains shut across it. He took a step towards her.

"Hold it right there!" She held up her hand. "Get those dirty boots off before you completely ruin my carpets!"

He wrenched the laces loose and peeled them off. He glanced down at his sodden, dirt-streaked shirt, peeled it off and tossed it aside. He herded her towards the bed wearing only his muddy jeans.

Ellen hastily stripped the antique rosebud quilt off her bed and tossed it over the footboard just in time. She turned to face him.

He loomed over her, his hard, muscular body streaked with dirt, soaked with rain, his dark eyes wild. He pushed her shoulders until she sat down on the bed, pushed her robe open and shoved it down.

She sat before him naked, still damp from her bath, her wet hair combed back off her forehead. Simon's hands skimmed reverently over her breasts, her waist, her hips. He hissed through his teeth when he saw the livid marks on her thighs and calves, and sank to his knees.

"Oh, baby. Your poor, precious legs. I'm so sorry." He covered them with gentle kisses, his lips warm and soft against her legs.

She bent over his head and pressed her face to his hair, shaking with a tenderness so deep it almost frightened her. When he pressed her thighs apart, she opened for him eagerly, with a low, pleading murmur. He probed delicately between her legs and looked up when he found her slick and yielding. His eyes were hot, glowing with desire.

"You're wet," he whispered. He slid his finger into the pool of moisture inside her and caressed her until she squirmed.

"It's the way you kissed my legs," she told him. "I get wet instantly when you're so sweet to me. I just can't help it."

He rose to his feet and wrenched the buttons of his jeans open, shoved them down. His penis jutted towards her. She reached out to caress him, but he shoved her back onto the bed.

"No, baby, I can't handle any games," he said. "Let me just . . . let me get inside you. Quick."

"Anything," she told him. "Anything you want."

He pulled a condom out of his pocket, tore it open with his teeth and sheathed himself with one swift, expert gesture. He scooped her legs up and braced her feet against his naked chest. "I've figured out the advantage of Great-grandma Kent's antique bed," he said. He fitted his penis against her and slowly, insistently prodded his way inside her. "It's the perfect height for me to fuck you on my feet. Most beds are too low, but this one, ah. It's like it was custom made just for me."

"I'm glad you've finally found something of Great-grandmother Kent's that you approve of," she told him. "Oh, Simon . . . oh."

"Is it OK?" He pushed himself deeper, caressing her with his hands and spreading her moisture lavishly around her labia to ease his way. She never quite got used to the sheer, unyielding breadth of him.

He pushed forward until he was completely seated inside her, then dragged himself out with agonizing slowness. "I don't have any control tonight," he said. "I want to go at you like a maniac."

"I don't want control," she told him. "I'm a maniac, too. Do it."

He gave her what she asked for, fierce and passionate. His

heavy, relentless thrusts churned her into a heated frenzy. She clutched his arms and hung on until all the tension the strange, violent day had wrought inside her stretched, tighter and tighter.

It broke, and flung her wide, into a dark, soaring nowhere.

When she opened her eyes, she found him sprawled beside her, dirty jeans still clinging to his hips. His somber eyes gazed into hers.

"Oh, no," she said. "Don't you dare. Don't even think of it."

He frowned. "Don't what? Dare what?"

"Whenever we make love, you get moody and inconsolable after. I won't stand for it anymore. Get . . . over . . . it. Right now. Understand?"

He smiled reluctantly. He pushed himself up onto his elbows and gazed around at the bed. "Jesus. Look at the mess I made."

She glanced down at the streaks of mud all over the fine white linen and shrugged. "No biggie. Dirt washes out."

He plucked at the sheets. "You know I'll always do that to you," he said. "Make messes. Get your perfect, clean life dirty."

She rolled her eyes. "If you'd calmed down a tiny bit, it might have occurred to you to take a bath before you leaped on me. I would have been happy to run you a bath myself. And wash you personally. My soapy hands, rubbing your body until you're squeaky clean. You like?"

"Sure," he said. "But I—"

"So you're creating problems that don't exist. Idiot man."

"And you're deliberately missing my point," Simon growled.

"Sure, I'm missing it. It's a stupid point. If you want me to get your point, make a better one." She slid off the bed and glared at him. "I'm going to go and run you a bubble bath." She reached down and pulled the condom off his penis. "I'll take care of this, if you would make yourself useful and strip the bed. Throw the dirty sheets in the corner, please. We'll put clean ones on after your bath."

She didn't look at him as she stalked into the bathroom. She left the door open as she set the tub running, and watched him out of the corner of her eye. He stood there, bemused and motionless for a few moments before he finally pulled off his jeans.

He disappeared into the alcove, and reappeared with an armful of sheets. He dumped them in the corner and walked into the bathroom, staring at the fragrant mounds of bubbles rising in the claw-foot tub.

"Wow," he said. "You want me to get into that? It's so . . . fluffy."

"Scented bubbles won't hurt you," she said. "I've wanted to give you a bath for years. Even back in the old days."

He frowned. "Come on. I wasn't that dirty."

"Oh, it wasn't just to get you clean." She looked up through her lashes. "My Simon fantasies were probably a lot less innocent than you might think. I loved the image of you naked and wet in the tub."

His penis lengthened. A wary grin stretched across his face.

She caressed his shaft, swirling her fingers around the bulbous tip. "When I petted your hair, it was always sticky with pitch," she went on. "I wanted to get that pitch out, but I knew you would smash all my mom's perfume bottles as soon as you turned around, so I never dared."

He rolled his eyes. "Did you Simon-proof your bathroom tonight?"

She shook her head. "No. You're very coordinated now. I noticed that when you were tossing bad guys right and left. Go on. Get in."

He stepped into the tub and sank down with a groan of delight. "Oh, yeah. Oh, wow. This is great."

Ellen soaped up the washcloth with her favorite lavender soap. She started on his arms, then his shoulders and his back, massaging him until he hummed with pleasure. "Dunk your hair, please."

When he came up, sputtering, she greeted him with a handful of rosemary mint shampoo, and worked the creamy lather into his hair.

It was heaven, to have Simon naked and wet and soapy under her hands. He was so beautiful and tempting when he was smiling and relaxed. But then again, he was beautiful and tempting in any mood.

She stepped into the tub with him and knelt between his legs, ignoring the sting of the hot water against her scratched legs. She abandoned the washcloth. She wanted to feel every delicious detail of his powerful, muscular body with her bare, soapy hands. She slid her hands beneath his butt and pulled until his hips floated to the surface. Beneath the bubbles, his thick erection lay stiff and crimson against his belly. She soaped up her hands again, and caressed his penis, swirling her fisted hand over his swollen glans, massaging his balls.

"My God, El," he murmured.

"I have to work hard on getting you nice and clean," she said, pumping and sliding. "This part of you needs lots of attention. Never let it be said that I'm not thorough when I start on a project."

"Oh, never," he gasped.

"Time to rinse," she announced. "Down you go. Hold your breath."

When he shook the water out of his eyes, he grinned at her and yanked her down on top of him. "My turn, now."

He soaped his hands up and slid his slick hands over her back, her bottom, her thighs, until she was limp and floating. She let her legs fall open when his hand slid between the cleft of her bottom, teasing and flicking. Delving inside her until she squirmed with excitement.

He nuzzled her neck, nibbled her earlobe. "You know what, El?"

"What?" she murmured.

"The good news is, I love bathing with you. The bad news is, I want to fuck you so bad, I'm going to faint from lack of blood to my brain."

She lifted her head. "And why is this bad news?"

"I don't have any more condoms," he said. "I have to get dressed and go down to the convenience store at the highway junction. Not that I'm complaining. I'm happy to do it. I just wish I'd gotten more at the tavern. I didn't want to jinx myself by being overambitious."

"Um, actually . . ." Ellen rose up onto her knees and reached for her fingernail scrubbing brush. She pulled one of his hands out of the floating suds and began to scrub at the half-moon of dirt beneath his nails. "I . . . a few years ago I had some problems with my cycle, and my doctor put me on the Pill to regulate it." Her voice trailed off.

Simon lunged upright. Soapy water slopped heavily over the tub and onto the bathroom floor. "You're on the Pill?"

She nodded. "I know that I'm safe. I always used a condom. And when I went on the Pill, I had all the bloodwork in the world done, including an HIV test. I was negative, so, um . . . there you go." She gave him a shy smile and fished for his other hand.

He stared into her face as she scrubbed each nail. "I've always used condoms," he said. "Always. I tested negative five months ago when I got a physical. I haven't slept with anyone but you since then."

She let his hand drop with a splash into the tub. "Well, then?" she asked. "What's the problem?"

"The problem is, technically, you shouldn't take my word for it."

"Well, technically, you shouldn't take mine, either, right?" she pointed out. "So we're even."

He snorted. "Hah. A million miles from even. Men hate condoms. All men hate them. A lot of men would lie like dogs not to use them."

"You wouldn't," she said.

"How would you know?" he demanded.

"I just know." She ran her fingers over his wet face. "I see it written all over you. I see right into you, Simon. And I love what I see."

His face went wary. "Don't read my mind."

"Why not? I'm not afraid of anything I might find," she said. "I've been in there before. I know my way around."

He pulled his face away from her hand and sank back into the water, his expression closed and hard. "Don't do this to me, El."

"Don't love you?" She got to her feet. "Too late. The damage is done, so deal with it." She grabbed a towel and wrapped it around herself. It hurt to be naked in front of him when he was being cold.

She stalked out of the bathroom, holding herself as straight and tall as she could. "You must be hungry," she said coolly. "Let me run down and make you some sandwiches—"

"Fuck the sandwiches." He appeared in the doorway, his naked body dripping. Anger blazed from his eyes. "You're punishing me."

She bristled. "Me? Punishing you? That's unfair and ridiculous! I'm just changing the subject, since that seems to be what you need—"

"This isn't about what I need," he said. "Let's talk about what *you* need. Never mind the sandwiches."

She wrapped her towel more tightly around her body. "I didn't mean to make you angry. What did I say that was so—"

"Come here, El, and I'll explain it to you."

The challenge in his voice stung her. She marched over to him, chin high. He jerked the towel off her body.

She fought down the urge to cover herself with her arms. "We have to put sheets on the bed if you want to—"

"Forget the sheets. Lie down. Right here."

"On the floor?" She frowned. "Simon, for heaven's sake.

I am not the type to have sex on the floor when there's a comfortable bed—"

"I know you're not," Simon said. "That's the whole point."

The look in his eyes aroused and frightened her in equal measures. When he looked at her like that, he was everything that was wild and perilous and unknown.

"I'll get down first," Simon said. He knelt on the rug, and spread out the towel he had taken from her. He grasped his penis, stroking himself slowly as he gazed at her body. "Come on, El. Come to me."

She sank down onto the towel, and batted at him with a murmur of protest when he seized her shoulders and pressed her down onto her back. He loomed over her. "Now open your legs," he commanded.

"Oh, stop it," she snapped. "You just love to order me around."

"Yeah. It turns me on when you trust me enough to do what I say. You're so sweet and selfless. You want to comfort me and save me and feed me, and give me everything I want. But what do *you* want, El?"

That glittering intensity in his eyes flustered her. "I want you," she said, tangling her fingers into his wet hair. "I love you, Simon."

He kissed her face, her throat, dragging his hot mouth down over her chest to suckle her breasts. The wet ends of his hair tickled her throat. "And you think your love can save me? You think you can clean me up and fix me so I can fit into the perfect El Kent universe?"

She jerked up onto her elbows. "What are you saying? What perfect universe? There's nothing perfect about my universe!"

"Yeah, right. The sheets are always clean and people are always polite, and there are five different kinds of iced tea and ten different types of muffins. Everything clean and pretty and perfect. But the world's not pretty and perfect, El. And neither . . . am . . . I."

"I know that!" she snapped. "I never asked you to be perfect! Not you, not me, not anyone! If I could figure out what the hell it is that you want from me, I'd give it to you, but I can't! So let go of me! Let me up!"

"You still don't get it. I want to get past the sweet, perfect angel act. This is me, Simon. You don't have to be an angel with me. You don't have to be so fucking perfect. You don't have to persuade me or impress me or enchant me. I want inside. I want the real, naked El."

Tears welled up in her eyes. "You are inside," she said softly. "It's all yours. Don't you see that?"

"Lie down on your back again." This time his voice was gentle, not commanding. She sank back, and was grateful that the floor was kind enough to hold her up. He pushed her wet hair away from her forehead, fanning it out behind her head. He pushed her legs wide, folding her open. "Open your eyes," he said.

She did as he asked, though her eyes swam with tears. She blinked them away and focused on his face. There was none of the smug, dominating triumph that she had feared to see. His face was rapt. Reverent. He was casting a spell over them both, and even he was half afraid of what the outcome might be.

The vulnerability on his face freed her. She moved sinuously beneath his stroking hands. She'd never known anything about being seductive before, but with Simon's eyes on her, it just came to her.

"Touch yourself," he said. "For me."

She put her hands between her legs, as she'd done so many times in the privacy of her own bed, but this felt so different. Everything she did and felt was reflected back to her in the mirror of his fascinated eyes, a feedback loop resonating to an unbearable pitch of arousal.

Her inhibitions were gone, melted away and forgotten. She parted her labia and caressed her clitoris, her hips moving in a subtle invitation. She opened herself so he could see every detail, the flushed, moist lips of her sex, puffy and soft, aching to be touched. She thrust her fingers inside herself and pulled them out gleaming with her juices.

She offered her hand to him. "See? That's all for you."

He made a wordless sound and seized her hand, sucking her fingers into his mouth. The hot, wet sucking of his lips and tongue made her body convulse.

"God, you taste good," he said. He thrust his finger inside her, and hooked it tenderly under her pubic bone, circling a spot deep inside her that softened and melted at his touch.

"Tell me again," he said. "Do you like this?"

"I love it," she gasped. "Oh, God, what are you doing?"

"My duty. Tell me again, El. I need to hear it. Do you need me?"

"Yes . . . I need . . . oh God . . ." She heaved against his thrusting hand, pressing both of her own down upon it. Pleasure burst inside her, and expanded into a rippling infinity, long and hot and lingering.

When he finally began to slide his penis into her, she trembled with delight and lifted her hips, gripping him deep inside herself.

Simon gasped. His body went rigid. "Oh, God. This is amazing. It's . . . you're so hot. El, you're killing me. I can't . . . please, don't move. Do not move. Let me get myself together. I don't want to come yet."

"Don't worry," she soothed. "It doesn't matter if you come. Just let go. My beautiful love." She undulated, clenching herself around him and loving the way the movement made him whimper and gasp. "I like it like this, with no condom, and you right on the edge. You can't play your teasing power games with me when you're out of control."

He hissed with pleasure and held her motionless. "Damn it, El, don't move!" He arched his body over hers, eyes squeezed shut, rigid with the strain of holding back his orgasm.

"Give me everything you've got. Everything you are," she commanded. "I need it. And I'll give you the same."

His control snapped. They lost themselves in a frenzy of writhing tenderness. His strength forged into hers, hers enveloped and contained his. Together they fused into perfect, dynamic shining oneness.

They stared at each other afterwards, silent and limp and tangled.

"I'm destroyed," he whispered.

She licked her dry, swollen lips. "That's two of us."

She watched him for the sadness that usually overtook him after sex. It didn't seem to be happening. He looked dazed. Tender and lost.

"Tonight, you're not going to run away from me," she said. Her voice had a quiet ring of command. "You're staying with me in my bed. You'll hold me all night and be there with me in the morning."

He nodded. "I don't want to be anywhere in the world but here."

She struggled to her feet and went to her bureau to pull out lavender-scented sheets. The best ones she had. Monogrammed linen, from the dowry of her grandmother, Ewan Kent's bride. The sheets she had always hoped to put on her bed for her wedding night.

"Would you help me make my bed?" she asked.

"Yeah." He sounded doubtful, but willing.

She tried not to smile as he followed her to the bed. Simon would have no idea of the symbolism of her choice of bed linens. He was a man. To him, sheets were just sheets. Nor would it be appropriate to tell him. He would probably run screaming, just when she'd finally lured him into sleeping in her bed. Skittish, wary wild animal that he was.

Ah, well. Subtle ancestor magic was most effective when done quietly, with no fuss. She directed the bedmaking with gentle bossiness. Simon followed her orders, dazed and meek.

She flicked off the bedside lamp and slid between the crisp, fragrant sheets. She lifted them up and invited him into her arms.

He crawled in and seized her, holding her against his hard,

hot body with a fierce intensity that made her heart melt with tenderness.

She had him in her arms right now. It would be stupid to wonder for how long. Even more stupid to hope for forever.

Chapter

15

*A*t first it was just another flying dream. He had a lot of those, and always welcomed them. It was fun, dipping and soaring up on air currents, floating and diving to skim over treetops. The sky still dark but starting to glow on one side with the first pale light of dawn.

He swooped high on an updraft, and that was where he saw it; a point of orange, glowing dully like an ember. As he swooped lower it came into focus. He knew this thing. He'd seen it in his dreams all his life, but deliberately let it fade from his memory when he woke. The circle of fire, huge and ravenous. He was bound to it with invisible chains. He swooped lower, until the flames were almost singeing his wings.

It left only blackened earth in its wake. A conscious entity. A monster in the dark. The one that had eaten his mother.

He was in the center of its black maw, and someone was in it, lying on the ground. A slender form, curled up with her back to him, the graceful sweep of her spine and the curve of her hip infinitely precious and familiar to him. El pushed herself up onto her knees. Her naked, beautiful body was smeared with dust and ash. She looked around the ring of flames that were closing in on her. There was no way out.

She held herself straight and proud. She looked up into

the sky. Her eyes met his, and the terrible knowledge filled
him, that it was all his fault, he should have saved her, and
he was helpless to save her now.

The fire reached for her. She screamed—

He jerked up in bed, his heart knocking furiously in his
chest.

"Simon? Are you OK?" Ellen jolted out of sleep and sat
up.

He couldn't answer, couldn't speak, just doubled over,
gasping.

El cuddled up to him. He leaned into her to show her that
he appreciated the gesture. He still didn't trust his voice.

El put her hand on his chest. "Good God, Simon. Your
heart is racing. That must have been a terrible nightmare."

He managed a short nod.

"Do you want to tell me—"

"No," he snarled.

Her arms circled him, and he felt her soft, tender lips
press against his shoulder. "Lie down with me," she coaxed.
"It'll relax you."

There was a suggestion that opened up a whole vista of
possibilities. Instantly the fight-and-flight drug pumping
through his blood channeled itself into a hard-on like a red
hot steel spike.

She murmured, startled, as he rolled her onto her back
and pushed her legs open. He covered her sweet mouth with
his own and mounted her, growling with wild, feral pleasure
at being able to forge right into her body. She was tight, but
slick and soft from his come, and it was so much easier with
all that extra lube to settle into the deep, plunging rhythm
that his body craved without hurting her.

She dug her nails into his shoulders, lifting her hips up to
accept his deep, thrusting glide. He tried not to be rough, but
the dream had blown away whatever remained of his self-
control. It got wilder, deeper, until he felt the power in her
body gather, and rise, and break. Her cunt clenched around

him, deep pulses that drew forth and demanded his own release. It flooded out of him. He gave it all to her.

She tried to move, eventually, but he pressed the small of her back and draped her thigh over his, keeping his cock inside her.

"No," he pleaded. "Let me stay inside. You're so hot and soft."

She shook with whispery laughter. "I cannot sleep with that huge thing shoved all the way inside me!"

"It'll get smaller," he promised. "Give it a minute. It'll get, um . . ."

"Bendable?"

"Yeah, exactly."

The laughter, the kisses, the cuddling all enabled him to shove the dream away and breathe again. El was fine. Alive and safe in her own warm bed, naked and soft in his arms, and he would stay shoved deep inside her body for as long as she would let him.

He had her, and he was holding her.

Ellen woke up in a state of grace, every muscle relaxed. Dawn glowed in the sky, the birds chattered outside her window.

Simon murmured in his sleep and rolled onto his side facing her. Her heart was so full, she could hardly breathe. It was just like all those nights back when she was young, staring at his long body stretched out on her bedroom floor, his limbs sprawled out in relaxed exhaustion.

She'd ached with a love for him that felt like it would burst the seams of her heart. Just as she did right now.

He was so beautiful, it hurt to look at him. Long and lean and perfect, the brown of his arms striking against the white linen. The top sheet was snarled around his waist, leaving his chest bare. His hair against the pillow was a tangled, dense black mass.

Asleep, his face lost its habitual wary tension. His sensual lips were almost smiling. A lock of hair trailed over his sharp cheekbone. A shadow of dark stubble accented the lines and angles of his jaw.

His big hands were capable-looking, long brown fingers, with the scars and battered nails of a man who used them for all kinds of work. She studied the dips and curves of his muscles, the jut of his rib cage, the hair on his chest that widened to a thick dark nest at his groin.

She tugged the edge of the sheet from under his thigh, careful not to wake him, and feasted her eyes on his powerful thighs, his flat belly. Masculine perfection. She wanted to kiss every inch of him, starting with his long brown toes, all the way to the tips of his black hair.

She wanted to watch him sleep, but she also wanted to wake him up and make his mouth stretch in a delighted grin. Her eyes strayed to his penis curled over his drawn-up thigh; dark and half-hard, soft as suede. Alluring her. She scooted down the bed until she lay with her face at his groin, and drew in the musky smell of sex that clung to him.

His penis seemed to sense her interest. It swelled before she even touched it, as if her breath alone were a caress. She licked his exquisitely sensitive flesh with tiny, delicate strokes of her tongue. He was salty, warm. Silky and tender. He murmured uneasily in his sleep.

She scooted closer, licking her lips, and drew the head of his penis into her mouth. It was much easier when he was only half-hard. When he was fully erect, he barely fit into her mouth at all.

He hardened instantly, and woke up with a gasp that sounded almost frightened. "What?"

She murmured soothing sounds and wrapped her arm around his hips, caressing the taut, clenched muscles of his butt.

She loved him with her mouth, and it got easier with every tender stroke. She flowed with it, rhythmic and sensual.

It was odd. What limited experience she'd had till now with this particular sexual technique had only served to convince her that it was not her specialty and never would be. This was different. No embarrassment, no painful tension in her jaw. No wondering if she was doing it correctly or how long it was going to take.

She felt sexy and wanton, purring with pleasure, flushed with power. She swirled her tongue around the thick head of his penis at the end of each long, suckling pull. A circuit of energy tingled and rushed through her body from his, to his, with each slow, dragging caress. She squirmed around a pulsing throb of excitement between her legs. She loved having him in thrall to her, moaning and helpless. She loved his vulnerability and his trust. She loved everything about him.

He lost control, thrust his hips against her face, and she caught the base of his penis in her hand to guide and control him. She shoved him until he rolled onto his back and pulled away just long enough to twist her hair back behind her neck. "You're right about long hair and oral sex," she told him. "It's complicated. Open your legs."

He obeyed her instantly, and she snuggled up between his thighs, cradling the heavy sac of his balls tenderly in her hand. He propped himself up onto his elbows, his high cheekbones streaked with a flush of arousal. He looked dazed. "Do you, uh . . ." His voice cracked. He cleared his throat. "Do you want to make love?"

She rubbed the head of his penis against her soft cheek, licking and nuzzling him with animal pleasure. "What do you want to do?"

He shook his head. "Anything. Any damn thing you want."

She flicked her tongue tenderly along the taut, shining underside of his penis. "Do you want to come in my mouth?"

He tightened and swelled against her tongue "You tell me, El."

She lifted her head and clucked her tongue. "Oh, no," she said. "We're not going to play that silly back-and-forth game. This is your blow job, Simon. You tell me exactly how you want it to go."

He flopped down onto his back. "I would love to come in your mouth," he said raggedly. "That is, if you really want—"

"Shh, then. Lucky for you, that's exactly what I want, too."

She curled up comfortably and settled into a deep, lazy rhythm. Slow and steady, making it last. Every time it looked like he was about to come, she eased off, nuzzling his groin until the wave eased down, and then she would suck him deep into her mouth while she caressed a tender place beneath his balls that she'd discovered made him thrash and writhe. His hands tightened in her hair, and his body shook.

"Please, El," he pleaded. "Let me come. I can't take anymore."

She smiled her assent, and let him guide her to the finish. He tightened his hand around hers, pumping it hard and fast, and the taste of him against her tongue changed, grew hotter, tighter, metallic.

He arched off the bed with a choking sound. She braced herself against the hot spurts of semen in her mouth.

Simon groped blindly for a pillow and flopped it over his face.

She wiped her mouth and nuzzled his thigh. "Simon?"

He held up his hand, silently begging her to wait. She couldn't. She crawled up his body and straddled him. "Are you OK?"

The hand gave her a silent thumbs-up.

She stretched out beside him and wrenched the pillow off his face. "Hey, you. Enough of that," she said sternly. "Be sociable."

He looked away, but not quickly enough to hide that his eyes were wet, his face red. "Damn," he muttered. "Give a man some privacy."

"There's no privacy to be had in my bed with me," she said. "Are you laughing or crying? Is something funny?"

He covered his face with his hand. "No. Yes. I feel like a live wire with the casing stripped off. I can't . . ." His voice trailed off, and he swallowed hard. "I can't keep my throat from shaking," he finished.

She nodded in perfect understanding. "I know the feeling. I've been in that condition for days. Ever since Peggy Hought told me you'd come home while she was checking my groceries at the Shopping Kart."

"It hasn't eased off?" He looked alarmed.

She shook her head. "It comes and goes. You get used to it."

He shook his head. "God help me."

"Cuddling helps," she informed him. "A lot."

He held out his arms. "Then get to it, babe."

Simon wrapped himself around her as she dozed, staring at her flushed cheek, her soft pink mouth, the curling fan of her lashes. He could have held her like that forever, but the rumbling in his belly made her murmur, eyes fluttering open. She rolled over to look at the clock, and jerked upright. "I cannot believe it! It's eight-twenty!"

"So? What's the emergency?"

"My guests! I have to make breakfast!" She jumped up and reached for a pair of jeans, but stopped short and slanted him an embarrassed glance. "I have to take a shower."

"Pretty juicy down there? Yum. Let me feel." He reached for her.

She skittered back. "Laugh and tease all you want. These people have paid me to make them breakfast, and it's my responsibility to—"

"Everybody knows that yesterday was a nightmare for you. Nobody in their right mind would blame you for taking it easy today," he said. "They can fix themselves breakfast. Calm down. You're entitled."

She looked unconvinced. "I, um, have to take a shower."

Simon luxuriated in her comfortable bed for a moment, but the image of El naked and wet in her shower soon proved to be irresistible.

She giggled helplessly when he muscled his way into the shower stall. "Simon! I'm in a hurry! Out! Get lost!"

"Just let me wash you," he pleaded. "I won't take advantage of the situation. That is, not unless you beg me to." He slid his soapy hand between her legs.

She squeaked, and shoved him back against the wall. "Let me rinse myself! You're too big! We're going to have a lake in here!"

"It's not my fault that I'm big." He batted his eyes innocently. "Here, let me rinse you—"

"Stop!" She swatted at him, snorting with laughter. "You're making a big mess, Simon. God, you are a handful!"

He grabbed both her hands and wrapped them around his throbbing hard-on. "More than a handful, babe. Check me out."

She fled the shower, laughing and sputtering.

He loved making her laugh. It made him giddy.

His triumph abated when it was time to follow her down the stairs. He had nothing to wear but his mud-crusted jeans. El gave him the pick of her sleep T-shirts so that he wouldn't have to put on his filthy shirt, but the only one big enough was a pink flowered thing.

He left his muddy boots by the front door mat, and followed El into the dining room. Muriel looked up from her newspaper and gave him a long, even look that made him squirm. Lionel just grinned.

"Well, well, well," Muriel said. "So you've found the nerve to stick around for breakfast. You're making progress, Simon."

"Mother!" Ellen exclaimed.

"Gee, thanks," Simon said sourly. "Nice of you to notice."

"You're quite welcome," Muriel said. "Oh, by the way, Ellen. Mary Ann, Alex and Boyd checked out early this morning, around seven. She said to tell you goodbye, and that she was very sorry, but things were just a wee bit too stressful around here."

"I don't blame her," Ellen said tightly.

"Cowardly female," Lionel grumbled. "Lily-livered."

El raised her nose into the air, sniffing. "What's . . . Mother?

Did you bake something? It smells like something's burning."

Muriel smiled. "No. Not me."

"Then what on earth—"

The kitchen doors burst open. Missy emerged, wreathed in smoke. She bore a basket of dark, irregularly shaped objects. Triumph beautified her thin face. "I made muffins," she announced.

Ellen gaped at her. "You . . . you what?"

"All on my own," Missy said proudly. "Lemon poppyseed. I just followed the instructions in the cookbook. See?"

Ellen blinked. "Missy, that's marvelous! I'm so impressed!"

Missy beamed. "I wanted to, you know, like, help."

"Well?" Simon asked. "Are you going to let us eat them, or what?"

The muffins were crunchy on the outside, gummy on the inside, and full of lumps of bitter, undissolved baking soda, but everyone exclaimed over their deliciousness, and Missy basked in their praise. Everyone ate one, except for Simon, who consumed the remaining eight.

"Good Lord," Muriel said faintly. "Ellen, honey, you'd better make the man some ham and eggs."

Missy leaped to her feet. "I'll do it!"

"Oh, no, thanks," Ellen said hastily. "You're a sweetheart to offer, but you've already worked so hard with the muffins. I'll take care of it."

Simon had polished off six fried eggs, three thick slabs of grilled ham, and was buttering up his fourth English muffin by the time he slowed down enough to feel self-conscious. He looked around the table.

Muriel looked discreetly horrifed. Missy was awestruck. El looked worried. Lionel looked wistful.

"I remember when I was a young fella, and could eat like that. I sure miss my teeth. Enjoy it while you can, bucko. Nothing lasts."

"I will." Simon shot Muriel a sideways glance. "I didn't eat at all yesterday," he muttered. "Just some watermelon."

"Don't feel like you have to explain yourself to me," Muriel said. "Bea called to find out if you're fit enough to help out with the pie table, Ellen. I'll give you a ride to the fairgrounds when you're ready."

"I'll take her," Simon said.

El's smile was radiant. "I'll go with Simon."

The look on Muriel's face gave Simon a thrill of embarrassed surprise. She didn't look suspicious, or disdainful. Her eyes were soft.

Just as quickly, the moment was gone. Disapproval was back. "Find him something more butch to wear before you go, Ellen," she said. "That pink thing is a disgrace."

Simon prowled through the fairgrounds until he saw the rainbow-striped tent awning with LARUE HIGH SCHOOL ART CLUB stenciled on it. Hank, his high school art teacher, was inside, chatting with a pair of elderly ladies. Hank was a short, froglike man with round glasses. His black ponytail and goatee had thinned and grayed.

Hank turned as the old ladies left. His round, homely face lit up. "You!" He hurried over to Simon and flung his arms around him.

Simon awkwardly hugged him back, embarrassed but pleased.

Hank held him out at arm's length. "I heard you were home! My best student ever! I was just about to hunt you down, but here you are!"

"Here I am," Simon repeated. "Good to see you, Hank."

"Yeah! Good to see you too!" Hank pounded Simon's back.

They grinned at each other like fools, until Simon gathered his thoughts. "I wanted to thank you," he said. "For sending me that letter."

Hank nodded. "Yeah, it was the least I could do. Terrible, what happened to Gus. Terrible. I'm so sorry, Simon."

Simon nodded his acknowledgment. "How did you find me?"

"Ah! That! Well, Gus came by the school a few years ago with some magazines under his arm—I think they were pictures of Bosnia—"

"Gus?" Simon was puzzled. "To the school?"

"Yeah, yeah. He was bursting with pride at what a great eye you had, what technique. Brass balls, too, going after the shots that you did. He had to share with someone, and I guess he figured I was worthy." Hank slapped Simon's arm. "What fine work. You kick butt!"

Simon grinned, flustered. "Uh . . . thanks."

"So anyhow, when Gus . . . ah, when it happened, I started making phone calls to the magazines, and hounding people until I tracked down an address for you," Hank said.

Simon nodded. "I really appreciate that."

Hank patted his arm. "Gus was real proud of you. Real proud."

Simon looked down at the ground. The roar of the crowd swelled in to fill the silence. "I, uh, wanted to ask you something, Hank."

Hank beamed. "Ask away, ask away!"

"Did you know Gus back in the late sixties, early seventies?"

The older man's brow creased. "Not well. We both grew up around here, but he was a few years older than me. Why?"

"Muriel Kent told me that Gus spent time in a mental hospital after Vietnam," Simon said. "I was curious about that."

Hank looked around to make sure they were alone, and leaned forward. "Well, the only thing I ever heard about that is pure gossip. I heard it was over a woman!" Hank's voice was a loud stage whisper.

Simon felt blank. "Come again? What woman?"

"Yeah! Gus was in love with Diana Archer, see? And oh, she was a looker. Like a movie star! But she dumped Gus, who was a hippie type. Real free spirit. She married Ray Mitchell. Rich boy, fresh out of Naval Academy. She had her son before Ray left for Vietnam. Then Gus ran off to Vietnam, too. To nurse his broken heart, they said."

"I can't picture Gus with a broken heart," Simon said.

Hank shrugged. "Yeah, he was a real tough guy. Anyhow, Gus got shot up, and he spent over a year in rehab and comes back with a hole in his head, see? Looking like a ghoul. He took one look at Diana the perfect society wife and had a breakdown. I heard they put him in the mental ward after he attacked Ray Mitchell. Jealousy, you know. But that's just hearsay." Hank shrugged. "That's all I ever heard."

"Thanks," Simon said thoughtfully. "That's interesting."

He gave Hank a hug and promised not to be a stranger.

It was hard to imagine Gus sick with love for Brad's bitchy mother. And it wasn't likely that whatever awful thing Gus had planned to tell him involved Ray Mitchell. He was the most influential man in LaRue. The local district attorney, for God's sake.

Another false lead.

Chapter

16

Ellen's body did everything it was supposed to do; it smiled, laughed, it engaged in chitchat, it passed slice after slice of pie to an endless stream of people, but everything had changed.

The sheltering glass bowl over her world was broken. Infinite possibilities stretched out in every direction, beautiful and threatening. The clouds seemed so soft, the aching blue behind them infinitely deep. The noise and chatter of the fair was a brilliant, dazzling mosaic. Every face was a window into another world.

She wished she could dress for this feeling. She'd picked out her dress because it covered her bruises, but it was excruciatingly ladylike. She wanted something eye-catching and bold. A flamenco gown with black and red ruffles. She wanted the world to know she was a woman who could spend the whole night in uninhibited erotic play.

How did a woman like that dress? She didn't even know. Her wardrobe was not equipped for this mood. Come to think of it, the stores and boutiques of LaRue probably weren't that well equipped for it either. Even if they weren't all closed for the festival.

At least she'd left off her underwear. The billowy skirt let currents of air swirl up and caress her bare bottom. It was a start.

"Hello, Ellen."

The acid voice made her shoulders stiffen. She looked into Diana Mitchell's face. "Hello, Mrs. Mitchell. Can I get you a piece of pie?"

"I wouldn't enjoy eating anything you'd baked, Ellen. Your irrational, immodest behavior would poison it for me."

Ellen pressed her lips together. "Maybe you would be more comfortable if you avoided me."

"You had Bradley in your grasp. Do you know how many women in this town would give up body parts to get Bradley's attention? And for what? For that no-good—"

"Giving up body parts would definitely get attention," Ellen said.

"Let's let these inflammatory topics go, ladies." Ray Mitchell stepped up to his wife's side. Deeply Concerned was firmly fixed on his face. "We didn't come here to hound you, young lady. Though I admit, I'm very disappointed in the choice that you made."

"Ah, well, there you go," Ellen said inanely. "I don't know what to say about that. Can I get you a piece of pie, Mr. Mitchell?"

"Give me some of your apple walnut, honey," Ray said. "Diana, sweetcakes, you know good and well that you want that lemon pie."

"Give me a piece of the lemon." Diana's face was sulky.

Ellen handed them pie and prayed for them to leave. They did not.

"Ellen, honey, I already warned you once, but I'm going to take this opportunity to say this to you now," Ray started.

"Please don't, Mr. Mitchell—"

"I heard what happened to you yesterday. I was appalled, but not surprised. I'm horrified that your, ah, association with this man has exposed you to violence. Violence which could have been deadly."

"What happened was not Simon's fault!"

"Oh, my," Diana said. "I've heard that refrain before. Not his fault that your property was destroyed, or that your life was put in danger."

"That's enough," Ellen said sharply. "I don't want to be rude to either of you, but I would appreciate it if you would both just go."

Diana ignored her. "And isn't it odd that Simon the big karate expert destroyed all four of these villains, but oops . . . they all got away! Such a shame they can't be questioned or identified, hmm?"

"He didn't chase them because he thought I might be hurt!"

Diana smiled. "Of course." She took a big bite of pie.

Ray patted her arm. "Honey, we're not suggesting that Simon is trying to deliberately hurt you—"

"Although I wouldn't rule it out," Diana said. "Since he didn't—"

"Rule it out." Ellen's voice was cold and abrupt.

Ray shook his head. "If you continue to associate with this man, you are going to get sucked into this vortex of violence that follows—"

"Afternoon, folks."

Diana shrieked and dropped her pie. She spun around.

Simon stood behind them, a wide, wicked grin on his face.

"You deliberately startled me!" she shrilled.

Simon gave her an apologetic shrug. "Sorry, ma'am. It's that pesky vortex of violence. Gets you every time. Hey, angel. How's it going?" He leaned across the table, caught the back of her head and scooped her close to give her a long, sweet, possessive kiss.

He smiled into her eyes when he let her up for air. "You're so cute when you defend my honor," he whispered. "It makes me hard." He turned to the Mitchells. "I made you drop your pie, Mrs. Mitchell. Can I buy you another piece?"

"Heavens, no," she muttered. "I've completely lost my appetite."

"My condolences for your loss, Simon," Ray Mitchell said stiffly.

Simon inclined his head. "I appreciate that. They told me you were the one who ruled it a suicide."

Ray's brow furrowed into Deeply Concerned. "Yes, that was my sad duty. The forensics and autopsy reports were conclusive—"

"Ray!" Diana shuddered. "Must we? It's so grisly."

"And yet, somebody's been through Gus's photographs," Simon said evenly. "Someone tried to breach his computer, too."

Ray's expression did not change. "That house has been abandoned for some time now. The responsibility for securing that property now rests with you, Simon."

"It just seems strange," Simon said. "I have an e-mail from Gus, dated the day he died. Not a suicide note. He told me to come home. That there was something important he needed to show me. Proof of some kind. Not the words of a man intent on killing himself."

Ray rested his hand on Simon's shoulder. "Son, your uncle had a history of mental illness," he said, in a sad, heavy voice. "He was also in the final stages of alcoholism, a fact which was corroborated by the autopsy. I'll be glad to take a look at this e-mail of yours, but you're just going to have to accept the sad truth that your uncle was—"

"Thanks, but I'm well aware of all the sad truths about my uncle. I don't need to be told again." Simon glanced down at Ray's hand.

Ray removed it hastily. "So . . . ahem. I imagine you're just in town long enough to deal with Gus's estate?"

Simon shrugged. "I don't know yet. I'm getting sort of fond of LaRue. Right now I'm real busy combing through Gus's stuff."

"It's not necessary to do all that work yourself," Ray said. "I know a woman who will take care of it. Very professional. She'll go through everything, sort out whatever has value, and send you an inventory. No sweat, no dust, no painful memories. Just efficient service."

"Thanks, but I'm trying to find whatever this proof was that Gus referred to in his e-mail. And an estate sale person wouldn't recognize stuff with sentimental value."

Diana snorted. "Sentimental value? Gus? Hah."

Simon gazed at her, his eyes calm and direct. "You might be surprised, ma'am. I've found some beautiful photographs that he took sometime around, oh, '67 or '68. Up at the waterfall. Lovely work."

Ellen watched the scene, puzzled. She felt like she was missing something important. Simon seemed to be waiting for a cue. Diana was staring stiffly into the distance. Ray was laughing heartily, as if someone had just cracked a joke. "Well, we should be on our way," Ray said. "Come on, honey. Almost time for the parade."

"Sir?" Simon asked. "You're a Vietnam veteran, right?"

Ray's face was overtaken by Hearty and Affable. "Why, yes, I am."

"Did you ever meet up with Gus when you were over there?"

Ray's smile was unwavering. "Sure didn't, son. Why do you ask?"

"I'm trying to put the pieces of Gus's life together," Simon said. "You know how it is. Curiosity."

"Sometimes it's best to let it go," Ray said. "Look to the future."

"You may have a point," Simon said. "Enjoy the parade."

They watched the Mitchells walk away. Simon slid around the pie table and slipped his arm around Ellen's waist. "That guy is strange," he said. "I can't read him. It's like trying to read a plastic doll. Weird."

"What on earth was that all about, anyway?" Ellen demanded.

He looked innocent. "What do you mean?"

She gestured towards the Mitchells' retreating forms. "Those undercurrents. You were poking at them. Trying to make them jump."

He kissed her again. "What do you expect? I come over here, all set to lure you into my vortex of violence, and I find them trying to poison you against me. You're surprised I didn't lick their shoes?"

"I don't expect you to lick anybody's shoes! You're avoiding my—"

"You're yummy in that granny dress. It's so prim, it's almost kinky. Did you go talk to the police about yesterday?"

She pressed her nose against the triangle of hard, bare chest revealed by his open shirt. "Yes. I talked to Wes Hamilton."

"Was Wes nice to you?"

She frowned. "What an odd question. Nice in what sense?"

"The usual sense." Simon's tone was light, but his eyes were keen and watchful. "Polite, helpful, respectful? All that good stuff?"

"Sure he was," she said, bewildered. "He was perfectly nice to me. Why do you ask?"

"No particular reason. I like it when people are nice to you, baby."

He leaned back against the table, crossing his long, jeans-clad legs. Her body clenched with longing at the sight of him. His hair was loose, ruffled by the warm breeze. He wore a thin, crumpled, white linen shirt buttoned halfway up his golden chest. His face was shadowed with bad-boy beard stubble. That indecent, give-me-sex-now smile on his face would be more appropriate if he were lounging stark naked in bed.

He beckoned her closer. "Come here. I want to tell you a secret."

She could just bet what kind of secret it would be. "There are people everywhere, Simon," she murmured. "Tell me tonight."

He grabbed her wrist and tugged her closer. "I want to tell you now," he wheedled. "I've been dreaming up new ways to make love to you all morning. It's driving me crazy. I want to run them all past you."

"Forget it," she said sternly. "Tell me tonight." She glanced down at the front of his jeans. "Whoa. You're in pretty bad shape, buddy."

He grinned. "I'm in agony," he confessed. "Only you can give me sweet relief. Cruel, beautiful El. Drape that huge skirt over my crotch and hide my shame, baby. Or better yet, how about if you just lean that perfect ass of yours . . . right against me. Oh, yeah. Give me all your weight. Oh, yeah. That's it."

She giggled. "We cannot have sex right now, Simon!" She grabbed a plate full of pie and offered it to him. "Compensate with sugar. That's what girls do. It works pretty well most of the time."

He waved it away. "I want El pie," he said stubbornly.

"Hey! Riley! Get your hand off that nice girl's bum, sleazebag!"

Cora grinned at them, stunning in a purple crisscross halter top and a miniskirt that showed off her graceful, muscular legs. Her curly hair was twisted up into an artful explosion of curly wisps. Cora was the only person Ellen had ever seen who managed to display extensive cleavage with no visible means of support. She defied natural laws.

Ellen glanced down at the lace-trimmed collar and the big, droopy silk bows that decorated her dress. Maybe she should dress like Cora to express her newfound knowledge about herself.

"Hey, Cora," she said. "Love your top."

"Thanks." Cora examined her face. "In spite of these stories I'm hearing about dumping your fiancé and fighting off assassins, you're looking good. Way better than the last time I saw you." Her eyes flicked to Simon's. "Keep up the good work, bozo. There's hope for you yet."

"Thanks, Cor," he said. "You're a pal."

"Want a piece of pie, Cora?" El asked.

Cora surveyed the array of pies with deep interest. "What's the most caloric thing you've got?"

"That would be the chocolate pecan with a shortbread crust," Ellen said. "Particularly once I heap it with whipped cream. It's too heavy for the summertime, but I always make one just in case."

"Oh, I love chocolate pecan. Bring it on."

Ellen cut her a generous wedge and heaped it with whipped cream. Cora took a bite and sighed with bliss. "I'm going to hell for this. God, Ellen, you're so good."

"Yeah, isn't she just?" Simon murmured. "Yummy."

"I didn't come by here just for the pie, guys. There's something I forgot to mention when I dropped off the sheets the other day. I saw Bebop and Scotty Webber turning onto the old logging road that leads up McNary Canyon that day. I walked down it a ways, and saw them staring down at your house with binoculars."

Simon scowled at her. "You should never have done that, Cor. Bebop and Scotty are scum."

Cora shrugged. "Yeah, no shit, but curiosity killed the cat. I didn't get close and I didn't stay long. I'm no fool." She turned back to Ellen. "Sorry I didn't tell you before. When I heard what happened, I thought, hmm." She tossed out her plate. "Who knows? Those two are slimy enough to pull a stunt like that, though I can't imagine why they would have it in for you two. But hey. For what it's worth. That's what I saw."

"I'll check it out." Simon's face had gone flint hard.

Ellen whirled on him. "No! You will let the police check it out!"

"And I'll just scoot along and let you two argue," Cora said briskly. "Watch out for those bad guys, Ellen. I just can't tell you how glad I am that you're finally having some fun."

"Thanks." Ellen waved away the two dollars that Cora proffered. "On the house. One question, though."

Cora raised an eyebrow as she tucked the money back into her purse. "Fire away."

"Did you buy that halter top here in LaRue?"

Cora's smile widened. "Hell, no. I got this in Portland. A great, trendy little shop on Sandy Boulevard. You like it?"

"Yes. A lot. I want one," Ellen said. "I want to change my look."

Cora looked intrigued. "I'll tell you the next time I go on a shopping spree. I know a bunch of swell places where we can get into all kinds of trouble." She slapped Simon's arm. "She starts dressing like me, you're gonna have a riot on your hands. Stay sharp, dude."

As soon as Cora was out of earshot, he grabbed a handful of her full skirt and tugged her back against his body. He frowned down into her face. "What the hell is this about changing your look?"

"You were the one who told me this dress is so prim it's almost kinky," she retorted. "I agree with you. I need a wardrobe change."

"You're not changing into that. I would never let you leave the house in a top like the one Cora's got on."

His vehemence startled her. "I thought men liked sexy outfits."

Simon scowled. "Sure I do, but not on my woman."

She flushed, and a shivering thrill went through her body as the implications of his remark sank in. Timid happiness tried to bloom in her chest, but there wasn't room enough for it to spread out. *Don't get all excited over a throwaway remark,* she chided herself.

She tried to joke her way past it. "It might be fun to shock you."

"Shock me all you want, babe. I'll take you someplace private where you can shock the clothes right off my body."

"Bea's not back from lunch yet, and Missy ran down to the Shopping Kart to get more makings for punch. Your clothes will just have to stay on your body for the time being, Simon."

He looked wistful. "As soon as we get home, then?"

She shook her head. "When I get home, I have to bake to-morrow's pies. I meant to get up and do it early this morning, but . . ."

He hugged her back against his body. "But instead, you decided to give me the most amazing blow job in sexual history." His laughter rumbled against her throat. "Glad to know your priorities are in order."

Simon prowled through the fair in full hunting mode, scanning for Bebop, Scotty, Eddie, or Max Webber. He finally spotted Eddie at the beer booth. Several brimming pint cups of foaming beer were poised in his beefy arms. "Yo, Eddie!" he called.

Eddie jumped, sloshing beer all over his arms and shirt. "Uh . . . d-d-dude," Eddie stammered. "Wha . . . what's up?"

Simon ambled up. "Not much. Can I have a word with you?"

"Sh-sure." Eddie's eyes darted from the left to the right, and then down to the beers he carried. "I'm kinda loaded up. Can I meet up with you in about twenty minutes?"

Like hell. "Nah. Leave the beers on the counter," Simon said calmly. "You can pick them up after we talk. This won't take long. Not long enough for them to go flat."

Eddie looked nervous. He turned back and unloaded the beers at the booth, with a mumbled apology to the guy behind the counter.

Simon herded Eddie around to the back of the booth.

"So, uh, what's this about?" Eddie asked. "You're acting weird, man. Lighten up."

"Where are Scotty and Bebop, Eddie?" Simon asked.

"Don't know," Eddie said promptly. "No idea where they— hey! What the fuck are you . . . *hey!*"

Simon grabbed Eddie's oversized football jersey and yanked it up over his ribs. Eddie stumbled back, pinwheeling his arms until his back thudded against the plywood wall of the beer booth.

Nothing. Just gingery chest hair and a pale, overhanging beer gut. No bruises to correspond with the blows Simon had delivered yesterday to whoever the fatter guy had been.

Simon's tension eased. The fat guy hadn't been Eddie. Not that it mattered, but still, he was glad. It would have truly sucked if one of those assholes had been Eddie.

"Jesus, man, you don't think I was one of those—" Eddie choked off his own words and looked hunted.

"One of those dickheads who jumped me and El on the canyon road?" Simon finished. "So you know all about that?"

"Everybody knows about that!" Eddie protested. "Everybody in town is talking about it!"

"What exactly are they saying, Eddie? Help me out, here."

"Just like you said." Eddie swallowed repeatedly. "That you guys got jumped. That you kicked the living shit out of 'em. That they trashed the truck after they saw you fucking Ellen at the waterfall."

Eddie squealed when he found Simon's fist against his throat, bunching up his football jersey and pinning him against the wall. "Don't ever use that language when you talk about her," Simon said. "Be very respectful when you speak her name. Is that clear?"

Eddie's Adam's apple jittered against Simon's knuckles. The whites of his eyes were visible all around his irises. He nodded rapidly.

Simon set Eddie back onto his tiptoes. "The only people who should know what Ellen and I were doing at the waterfall are the assholes who were spying on us. So who'd you hear it from?"

"Everybody," Eddie insisted hoarsely. "Nobody in particular. They're talking about it all over town. I swear. Everybody."

Simon sighed. "Where are Bebop and Scotty?" he repeated.

Eddie's eyes dropped. "They're gone. Left town."

"When?"

"Last night sometime, I think. Down to the coast. I don't

know where. I swear, I don't know. They never tell me stuff, 'cause they think I'm a moron. Hey, man. Chill. Don't . . . don't hit me."

Simon let go of him. Eddie rubbed his throat, wheezing.

"I would never hit you, Eddie," Simon said quietly. "I know it wasn't you. And you used to be my friend, so I won't come after you. But I am going to give you a message for them."

"I tell you, man, they don't talk to me! I swear, Simon—"

"Remember yesterday at the dump, when we talked about what happened when we were kids? And I told you not to sweat it?"

Eddie nodded nervously. "Sure. But I—"

"This is different. This, I do give a shit about. I want you to tell your brothers, tell your dad, tell your friends, tell your enemies. Tell everyone you know. Those guys hurt Ellen. They scared her, and they trashed her truck, and they knocked her down. And when I find them, I am going to tear their heads off. And rip their guts out. Through their necks. Will you pass that along for me?"

Eddie's mouth worked. Simon patted him on the shoulder and jerked his chin towards the noisy thoroughfare. "Go on back and pick up your beers, Eddie," he urged gently. "They're getting flat."

Chapter

17

"These are the last of the pies, right? Tell me that's all. Please."

Ellen laughed at Simon's plaintive tone as she pulled the last of the bubbling strawberry rhubarb pies out of the oven. "I have to do the meringues for the lemon pies, but I guess I can do that tomorrow morning," she said. "Since you're so desperate."

"Thank God." Simon swung his long legs from his perch on the marble kitchen counter, the only corner of the kitchen that Ellen had conceded to him. "I missed you."

"What do you mean, missed me? You've been right under my feet, for three hours! And it would have been less if you hadn't constantly gotten in my way! Teasing me, distracting me, harrassing me! Argh!"

"You've been thinking about nothing but pastry," he complained. "Come here, babe. Come pay attention to me, me, me."

She tried not to smile. "Looks like I've already spoiled you rotten."

"You've been warned about my vortex of violence, pretty girl," he murmured. "Step inside. Let me frappe you into a delicious liquid froth."

Ellen leaned against his legs and waggled her chocolate-smeared fingers in his face. "Ah, the famous vortex of violence. Can you whip cream or stiffen egg whites in your vortex?"

He wrapped his strong legs around her waist, trapping her against him, and sucked the chocolate off her fingers eagerly. "I don't know about that, but the words 'stiffen' and 'cream' both have really happy associations for me, so, ah . . ."

She snickered, and tugged her hand back. "Let's go upstairs."

He slid off the counter, and they walked hand in hand through the darkened, silent house. Everyone else had long since gone to bed.

She flipped on her silk-shaded, fringed Victorian lamp. "Is that lamp another one of Great-grandma Kent's antique things?" he asked.

His suspicious tone made her smile. "Certainly not. I got this at an antique shop on the coast because I thought it was sexy. Great-grandmother's stuff is very good quality, but never sexy."

"A lamp? Sexy?" He looked intrigued as he unbuttoned his shirt.

"The way a laced-up ivory satin corset over a cotton chemise is sexy," she said. "Mystery. Restraint. The tantalizing unknown."

"Ah." He flung his shirt to the floor. "Like that granny dress you're wearing. It hides your shape, but all those ribbons and lace don't fool me for a second. The more you hide it, the brighter it shines out at me."

"Then maybe I shouldn't bother hiding it anymore." She pulled the pins out of the braided knot at the nape of her neck, pulled the elastic off the end and unraveled the braid. She combed her fingers so that the crimped, wavy locks rippled around her face and shoulders.

He lifted a handful of her hair, winding it around his hand. "I've been fantasizing all day about ripping that dress off you."

She shook her hair back over her shoulders. "You can, if you like," she announced. "I'm never going to wear this dress again."

His brows snapped together. "Why the hell not?"

"I told you. I want to change my look. I feel wild and sexy, not dull and prim. I'd like to attract some attention."

"You've got me to make you feel wild and sexy," Simon said. "And you've already got my attention. One hundred and fifty percent of it."

Ellen cupped her breasts through the layers of cotton and lace, and looked up through her lashes. "Fascinating," she murmured. "Have I found your Puritan streak, Simon? Can't I wear a scrap of something that covers just my nipples and ties around the back with ribbon ties? Other girls do. Don't you think I would look good?"

"Whether or not you would look good is not the issue," he said curtly. "I don't want other men gawking at your tits. And I don't appreciate being jerked around like this."

His tone made her eyes widen. "So macho and controlling! Why haven't you ripped my dress off? I gave you permission."

"If I wanted to rip your dress off, I wouldn't wait for your permission. Permission would defeat the purpose." His hands clasped her waist. "But that's not how I want it to be tonight."

"Oh." She feigned disappointment. "So there'll be no savage wild man climbing in my window and ravishing me tonight?"

His face hardened. "You tell me, El. Don't provoke me. If that's what you want, just ask for it. Some women like it really rough."

The thought of him with other women made her prickly and furious. "And I suppose you did your very best to oblige all these kinky women who like it rough?" she demanded.

"Up to a point," he said guardedly. "It's not my preference. But if it's the only way to make a woman come, then I did what I had to do."

"Oh! How noble and manly! Are you trying to shove me away?"

"Hell no," he said. "Why would I—"

"It never occurred to you that telling me the details of your other women's insatiable sexual demands would make me, oh, just a *smidgen* uncomfortable?" She shoved at his chest. He stumbled back a step.

"I didn't mean to piss you off," he growled. "But I'm not in the habit of censoring myself. This is who I am, El. Deal with it."

"This isn't fair," she said. "This is the part where I should make you squirm with jealousy over all of my past erotic adventures. But I've got practically nothing to torture you with. Just a bunch of bad dates, dead ends, and one failed engagement."

"Oh yeah. That." Simon's voice was heavy with irony. "About that engagement, El. I think I've got the jealous, squirming bit all covered."

"That's different! I never had sex with Brad."

"Your choice," he said. "It was your choice all along, babe. It's not my fault your sexual experience is so limited."

"You're right! Thanks so much for pointing that out to me, Simon. Now that you've broken the spell, maybe I can finally do something about it! Maybe it's not too late!"

She spun around and marched for the door. She couldn't bear to stay in the same room with him when she was so angry.

He seized her around the waist and jerked her back against his hard, half-naked body just as she was reaching for the doorknob.

"Like *hell* it's not too late!" He spun her around to face him and pinned her back against the wall.

"Simon!" she gasped. "What are you—"

"Are you trying to make me jealous, with this bullshit about sexy clothes and other men? What's that about, El?"

"I—I—"

"Are you?" He thrust his face close to hers.

She shook her head. Her voice was stuck in her throat.

"Don't." The word was hard and flat. "I work real hard at controlling my temper, El. I do not need you to provoke me. It's a bad idea. Do we understand each other?"

She nodded hastily. "Of course. Calm down."

He made a rough sound in his throat and dragged her into his arms. His heart pounded against hers. The desperate embrace felt urgent, as if he were trying to extract a silent promise from her.

She reached up and cupped his head, pulling his face down until she could kiss his cheeks, his jaw, his throat. He sagged over her and draped his head over her shoulder.

"Sorry," he said. "I didn't mean to—aw, shit. Did I scare you?"

She tightened her arms. "No," she lied.

They rocked silently for a minute, wound tightly together.

Simon lifted his head. He looked embarrassed. "I was trying so hard to be good. And then you poke at me, and it all goes to hell."

"I didn't mean to upset you," she said. "I was just teasing. Trying to excite you. We just . . . took a wrong turn."

"You don't have to try to excite me," he told her. "I'm in a constant state of arousal already. Just be your own sweet self, and my dick will be perpetually hard for you."

She giggled. "You're so crude."

He grinned unrepentently as he untied the floppy bow at the top of the modest neckline. "Hey!" he snapped. "You're not wearing a bra!"

She rolled her eyes. "Underneath all that lace, who can tell?"

He frowned. "That's not the point! It's the principle of the thing!" He spread the bodice open and cupped his hands over her breasts.

His eyes narrowed with a sudden suspicion, and he yanked her skirt up. "Jesus!" His voice was outraged. "You went out to sell pies to the whole goddamn town, bare-assed! And you never told me!"

"I wanted to feel naughty," she confessed, as he pulled the dress up over her head. "I wanted to feel the air moving under my skirt."

He wrenched open the buttons on his jeans and shoved them down, freeing his thick erection. It sprang out before him eagerly.

"And the whole time I was talking to you in the pie booth, you never said anything!" He sounded almost hurt.

She laughed, but the sound broke and shivered into a soft moan as he slid his fingers between her legs. He teased and slipped them gently inside her. "What—what would you have done if I'd told you?"

"I would have kidnapped you," he admitted. "Carried you off over my shoulder to the first private place I could find. Laid you down and fucked you senseless." He scooped her up into his arms and carried her over onto the bed, laying her down onto the tangle of crumpled sheets.

He knelt between her thighs, looming over her. Ellen braced her hands on his chest. "All hail the conqueror," she mocked. "Mr. Macho."

He thrust his finger inside her, sliding it tenderly in and out. "You get off on it, big-time. You provoke me into it, El. Feel how wet you are?"

"You get off on controlling me." She squirmed as he searched inside her for that delicious hot spot, and unerringly found it.

He kissed her belly as his hand worked its wicked magic. "You're in a contentious mood tonight. Complain all you want, sweetheart. I'll just keep doing whatever makes you come. After I'm done, when you're all soft and glowing, we can have the serious conversation about what's politically correct and what's OK." He laid his teeth delicately against her throat. "Then I'll roll you over and take you from behind."

"Oh, stop it," she snapped. "Admit it. You're incredibly dominating. I will not be your sex slave. So behave yourself."

"Sure, I'm dominating." He stroked her with the head of his penis and then pressed forward, until he was wedged inside her. "I like to be on top." He pulsed inside her with shallow, teasing thrusts to ease his way, and ran his hands over her breasts, her ribs, the dip of her waist. His hands settled on her hips, gripping her. "I love the differences between us. I love being bigger and stronger. I love it that you're so soft and smooth and delicate. I love penetrating you. Just . . . like . . . this."

She splayed her hands against his chest and arched herself to accept his insistent invasion. "I love it, too. Oh, God."

He rocked slowly and lazily inside her, and leaned over, drawing her nipple into his hot mouth. "I like to hook you into my spell," he murmured as he licked her. "I love it when your face gets pink and your eyes glow. When your eyes are like that, you'll do anything I tell you. It makes me feel like a god. Like you're all mine. I *love* that, El."

I am all yours, she wanted to say, but the words fell apart. She convulsed around him as the rushing wave of pleasure broke over her.

When she opened her eyes, he was gazing into her face, fascinated. "I love to hear you gasp and whimper when I shove my cock into you—like this." His deep, hard lunge made her cry out and clutch his shoulders. It wasn't painful, just overwhelming. He swiveled his hips against hers, pressing against every sensitive point.

"I love to feel your pussy hugging every inch of me," he went on. "Clutching at me." He dragged himself out slowly, and drove back inside, and then stopped, poised on top of her.

Her eyes fluttered open. "Simon?" She tugged at his shoulders, dazed and hungry for completion. "Don't stop. Move!"

His eyes gleamed with teasing laughter. "Ah, but you know what else I love?"

She started to laugh. "You bastard. You dirty, rotten tease. Tell me quick, and get the hell on with it!"

"I get just as hot when you shove me around, yell at me to shut up and fuck you already. Like you're doing now. That makes me nuts."

"Then do it!" she demanded. "Damn it, Simon!"

Her voice choked into a gasp as Simon rolled over so he was on his back and she was sprawled on top of him.

"I love it when you ride me like some deranged, horny cowgirl on her bucking bronco. I'm happy to be your sex slave, El. So what does that mean? What does that make me? Dominant? Or submissive?"

She rearranged herself until she was upright, riding him, and squirmed with delight around his thick, throbbing shaft. "I think it just makes you horny and oversexed," she informed him.

"Oh, that goes without saying," he assured her.

"So it's just a question of who makes the first move?" Ellen sank down onto his erection, taking him in as deeply as she could.

He groaned, bucking his hips beneath hers. "Somebody's got to lead the dance," he said. "I'm a more aggressive person, so it ends up being me, more often than not. But I'm flex. I want to please you. I'll do any goddamn thing you can dream of. Just tell me what you want, and what you don't want. And I promise, I'll listen."

She stared into his somber, intense gaze, and leaned down to kiss him. "OK, then. Last one in the pool gets to be on the bottom."

The laughter that rippled through them melded with the slow, pulsing dance of their bodies. "I'm going to get you a cowboy hat and boots," Simon said. "And a lasso. Think of all the possibilities. A four-poster bed. A length of rope. Hmm."

She flung her head back, shaking with laughter, and spiraled her hips, grinding herself over him. "You have a very dirty mind," she said.

"That's what you get for picking out an ex–juvenile delinquent for a lover. I get off on transgression. But really. Do you think you'd like it?"

"Like what?" She poised herself above him.

"Being tied down. Would you let me? Do you trust me?"

She stared into his beautiful eyes. Every question from him had a hidden meaning to decode. Everything was a challenge, a subtle demand to yield up even more of herself. To offer it all to him.

She grabbed his hand, brought it up to her lips and drew his finger into her mouth. She sank down until his throbbing shaft was shoved deep inside her, pressing against her womb. "Only if you knew good and well that your turn came next," she conceded.

His grin was instantaneous and joyful. "Deal."

"And now that we have that matter settled, it's time for you to get your ass in gear," she told him.

She laughed at his look of puzzlement, and grabbed his hands, splaying them against her hips. "I'm happy to be your deranged, horny cowgirl, Simon, but you have to give me something wild to ride."

He rose to the challenge with a growl of eagerness, and gave her everything he had, as rough and wild as she thought she could take, and then he pushed her further. He knew just how to angle her body so that his penis stroked all of her melting, tingling pleasure spots.

She shook apart over him. Power pulsed upwards through her body, from the glow in her sex up to her belly, swirling into a blooming, rose-tinted flower that unfurled in her chest, swelling into a knot of pure feeling that only tears could possibly release.

The tears broke, and so did she, shivering and sobbing. She collapsed over his body. He rolled her over and held her tightly beneath him as he drove himself hard to his own explosive climax.

They dozed and drifted together, through a timeless fog of lazy kisses, soft caresses, maintaining constant contact.

Ellen finally sat up and perched on the edge of the bed. "I should wash," she murmured.

He tugged at her arm. "Why? What for? Come back here."

She shot him a wry glance. "I'm all slippery, Simon."

"But I love it when you're all slippery. The wetter, the better," he said. "That way, when I wake up in the night with a raging hard-on, I can just slide my cock right into you, in one slick, hot plunge."

She batted his hand away and slid off the bed. "Too easy, Simon," she said. "I would rather present more of a challenge to you."

He got up and trailed after her towards the bathroom. "Believe me, you are a challenge," he told her. "The biggest challenge I've ever had in my life." He grabbed her shoulder as she opened the shower stall. "I've got a better idea. Sit down with your feet in the tub, and let me wash you with the detachable shower head. You'll love it."

She laughed in his face. "Get real! Enough! I'm exhausted!"

"I swear, I just want to kneel before you and wash you," he protested. "I've got no ulterior motives. I just want to serve you. Like a proper submissive sex slave. Sit down. You'll see. I'll be so good."

She was too tired to argue, particularly when he smiled like that.

He was fussy and ceremonious about finding the perfect water temperature. He frowned with concentration as he soaped his penis and rinsed it to test the water. "Perfect," he said. He knelt in front of her and lathered his hands. "Open up your legs for me, oh exalted mistress."

She obliged him, and he pressed them even wider, gazing at her with the fascinated attention that he always gave to her body.

"I love to see you like this," he said. "Dripping with my come. Makes me hard, all over again. Must be some caveman instinct."

"No doubt." She murmured as he caressed her with his

soapy hand. "Careful. I'm sore. It's been intense, these last few days."

He kissed the tops of her thighs. "I'm sorry. I'll be gentle."

She leaned back against the cold tiles and gave herself up to luxury. Simon petted her, soapy fingers sliding along every fold of her sex, caressing and laving her with exquisite gentle care. He followed it up with a stream of warm water from the shower nozzle to rinse her.

Oh, he was wickedly good with that shower head. He was incredibly intuitive, directing the stream as unerringly as if she were doing it for herself. He coaxed and caressed her right into another soft, lovely orgasm. It burst over her like a rainstorm, followed by dazzling rainbows, glittering drops, the steamy perfume of wet, fertile earth.

He shut the water off, grabbed a towel and patted her dry, and leaned closer. She put her hands on his face and stopped him.

"No. You promised," she whispered.

"I just want to kiss you in that secret, tender woman place," he coaxed. "Your pussy is so beautiful, El. No fingers, no tongue, no penetration. Just soft, reverent, worshipful kisses."

She was helpless to withstand his teasing charm. Her hands cupped his face. "You are not to be trusted," she said softly. "And it's not good for you to always get your way."

"But it's good for you, El." He stared into her eyes as he leaned closer, pressing his warm lips against her sex. Just as he had said. Soft, reverent kisses, his warm breath blowing across her sensitive flesh.

He smiled, and she knew instantly from the gleam in his eyes he was about to cheat. He parted her labia with two fingers, and slid his tongue deep inside her, seeking that well of liquid softness that had filled up again from all the pleasure he had lavished on her.

She held his head in her hands and stared down at the tender, intimate thrusting and lapping. It felt too lovely to protest.

He leaned back and wiped his mouth and chin, grinning

shamelessly. "I had to sneak a tiny sip to hold me till next time."

"You're terribly naughty," she said. "Bad to the bone. I'm so limp."

Simon clasped her waist, and lifted her gently to her feet. She followed him out of the bathroom on wobbly legs, and stopped to pick up the dress crumpled on the floor. She turned it right side out.

Simon pulled it out of her hands, and buried his face in it. "Don't get rid of this dress." His voice was muffled. "I like this dress."

"OK," she agreed. She waited for him to look up. "What's wrong?"

He lifted his head. His face looked worried. "I've never been jealous before," he said. "It feels strange."

"Jealous?" She was baffled. "Jealous of what?"

"I can't stand the thought of you with another man."

Ellen laughed. "What other men? Do you see any other men in here? Come on. You need rest. You're not making sense."

She was just pulling him onto her bed when they heard the violent crash, and the shatter and rattle of broken glass falling.

Chapter

18

They sprang for their clothes and yanked them on. Ellen dove for the door, but Simon grabbed her arm. "Put your shoes on," he demanded. "There's broken glass out there."

El flipped on the light at the top of the staircase. The stairway glittered with shards of colored glass. A big, ragged hole in the stained-glass window over the staircase showed a patch of black night sky. An irregularly shaped, grayish bundle lay at the foot of the stairs, hissing and spitting like a live thing.

"Get back!" Simon grabbed El's arm and yanked her back up the stairs and into his arms, just as all hell broke loose.

Thunderclaps, cannon blasts, pistol shots, mortar fire. Hissing sparks. Sulphurous clouds of foul, noxious smoke billowed up.

The ear-splitting chaos finally eased off. Ellen took her hands off her ears and lifted her face from where it was pressed to his chest.

"Is the house on fire?" she whispered.

He could barely hear her words, his ears were ringing so hard. "I don't think so." Simon tried to keep his voice low and calm. "I'll check it out. Stay right here. Don't you dare move."

She followed him anyway, of course, straight into the stinking yellow fog that filled the stairwell. Her sandals and his boots crunched over broken glass. Her cold, slender hand clutched his bare shoulder.

The smoke made his eyes water. He'd taken the time only to fling on his jeans and shove his feet into his boots without lacing them. They flapped open, laces dragging through the shards of glass.

"What the hell was that?" Chuck stood at the top of the stairs, with Suzie beside him. Both of them looked pale and terrified.

"Stay back until I check it out, please." Simon nudged the burned, blackened shreds of paper and plastic with his foot. "Homemade firecrackers," he said quietly. "You pack black powder into a toilet-paper roll with a fuse waxed into it and cover it up with duct tape. I used to make these when I was a kid."

"Jeeminy Christmas, what's happening around here?"

"What in heaven's name?"

"Mother of God—"

The chorus of excited voices grew as Muriel, Lionel and Phil converged with Chuck and Suzie at the top of the stairs. Simon tuned them all out and stared down into the smoke and the stink.

"It was just a nasty prank," Ellen announced, but her voice shook. "Firecrackers, folks. Nothing to get alarmed about."

"A prank that could have burned your house to the ground." He said the words quietly, so that only she could hear.

El shot him a miserable glance as she backed away from the mess. She looked besieged. There were bruised-looking shadows under her eyes, and the cut-offs she'd thrown on showed off every last one of the cruel scrapes and bruises that yesterday's misadventures had left on her slim legs. "I'll just, ah, go get the broom," she said. "Stay off the glass, please, folks, until I clean it up."

"I'll call the police." Muriel's voice was subdued and quavering. Simon stared down at the blackened filth, the broken glass, the foul smoke. He stalked out onto the lawn and stared into the wet, rustling darkness. Whoever had done it was long gone, of course.

His gut cramped with impotent fury. He just wanted to protect and cherish her, but the closer he got, the more the chaos escalated.

Yeah, big fucking surprise, that.

He and El worked quickly, sweeping and scooping shards of glass into the plastic bucket. They heard a nervous "ahem."

Phil Endicott stood at the top of the stairs, looking shamefaced. He picked his way downstairs, suitcase in hand. "Ellen, I'm so sorry."

"I understand." Ellen straightened, dignity personified. "I suggest the Hampton in Wheaton. Turn right, follow the signs for Wheaton, and take a right at Shearer. I'll credit you for tonight's stay, of course."

Chuck and Suzie were hard on Phil's heels, loaded with towering backpacks and bristling with sports equipment.

"Uh, dudes. We are so outta here. This scene is just way too weird for us," Chuck said. His voice quivered with tension.

Muriel was blocked on the stairs behind Suzie, who was frozen in awe as she stared at Simon's naked torso. Her mouth dangled open.

Muriel shot him a sly glance, and winked. "Simon, for God's sake, cover yourself. You're causing a traffic jam."

Chuck spun around to glare at Suzie, then at Simon. He grabbed Suzie's arm and dragged her downstairs and out the door. Their voices receded into the distance, his low and furious, hers shrill and defensive.

Ellen looked up at Lionel, who stood at the top of the stairs in his pin-striped pajamas. "Would you like to go, too, Lionel?" she asked. "I promise, I wouldn't blame you one bit if you did."

"Hell, no, girlie. You know me. I like being where the action is. Couldn't drag me away. Sounds like the cops are here, folks."

"Simon. A shirt. Please," Muriel said.

Simon was heading down the stairs buttoning his shirt as Sergeant Al Shephard came through the door. Al had always proven to be a mellow and reasonable guy, but Simon's heart sank when he saw who followed him in. Wes Hamilton. Of course. Who else.

Shit. His conflictual relationship with the LaRue Police Department was an issue he would prefer not to share with El and her mother, but what the hell. They would all live through it.

Wes looked up and nodded, as if he'd just been proven right. "Well, well, well. Why am I not surprised to see you, Riley?"

Simon shrugged, and declined to answer.

"Things were mellow around here till you showed up," Wes said.

"This is not Simon's fault!" El's voice rose dangerously in pitch. "None of it was! And I do not appreciate your insinuations!"

Wes grunted. "Where were you when this occurred, Riley?"

Simon hesitated, looked at El.

"He was with me," El said sharply. "In my bed. Any more questions? Do I need to elaborate? Do you want details?"

"Ah, no, miss. That's fine." Al looked at Wes. Wes looked at Al.

"What?" El snarled. "What's that look about? What are you implying? That Simon tried to blow up my house?"

Wes sighed. "Mr. Riley here has a history of playing pranks involving firecrackers. And you, miss, have a history of providing questionable alibis for—"

"Questionable? What's questionable about it? Would you like to go up and check the wet spot? It's still fresh. Please, feel free."

"Ellen!" Muriel exclaimed. "That is *crude!*"

Simon convulsed and hid his face in his hands.

"Does this amuse you, Riley?" Wes asked.

Simon pulled himself together and lifted an absolutely straight face. "Certainly not, Lieutenant."

"I don't understand," El yelled. "My house is attacked, and you waste my time making bizarre accusations? How stupid is that?"

"El, calm down," Simon soothed. "Take a deep breath."

She whirled on him. "They are supposed to be helping me!" she bellowed. "Not pissing me off!"

And so they would be, if I weren't here. He swallowed the words back and wrapped his arm around her from behind. "If there's one thing I learned in this town, it's not to mouth off to cops," he told her quietly. "It's an impulse to suppress, El."

She wrenched away from him. "I've been suppressing too many impulses for too many years! Let them put me in jail for being a smart-ass if they want! We'll just see how long the police chief can hold out without my cinnamon pecan pull-aparts!"

"No one's going to be putting anyone in jail, Miss Kent," Al said patiently. "Let's just go through this again from the top."

Ellen recounted Cora's sighting of Bebop and Scotty in the woods in the course of going through it again and again. The two policemen regarded each other silently. "We'll check this out right away," Al said. "We'll be talking to your ex-fiancé, too—"

"I never suggested it was Brad! That's impossible!"

Al cleared his throat uncomfortably. "Well, er, a disgruntled ex is usually the easiest place to start in cases like this—"

"Brad is not a thug!" Ellen said sharply. "Don't waste your time."

Al and Wes exchanged looks again. "I just want you to understand that we'll be very thorough, Miss Kent," Al said carefully. "We'll check all avenues, and we'll get to the bottom of this."

"Fine," El said. "Good night. Thanks very much for your help."

The four of them listened to the police car receding into

the distance. "Well," Lionel said heartily. "That's that, eh? How about if I put my insomnia to good use and keep watch out here on the porch?"

"That's an excellent idea, Lionel," Muriel said. "I'll get Frank's shotgun out of the gun safe and sit with you. I'm certainly not going to sleep tonight. You young folks go on upstairs and get some rest."

"If I left, all this bullshit would stop dead," Simon said quietly.

There was a strained silence after his words.

Muriel sniffed. "Do not flatter yourself, young man. For heaven's sake. You are not necessarily the center of the universe."

Ellen grabbed his shirt and yanked him closer, hard. "Don't even start with that. Or I will clobber you. Flatten you. Into jelly."

"Take him on upstairs, girlie, and give him a good reason to stick around," Lionel suggested. "Best way to make a man feel needed."

El turned her glare to Lionel. "I'll pass on couples counseling."

Lionel just smiled and patted her arm, unoffended. "Go on, hon," he said gently. "I don't hardly sleep at all even when there aren't maniac firebombers running around. Doesn't cost me a damn thing."

"Me neither," Muriel said. "Be a dear and get me a shot of Glenlivet while I fetch the gun, would you, Lionel?"

"Coming right up, Muriel. Ashamed I didn't think of it myself." Lionel hobbled over to the liquor cabinet and pulled down two tumblers.

"For God's sake, Mother. Don't mix whiskey with guns!"

"Good night, sweetheart." Muriel dismissed them with a flutter of her hands. "Off with you two. Go on, now. Chop chop."

Ellen started up the stairs. She stopped halfway up and glared down at him. "Well? Simon? Get your butt up here. What are you waiting for? Christmas?"

Lionel clapped. "That's tellin' him. Show him who's boss."

Simon followed her up the stairs. He closed the door behind them and stared at El as she paced back and forth across the room. She was wringing her hands, muttering. "Uh, babe?" he ventured cautiously.

"I am so angry!" She spun around, eyes blazing. "I want to destroy someone! When I find the asshole who did this to my house, he is going to be wearing his dick for a tie!"

"Ouch." The image made him wince.

"You!" She pointed an imperious finger at him. "That's enough sass out of you, Simon Riley! Get those jeans off this minute! Who told you that you could wear clothes?"

He stripped off his shirt and dropped his jeans as a nervous burst of laughter relieved some of the tension accumulated inside him. "Here's the unexpected bonus to being pelted with firecrackers," he said. "You turn into the empress of everything when you're pissed. You scare me."

"Good." El peeled off her T-shirt and flung it away. She stroked her fingertip down the length of his cock, which sprang obediently to attention for her. "Be afraid," she said. "Be very afraid." She ripped open the buttons of her cut-offs and let them drop to the ground. She stood there, legs wide, eyes wild, his cock in her strong grip.

"So, your worship? How do you want it?" he asked meekly. "Should I fall to my knees and pay homage to your beauty?"

Her hand tightened around him. "Keep your mouth shut and do exactly as you're told." She shoved him backwards, driving him across the room. He fell down backwards onto the bed, arms wide, and stared up at her, transfixed. God, she was stunning. Sexual heat rolled off her in scorching waves. She blazed, she shot sparks.

"Touch yourself," she said. "I want to watch you do it."

He was blank for a moment. "Huh? You mean, my cock?"

"Of course," she said. "Show me how you do it. Look at me . . ." She stroked her breasts in her hands, then slid her

hand down between her legs, opening her pussy and showing it to him. ". . . and show me."

He stroked his cock and stared at her. She was a constant
discovery, her sensuality unfolding and evolving continually.
Burning hotter every minute that passed. There was a shining core of power inside her that called to him. It made him
dazed and desperate.

Willing to risk anything just to have some more.

El climbed onto the bed and straddled his thighs. "You're
wet." She circled the head of his cock with her fingertip. It
was dripping with pre-come. She lifted her wet finger to her
lips and sucked it clean.

"I can't help it," he told her. "Staring at you makes my
dick drool. It wants to be slick and at the ready, just in case it
gets lucky."

"Did you ever fantasize about me when you masturbated?"

"Oh, sweetheart. Like crazy." He grabbed her hand and
wrapped her fingers around his cock, dragging them slowly
up and down his throbbing length. "I imagined how it would
have been if I hadn't left," he said. "If I'd gotten a clue, and
seduced you sooner. All those nights I spent on the floor of
your room, I could have been on top of you, inside of you. I
imagined climbing that tree and sneaking into your room,
waking you up by licking your clit. I imagined every position, every technique I've ever heard of or read of or dreamed
of."

"Hmm." She pumped him, a little roughly, just how he
liked it. "Sounds like your fantasies and mine were pretty
much the same."

"I bet mine were raunchier," he said. "Girls are more romantic."

She laughed. Her throat was so graceful, thrown back like
that. "You'd be surprised how raunchy I can be, if I put my
mind to it."

He panted and writhed. "Put your mind to it," he gasped.

She rose up over him. "OK," she whispered. "Serve me,

Simon. Pet me with the tip of your penis. Don't penetrate me, just pet me. As if your penis were a tongue, licking me."

He gripped his cock firmly and did exactly as he was told.

It was heavenly torture. She touched her breasts and played with her clit as she stared into his eyes. She anointed the sensitive tip of his cock with her hot lube, but never let him slide inside. She hovered just out of his reach, her perfect body swaying over his.

He knew that she needed to be in control, but his own control was slipping away. He was desperate to roll her over and take the plunge.

Just in time, she sank down onto his cock and took him inside. He almost wept with relief, but when he grasped her hips and started moving beneath her, she seized his wrists and jerked his hands wide.

"No! If I want you to move, I'll tell you where, how, and exactly how much. Give me your hands, Simon. Let me brace myself."

He gritted his teeth while she worked herself over his rigid body, to a long, deep climax. That was it. He rolled her onto her back.

Her eyes flew open, and she slapped and swatted at him. "Hey! I never said you could—"

"That's just too bad." He grabbed her flailing wrists, and jerked them up over her head. "It's my turn."

She writhed furiously beneath him. "But you said—"

"Babe, if you want me to stay down, you better tie me down. I was born to break the rules." He drove himself inside her.

She came again within seconds, and he followed her. They shot over the edge of a waterfall into a cauldron of white, pounding foam. He was tumbled and tossed, battered by sensation. When he came back, El was crying, her arms wrapped tight around his neck.

This time her tears didn't scare him at all. For once, it was he who comforted her, he who lulled her, stroking her hair and kissing the tears off her soft, hot cheek until she sank into an exhausted sleep.

He buried his nose in her hair and hung on tight. The world had said "no" to him a lot in the course of his lifetime. He never had learned how to take it gracefully, and he wasn't about to start now.

He was flying again, but with a sickening ache of foreboding. Something horrible was going to happen, and there was nothing he could do to stop it. He was only a child; too small to challenge the monster. It was hidden by black magic. He could not break the spell.

He caught a downdraft and swooped towards the A-frame house on the bluffs where he lived with his mother. The light grew stronger, but not the glow of dawn. It was a red, sullen light, smeared by smoke.

His mother was perched on the tip of the roof. She held the eagle sculpture in her arms. She launched it into the air. It became a real eagle that whooshed past him, a storm of wings flapping like a cold ghost wind. When he looked again, his mother had become a statue herself. She had flung her warm, vibrant life into the bird that had taken wing. Now she was a graven image, regarding him with stony compassion.

The fire monster had engulfed the house. It licked at her long stone skirt, streaking it with black. He flew closer, becoming infinitely small as she became infinitely huge. The mottled gray and yellow and orange pattern of the lichen on the surface of her face revealed itself to be a mottled landscape covered with trees. He was flying over the curve of the hillside that had been her eye. There was a spark of sullen fire in it.

It grew larger. Horror exploded inside him. It was the fire monster again, and El was inside this circle, naked and helpless and sleeping while the fire moved in. Flames leaped and roared, ravenous.

El woke, and screamed, as the flames reached for her.

He jerked out of the dream with a hoarse gasp. His heart tore a hole in his chest. His lungs heaved, but wouldn't take in air.

He knew this feeling in his gut. He remembered it with crystal clarity, twenty-eight years later. It was the feeling he'd had all day long before they came to tell him that his mother was dead.

El raised her head with a questioning murmur. He flinched away from her hand. "No. Please." His voice was ragged. "Don't touch me."

"But you're trembling. Let me—"

"No." He wrenched away from her and stumbled off the bed. "I'm sorry. You can't. It's not your fault."

"Let me help," she begged him. "Let me—"

"You can't help."

She shrank back. "Why can't I?" Her voice was small.

He groped around in the darkness for his jeans, his boots, his shirt. "I don't know. I'm sorry."

"It's just a dream, Simon," she said.

Hah. If only. He jerked his jeans on, then one boot. "I have to go out," he said. "I have to breathe."

"Can I come with you?"

The breath he dragged in felt more like a sob. "No."

He felt her hurt and confusion in the dark as clearly as if he could see her face. He had to offer her something. The words just fell out of him, desperate and unplanned. "I love you, El. I love you, but just . . . please, let me go. I have to go outside. I have to breathe. I'm sorry."

I love you. He felt how true the words were the instant they left his mouth. El clamped her hands over her mouth and hunched over her knees. He pulled on his other boot and tried to lace it up with trembling fingers. He yanked the shirt on, but the buttons didn't come together. He'd put the thing on inside out. He left it open.

El slid off the bed and stood before the window. "It's raining," she said. "I hear it rustling against the leaves."

"Rain won't hurt me." He was transfixed, in her magnetic grip. She took pity on him and broke the spell by turning her back. She became just a beautiful, dark silhouette against the window curtains.

Waiting for him to get the fuck on with it and leave.

He slunk down the stairs and out the kitchen door, plunging through the lilacs into the wilder, rougher world of the Riley property. He didn't need light to make his way through the scrub oak and blackberry brambles down to the creek. He'd walked it and run it countless times, but for the first time ever, the darkness menaced him.

McNary Creek gurgled a liquid lullaby, but he was not soothed. The roiling water looked as if it were hiding something in its gleaming depths. There was urgency to the scudding clouds, panic in the wind. He'd never been afraid of the dark in his life, but tonight, his skin was crawling. The dark seemed to be watching him. Biding its time, licking its chops. He no longer wanted a breath of air. His lungs wouldn't take it in anyway. He wanted to run back to El's bed.

A lifetime of steeling himself against fear prevailed. He had to face this dream, and the perceptions that were behind it. He had to stand in the midst of his mother's statues and beg her to help him decipher its message. To give him the strength to face what he feared it might mean.

That the only way to protect El from the violence that dogged him was to take himself away from her.

El deserved a husband she could lean on, build a family and future with. Not a loser who fled her bedroom gasping for air in the middle of the night, tortured by dreams, scared of his own fucking bad-luck shadow. The explosions of the firecrackers echoed in his mind, and he thought of the gunshot that had killed Gus. Maybe the darkness pressing down on him was the same darkness that had pulled Gus under.

If it was, he could almost understand pulling the trigger.

He didn't want to understand it. He didn't want the dark to whisper to him. He didn't want to hear what it might say.

He reached the pine grove. He could barely make out the individual figures of the animals scattered through the trees. The wind rushed and tossed the boughs high above.

He sank down onto his knees. Mud soaked through the knees of his jeans. He opened his mind, and tried to let the silence and calm fill his mind like a cup. To let a quiet space open up inside him where messages could be heard. He sent out his silent plea.

Help me with this. Help me understand. Help me to do the right thing, whatever the fuck it is. However much it hurts me. Or her.

He waited, but all that came to him was grief so deep it cut him like a blade. This place was a refuge no longer.

Chapter

19

Ray pushed through the wet pine boughs on the creek bank and pressed his hand over his mouth to muffle the helpless giggling. He lowered the infrared goggles and pressed his hand against the glow of fire in his belly. Riley was playing right into his hands, unasked, unpushed, just like he had seventeen years ago.

It thrilled him. It was so perfect. Like magic.

Ray was tempted to just eliminate him, as he had eliminated Gus, but Simon was young and strong and quick on his feet, according to the battered and sullen Scotty and Bebop. A karate expert of some sort, no less. Ray was fit for his age, but he'd barely managed to overpower Gus.

Taking out Simon would be riskier. He would have to use his gun. The conditions were not right, the risk factor too high. It would be self-indulgent to depart from the plan just for the instant gratification of a quick kill. Simon Riley dead created questions, furor, a criminal investigation, whereas Simon Riley alive and wandering around in the dark with no alibi was offering himself up as the perfect scapegoat.

Just as he had done for the stable fire. His sacred role in life seemed to be to absorb blame and create diversions.

Ray pulled out the cell phone and dialed the number as he

stepped into the creek. He walked through the water in his rubber galoshes until he reached the grove where he had hidden Brad's motorcycle. Brad had purchased the thing in a fitful rebellious moment and then largely abandoned it. It was a BMW, the same model and make as Riley's. There was no end to the gifts this night was giving him.

The phone was picked up on the first ring. "Boss?"

It was Scotty, to his relief. The younger one. Slightly more intelligent than Bebop, but he tended to ask too many questions.

"Meet me at the usual place," Ray said. "Headlights off."

"Hey, we did what you said. We threw the firecrack—"

"Shut up. I've told you not to talk business on a cell phone."

"OK," Scotty said sullenly. "We'll be there in twenty."

Ray accelerated up the old logging road and turned onto the highway. This glow of anticipation felt sexual. He liked the motorcycle between his legs, the noise, the power, but the pleasure, the freedom, eroded his mask. It was crumbling, and that struck him as funny. The wind in his face whipped the peals of laughter away from his lips.

There was an earthquake of screaming laughter inside him.

He turned off the highway onto the road that followed the LaRue River under the highway overpass. He switched off his headlights, cutting speed until his eyes adjusted to darkness. The roar of the river and the roar of the freeway was another screen of privacy.

Ray coasted to a stop when he saw the hulking shape of Bebop's truck. The tires of his motorcycle would make a track in the mud, with the exact same treads as Riley's motorcycle. Beautiful. He choked the laughter down to chuckles and pulled on the rubber gloves.

"Hey. Boss. That you?"

Ray fingered the knife in his pocket. This was the last time he had to tolerate such vacuous stupidity. He should never have enlisted the Webber boys to begin with, but they had been so useful in engineering the firecracker cover story for the stables. They were a weak link now. Tools that had served their purpose. Swords that he was about to beat into ploughshares.

Scotty limped towards him. A splash of moonlight illuminated Scotty's battered face. Both eyes blackened, nose and lips swollen.

"Hello, Scotty," Ray greeted him. "You look just terrible."

"Hey, Boss." Scotty sounded nervous.

"Where's Bebop?" Ray asked.

"He's in the truck. His knee's fucked up. He can't stay on his feet too good," Scotty said.

The truck window rolled down. "Hey," Bebop said.

"Evening, Bebop. Sorry to hear you're not feeling well."

Bebop grunted and lifted a flask to his lips. Perfect. Drunk, too.

"Uh, Boss? You never said anything about Riley turning into some kind of fuckin' ninja." Scotty's voice edged towards a whine.

Ray lifted his hands. "I'm very sorry, Scotty. Bebop assured me that you boys would be able to handle him. Why should I doubt you?"

"Sure, we used to slam him back in school, but he's different now. He's like, fuck me."

"Well, you both survived, didn't you?" Ray said bracingly.

"Yeah, but Eddie told us Riley knows it was us. He said Riley's gonna get us for messing with Ellen," Scotty said. "He said Riley's gonna rip our heads off. Rip our guts out. And he's not kidding."

"Oh? Really?" Interesting. Better than the usual class of tidbits that he pried out of Scotty and Bebop. "How frightening for you."

"Yeah, man, no shit. And I mean, the guy could do it. Easy. He comes for us, man? We are, like, so fucked."

"I'll certainly take that into account," Ray said.

Scotty paused with the air of a man who was gathering

his courage. "Uh, boss? Bebop and I, we've been thinking . . ." he began.

"I wasn't aware that you two boys often engaged in that activity," Ray said, in his jolliest voice.

Scotty snorted nervously. "Hah, yeah, very funny, boss. We've decided, uh, that this firecracker thing? This is it for us. We don't want to tangle with Riley. We're good to go on anything else you got for us, but we don't want to mess with that guy no more."

"I understand completely." Ray's voice was all sympathy. "In fact, I think your decision shows very good judgment. Considering."

Scotty appeared to be stumped by that. "Uh . . . yeah. So anyhow. We, uh, decided something else, too. We think maybe our arrangement with you, uh . . . that maybe we should, you know, update it."

"Really? How exactly should we do that, Scotty?"

Scotty was emboldened by the question. "Well, we didn't expect to get fucked up like this. It hurts, and we're out of circulation until we heal up. It makes our lives real compli-cated. And to have a guy like Riley on our backs, man . . . that's bad news. That's worth more than a couple thou every now and then for the odd job, you know? And, uh, we do know some stuff that you wouldn't want us to talk about, right? But we would never tell, would we, Bebop?"

"Fuck, no," Bebop rasped. "No way, man. We're totally zipped."

"That kinda loyalty, boss, it's worth something, you know?" Scotty's voice had lost its quaver and become self-righteous. "Christ, this hurts. Sumbitch smashed a couple of my ribs."

"And what would you and Bebop think would be fair?"

"Well, to start with, you can give us enough dough to get out of town for a while, till we're back to normal," Scotty said. "A couple of tickets to someplace nice with a beach, where we can suck down some beers and relax. Maybe, like, fifteen, twenty grand?"

"My, my." Ray clucked his tongue. "That's some beach, fellows."

"Hey. Bebop's got a fucked-up knee. My nose is broken, and my ribs, and my balls feel like a truck ran over 'em. It really don't sound like all that much to me right now."

"Don't get upset," Ray said. "Have I ever been anything but fair with you two boys?"

"I guess not," Scotty muttered.

Bebop grunted again, and took another deep pull on his flask.

Ray clapped Scotty heartily on the shoulder. The younger man flinched, and hissed. "Hey, watch it. I'm all fucked up, remember!"

"Sorry, Scotty. I appreciate your candor." Ray reached into his pocket. "Both of you will get exactly what's coming to you."

"Huh?" Scotty sounded baffled. "What, have you got that kinda money on you right now, boss? You can give it to us— *unghh!*"

Ray drove the blade deep, angled it up, rotated it to catch as many vital organs as possible.

"Holy—what the *fuck* are you doin', man?" Bebop squawked. "What are you—Jesus! Hey! Stop!"

Scotty gasped, eyes wide, and sagged over his hand. Ray let him drop, and wrenched the truck door open before Bebop could slide out the other side. He seized Bebop's shirt, parried his wild blow, and stabbed the drenched knife into the most vulnerable spot in Bebop's gut. In. Up. Around. Twist. He took Bebop by the scruff of the neck and pitched him face first down onto the wet river rocks.

He used his unbloodied hand to pluck the heavy-duty garbage bag out of his pocket and drape it over the opened truck door, at the ready for when it was time to strip off the blood-smeared plastic. There was a nice, deep hole at the municipal dump all ready for it. He had ordered Scotty and Bebop to prepare it for him days ago, as soon as he had heard about Riley's return. It was always good to think ahead.

He knelt down and yanked Scotty's head up by his long, greasy hair. He was still alive, but only just.

"So Riley said he'd rip your heads off and your guts out?" Ray repeated. "My, that sounds strenuous. But remember when I ran for mayor, Scotty? Do you remember what my campaign slogan was? You should. You and Bebop put up most of the posters."

Scotty's eyes rolled. Ray patted Scotty's cheek with his bloody hand. He put his mouth to Scotty's ear and breathed the words out.

"It was 'Ray Mitchell never backs down from a challenge.' "

Done. Gus's house was empty, but for a stack of boxes and the cobwebs that hung from the rafters. He'd swept the place out, searching every nook, every drawer, every closet, every corner. Every photo.

Nothing. No clues, no more letters, no messages from beyond the grave. No revelations that explained everything. No proof of any kind. Nothing that had belonged to his mother. Nothing about Vietnam.

Not one fucking thing to solve this mystery.

Gus's house was as stubbornly silent as his mother's animal sculptures had been last night. No miracles. No epiphanies. Just futile, back-breaking work. He hadn't eaten, but he was too jittery to think of food. He'd been back and forth to the dump all day. It had been closed, but picking the padlock was no big deal to a guy with a misspent youth, and he'd left the fees folded into a scrap of paper and shoved under the door of the cottage. The boxes of books he'd left under the breezeway outside the library. The furniture, dishes, pots and pans and silverware he had left under the awning of the Salvation Army.

Nothing was left but the photos, the cameras, the darkroom

equipment, Gus's laptop, and the childhood albums that Gus had made. He hadn't been able to bring himself to throw away the sheaf of correspondence with the detective agency, either. It was proof that Gus had cared enough to keep tabs on him. A small thing, but if it was all you had, you hung on to small things.

Ellen's love was no small thing.

Yeah, right. It was a huge thing, it blew his mind wide open, made him see stars, made his eyes water, his heart hurt, his dick throb.

But it didn't change this feeling in his gut. It had been building ever since he got to LaRue, and since last night's dream, it was getting worse. The knot of dread that had never failed to presage danger and tragedy. It had been so bad the day his mother died, he'd thrown up in the playground during recess. It was just as bad today.

He'd felt that dread the day of the fire at the stables, too. He'd felt it in varying degrees when he'd been in combat, and on the job in war zones. When death brushed close enough so that he could smell the stink of its breath, he felt it. That feeling had helped him dodge bullets and bombs. If he followed its warnings, he could evade disaster.

But evading disaster meant evading El. He didn't want to. He wanted to throw himself at her feet and just lie there, come what may.

Simon sank down onto the sagging porch steps, and buried his face in his filthy hands. From here, he had a great view of the jagged hole in El's stained-glass window. It mirrored the bruises on her legs.

He'd thought of begging her to go away with him, but to where? His haphazard life on the road would be a nightmare for a woman like her. She wanted babies. She liked antiques. She would never be able to grow roses or bake muffins ever again. He didn't want to expose her to the danger and stress of that lifestyle, even assuming she was willing to try it. Which brought him to the option of finding another place to be where El could be happy. But she owned her beautiful house, she'd worked hard to build her business. Her roots ran deep here.

Besides, his biggest dread was that the chaos and danger was inside him, like a virus or a curse. That the outcome would be always, eternally the same. *Fate. You can't outrun it,* her mother had said.

His throat was thick with dust. He wished he could bathe, but there was no water at Gus's place. He climbed onto the motorcycle and pointed himself towards the gas station at the junction. He had to get something to drink. So what if LaRue saw him dirty and filthy. They'd made up their minds about him years ago.

He bought a sports drink in the convenience store and poured half of it down his throat as he walked outside. As soon as he swallowed and started to breathe again, he became aware of a sensory stimuli that was about to kick his ass hard with a painful memory. It was a smell. A fresh, faint scent that made his tired body stir, way down deep.

He turned his head, almost fearfully, to identify it.

Petunias. Racks and racks of blooming petunias for sale in plastic tubs. Purple, pink, white, candy-striped.

He turned away, closed his eyes and breathed through his mouth.

When he opened his eyes, an SUV was pulling up. A guy with a little girl got out. She tagged behind her dad, and gave him a gap-toothed smile. She had freckles. Big brown eyes. Long blonde hair. The guy gave him a dirty look and jerked his little girl closer to him.

This was hell. Knives jabbing him. Reminders of the life he should have had. The wife he should have had. He snagged the key to the small, foul men's room out back, where he splashed his face and stared at himself in the mirror. He looked like a zombie. Dirty and haggard.

He saw it written in his eyes. Exactly what he had to look forward to. An infinity of empty days and lonely nights. Casual sex now and then to alleviate the boredom, quickly forgotten. Skimming over the surface of life, a dispassionate observer with his camera.

Taking risks because he had nothing better to do with himself. Because the adrenaline reminded him that he was still alive. If he felt blank and let down afterwards, what the fuck. He would just do it again, and again, and again. Like an addict getting his fix.

Until he reached the critical point where the balance of ugly images in his mind so far outweighed the good ones that he ended up like Gus, embittered and alone. Staring at a pistol in his hand.

A strange feeling came over him. A melting feeling in his bones, like the starch had just gone out of him.

He couldn't do it. He couldn't turn away from her. He didn't have the strength. If leaving was the right thing to do, then fuck it. He wasn't man enough to do it. He didn't have the balls. End of story.

He started to laugh, in euphoric relief. The laughter degenerated into silent tears. Somone pounded on the bathroom door, yelling obscenities. He ignored them. He tried to keep it quiet, but he couldn't make it stop. It racked his whole body.

He was going back to El. He would throw himself on her mercy and spend the rest of his life trying with every ounce of intelligence God gave him not to fuck it up. If this queasy dread in his belly never went away, he would learn to live with it.

The way people lived with bunions, or back pain.

Ellen kept a bright smile on her face as she passed a slice of lemon meringue and a slice of strawberry rhubarb to Mae Ann and Willard Blair. Her smile muscles burned and ached, but if she stopped smiling, even for a second, there would be hell to pay.

Push on, she told herself. It's almost over. The whole long, endless day in which Simon was avoiding her again, this time after telling her that he loved her. If he wanted to baffle and torture her, he'd succeeded.

She looked over at Missy, who presided over a huge punch bowl. "Looks like it's getting low, Missy. Shall we mix up another batch?"

"I can do it! I've got the recipe right here."

"Whatever you say," Ellen said.

Missy scampered to the cooler, pulling ice cream, bottles of soda and fruit juice out of their beds of ice. Missy had been behaving so oddly. Insisting on doing everything by herself. It was a positive change, to be sure, but sudden enough to be disconcerting. Especially considering the number of spectacular mistakes that she made.

"Hey, girlfriend. Got any more chocolate pecan pie lying around?"

The smile that came to Ellen's face was a real one, and the sensation was a blessed relief. "Actually, Cait Gillis wanted to buy the whole pie for her dad, but I saved the last piece just for you."

"You're an angel," Cora said. "Lay it on me, babe, and don't skimp the cream. Eat, drink and be merry, for tomorrow we diet. As soon as the Peach Fest is over, I'm back to celery sticks and rice cakes."

Ellen's eyes flicked over Cora's body, splendidly displayed in a denim miniskirt and a halter top that looked like it was made out of a white Ace bandage. She glopped an extra spoonful of whipped cream onto the pie. "Please," she said. "Spare me."

Cora took a big bite of pie. "Everything has its price. Hey, where's Simon? I thought you lovebirds were joined at the hip."

The question took Ellen by surprise. Her face crumpled.

Cora sprinted around the pie table and put her arms around El's shoulder. "Oh, shoot, sweetie. I'm sorry. I put my big foot in my big mouth all the way up to my knee, didn't I?"

"Ellen? Are you all right?"

Ellen dashed her tears away, and smiled at the mayor, Owen Watson, and Wilma Watson, his wife. "Just fine, thanks," she said. "Banana cream for you today?"

"Yes, thank you," Wilma said. "And Dutch apple for Owen. I heard about your ordeal, Ellen. How terrifying. I would still be laid out in bed after a shock like that, but look at you! Here you are, tough as nails! Selling pie like a trooper!"

"Yes, it was pretty bad." Ellen passed over the plates. "But as you can see, I'm fine."

"You don't look fine, honey." Wilma studied Ellen with a critical eye and darted an unfriendly glance towards Cora. "Frankly, you look like something the cat dragged in."

Ellen looked down at her baggy gray jumper. It was the plainest, most sexless thing she had in her closet. Perfect for her mood. So was the crown of braids, pinned cruelly tight. No wisps, no curls, just hard, cold, sexless practicality. That was the new Ellen. Hard as gunmetal.

She dragged in a deep breath and smiled. "Bad hair day."

"Hmmph." Wilma studied Ellen's hair. "Is it true, then, that your engagement to Brad Mitchell is off? I was so disappointed to hear it. He's such a fine, successful, *respectable* young man. A real prize."

Cora let out an audible snort. Ellen smiled until her jaw muscles burned. "Brad and I decided that we just didn't suit."

"That's not what I heard," Wilma said. "Rumors are flying about you."

"You shouldn't listen to rumors, Mrs. Watson."

"There's a lot of things that a nice girl shouldn't do," Wilma said. "And it looks like you're working right through the list. Watch your step, hon." She frowned at Cora. "And the company you keep, too."

Cora stretched her arms up over her head, a langorous, sensual movement that displayed an extra few inches of taut, tanned belly. She fluttered her mascaraed eyelashes at Owen

Watson. Wilma elbowed the gawking mayor. He choked on his pie and began to cough.

Wilma's eyes glittered avidly. "So? Are you an item with that photographer fellow, then? Simon Riley?"

Ellen stuck her chin out. "I'm a free woman."

Wilma clucked her tongue. "Oh, dear. Why do girls do this to themselves? So you let go of your bird in the hand in favor of a bird in the bush . . . or should I say, waterfall? And now you've got squat."

The need to be polite fell away from Ellen like an unwanted garment. She opened her mouth to reply, but Cora beat her to it.

"Oh, I wouldn't say she's got squat, Wilma," Cora said. "She's had something that most of us only dream about with our vibrators."

The mayor began to cough again. Wilma turned an unbecoming purple. "And who asked you for your opinion, Cora MacComber?"

Cora leaned over at a ninety-degree angle, displaying her bosom, and scooped up a fingerful of whipped cream off of the mayor's pie. She licked it off her finger. "Come on, Wilma, 'fess up," Cora cooed. "How long has it been since a hot, sexy stud gave you multiple screaming orgasms at a waterfall? Aren't you just the teensiest bit jealous?"

Wilma made a furious huffing sound. She seized her crimson, hiccuping husband by the arm and dragged him away.

"I don't think you paid for that pie, folks!" Cora called after them.

Ellen tried to muffle spasms of laughter with her hands, and failed. "How do you do that?" she gasped out. "How do you dare?"

Cora's smile was mysterious. "Practice, grasshopper."

Missy stared at them, eyes frozen wide and mouth hanging open. She clutched an open carton of strawberry ice cream at such an angle that it dripped down over her skirt in long pink streamers.

"Missy? Sweetie? The punch?" Ellen reminded her gently.

"Oh! Ah, yeah!" Missy sprang into action and hustled about with an air of immense importance, emptying bottles of soda and cans of juice into the punch bowl. She tossed in a big handful of strawberries, and pried the soft, goopy cube of ice cream out of the carton.

Ellen winced as it splashed into the punch, displacing at least a third of the liquid all over the table and napkins.

Missy grinned triumphantly. "I did it all myself!"

"You certainly did, Missy. Good job!" Ellen lunged for the roll of paper towels. "Your attitude is really changing. What happened?"

"Simon said I had to practice." Missy tested a spoonful of the punch with a frown of concentration. "So I'm practicing."

Ellen checked the position of her face, making sure her serene expression did not slip. "What did Simon say to practice?"

"To pretend not to be scared," Missy said. "And to give myself points for every time I did something on my own. Works, too."

"That was excellent advice," Cora said gravely. "You're smart to take it. And that brings me to the real reason that I came by today, Ellen, aside from the pie. Advice. Because I've been hearing the same rumors that Wilma heard. Yowsa. You go, girl."

Ellen felt her face go hot. "Oh? So? And?"

"I decided it's time to give you some pointers on how to conduct yourself now that you're a sexpot bad girl." Cora's eyes flicked over Ellen's hair and dress. "Looks like I didn't get here a moment too soon."

Ellen tried to look nonchalant. "My policy is just to ignore it."

"Not enough. If you're going to join the sisterhood of women who make decisions with their pelvises, you've gotta look sharp, girl."

Ellen giggled, and then sobered. "You, uh . . . are kidding, right?"

"Only partly," Cora said. "Hardly at all, actually."

Ellen glanced over to make sure that Missy was busy serving punch. "Are they really saying . . . you know? About the waterfall?"

Cora shook her head. "You don't want to know what they're saying. Before you know it, they'll be telling stories that involve dog collars, mayonnaise and rope."

Ellen's stomach tightened. "Ouch."

"Yeah. Right. The first thing you need to do is dress the part. So I brought you this." She reached into her purse and pulled out a handful of white gauze, ribbons and lace. "I settled on white for two reasons," she said, in a businesslike tone. "One, it'll look fab with your tan and your blonde hair. Two, the virginal color and the white lace combined with the sexy cut gives the outfit more ironic impact, particularly when it's filled out with those great tits of yours. A sort of a fashion fuck-you to the Wilmas of the world." Cora draped the brief little garments over Ellen's hand. "So?" she urged. "Go on. The Kountry Kitchen has a bathroom behind the jams and jellies section. Go change."

Ellen stared down at the garments. "Ah, Cora? You're, um, sweet to try and help, but the truth is, I feel really low today. Definitely not brazen enough to pull off an outfit like this. So I'll just pass on the—"

"That's another thing," Cora said. "You can't afford to be low. Not in public, anyway. You can't show a moment's weakness. No regrets, no embarrassment, no shame. Keep your thumb to your nose at all times, or the vultures will circle in and pick your bones clean. Got it?"

The look in Cora's eye hinted at old pain. Ellen nodded. "Got it."

"That dress you're wearing? It's an apologetic dress, hon. It says to me, OK. I know I was wrong to break free and have fun and be sexy, and I'm oh, so sorry, and can I please crawl back under my rock now?"

Ellen winced. "Oh, dear."

Cora patted her shoulder. "So I'm going to give you the bad girl's mantra. Missy, you're too young, so this doesn't apply to you yet, but listen up anyhow. It's sure to come in handy someday. 'Kay?"

"I'm listening." Missy was enraptured. "You bet I'm listening."

"OK." Cora rested her hand on Ellen's shoulder. "Repeat, 'I don't give a shit what anybody thinks of me. I know my own worth.' A hundred times before bed, a hundred in the morning, and a hundred more whenever a frigid, shriveled-tit harpy like Wilma snarks on you."

Ellen stared into Cora's eyes. "Thank you," she said quietly. "That's an excellent mantra."

"How about that outfit, then? You up for it?" Cora's hazel eyes were full of good-humored challenge.

Ellen's back straightened in response. "Would you help Missy with the pie table while I'm gone?"

Cora's grin was radiant. "Sure thing, girlfriend."

The Kountry Kitchen's cramped bathroom was smaller than a broom closet, a difficult place to slough off her dull gray dress and shimmy into Cora's intricate outfit. The top was like a complicated puzzle. It was a corset, impossible to wear without shedding one's bra. It laced up the front, leaving an inch-wide strip of bare skin all down her chest so that the valley between her tightly compressed breasts was visible behind the crisscross of ivory ribbon. The tops of her boobs popped out over the frothy lace trim, and the bottom was cropped over her navel, leaving a long expanse of pale, naked belly beneath. The top was clearly designed for a woman with smaller breasts than hers.

The flirty white skirt was designed to ride shockingly low on her hips, forcing her to shove down the elastic of her underpants. It showed all the bruises on her legs, but whatever. Let them look. This was the new Ellen. No shame, no illusions, no regrets.

Wow. She stared into the small mirror at her anxious face,

and wished she had some makeup. She pulled the pins out of her hair and unraveled it until it billowed out into a wavy mass. That helped a little.

She thumbed her nose at herself, just for practice. She stuck out her tongue. She put her thumbs in her ears, waggled her fingers, crossed her eyes, blew a raspberry. At Simon, LaRue, the whole world.

"I don't give a shit what anybody thinks of me," she said to her own reflection. "I know my own worth."

She walked through the fair, head up, chin out, shoulders back. People fell silent, mouths dropped open, heads turned to watch her pass. A rustling murmur started up in her wake. It was eerie.

When she reached the pie booth, she curtseyed to Cora and Missy and thumbed her nose. "Ta da."

Cora applauded, grinning. Missy bounced with excitement. "Omigod, Ellen, you look just like one of the girls in *Cosmo* magazine!"

"Yeah. Watch out, boys. Here she comes. Before, you looked like a victim," Cora said. "Now, you look like trouble."

"I don't feel like trouble. I feel like I'm in one of those dreams where I find myself naked in the middle of the LaRue Shopping Kart."

"You get used to it," Cora assured her. "You'll sell out on pie in a half hour. Sex sells."

"And you should know, shouldn't you, Cor?"

All three of them stiffened at the familiar voice. Brad Mitchell stepped out of the shadows beside the booth, looking fresh and crisp and intimidating in a snow white polo shirt and designer jeans.

"I'm dazzled." He feigned shielding his eyes with his hand. "Blinded by your combined explosive sexuality, ladies."

"Maybe you'd better piss off before you suffer permanent injury to your retinas," Cora suggested.

Ellen forcibly controlled the powerful urge to wrap her

arms across her half-exposed breasts. "Don't be snide, please, Brad."

"Why not?" he said. "What have I got to lose at this point? So Cor is coaching you? That's appropriate." His narrow green gaze flicked over Ellen's body. "This must be the real you."

Ellen flung her hair back. "Yes, this would be the real me."

"I was wondering if you'd have the nerve to show your face today," he said. "Ellen Kent, domestic goddess. Feeding the world with her pies, when she's not too busy having wild sex in public."

Ellen's fists clenched. "Brad, please don't—"

"I don't appreciate getting dragged into a police investigation whenever your poor judgment and bad choices in bed partners gets you into trouble, Ellen."

Ellen bristled. "I did not ask them to bother you! I know you would never be involved in a thing like that! And I told them so!"

"Oh, I'm so touched by your faith in me. Too bad they didn't take you seriously, but who can blame them? Did you make your statement dressed like that?"

"Fuck off, Brad," Cora said.

He turned his laser-sharp gaze on her. "And you. Jesus, Cor. Could you possibly show any more skin? I think you're violating the city ordinance on decency with that thing."

Cora pursed her full lips at him and blew him a lazy, deliberate kiss. "I never worry about pesky rules when my pleasure is at stake," she cooed. "Want to make a citizen's arrest, big boy? Go on, cuff me. Let's see if you're man enough to take me down."

"Don't tempt me." Brad's voice was menacingly soft. "I've had a shitty week, and it's not getting better." He turned back to Ellen. "So where's your stray dog? Has he already gotten bored?"

"Leave her alone, you stupid bully!"

The trembling voice came from Missy. Ellen and Cora both turned to look at her, their mouths agape.

Brad's eyes narrowed. He sauntered over to stand in front of her. Missy stuck out her chin and glared over her lake of punch.

"Well, now," he said. "Aren't you sassy." He glanced at Ellen. "I'm surprised you trust her with the punch. That's a heavy responsibility for Missy." He picked up a cup and held it out. "Come on, sweetheart. See if you can fill this up without spilling it. Try not to drown yourself."

Missy's face turned a splotchy red. She stared down at Brad's outstretched hand. She looked up into his face.

She tilted the punch bowl and heaved its contents, complete with the lump of ice cream, all over Brad's chest.

The stupefied silence was broken by assorted titters and snorts. The band down the way launched into a rowdy two-step.

Brad stared down at himself. His white shirt was streaked with pink. The lump of ice cream had landed on his shoes. He kicked it off, his face expressionless. He turned and stalked away.

Missy clapped her hands over her mouth, and gave Ellen a timorous look. "I'm so sorry about the punch," she whispered.

"Oh, Missy, it was so worth it," Ellen said fervently.

Cora started giggling, and suddenly they were laughing like fools.

Ellen patted Missy's shoulder. "Thanks for standing by me."

"It felt great," Missy said. "Simon says to pretend you're not afraid, even if you are, and then eventually, you really aren't."

"Is that what you were doing?" Ellen asked. "Pretending?"

"Yeah," Missy said, blushing.

"Could have fooled us," Cora said warmly. "Keep on pretending like that, sweetie, and you'll take over the world."

Ellen bit back a scathing and inappropriate comment about Simon and cowardice as she scooped up the lump of melting ice cream.

She wished he would take his own goddamn advice.

Chapter

20

Simon had it all worked out by the time he got down to the fairgrounds. All the reasons it could work if he retired from freelancing and settled down here, in LaRue, in her house, in her bed.

Even without Gus's inheritance, he was in a good place for a career change. He could afford to do impractical things like still-art photography, which he hadn't had time for in years. Or producing his own documentaries, with full control of the story from start to finish, and no spin doctor or TV producer to whitewash it.

The idea filled him with creative excitement. For the first time in he didn't know how long, he wanted to work again.

He was still dizzy with the euphoria that had seized him in the gas station. He'd psyched himself up into such a state, he could almost ignore the sick dread in his gut, but as he got closer to the fairgrounds, the euphoria drained away and the dread got heavier and colder.

Doubts began to whisper to him. Maybe he was fooling himself, and LaRue would spit him out, like a watermelon seed. Maybe El wouldn't even want a husband who had to travel around making documentaries. Maybe he was just prolonging the agony.

He parked his bike by the riverside park boat ramp, and walked through the carnival that was stretched out along its length. A country band twanged and throbbed in the distance, competing with the tinny carousel music. People laughed and shrieked on the Ferris Wheel, the Hammer. The smell of popcorn and cotton candy and beer.

He walked past the food booths, and picnic tables full of people eating hot dogs, chicken and burgers. Fry bread and elephant ears and corn on the cob. It had a brilliant, surreal clarity in the fading twilight.

He saw Eddie there, with the chubby brunette that Simon had seen with him at the restaurant. Simon nodded politely to Eddie. Eddie swallowed his mouthful, wiped his mouth, and slowly nodded back.

". . . should have known better than to get anywhere near that slut now that you know what she's really like, Bradley!"

A dismayed breath hissed in between his teeth. He turned around, and found himself right in the path of Brad Mitchell, who was being followed and scolded by his mother. Ray Mitchell followed close behind, making ineffectual soothing noises.

Simon braced himself. Brad looked furious, his face pale and rigid. He was soaked from neck to knees with sticky, pinkish liquid, with streaks of deeper pink adorning his white shirt.

He stopped when he saw Simon. "You," he said. "So you're still around. I thought you'd gotten it through your thick head, but no. The stray dog is still hanging around hoping for some more scraps."

"Hey, Brad." Simon nodded to Brad's parents. "Evening, Mrs. Mitchell, Mr. Mitchell."

"I've been hearing wild stories about the waterfall," Brad said. "Who would have thought that Ellen would—"

"One more word about El, and I take you to pieces," Simon said.

Ray Mitchell stepped out in front of Brad and lifted his hands in a placating gesture. "Now, boys. We don't want any unpleasantness. Simon, you just take a deep breath, and—"

"Did you arrange for that firecracker stunt, Brad?" Simon asked.

Brad's eyes did not waver or drop. He let out a short, bitter laugh. "No, Riley, I'm not the outlaw type. I prefer to work within the system. I recommend you try it sometime."

"And those guys who attacked us on the canyon road?" Simon persisted, still studying him. "You don't know anything about that?"

"Of course he didn't!" Diana Mitchell pushed forward. "You have a lot of nerve to accuse my son, after burning down the—"

"No!" Eddie bellowed.

A crowd was forming around the melodrama. All eyes turned to Eddie. Eddie shook off his girlfriend's hand and weaved, somewhat unsteadily, to stand in front of them. His breath was heavy with beer.

He shoved Ray Mitchell's chest, forcing him back a step. "It was *you* that burned the stables. You lying fuck. It was *you*."

"Eddie, you're drunk." Ray's voice was soothing.

"You burned it yourself for the insurance money, you asshole!"

"This is ridiculous!" Diana shrilled. "This fair is becoming a free-for-all! Someone call the police! Right now!"

"It was you and Bebop and Scotty set it up!" Eddie yelled. "The whole fuckin' thing was a setup! I know 'cause they gave me a hundred bucks to get a bunch of my buddies together to shoot off bottle rockets behind the stables—"

"Shut up!" Diana shrieked. "You stupid *drunk!*"

"I'm sick of being told to shut up!" Eddie bellowed back. "We were already gone and halfway up the hill before we saw the fire. And of course Simon the stupid fuckin' *hero* just has to run back because of the stupid fuckin' *horses* . . ." Eddie's voice choked off.

Simon laid his hand on Eddie's shoulder. "Take it easy, man."

Eddie wiped his runny nose on his arm. "But I didn't go

back with you," he said forlornly. "I let you go back there all alone."

Simon let his hand rest where it was. "We do what we can."

Ray slapped Eddie on the back. "See, Eddie? Simon's not blaming you. Nobody is. You just go home and sleep it off, and it'll all be—"

"Don't touch me, asshole!" Eddie wrenched away. "I figured it out when Bebop got his new truck and the job at the country club. And Scotty made foreman, and bought a wide-screen TV. And Simon took the rap, but Bebop and Scotty said keep your big mouth shut or we'll kick your ass." He turned to Simon. "And I figured, fuck it. You were already gone, man, right? What did it matter if they blamed you? Why get my ass kicked for nothing?" His red, fleshy face was heavy with old unhappiness. "But I was wrong. I'm sorry, man."

"It's OK," Simon repeated gently.

Eddie shook his head. "Fuck. Bebop got a truck and Scotty got a wide-screen TV, and what did I get? A hundred lousy bucks and my best friend blamed for something he never did, and me feeling like a piece of shit. For years."

Eddie looked back at Ray, who was chuckling with his hand over his mouth. "You think this is funny?" Eddie demanded. "I bet you all just figured, Eddie's such a fuckin' clown, he won't even notice when he's being used, right? But nobody's using me anymore. No one's kicking my ass anymore, you lying arsonist asshole. Torching your own goddamn horses. Stop laughing. You make me sick. You sick fuck."

Ray shook his head. "Eddie," he gasped out, between peals of laughter, "You're very innocent to think that I might have . . . I don't mean to be crass, but I am a very wealthy man. I had no need for such an . . . an insignificant sum as that . . . insurance money . . ." His voice degenerated. He covered his face, waving his hand.

The crowd had grown to twenty or so, all watching the trainwreck with looky-loo fascination. Simon's eyes met

Cora's. She looked tense and sad, which was exactly how he felt. A guy like Eddie couldn't challenge someone like Ray Mitchell without paying through the nose for it. It was going to be ugly for poor Eddie once this shook down.

Ray Mitchell was still laughing, even harder now. "It's just . . . the most ridiculous thing I've ever heard," he gasped. "It's just . . . excuse me please, I can't seem to . . ." He took off his glasses, wiped his streaming eyes, his reddened face. "It's just so . . . so ludicrous—" He doubled over, snorting, and hid his face in both hands.

"Ray?" Diana's tone was sharp. "I don't think it's funny."

Ray lifted his hand and waved her down. "I know," he gasped. "I know it isn't. I just can't . . . I can't . . ."

All anyone could see of his face were the purplish veins pulsing in his forehead. His laughter grew louder. Great, gasping, whooping sobs, terribly audible in the deepening silence around him.

"Honey? Are you . . . dear God, he's having some sort of an attack. Someone call a doctor. Ray? Honey?"

Ray was clearly trying to stop, but the laughter exploded out of him. It was high pitched and loud, like the whinny of a terrified horse. He backed blindly through the crowd. People shrank away from him. He turned and ran, disappearing into the shadows beneath the willows.

There was a shocked silence. A murmuring buzz of speculation began to rise. Diana yanked on Brad's arm. "Hurry! Go after him, honey! Bring him to the car while I go call Dr. Marcos, and we'll—"

"No," Brad said. "I'm not going after him."

Diana's bright red mouth fell open. "Bradley! What are you thinking? Don't tell me you actually believe this . . . this idiot?"

"Forget it, Mom," Brad said. "He's on his own."

Diana's mouth worked. She whirled on Eddie. "I will destroy you for this! If you think you can slander my husband, and—"

"Shut up, you poisonous bitch," Eddie spat back. "You're

just as bad as him. You paid Bebop and Scotty to spread rumors about Cora. They used to compete for who could make
up the filthiest stories when they got stoned. Just because
she wasn't good enough for your precious baby boy." Eddie
looked at Brad. "And you bought it," he jeered. "Mr. Stuck-
Up Ivy League. You bought all of it. Asshole."

Brad pulled his arm away from his mother's clutching
hand. His face looked stiff and gray. "Mom?"

Diana's makeup looked like a garish mask. "Don't look at
me like that!" she hissed. "You were so young, and so stubborn and intense. I couldn't stand to see you clip your wings
for a cheap tramp like that. I did what I had to do!" She
reached for his arm.

Brad jerked out of her reach. "Do not ever touch me
again."

Brad looked over at Cora. Tears streamed down her face,
making her mascara run. She shook her head, turned and
marched away. Pride and dignity radiated from every line of
her bare, gracefully upright back.

Brad looked around at the crowd. At Simon, at Eddie, at
his mother. His face contracted. He stumbled away from them
towards the river. He stepped out of his loafers. Stripped off
his sticky polo shirt and flung it onto the grass. He splashed
into the water, wearing only his jeans, dove in and headed
for where the swift current was strongest.

He cut across it with strong, steady strokes and disappeared into the gloom. Diana Mitchell burst into hysterical
tears. No one rushed to comfort her. The space around her
widened.

Eddie swayed on his feet. "What a dumb shit," he said.
"Keeping my mouth shut. All those years, about all of it.
You, Cora, everything."

"Forget about it," Simon said. "You spoke up now. It was
all you could do to make things right. And I'm glad you did.
Thanks, man."

Eddie looked so empty and lost that Simon felt his throat
start to tighten. He grabbed Eddie, gave him a brief, rough

hug, and then turned away before he could choke up again. Bad enough to break down crying in a stinking gas station bathroom. Doing it in public at the LaRue Peach Festival would be his idea of hell.

He pushed on through the crowd. Everywhere he turned, the world fell apart at the seams. Then somebody grabbed him by the arm, someone else pounded him on the back, and suddenly, a bunch of people had completely encircled him, talking all at once.

"I knew you didn't do it, man," one guy assured him.

Another guy Simon couldn't quite place pumped his hand. "I never believed that crap they said about you. No way, dude!"

"I always said there was something fishy about the whole thing," said a tall brunette whom Simon dimly recognized as the head cheerleader of his high school football team. Before he knew it, Simon had an offer to play football that weekend with a bunch of guys whose names he was struggling to remember. A guy named Vern was trying to convince him to shoot a video for his sister's upcoming wedding. The brunette wanted his phone number.

Simon extricated himself as politely as he could. This was all very touching, but at the moment, he couldn't give a shit. He wanted El.

A hand seized his wrist and dug in with long, sharp nails. "Ah. There you are, Simon," said Muriel. "I heard you were out here, causing a ruckus, as usual. I've been looking all over for you!"

"Later. I need to go find El."

She looked smug. "I should think you do! About time you saw reason. I was worried for a while today! Let me take your arm, and—"

"Not now, Mrs. Kent," he said between set teeth.

She frowned. "Stop being difficult. Let me take your arm, so we can show everyone you're part of the family, and—"

"El will be the one to decide that."

She towed him along. "Gossip is flying about you and my

daughter," she said. "I'm relieved to hear that business about the fire is finally settled. Of course, I never doubted you."

"Uh, thanks. Mrs. Kent, I have to go—"

"Now you can make an honest woman of her." She raked him with a disapproving glance. "For heaven's sake, Simon. You might have come up with a clean shirt for the occasion."

Simon glanced down at himself. He was dressed in the dusty, sweaty shirt and jeans that he had been working in all day.

He looked her straight in the eye. "Muriel, let go of my arm. I don't want to be rude, but I'm going to talk to El. And you're not invited."

Her eyebrow shot up. She let go of his arm. "Well! Get to it, then!" She made a shooing motion. "Chop chop!"

He plunged into the crowd again.

He saw her from a few booths down, laughing as she passed some creamy confection to a customer. His mind emptied like a sieve.

Where the fuck did she get those clothes? That white lace thing must have come straight out of a sex fetishist's catalog. Her tits bulged out of a white corset. The skirt threatened to drop right off her ass. Her hair was frizzy and tangled and loose. The naughty peasant vixen bride, selling goodies in her underwear. Tantalizing every man she saw.

It made him want to jerk that skirt down—it wouldn't take much of a tug—and put her over his knee. Swat her round, rosy ass until it tingled, until she wiggled and squealed. God help him. He did not need an erection to embarrass and distract him in these next few crucial moments that would determine the entire course of his life.

El caught sight of him. Her arm flew up to hide her breasts. She stuck her chin out. Even in her white sex-kitten outfit, she looked as proud and lofty as a queen.

"Hello, Simon." There was a breathless catch in her voice. "What a shocking surprise. Would you care for a piece of pie? We still have banana cream, huckleberry and—"

"I want it all," he said.

Her eyes got very big. She looked almost frightened. "Do you mean . . . you want a piece of each kind?"

"No." He took a deep breath and gathered himself to tell her what he really meant, what he really wanted. To love her, cherish her, stand by her, have kids with her. To worship her body every night in their bed, to give her everything he had, everything he was. "I want—"

A scream ripped the air. It was followed by a long, gurgling wail, from the direction of the bandstand. There was a murmur, a rustle of movement. Everyone began to talk at once in hushed voices.

A knot of people started to move down the midway. Millie Webber was in the midst of the crowd, still screaming. One of her arms was held by her husband Max. A gray-faced Eddie held the other. She shrieked, flailed, fell to her knees. They lifted her up and hustled her away.

Something horrible had happened.

Simon felt the ghost wind rising, cold and implacable. It swirled around his neck, raising his short hairs. Disaster breathing down his neck. It had been playing a game of cat and mouse with him.

"You folks hear the news?" Lionel said from behind him.

"What news?" El demanded.

"Some hikers found Scotty and Bebop. Down by the river, towards Wheaton. Someone decapitated them. And disemboweled them."

A chill snaked down Simon's spine. He turned his head.

Detective Wes Hamilton was striding towards him.

Ellen's first instinct was to protect Simon as the purpose drained out of his face, leaving it a strained mask. She wanted to leap in front of him and shriek a challenge at anyone who dared to hurt him.

He looked like a refugee from a jungle war movie, with his hair a wild, tangled mane, his face shadowed with stubble.

Wes stopped in front of them. His face was damp with sweat. His eyes looked hollow. "I see from your faces that you folks have heard."

Ellen reached across the table and seized Simon's hand. His fingers curled around hers. His hand was ice cold.

"Mr. Riley, where were you between the hours of four and six this morning?" Wes's tone was stiff and formal.

Simon let out a silent sigh. He opened his mouth to reply.

"With me," Ellen cut in. "As always. He spends every night in my bed, Lieutenant. Consider it a given."

"I don't consider anything a given, Miss Kent," Wes said heavily. "Not when there are mutilated bodies involved."

Ellen's eyes fell. Simon's fingers tightened around hers.

Wes fixed his eyes on Simon. "They say you threatened those two men. Word is you said you'd rip their heads off, and their guts out. And damned if somebody didn't do just exactly that. Isn't that funny?"

"Not me, Wes," Simon said quietly.

Wes grunted. "Don't leave town."

They watched him walk away. Ellen looked at Simon's shuttered face. He would not meet her eyes. The door she had sensed swinging open had slammed shut again. "Simon?" she asked. "You . . . you were about to say something to me?"

His eyes met hers, hollow and sad. He lifted her hand to his lips and pressed a soft, lingering kiss against it. "No, baby. Not now."

"Then when?" Her voice was shrill. "When, Simon, if not now?"

He shook his head and let go of her hand. "I'm sorry, El."

He walked away, disappearing between the booths.

Ellen stared after him. She wanted to shriek, throw pies, bite her own hands. She couldn't believe it. So close, and then nothing.

"Well?" Lionel said. "You just going to stand there with your teeth in your mouth and let him walk off into the sunset?"

Ellen looked wildly around the booth. "Would you find my

mother to help Missy?" she asked him. "Someone has to help her pack up, and take care of the cash box, and give her a ride home, and—"

"Run along." Lionel waved her away. "We're covered. Missy will be fine. Move, now! Step lively!"

Ellen needed no further urging. She bolted through the break in the booths where she had last seen him and sprinted down the midway. She wove through the crowd, hair flying behind her like a flag, breasts flopping, sandals flapping, oblivious to the staring crowd.

He wasn't in this aisle of booths, so she ducked through the display tents and tried the next one. One of her slip-on sandals flew off. She kicked off the other rather than bothering to look for it. She could sprint faster on the balls of her bare feet. She was flying over the ground, and the roaring engine that powered her was in her chest. Her legs churned under her, beyond conscious control as she scanned the crowd for the tall, graceful lines of his body, the gleam of his hair.

She finally spotted him in the riverfront park, climbing onto his motorcycle. The sight gave her one last final burst of desperate energy.

"Simon!" she shrieked. "Stop!"

He turned and shook his head. He pulled out of the parking lot onto the street. She cut across the road to head him off, and two cars squealed to a stop to avoid hitting her, honking angrily. She dove for him, grabbed his arm before he picked up enough speed to evade her.

He braked. "What the hell do you think you're—"

"Catching you," she gasped. She clambered onto the motorcycle behind him. "I won't let you run away from me!"

"Goddamn it, El, get off!" He tried to pry her arms from around his waist, but she just hung on tighter. "You're making it worse!"

"You better believe I'm making it worse! You're not sneaking off like this, Simon Riley, so just forget it! Forget it!"

Simon's head sagged down between his broad, hunched shoulders. "Fucking hell," he muttered. "Shit, shit, *shit!*"

The bike surged forward. Ellen pressed her face against his back.

His loose hair whipped and stung her face. She squeezed her eyes shut and tried to gulp up as much as she could of him, with every inch of skin that touched his beautiful body. Her chest pressed against the thin, sweat-soaked cloth of his shirt, the feel of the lean, hard muscles moving beneath it. Her naked thighs pressed against his jeans-clad butt. Her hands clutched the clenched muscles of his belly. Anger and frustration rolled off him in hot waves. She didn't care. She'd take him angry, if that was the only way she could have him.

Chapter

21

B rad had wanted to fight the current, and the current obliged him. He was a strong swimmer, but he barely dragged himself out of the swift rushing water and struggled to the side before it swept him into the chutes, at which point he would have been thoroughly screwed.

But then again, he already had been.

The muscular pull of the dark water was something to resist. Something to throw his anger at. He fought his way to the side, where the water was chest deep and ran slightly slower. His heart pounded.

Cora came into view as he drifted around the curve. She stood on the rock shelf of the riverbank and waited as he stumbled his way through the rocks to the shore. He felt naked and exposed with Cora's eyes on him. Pathetic, like a drowned rat. The water was so cold against his skin. He was conscious of the drag of his wet jeans against his legs, the jagged rocks against his hands, the hungry pull of the water.

He felt every detail. The river deafened him. He felt cracked open, flung wide. The world was rushing into him, noisy and unruly. He was overrun. The gold coins of Cora's earrings gleamed against her cloud of dark hair. His eyes dropped to her feet. Slender, brown and dusty. Toenails painted a silvery green. Her flip-flops sported plastic daisies.

She had beautiful feet. Long and fine boned. The sight of those brave, cheerful plastic daisies made his chest tighten.

The pressure was turning him molten, liquid and unstable inside.

He reached for the rocky shelf of the riverbank and hoisted himself up so that his torso was over it. He laid his cold, wet hands on either side of her feet. He sank down and kissed them.

She wobbled and tried to step back, but he held her ankles and pressed his wet face against her feet. She tasted of powdery road dust, but the water that dripped from his hair washed it away. Soft, silky skin. Brown on top, pink on the sides.

He kissed every part of her feet that he could reach. The sweep of her metatarsals, the curves and hollows of her ankles. He kissed them more passionately than he had ever kissed any woman's face.

He'd never known until this moment what a kiss was. Not titillation, not sensation. It was a conduit for passion. He was pouring it over her feet like wine over an altar. Lavishing it on her.

His dick was harder than it had ever been in his entire life. When he slid his tongue between the crevices of her slender brown toes, he imagined opening her thighs, sliding his tongue inside her.

He'd never done that to her. The realization was accompanied by a rush of dumb amazement. He'd had lots of sex with Cora, explosive sex, but he didn't know what she tasted like. He'd seldom gone down on his lovers. It never occurred to him to do so, unless his partner prodded him. But he wanted to taste Cora's body.

He vaulted up from the river onto the stone ledge and stayed crouched on his knees. He didn't dare stand up. He was too tall. He would tower over her, and he sensed that would wreck it. It was too delicate, too unstable, this wild, fragile thing that was blooming out of nowhere. He couldn't bear for her to run away. He would do anything.

He crouched there, dripping, waiting. She started to back away. His hands flashed out and grabbed both of hers.

She stiffened. "Hey! Don't think for one second that you can—"

"I don't think anything," he said. "I'm not thinking at all. Don't run away. Don't leave me alone. Please."

Her hands trembled in his grip. "I can't believe you just said 'please.' I didn't even know that word was in your vocabulary."

"It is," he assured her.

He drew her hands to his mouth and kissed them. She yanked one away so she could wipe her face.

"Cor?" He kissed the palm of the hand she had left to him.

She sniffed, hard. "Yeah?"

"You said you were a lifeguard. If I were drowning, would you save me? Would you do CPR on me?"

She gazed down at him, mouth quivering. "Yes."

"Why?" He kissed her tender wrist. "I thought you hated my guts."

"I do," she said. "You're horrible. But we all deserve to be saved. We all deserve one last chance to get things right."

"Are you going to give me that chance?"

"You used up all your chances," Cora whispered. "Years ago."

He grabbed her other hand. "Give me another one. I'm drowning, Cor."

He leaned closer, so that her perfect thighs were in his face. She was wearing a denim miniskirt trimmed with shells. Her hands were brown, chapped and callused. Cheap silver rings on every finger. He kissed every joint, every knuckle, front and back. All the tender junctions and sensitive inner places. He took his time, sought out every detail, and pressed the tender tribute of his kisses against them.

He pressed his face to her thighs. She stiffened, so he moved down and not up, kissing his way down the long, elegant sweep of muscle that led to her knee. He pulled on her hands, a beseeching tug. He could hardly believe his luck when she sank to her knees.

She was so warm and soft. She smelled sweet, a spicy perfume like something good to eat. He pulled her closer, leaned his dripping forehead against hers until her curls brushed his face and shoulders.

He kissed her hands like he couldn't bear to stop.

She'd gone insane. It was the only explanation for why she was allowing Brad Mitchell to touch her. As if he could make up for all the ugliness of the last seventeen years. As if she didn't know any better, hadn't grown up long ago and stopped believing in fairy tales.

And now he had pulled her white halter top down until one brown, taut nipple was revealed. She meant to smack him and scream bloody murder, but his lips fastened over her nipple, engulfing it in a scalding swirl of sensation. It felt intense and strange and wonderful, combined with the icy cold that dripped off his body.

Her words disintegrated. Instead of smacking him, she was holding his head, her fingers sliding through his short, thick wet hair.

He kissed her breasts the way he'd kissed her feet. Cherishing them. He'd never touched her that way, even in the old days. He'd only been nineteen, he'd been in too much of a hurry to get his dick a mile or so inside of her. Which had been no problem for her, since she'd wanted the same thing. She'd been young and dumb, she'd known no better.

His wet hand slid between her thighs and brushed over her satin panties. She threw her arm around his big shoulders, suspended between pleasures, the pleading pull of his mouth at her breasts, and his fingers brushing over the damp glow of need between her thighs, teasing, coaxing. His hand slid beneath the elastic of her panties.

"Cor. My God," he groaned. "You're completely . . ."

"Yeah," she whispered. "You bet I am. I get a Brazilian wax every few weeks in Portland. I love to be bare down there. You like it?"

"Oh, God." He slid his hand beneath the fabric and cupped her.

And she went off, just like that, in an orgasm that felt like it had been years in the making. Long and wrenching, and yet soft, like a fountain sobbing inside her. She would have fallen if he hadn't caught her against his wet body. He cupped his hand against her pussy as if he wanted to trap her pleasure in his hand and keep it for himself.

"God," he rasped. "Cor, please."

Before she knew it, she was sprawled out on the flat rock. He'd dragged her panties off in one practiced sweep and tossed them away.

And here she was, just like old times. Breasts popping out of her top, skirt around her waist, and him with that look on his face, that wild look that had always driven her out of her mind with excitement.

She tried to wiggle away from him, but he caught her waist.

"Wait," he pleaded. "Just let me look. It felt so good to touch. So amazingly sweet and soft and tender. I just have to see it."

He pushed her legs apart, and slid his hand between her thighs. Opening her like the petals of a flower, with his fingertip and thumb. He bent down, like he was going to kiss her there.

She panicked. It crashed down on her; how alone they were in the darkness, how big and strong he was. How easy it would be for him to just open his jeans and shove himself inside her. And then, dear God.

She twisted out of his grip, scrambled back and stumbled

to her feet. She lost her balance, tripped and banged her knees, hard.

He leaped to his feet. "Damn it, Cor! Don't be stupid—"

"Do not ever call me stupid!" she hissed. "Don't touch me!"

"I wasn't going to rape you." His arrogant tone was back. "I was going to make you come. Since you seemed to like it the first time."

She backed away. "You know what would happen if you did that?"

"Yeah? What?"

She locked her knees to keep her legs from buckling. "We would end up having sex."

"Yeah. Incredible sex. And you would've loved it."

She backed away. "No freaking way! I can't have sex with you! I'm too mad at you! I've been mad for years! I can't just make that go away just because . . . because you feel like it!"

He studied her with narrowed eyes. "So how long will it take for you to get over being mad?"

"I don't know," she said helplessly. "Maybe never. How could I? I should never have put out for you in the first place. I was so stupid. Rich boy bound for Princeton, fooling around with the girl from the trailer park before he sets off for his bright future. What a cliché."

"Is that what you thought?" He had the gall to sound offended.

"No," she said. "It's not what I thought. It's what I feared."

The twilit shadows accentuated his arrogantly handsome face. She knew that look so well. The sulky little boy who wasn't getting his own way. It made her want to slap him silly, and then shove him down onto a bed and torment him until he was begging and pleading.

Until he admitted how much he needed her.

She backed away, alarmed by the dangerous drift of her thoughts. "This is insane. I shouldn't be here. I have to go home. I shouldn't—"

"I'll take you home."

His presumption made her laugh. "In a pig's eye! One, I would never let you take me home. Two, you're half naked and barefoot and dripping, so cut out the lord-of-the-manor routine."

He dug his hand into his wet jeans with some difficulty, and fished out a string of keys. "I've still got my car keys."

"You're going to plant your sopping wet ass on that Porsche's leather seat?" Cora clucked her tongue at him. "You'll regret it, buddy."

"It's that or stripping them off on the street and driving home stark naked," he said.

It came to her in a rush, an image of Brad naked, his powerful, muscular body stretched out on the soft leather of the Porsche. His nice, thick dick all stiff and hot and ready in his hand, his slanted green cat-eyes heavy with arousal. The look on his face that silently said *come over here and pleasure me, as is my royal privilege.*

She could tell from the charged silence that stretched out that he was thinking something very similar.

She turned away and pushed through the bushes. He followed doggedly in her wake, cursing as his bare feet found all the hidden obstacles. He caught up with her once they got to the smooth grass of the high school football field. His wet jeans squeaked every step he took. She felt his intense gaze on the side of her face.

They made it all the way to the fifty-yard line before he came out with it. "I want to stay with you tonight."

Well. Couldn't fault the guy for not being clear and direct.

"No," she said baldly.

"Cor. I want you to give me another chance. I never meant to—"

"I would never dream of having sex with you again unless we were married," she said. "I've learned that much, at least."

She'd figured that sally ought to cool his ardor pretty damn quick. Sure enough, he stopped. She left him and strode briskly onward.

He caught up with her a few seconds later. "Married?"

"See how ridiculous it is? Give it up, Brad. You have political ambitions, right? Even if you wanted to, which of course you don't, you couldn't ever marry a person like me. Lush Lips MacComber is not cut out to be a politician's wife. For one thing, I wouldn't be caught dead in a power suit. I like spandex. And for another, I would never be able to say I didn't inhale and keep a straight face. See? It's hopeless. You can't marry me. Ever. Ergo? No sex. Ever. Case closed."

The football field segued into the baseball diamond, after which the riverside park stretched out before them. They could see the glow of the carnival and hear the noise of the crowd at the far end of it.

"But you want it, too," he said.

The bafflement in his voice made her furious. "God, Brad! I know you're not dumb, so how could you be so goddamn *stupid?*"

He opened his mouth to answer, and closed it again. He gave her a hard, angry little shrug, and shook his head. Confused and clueless.

She stabbed an angry finger towards his chest, and he shrank back. "You know something?" she demanded. "After your mother did her bit, and you dumped me, and word got around? I was done in this town. Trashed. Guys were willing to take me into a dark alley or a bar bathroom, but nobody wanted to be seen at the Peach Festival dance or in a nice restaurant with Lush Lips MacComber."

He looked defensive. "I never meant to—"

"I don't give a good goddamn what you meant. Let me finish. I had to leave this town, just to keep my sanity. I put myself through school. I worked three jobs. I partied real hard to blow off steam. I've had a lot of lovers since you, and I think I can safely say, without vanity, that by now, I have fully earned my honorary title as queen of the blow job. And I wear the crown with pride."

He seized her shoulders. "I'm sick of your provocation games!"

She slapped his hands away. "I'm just rubbing your face in your own rotten double standard! If you can't handle the fact that I'm a sexual, flesh-and-blood woman with a checkered past, then I don't want to waste another second of my time on a tight-ass loser like you!"

He was silent for a minute, working through it. "By this, can I infer that if I can handle your checkered past, that you might be willing to waste some more seconds of your time on a tight-ass loser like me?"

She grunted. "You are such a goddamn lawyer."

"To the bone," he agreed.

"Don't even try your sneaky lawyer tricks on me," she snapped.

"Then stop messing with my head. You tell me you're so great at giving head? I'll believe it when I feel it."

"In your dreams, bozo."

"You bet it's in my dreams," he said. "Every night. So? It's just you, me, and an empty baseball diamond, Cor. Show me this amazing skill of yours. I'm all ready to be impressed by your technique. My dick is as hard as steel. Let's do it right here on home plate."

She groped around for a put-down that was as harsh as he deserved, but her mind was muddled with erotic images. She contented herself with tossing her hair. "Don't hold your breath. Pig."

They left the baseball diamond and headed into the park. "So what do you do differently now that you didn't do before?" he asked.

She floundered, and realized belatedly that he was still talking about oral sex. "Oh, for God's sake, don't fixate."

"Just tell me," he insisted. "I'm dying to know."

She forced all the trapped air out of her lungs so she could start breathing again. "Well," she began. "One thing I do is demand one hundred percent reciprocation. A man has to be a master at the art of cunnilingus to satisfy me. And as I recall, Brad, it's not your specialty. Another example of the uncrossable abyss between us."

"So teach me," he said. "I can make it my specialty."

She tripped over her feet, and he stuck out a swift hand to steady her. Her eyes flicked nervously over his glowing, tilted eyes, down over his muscular chest. His thick erection strained against his wet jeans.

So. The thought of licking her turned him on. She pressed her thighs together hard.

"I'm a quick learner," Brad said. "Very focused. Very motivated. I'd do it right here, right now. How about under that willow? Lie down on the grass and spread your legs, Cor. Give me my first lesson."

She backed away from the aggressive sex vibes pulsing off him. "Not so fast, buddy. We shouldn't even be talking about sex yet. We've got way too many other issues to deal with—"

"List them. Let's deal with them right now."

"Hah!" She shoved at his chest, and snatched her hand away, alarmed at how it tingled at the contact with his skin. "Just like that, huh? You think it's so simple?"

"It can be, if you let it be."

"Well, for starters, if you want to even talk about nooky with me, you have to start acting like a civilized human being."

He frowned. "Meaning?"

"Meaning you should apologize to Missy and Ellen. Simon, too."

He stiffened. "Fuck no!"

"OK." She lifted her hand in a fluttering wave. "This is where we part ways, then. Bye-bye, Brad. Have a nice life."

She turned away. He grabbed her wrist and yanked her back. She reacted without thinking, and swung her other hand up to smack his face. "Put your hand on me again in a bullying way, and I'll cut it off!"

He let go of her instantly. "Jesus, Cor! Lighten up!"

"I'm dead serious! I have nothing to lose, and I have no reason to compromise. And I am tired of your bullshit. Good night."

"Wait!" He reached for her, stopped himself, and held up his hands in surrender. "Hold on. I admit, I was harder on Missy than I should have been. Her cringing and cowering got on my nerves."

She made a disgusted sound. "That poor girl. You are evil, Brad."

"Fine, I'll tell her I'm sorry. But Simon and Ellen?" His voice was outraged. "They were screwing around while she was engaged to me!"

"That's your karma, Brad," she said. "You've been an ass-hole too many times in your life, evidently. You've got a lot to answer for."

"I do not owe them a goddamn apology!"

Cora shrugged. "Fine. You are so right. Nobody owes anybody anything. Being courteous and kind to one's fellow human beings is not a requirement in this shitty world. It's entirely optional. You are free to be a dickhead if you so please. Just don't make me watch."

"Cor—"

"And now, I must leave you. This is my turn-off." She gestured up at the curve of Twin Lakes Road that disappeared into the dark woods. "I'm heading home. I've had enough soap opera drama for one day."

"On foot?" He sounded shocked.

"Truck's in the shop," she said. "I'd planned on getting a ride home from the fair with a friend."

"Friend?" Brad scowled. "What kind of friend?"

A sweet seventy-five-year-old neighbor lady friend, she declined to tell him, it being none of his goddamn business. "Give it up, Brad."

"It's two miles to the trailer park, and it's a bad neighbor-hood!"

"It's a community of manufactured homes, if you please,

not a trailer park," she said. "And it's a perfectly fine neighborhood. Full of respectable working-class people just like me, you uptight snob."

"And it's dark, and you're wearing flip-flops, and the roads are full of pickups driven by assholes who have been drinking," he said angrily. "Plus, your ass is bare underneath that thing you call a skirt. I'll drive you home. Don't bother arguing. My car is parked at the municipal building. Come with me, and—"

"It's your own damn fault that my ass lacks panties," she said. "Don't worry about me, Brad. I've taken care of myself alone for a long time. I can do it again tonight." She set off up the road.

"I'll get the car and pick you up on the road," he snarled.

"Don't bother," she called back. "If I see headlights coming I'll dive for the bushes. You'll never find me, so don't waste your time. The pickups full of drunken assholes won't see me either, though. So relax."

He threw back his head and let out a roar of frustration. The tendons in his neck stood out. "You drive me fucking *crazy* with your smart mouth, Cor!"

She skittered back, putting distance between them. "Good night."

His eyes burned into her bare back. She held herself very straight, walked very fast, concentrated on not looking back.

She turned the corner. Her shoulders sagged, her eyes filled, and she started to trot down the dark road, as fast as her flip-flops would allow. She wanted to curl up and lick her wounds in her safe, quiet nest at home. He'd scoffed at the trailer park, but she was proud of the pretty, tidy way that she'd fixed up her nice doublewide. Her deck, her barbecue, her veggie garden and flower beds. She'd fixed the inside just the way she liked it, too. Each piece of furniture and art was carefully chosen, right down to the orthopedic splurge of her king-sized bed.

She tried not to imagine Brad sprawled in it, naked

against her ice-blue satin sheets. She couldn't even let herself fantasize about it.

She was about to cross the Dry Creek Bridge when she saw the lights from a car coming up behind her. She scrambled down a gravel and dirt slide into the gully beneath it in a burst of unreasoning panic.

She fetched up in a tangle of thorny blackberry bushes, and hoped to God she wasn't sitting in a rattlesnake nest.

A car passed slowly over the bridge, the purring hum of a powerful engine. It slowed, stopped. A window whirred, coming down.

"Cor? Come on, just let me drive you home. I swear to God I won't touch you and I won't be rude. I just can't stand to think of you on the road at night." He waited for a moment. "Please," he added loudly.

Cora crouched in the gravel and pressed her wet face against her scratched knees. The car door popped open. He got out and leaned over the bridge. "Cora!" he yelled. Anger and frustration pulsed off of him.

She was amazed he couldn't hear her heart, it was beating so loudly. She wanted to call out to him so badly she ached. She also knew that if he took her home, he would spend the night in her bed.

Her defenses were too low to risk it. He could wreck her if he wanted to. And she knew just exactly how cruel he could be.

If he didn't learn to respect her now, then she had no business with him anyway. She wasn't going to be just a quick, easy lay, handy for a dry spell. He was going to treat her with respect, like a lady, cherished and special. Or else he could stick it where the sun didn't shine and spin on it like a freaking dervish.

He started cursing, starting soft and getting louder. He knew damn well she was hiding and could hear him. The door slammed, the engine surged, the tires squealed. The car roared off. One last, furious blatt of his horn echoed and faded away into the rustling darkness.

Chapter

22

They pulled into the long, bumpy driveway that led down to Gus's house, and pulled up next to a U-Haul that was backed up to the porch.

Simon turned off the engine and put down the kickstand. His chest heaved beneath her clutching hands. She felt his rapid heartbeat.

Ellen slid off the motorcycle and leaned against him, pressing her face against his hair. He lifted his head and pulled away, looking her over. She suddenly remembered the clothing that Cora had given her.

She felt more exposed in that outfit than if she were stark naked.

He did not comment, just stared at her body. "You're barefoot," he said. "What happened to your shoes?"

"I lost them running after you."

Simon swung his leg over the motorcycle and knelt down next to her. He lifted one of her feet, bending it at the knee and running his fingers gently over her entire foot. He did the same with the other, and then stood up and scooped her into his arms.

"Simon, my feet are fine," she protested. "I can—"

"No, you can't. The yard is full of old pop-tops and broken glass."

She wrapped her arms around his shoulders and let herself enjoy the ease with which he carried her, the powerful muscles bunching and flexing beneath her hands. He jerked the screen door open and stepped into the dark. He set her gently on her feet.

She waited in the pitch darkness. A match hissed, and a brief orange flare lit Simon's face as he bent over the kerosene lamp. The flame leaped, high and smoky. He adjusted the wick and set the glass chimney in its place on the bare kitchen table.

Shadows danced on the discolored walls. The room seemed even more desolate now that it was empty. Simon regarded her with inscrutable eyes. "Did you opt for no underwear under that outfit, too?"

She threw up her arms. "Of course. With all the things we have to talk about, you have to fixate on that. How typical."

"You're shoving it in my face," he said. "So? Answer me."

"Would you prefer if I had no underwear? I can arrange that." She hiked up her skirt, dug her thumbs under the waistband of her panties, and shimmied them down. She stepped out of them and held them up. "See? I'm completely without underwear now. Is that burning question finally settled for you, Simon? Can we move on?"

She flung the panties at him. He plucked them out of the air without looking at them and crumpled them in his big fist.

"Are you trying to drive me nuts?" he asked.

A sound came out of her, half growl, half shriek. "No, you big idiot! I'm trying to seduce you!"

"Don't." He picked up a box from the pile in the corner of the kitchen and carried it out the door. She heard it thud into the bed of the U-Haul outside. He came back in for another box.

The next time he came in, she seized his arm. "Are you going to ignore me?"

He stared down at her hand. She dug her fingers in.

"I'm busy," he said. "I didn't invite you to follow me. You shouldn't be here at all." He wrenched his arm away, and picked up another box.

Each box he carried out felt like a brick in a wall he was building against her. She wanted to knock them out of his arms, but she knew better than to challenge him physically. The next time he came in, she placed herself between him and the few boxes that remained.

"Stop, Simon," she said. "You can't just run away like this."

He turned his back and stalked outside. She followed him out and watched him lift the nose of his motorcycle into the truckbed. He hoisted up the back, shoved it in and wiped his hands on his jeans.

She planted herself in front of the door. "You belong here, with me. You can't go. I won't let you."

He lifted her and set her aside like a doll. "Tell me something, El."

This sounded promising. At least he was initiating conversation. She followed him back into the kitchen. "Anything you want."

He heaved another box into his arms. "Why did you tell Wes that I was with you this morning? Do you think I need you to lie for me?"

"No," she said.

"Then why?" His voice was harsh.

"Because I knew Wes would never buy it if you told him you were out moping in the rain because you had a goddamn bad dream!" she yelled. "Only someone who knows you like I do would buy it!"

"Is that so?" He kicked the screen door open with his foot. It whacked against the wall. He disappeared outside. She waited for the thud into the truckbed.

"Yes, that's so!" she said when he reappeared in the door. "It sounds improbable and ridiculous and stupid! Which it *was!*"

His face was taut. "So you don't think it was me, then?" he asked. "You don't think I killed those men?"

Her jaw dropped. "Oh, for the love of God, Simon. Of course not!"

He let out a ragged sigh. His hands relaxed. His shoulders sagged.

"Of course, it doesn't help that you'd gone strutting around town like a turkey cock, putting it about that you wanted to rip them to pieces! I told you to let the police handle it, but no! Mr. Macho just had to take matters into his own hands!"

"I wanted them to stay away from you," Simon said. "That's the only language guys like Bebop and Scotty understand. If I'd gotten my hands on them, I would have pounded them, yes, but not . . . not that."

She growled through her teeth. "Idiot."

His face was bleak. "I can kill if I'm forced to, El. I've had the training. But it's not something I would do in cold blood, or for fun."

"I know you wouldn't," she said. "You don't have to convince me."

"No? How about Lionel?" Simon asked. "He probably heard me leave the house. How about your mother? The woman never sleeps. She probably heard me, too. They're both smart people. You think they're going to buy the moping-in-the-woods story? You think they'll want to sleep under the same roof with me once they think about it for a while?"

"They'll find the real killer and it'll be irrelevant," she said.

Simon shook his head. "My life never works that way."

"Oh, don't start with the poor Simon routine—"

"It's not a routine!" He slammed his hand down onto the table. The kerosene lamp teetered, and he grabbed the chimney to steady it, hissing in pain when the glass burned his hand. "Fuck!"

Ellen picked the lamp up and placed it on the kitchen counter, out of harm's way. She took his hand, examined the welts across his fingers and dropped a kiss on his palm. "Poor baby," she whispered.

He pulled his hand away. "It's not a routine," he repeated.

"I felt it, as soon as I came here. Like . . . like something is lying in wait for me. I tried to ignore it but the harder I try, the worse things get. Whatever I touch gets trashed. And now there are bodies lying around."

"But what do Bebop and Scotty being killed have to do with you?"

"I don't know! It doesn't matter! I can't figure how it could have anything to do with me. I barely knew those guys. I might not have recognized them if I met them on the street, unless they were wearing nylons over their heads. But that's not the point. They're dead, El. Every day it's a new disaster, and the disasters are getting worse. The only way to make it stop is to haul ass out of here!"

"Simon, none of this is your fault!" she yelled.

"Yeah?" he snarled. "Look at your house, El. Your fancy window. Thousands of dollars of damage to your home. Look at your legs. The state of your business. Your hotel guests are gone. Your truck is trashed and sunk in the mud. What more will it take to convince you?"

"I don't regret one single thing," she said stubbornly. "It would be worth it to be with you, even if that was the price I had to pay. But it's not. It doesn't work that way. You're being ridiculous."

He looked around the house, his face tense. "I've been trying to convince myself that it's just a puzzle that I could solve if I tried hard enough," he said. "If I could figure out why Gus killed himself, or what the fuck that e-mail was about. Anything at all that might give me a handle on why this place is so fucking poisonous to me. But I can't. I've been through this place with a fine-tooth comb, El, and I can't find a goddamn thing!"

She hesitated. "And since you can't find anything, that means you think that you're, ah, cursed, or something?"

He turned his face away. "I'm embarrassed to think of it in those terms, but once you get beaten over the head one too many times . . ."

She grabbed his hand. "But you're forgetting all the good

things that you do. You're a catalyst, Simon. Look what you did for Missy. She's transformed. She defended me like a tiger tonight. She dumped a half-gallon of ice cream all over Brad Mitchell's shoes."

He laughed sourly. "Great. So now I'm the catalyst for Missy getting in touch with her aggressive urges. It starts with her hurling ice cream, and you think it's so cute, like a kitten hissing. But where does it end? Before you know it, she'll be opening fire with an M-16."

"Oh, shut up!" she spat. "You're so quick to see the hidden meanings in things when it suits your mystical loner fantasy bullshit. But if it doesn't, you're blind and deaf and dumb as a rock!"

"It's not my fantasy that doesn't fit with reality." He pointed his finger at her. "It's yours, El. Your happily-ever-after fantasy."

She stiffened. "So you think that's all my love is? A fantasy?"

Simon let his hand drop. "Yes," he said. "That's what I think."

She reached out to him. "That's not true, and you know it."

He stepped back, eluding her embrace. "Watch a self-fulfilling prophecy fulfill itself before your eyes. I am leaving. Now, before anything else explodes. I do not love you. Read my lips. Go away."

She wound her arms around his neck. "I don't believe you."

He wrenched her hands down. "Goddamn it, El." His voice vibrated with strain. "Do not force me to be ugly with you."

"You told me that you loved me," she said. "Last night, you—"

"Grow up." He shoved her back against the table. "Sure I did. Men say that sometimes to the woman that they're fucking."

She refused to flinch. She wrenched the buttons of his

shirt open and shoved it off his shoulders. "Then . . . then fuck me again, Simon," said. "Because I want to hear you say it again."

He lifted her up onto the table and shoved her legs wide. "I'll fuck you again if you want me to. But that's all it'll be. That's all it ever was."

She wound her arm around his neck and kissed his chest. "You've compromised yourself too much already, my love. You can't fool me now. You just look silly when you try. All that bluster. Posturing idiot."

He shoved her down onto her back on the kitchen table. She clasped the hand that held her down and twisted around to kiss it. "I want you so much."

"Oh, yeah?" He shoved her skirt up and ran his hands down the inside of her thighs. "You're doing it again, El. Your angel act. Sweet and selfless. Sacrificing yourself on the altar of my lust."

She writhed sensuously in his hard grip. "I love the altar of your lust, Simon Riley. I want to drape a nice quilt over it, toss on some pillows and make it into my permanent bed."

He doubled over in a spasm of bitter laughter. "Oh, man. Shoved right into my own trap," he muttered. "You're nuts, El."

"For you, yes," she say. "Always have been."

He lifted his head and hooked his finger into the bow of the ivory satin that laced the corset together. "This thing should be illegal. Where the hell did it come from?"

"Cora," she admitted. "She told me I should dress, ah . . . unapologetically was the exact term that she used."

"I should have known." He slid his finger into her cleavage. "This isn't unapologetic. This is shameless, in-your-face provocation."

"Shameless is right," she said. "I'm not the least bit ashamed about anything I've done. Not since you got here, anyway."

He pulled the bow loose, and watched with intense fascination as the pressure of her breasts against the tightly pulled fabric unraveled the slippery satin ribbon lacing. "When I saw you wearing this thing, I thought you were trying to punish me."

"What? I wasn't!" she sputtered. "I—"

"Showing your body to the whole world, to make me jealous and crazy. To provoke me into doing something stupid. Well, you won. I'm about to do something real stupid, babe. Both of us are."

"I can hardly wait. And yes, I wanted to excite you, if that's what you mean by provoking you."

He wrenched the laces down to expose her heaving breasts, framed by a tangle of ribbons and lace. "Look at you. You're killing me."

"You're worse," she flung back. "You always tease me, Simon, but I'm not teasing you. I'm offering you everything. So take it. Take me."

He closed his eyes, and for a moment, his face was so tight with misery, she felt almost guilty for torturing him.

She thought of the U-Haul outside and her resolve hardened. Everything hung on this. She could not let him run from her tonight.

She slid her hand between her parted legs, between the folds of her labia, caressing and opening herself for him. "I'm already wet," she said. "I'm ready for you right now. I'm aching for you."

"Fuck it." He wrenched the buttons of his jeans open and freed his erection. "Don't blame me if this doesn't fit your fantasies."

She reached for him. "I don't blame you. I never have."

He shoved her back down. "Shut up, El. Not another word."

He fitted himself against her, grabbed her dusty feet and braced them against his chest. He drove himself inside her.

She came instantly, a match to gunpowder. She arched off the table, crying out. Simon held on to her, staring into her face while the jolts of pleasure racked her. Then he began to move.

She clutched his upper arms to brace herself. She'd never thought, in all their loveplay, of how immensely strong he was, but she felt it now, in the grip of his big hands, the relentless driving of his hips against hers. The table rattled and shook with the force of his passion.

She loved it. He couldn't help but please her. She knew in every cell of her body that he loved her, no matter what he said. She pulled him down to cover her. He scooped her up against him, still joined.

He carried her over to the wall. He pinned her there with his body, driving into her from below, and she liked that even better. That way she could wrap her arms around his neck, press her face against his hair, feel his ragged breath against her throat. She abandoned herself to his power with total trust. It melted and yielded and transformed her.

He felt it too. He fought it, in vain. She felt his desperate resistance in the steely tension of his body, but he was as helpless as she to resist the magic, the melding, the sweetness that blended them into one desperate agony of need.

Both of them cried out in terror and wonder as the storm broke.

He hid his face against her throat, waiting for the echoes of their violent mutual orgasm to subside. Ellen nuzzled the top of his head and hugged him with all the strength she had left in her body.

He pulled himself slowly out of her body, and set her on her feet. "I'm still hard." His voice was unsteady. "I can't believe I can come like that, and still be hard. It's insane. I could take you again right now."

Her knees buckled. She grabbed him to steady herself. "I would love it if you did."

He plucked her hand off his shoulder and pushed her back against the wall. "You haven't proved anything with this. Just that I love nailing you, and I'll do it at any opportunity. Big surprise."

His semen trickled down her shaking thighs. She pressed

them together. "I know the truth about you," she said. "There's nothing you could say that would convince me that you don't care for me."

"Nothing I can say," he repeated. "How about what I do?" He turned her around and bent her over the table facedown. He slid one arm around her waist. His penis prodded her, and thrust deep inside.

"What if I do this?" he said. "And when I'm done, I'll button up my pants, get into that U-Haul, and go. Does that convince you? What do you say, babe? One more for the road?"

That was it. She recoiled from the dark cruelty inside him that lashed out when he was cornered. She couldn't take any more.

"No," she said. "Stop. I cannot stand you when you are like this."

He withdrew himself. She stood up, smoothed her skirt down. When she dared to turn around, he was buttoning his jeans over his straining erection. He was careful not to look her in the eye. They stood in the flickering shadows until the silence became unbearable.

"Tell your mother she can buy the house," he said. "I'm through with this place. Contact Plimpton's firm, I guess. I'll have them handle it. Assuming I don't become a fugitive from justice."

She opened her mouth, but Simon held up his hands and took a step back. "No. Don't, El. Leave it like this. Don't make it worse."

"How could it possibly be worse?" she asked.

He leaned over the counter and blew out the lamp. Darkness fell onto them, heavy and smothering. "You don't want to know," he said.

He walked out the screen door. It slammed shut behind him, leaving her alone in the dark. She followed him out onto the porch and picked her way down the sagging steps.

Simon closed and latched the U-Haul's doors. He got into the cab, started up the truck, and drove away.

Ellen watched the red taillights recede down the winding driveway, pause at the road and turn towards the highway. Over the rise, around the hillside, and the lights disappeared.

She stumbled over rocks and roots, thistles and brambles as she picked her way up the hillside towards home. She wrenched her tangled hair free of the lilac bushes and staggered across the smooth lawn.

The porch light snapped on. She blinked until her eyes adjusted enough to make out her mother standing in the door.

"Mercy. It's about time you—good God! What did he do to you?"

Ellen tried to hold the two sides of Cora's tiny corset together over her bare breasts. "Nothing I didn't beg him for."

Lionel poked his head out from behind her mother. He jerked it back in just as quickly. "Sweet holy Jesus," he gasped. "Is that young man of yours being a dirty dog? I'll just go right down there and—"

"No." Ellen abandoned the effort to hold the top together, and wrapped her arms across her breasts as she pushed past them. "Don't bother. He's gone, and he's not coming back." She started up the stairs. "Oh, yeah. You can buy his house if you want it, Mother."

"Ah . . . honey? Are you OK?"

Ellen looked down at her mother's and Lionel's anxious faces. This was her cue to smile and say something brave and reassuring.

She shook her head, and continued up the stairs.

Chapter

23

The highway raced beneath the U-Haul's wheels, the headlights illuminating just a small pool of the tumble-weed desert. One small chunk, as much reality as he could take at one time. Morning was supposed to be near, but what sullen light managed to sift through the clouds only served to show how dark and menacing they were.

He had to stop for a while. He was starting to hallucinate. Some bad coffee would make the cramping agony in his belly complete. Maybe the pain would help keep him awake.

He pulled off at a truck stop and stumbled into the restaurant. He sat down at the counter, and an older woman with large jowls and a brassy bouffant poured him some coffee. Her name tag read DARLA.

Darla looked him over with sympathetic concern. "Jeez, honey, you look wasted. You spend the night in jail or something?"

Simon sipped his coffee. "Not yet," he muttered. "Maybe later."

"On the run from the cops? Don't worry, I never tell. I seen all types come through here."

Simon rubbed his face. "I wish it were that simple."

Darla clucked her tongue. "The Feds?"

He shook his head. "A woman."

Darla's face softened. "Aw, honey. Too bad we don't have booze in this joint. How about some dessert? Sometimes sugar helps."

"What have you got?"

"Oh, we got all kinds of pie," she told him. "Huckleberry and—"

"Christ, no." Simon covered his face with his hand. "No pie."

Darla left him be. He nursed the coffee and watched the short-order cook break eggs, throw them on the griddle. The sizzling was horribly loud, and the smell of the food made him nauseous. Flames leaped under a grill full of burgers, bringing his dream back to mind. El lying naked on the blackened ground. The circle of fire closing in.

The sickening dread in his belly wasn't getting any better with distance. If anything, it was worse.

Darla had been making the rounds of the restaurant with her coffeepot. She paused behind his shoulder, refilled his cup, and gave his ass a friendly, lingering pat. "You know, we got pay showers back there for the truckers, honey. You could use a wash," Darla advised. "Might make you feel better. And you look like you'd clean up real nice."

"Thanks." He gulped the rest of the coffee, left a couple of bucks on the counter and did the zombie shuffle out to the truck.

He stared at the big, unwieldy truck with unfriendly eyes. He missed traveling on the motorcycle. The constant roar and pressure of the wind against his body blew memories and feelings away.

Alone in the quiet cab of a truck, they jostled around him and clamored for attention every goddamn second.

Maybe he should get the bike out of the back and just leave the truck behind. He didn't really need that stuff. He had no place to set up the darkroom equipment, no one to show the albums to. He would just have to shove all the stuff into a rental storage unit somewhere and then remember to pay the bill. What was the point?

Maybe dumping it would be the perfect gesture. Let go. Move on. Just take off like a bird.

He would decide after he closed his eyes for a few minutes. He climbed into the cab, rolled the window down for air and leaned his head back. The coffee burned in his belly, but did not brace him.

A brilliant flash of lightning startled his eyes into opening.

His mother was standing in the truck stop parking lot, in front of the U-Haul. Young and beautiful, as she was in his blurry memories, as she'd been in Gus's photos. Her long dark hair whipped in the rising storm wind. She held something cupped in her graceful hands. She held it up for him to see. It was his clay homing pigeon sculpture.

As he watched, it rippled and stretched and grew, became the eagle statue. She lifted it effortlessly, launched it. It took off in an explosion of flapping wings and bolted westward, into a blazing sunset.

Her dark eyes were solemn. *"Hurry."* Her lips formed the word, and he heard her low, musical voice inside his head. *"Go."*

He knew what would happen next, and he could hardly bear to watch it. She was turning into a stone statue, eternally lost to him. He was spinning through space, becoming smaller, and she was growing bigger, as big as the whole earth. He soared into the faint glint in her eye but it wasn't a glint, it was a fire, it was the monster—

Getting bigger, closer. He hurtled towards the blackened earth and saw El, curled up naked. Sleeping in its black maw while the jaws of fire closed around her.

A deafening crash of thunder jerked him awake. Lightning flashed. In that split second of brilliance, Gus stood outside the truck, his beard blowing behind him. His eyes burned with terrible urgency.

Then he was gone.

Simon's heart thudded. Thunder cracked the skies open. Lightning flashed again. This time Simon kept his eyes squeezed shut. If Gus was still out there, he didn't want to see him.

A heavy drop of rain plopped down onto the windshield, then another, then a huge, rustling, torrential roar, slashing sideways into the window and bringing a wave of humid wind, heavy with the sweet smell of hot dust turning into mud. He rolled up the window.

Hurry. Go.

The bird. The homing pigeon. Home. His mother, becoming a statue covered with lichen. The eagle statue, coming to life, flying west into the blazing sunset. The circle of fire, closing in on El.

yr mother guards proof

Oh, God. Of course. How stupid. Blind, deaf and dumb as a rock, just like El had said. He'd been begging for help and guidance, and they'd been trying so hard to give it to him. Flogging him over the head with their dreams, but he'd been so wound up in his own self-pity and raging hormones, he hadn't been able to see it. Of *course.*

He started the engine and slewed the truck around till it pointed homeward. He hit the wet asphalt so fast he started fishtailing.

Her sheets were washed and bleached, her room scoured, but the post-Simon purification ritual wasn't making Ellen feel any better.

She heard a car pull up, and peered over the sheets she was hanging on the line. Her heart sank when she saw the Porsche. Oh, Lord. A run-in with Brad was all she needed to make her misery complete. She braced herself to be dignified, no matter what.

Brad got out of his car and started up the path towards her. She forced herself to nod politely. He nodded politely back. So far, so good.

She grabbed a pillowcase out of the basket. "Hello, Brad."

"Uh, hi." Brad had none of his usual arrogant self-posses-sion. He looked like he was psyching himself up to do some-thing that scared him. He looked up at the stained-glass window. "So that's what happened the other night?"

She nodded.

"Can you fix it?"

"I found the original artist's sketches that were sent to my grandfather back in the '30s, fortunately," she said. "And I've already gotten in touch with a stained-glass artist in Olympia who's going to come down and take a look. I'll just have him make us the closest match he can of the same de-sign."

"Oh. Well. That's good, then."

"Yes, I'll be relieved once it's replaced." She noticed that he was staring down at her legs. "What is it?"

He gestured towards her bruises, which had blossomed into a brilliant rainbow of colors. "That looks painful."

"They're much better," she assured him. "Hardly hurt at all."

Seconds ticked by. She wanted to stamp her feet with im-patience. "Brad, what is it?" she demanded. "You're acting strange."

"I'm sorry I was a dickhead to you." The words burst out of him.

The pillowcase she was holding plopped onto the grass.

Brad picked it up and offered it to her. "I'm not so great at apologizing. But I know I said stuff to you that I shouldn't have said."

She stared at him, flabbergasted. "I . . . uh—"

"Don't worry. I know it's over between us," he said hastily. "I'm not trying to patch things up or anything like that. I know that you want Simon. I just wanted to . . . you know. I'm sorry." He draped the pillowcase over the clothesline. "Where is Simon, by the way?"

She looked down. "Gone. Last night. You missed him."

"Ah. Well, if you should hear from him—"

"I won't," she said. "Believe me, I won't."

There was an awkward pause. "Uh, OK. But if you should, just tell him I only pounded him in high school because I thought he was poaching on Cora. Which he wasn't. And I'm sorry."

"Oh. OK." She grabbed another pillowcase out of the basket.

"And for the stable fire, too," he said. "I wish I could tell him—"

"What about the stable fire?"

"You mean you haven't heard?" Brad looked incredulous.

"I was distracted last night," she said. "There was a lot going on."

"My dad was the one who set that fire at the stables," Brad said gruffly. "He did it himself. I have no idea why."

"Oh, my God."

"It all came out last night. No one's seen him since. No great loss. I don't have much of a desire to see him anyway."

"I'm so sorry, Brad."

His shrug was a hard, angry gesture. "This may sound weird, but I'm not that surprised. I never . . . I tried so hard to convince myself that there was something in there. That he had real, normal feelings hidden away somewhere. Finally, I stopped trying. It was easier."

"I'm sorry," she said again. "That's just so awful."

Brad stuck his hands in the pockets of his khaki pants and stared down at his shoes. "Is Missy around?"

Here was another puzzle. "Why?" she demanded.

He looked away. "Just wanted to have a word with her."

Ellen yelled towards the kitchen. "Missy? Come on out here!"

Missy emerged onto the back porch, wiping her hands on her apron. She saw Brad and her eyes widened. Ellen beckoned.

She approached, after a long, suspicious pause.

"I'm sorry I was rude to you," Brad blurted out.

Missy's mouth shut and tightened. "Don't ever do it again."

Brad's mouth twitched. "Hell, no. I wouldn't dare." He took a step back, hands twitching in his pockets. "Uh, anyhow. Thank God, that's done. I'm gone. Let me know if you need help with anything."

"OK, I will. Thanks," she said faintly.

They watched him run down the sloping lawn. He waved, and got into his car and drove away. Ellen and Missy looked at each other.

"Did a flock of pigs just go by on roller skates?" Ellen asked.

Missy burst out laughing. Ellen tried not to follow suit. The minute she let go of her laugh muscles, she'd let go of her cry muscles too, since they were the same muscles.

Sure enough. It took about a half a second to reach total meltdown. Missy threw her arms around Ellen and promptly burst into tears to keep Ellen company, helpful sweetheart that she was.

Cora had psyched herself up to play it super-cool, no matter what happened, but when the Porsche pulled up outside the Wash-n-Shop, all the boxes of detergent she was loading into the coin-op machine slid right out of her hands and tumbled to the floor.

Of course, she was still down on the floor picking them up, crouching carefully so as not to flash her underwear at anybody from under her pink minidress. She pretended not to notice him. His Ferragamo loafers stopped inches from her bare knees.

She rose up in one slow, sinuous movement and gave him her best femme fatale smile. "Hey, Brad. What's up?"

"I did it."

She finished shoving the boxes into the machine, shut it, locked it and reset it before she dared reply. "Exactly what was it that you did?"

"Apologized. To all three of them. Or, well, Simon technically wasn't there, but I told Ellen to tell him I was sorry if she heard from him." He gazed at her expectantly. "That should count."

She raised her eyebrows. "So? Good for you, Brad. You're making progress." She marched over to the big washers and started dragging an armful of wet sheets out of the washer and into the cart. She turned around to grab another armful, and found their bodies almost touching.

"What?" she snapped. "What do you want from me?"

"I did what you told me to do," Brad said.

She glared up at him. "What do you want, a medal? You want to know if you've earned enough humanity points to fuck me yet? Dream on, buddy. I'm real glad for you, that you're acting better, but I'm still mad. So don't get any ideas." She shoved the cart over to the dryer.

He followed her. "You said you'd have sex with me if we were married."

She went motionless, up to her elbows in wet sheets. "I did not say that. I said I would *not* have sex with you if we *weren't* married."

"What's the difference?"

She shoved the sheets into the dryer. "The difference is characterized by my level of choice and control in the situation," she said. "Which is to say, complete and absolute."

"Will you at least concede that my chances of having sex with you rise sharply if we're married?" he demanded.

She shook her head, openmouthed. "Am I having a nightmare? Or did I just hear you make the most crass, rude, unclassy wedding proposal in all of human history? Congratulations, Brad. You never cease to amaze me."

He looked irritated and defensive. "That wasn't the official proposal. I'm just sussing you out. Trying to get the rules straight."

"Rules? This is not a game of tennis! Think it through, for God's sake! What are your hoity-toity parents going to—"

"I could give a flying fuck."

She paused, startled. "You're not using me to punish them, are you?"

"Absolutely not. I'm not factoring them at all. They lied to me. They can both go to hell. I don't want to see either one of them."

"Oh. Well, that might be tough, considering that you live—"

"I do not live there," he said. "I moved out last night. I checked into the Days Inn out on Sammett. Until I find another place."

"Uh-oh." She yanked the rolling basket towards her, and he leaped back to keep from getting swiped. "What is that cheesy grin about? Don't think for one second that I would invite you to stay with me, bozo. This is not a done deal. By no means."

"It's not?" He sounded faintly hurt.

She gave him a narrow look. "You are at the foot of a very high mountain, buddy. This is going to be a long, tough, expensive courtship with no guarantees. I have no idea what I'll decide in the end. Yes? No? Sex? No sex? It all depends on my mood."

"You can be such a bitch, Cor." His tone was admiring.

"Call me a bitch again and I'll knock out all your teeth."

He pushed her back against the dryer. "I'd like to see you try it."

"Let me get my baseball bat, and I'll show you," she suggested.

The heat rose as they stared at each other, prickly and wild and strange. Brad let out a shaky, ragged breath. "OK, so what'll it take?"

"What are you talking about?" she snapped.

"You said expensive courtship," Brad said. "Good thing I've got money to spend. What do I have to buy?"

She gave his chest a violent shove. "It's really a shame that sensitivity, imagination and good taste cannot be bought!"

He looked chastened. "Uh . . . flowers?"

"Oh!" She threw her hands up. "Look, everyone! A flash of genius!"

"Expensive flowers?" he ventured. "Orchids?"

She sighed. "Get out of here, Brad. I'm trying to work."

"Chocolates?"

"Out!" she yelled. "Get lost!" She spun him around and shoved his broad back in the direction of the door. Wow, he must work out hard to get lats like that. Nice. She gave him another hard shove, just so she could touch them again.

"Jewelry?" Brad said, in a long-suffering voice.

Cora lifted her hands off his tempting lats. "Ah, that reminds me, Brad. Don't even think about palming Ellen's engagement ring off on me. That would be the final nail in your coffin. Eeeuw."

"That was a very expensive ring!" he protested.

"Butt-ugly," she said. "Out, Brad."

He turned back at the door. "One more question, Cor."

She rolled her eyes. "Make it quick."

"I know you said no sex till we're married—"

"I meant every word of it," she assured him.

"Does that cover cunnilingus, too?"

Cora looked around the laundromat. Candy Hanks was doubled over, trying not to laugh. Joanna Pilsner dragged her four-year-old girl out the door and slammed it. The bell tinkled angrily.

"I want to start practicing," Brad said. "I mean to be the best you've ever had by our wedding night. But I don't feel like practicing on anybody but you—"

"You better not, if you want to keep the family jewels intact."

"So that leaves me with a real dilemma," Brad concluded.

Unthinkable. She, Cora, the scarlet woman of LaRue, the queen of the blow job, she of the thumb permanently attached to her nose, was blushing. "Keep your voice down," she hissed. "Get your ass in here."

She beckoned him into her office nook, fully intending to scold him. As soon as he wedged himself into the tiny space, he overwhelmed her. He blocked out the light, took up all the air. He generated so much heat, she started to sweat. She was dizzy with his piney scent.

He leaned down, so that his mouth was inches from her ear. "I know you're mad, Cor," he said. "I know I was a dick, and I want to redeem myself. So this is my scheme. Every evening, we go someplace private for a couple of hours, and you let me be your slave boy. Someplace with a soft couch where you can recline, and I'll pull your panties off and lick away at that beautiful bare naked pussy until you come, and come and come. That's my fantasy."

"Whoa. Back off, buddy," she whispered. "Slow down."

"Oh, sure. I'll be real slow," he promised. "I'll do it however you want. I've got a long, strong tongue. I've got a long, strong everything."

"I know exactly what you've got," she said. "Don't boast."

Somehow the sneaky bastard had insinuated himself against her so that she was leaning backwards over her desk and he was standing between her legs. "So?" he said. "You up for it?"

Play it cool, she reminded herself. "I'll make you suffer the tortures of the damned," she said. "I'm not going to break down and say, oh, what the hell, let's just have sex. Forget it. No way."

"I would expect nothing less of you," Brad said.

"Slave boy, huh?" The possibilities began to unfold. "Does that mean you'll massage me with scented oils? Mix my drinks? Paint my toenails? Alphebetize my CD's? Organize my underwear drawer?"

His eyes gleamed. "What have you got in that underwear drawer?"

She stretched up on her tiptoes so that now it was her breath tickling his ear. "Wouldn't you love to know, big boy?" she crooned. "If you want to look inside, I'll make you wash out all my lace-trimmed nylon thigh-high stockings first. And then you have to hang them out to dry on the clothesline outside while the neighbors are watching."

"Whoa," he breathed. "Now you're getting kinky."

"If it's too much, just run away, Brad. Nobody's stopping you. But I can just see you in my kitchen. Stark naked. Fully erect. Wearing nothing but a pair of yellow rubber gloves. Running a soapy sponge mop over and over my linoleum . . . until it beams."

He vibrated with suppressed laughter. "Oh, shit. I'm in trouble. Will it get you over being mad?"

She took his earlobe between her teeth and nipped it hard enough to make him gasp. "We'll just have to wait and see."

"Ouch. You're as hard as nails," he complained.

"You better be, too, when the time comes."

A grin split his handsome face. "Count on it. But don't think you're getting any of that before our wedding night. Don't even bother begging and pleading. No matter how hard it gets."

She glanced down at the bulge in his jeans and ran her forefinger along the entire turgid length of him. "Something tells me that I'm not the one who's going to be begging and pleading."

"We'll just have to wait and see, won't we?" Brad said.

They stared at each other, spellbound. The sexual energy vibrating between them was heavy, palpable. As thick as honey.

"Wow," he murmured. "You better marry me quick."

"Get to work, then," she said. "Now. Go on. Convince me."

He slid his arms around her and kissed her.

She was so switched on. So lit up. The power of her feelings thrummed through her body, and he met her power with his own. All the hunger, the longing, the angry passion, the hopeless waiting.

It locked together and suddenly became something bright and startling and brand new. He pressed his big body against hers, the bulge of his cock pressing where she was most sensitive, his warm lips moving over hers, coaxing for tenderness, pleading for forgiveness. For the passion that flared up, wild and hot and wonderful.

She couldn't help but give it to him. She couldn't deny how she felt. When he pulled away, she felt so bereft, she wanted to drag him back. "Just where the hell do you think you're going, buddy?"

"The florist," he said. "And the candy shop. Milk chocolate or dark?"

"Dark," she said breathlessly. "Rum and champagne truffles."

"Any particular color preference on the orchids?"

"Pink," she said.

"Speaking of which, I like that outfit. You look good today, Cor."

She smoothed her rumpled pink dress down over her body. "Uh, Brad? What about . . . didn't you want to go into politics? It's true, what I said about me not being a good bet for a politician's—"

"I have no idea if that is what I want," he said. "The only thing in the whole world that I'm absolutely sure that I want is you."

The expression on his face struck her speechless. She, Lush Lips, who was always ready with a smart comeback. He couldn't control the grin on his face. He didn't look smug, or triumphant, or superior.

He just looked happy.

Before she knew it, she was laughing, leaking and mopping her eyes. Good thing she'd worn waterproof mascara, in case anything dramatic happened.

"Preferences in gems?" His voice was businesslike. "I know you hate diamonds. How do you feel about rubies, emeralds, sapphires?"

"Three words, Brad," she said. "Bold. Colorful. Unique."

He grinned at her. "Just like you."

Chapter

24

Ellen had been dreading twilight. She could think of nothing else that needed doing. It didn't help that her bedroom window looked out over Gus's house. Her eyes kept straying down that way, trying to pick out the expanse of roof among the tossing sea of trees.

Maybe she should go sleep in one of the other rooms, with the view of the mountain. There were four vacant bedrooms to choose from. Now there was a worthy thing to feel depressed about. Four vacant rooms. Hundreds of dollars of lost revenue, night after night.

She tried to work up a fit of proper anxiety about it, but finally she just had to admit to herself that she didn't give a damn. Compared to how she felt about Simon, it seemed transient and silly. And—

She saw something strange and spun around. It must have been some odd reflection, or—

No. There it was again. A flicker of light from the upstairs room of Gus's house, the one that used to be Simon's bedroom. A muted yellow glow. Shadows dancing on the walls. Someone was walking around up there with the kerosene lamp.

Her heart pounded. She didn't dare let herself hope—no.

Cancel the thought before it even formed. But if it wasn't Simon, then she should report an intruder to the police immediately.

But then again, if by some crazy miracle it was Simon, the police would be the very last people he would want to chat with.

The only solution was to take a closer look and see what vehicle was parked outside. That would inform her next course of action.

She congratulated herself for being so sensible as she tugged on her sandals, but she sneaked down the stairs on the non-creaking side. She didn't want to enter into a debate with her mother or Lionel about the dubious wisdom of investigating an intruder to Gus's house.

She stepped out the kitchen door and let the screen door click ever so delicately into its frame. She darted across the lawn, staying in the shadows of the trees like a fugitive, and pushed through the lilac bushes. Her heart raced so fast, she felt dizzy.

There was just enough light left to make her way through Gus's meadow. She circled around until she could see what was parked in the gloom beneath the big pine.

A big black and silver BMW motorcycle. Oh, God. Frantic joy bore her up and carried her on a floating cloud the rest of the way to the house. She bounded over the sagging porch and pushed through the creaking screen door into the dark kitchen.

"Simon? Are you up there?" she called out.

No answer. A flash of sickening doubt slowed her down. Maybe he didn't want to see her at all, and he was silently cursing his luck up there, hoping she would just disappear.

She shoved the thought away. If he'd worked up the nerve to come back here, then he had to deal with her. That was all there was to it. She pushed her way through almost pitch blackness with her hand on the wall, navigating by feel. "Simon? Please answer me."

Then she noticed the smell. Heavy, sharp fumes that made

her eyes water and her stomach roll. Kerosene. Simon must have spilled some of it on the stairs, where the smell was strongest.

She climbed slowly up the stairs. The blaze of joy that had borne her along had drained completely away. Maybe the bedroom door was closed, and that was why he hadn't heard—

No. As she climbed the stairs, she saw shadows dancing on the ceiling. That bedroom door was open.

It came over her all at once. A wave of fear and dread that swelled up underneath her, deep and cold. Crawling panic froze her into place.

The motorcycle had fooled her. This was not Simon. She knew the quality of the energy that radiated from Simon.

This sickening, toxic wave of fear was something utterly different.

She exerted a huge effort of will over her paralyzed muscles, and stepped silently back down onto the tip of her toe. If she could just creep back the way she came, sneak out the door and—

"Hello there, Ellen. What a nice surprise."

Ray Mitchell appeared at the head of the stairs. His clothing looked rumpled and stained. He held a kerosene lantern in one hand. Points of reflected fire danced in the lenses of his bifocals. He held a pistol in his other hand, pointed at her.

"Don't move, honey." He sounded jovial. "Or I'll kill you."

Simon parked on the side of the road at the quickest short-cut down to the patch of woods where his mother's sculpture garden was located. He loaded the batteries he'd just bought into his flashlight and slid down the gravel shoulder. He vaulted over the barbed-wire fence and took off through the woods at a pace he knew was dangerous in the dark. Slower wasn't an option. This was the only setting his nerves had.

He skidded to a stop in the pine grove and flicked on the

flashlight. The dark grew denser and more unfriendly for being pushed away. He swept the light around until he found the eagle sculpture and knelt beside it. His hands shook so violently, he almost laughed.

Take it easy. He was only trying to solve the riddle of his whole existence. Only trying to save what little sanity he might have left.

He took the heavy ceramic object in both hands and dislodged it from where it was embedded in loam. He laid it gently on the ground and shone the flashlight into the cavity.

The light gleamed on a fold of clear plastic. He drew it out. A Ziploc bag, full of photographs. Negatives. A sheet of paper. He pulled them out, and leafed through the photos.

They were in sequence, a black-and-white filmstrip from hell. Some were out of focus, but the story they told was stark and clear.

A young man in combat gear, dragging a screaming Vietnamese girl along the ground by the armpits. The same man standing over the girl and an older man, pouring liquid from a white plastic container over the two of them. The girl and the old man's eyes were wide with terror.

In the last photo, the two figures on the ground were both in flames, and the face of the uniformed man was crystal clear. His eyes were alight with ecstasy as he watched his victims burn.

Simon dropped the photos back into the envelope and looked at the letter, in Gus's bold, familiar script.

Dear Simon,

If you have found this, I am dead. The man in the photos, Ray Mitchell, is my killer. He killed your mother, too. He loves to kill. They called me crazy, so no one would believe me. Maybe with these photos, they will believe you.

Be careful. I wish we could have seen each other again.

Your affectionate uncle,
Augustus Patrick Riley

Simon's vision went black. The note fell to the ground. He sank down to retrieve it, keeping his head down until the head rush passed.

He rose to his feet and shoved it all back into the plastic envelope. His legs felt rubbery, and his skull pounded. A heavy hammer beat on it with each throb of his heart. There was a real monster on the prowl, not a phantasm from his nightmares, and he had left El alone with it.

As soon as he turned his body towards El, his legs picked up speed, weaving around obstacles he barely saw, leaping over ditches and landing like a cat. He reached the path that led to Gus's house, and saw the light in the window.

A gunshot. Glass exploded out of the upstairs window.

A shriek of terror. *El.*

He took off like a lightning bolt.

Ellen stared into the fire flickering in Ray's eyes. She thought of that time she'd stepped too close to a rattler. She's seen it rise, tail buzzing, and pull back to strike—until Simon had let fly with his knife.

This was worse. The snake had been an innocent wild creature just trying to survive. Her misstep had been its bad luck far more than it had been hers. Ray Mitchell was a monster, corrupt and festering.

And there was no one to save her this time.

"Come on up the stairs, Ellen. Since you're here, we might as well have a talk, just to clear the air. I'd be happy for some company."

She had always privately made fun of the masks Ray wore. Now they were fragmented. Bits of one and then another floated across his face, but the burning madness in his eyes was constant. She finally understood why he showed only a public persona.

His private one was totally insane.

"Actually, Ray, I only came over because I thought you

were Simon," she said desperately. "So I'll just, ah, be on my way—"

"Do . . . not . . . move."

She stopped. There was death in his voice.

"You thought I was Simon?" he asked. "That's pathetic. I saw you two come back here last night. I saw you go into this house and then come out half naked. You let him have his way with you, didn't you?" Ray clucked his tongue. "Letting him take advantage of you like that. It makes me sad. Angry, too. Men are such pigs sometimes."

His voice was admonishing, fatherly. It made the wild look in his eyes that much more horribly surreal.

"What are you doing here, Ray?" she asked.

"Cleaning up," he said. "Settling accounts. Come on up, Ellen. I would never have involved you in this if you hadn't insisted. You would have been fine if you'd just managed to stay away from Riley."

"You can't do this."

"Come on, honey. One foot after the other. It's your own fault for misbehaving. You've been very bad, and now you have to pay. Don't make me shoot you, now. That's not how I want this to go."

She started slowly up the stairs. "You can't get away with this."

"I certainly have so far." His jolly laugh was a funhouse parody of mirth. "I've gotten away with it all my life. I like fire, you see. I started playing with it when I was little. Small animals, at first. My secret childhood hobby. Ever hear of lighting cats?"

She cringed. "Please don't tell me."

"It's just a matter of dousing them with gasoline and—"

"No!" She put her hands over her ears. "Please!"

Ray giggled at her response. "Weak stomach, eh? Not me. But cats don't satisfy anymore. Once you move on, there's no going back. The horses would have been good, but Simon ruined it. He let them all out. He ruined it for me. Simon ruins everything."

She cowered against the wall of the corridor. "So that was why? You just wanted to kill . . . oh, Lord."

"The horses. I wanted to hear them screaming." He jerked his chin towards the bedroom. "Don't distract me. In you go, there's a good girl."

She edged reluctantly into the bedroom. The barrel of the gun slid through her hair and settled at the nape of her neck. It felt very cold.

The room was empty, but for a can of kerosene. The windows were shut. The floor was splashed with the foul-smelling stuff.

Ray circled slowly around her. "I knew, even when I was little that I would have to see how it would be to light a person someday." His tone was conversational.

"Ray, please," she whispered. "I don't want to know."

"But it's such a relief to talk about it," he said plaintively. "It's a constant stress, keeping it secret. It's just bursting out of me, Ellen."

She stared at the gun trained on her face. "So Brad and Diana . . . don't know this about you?"

His face changed. Solemnly Sincere obscured the madness on his face. For a moment, he looked just as he always had, a pleasant, mild-faced middle-aged man. "Good gracious, no." He blinked as if she'd said something shocking. "Brad and Diana are impeccable. The only way for a thing like this to work is if the conditions are right. The mask has to be perfect. Brad and Diana are perfect. I adore Brad and Diana."

"Ah." She thought of the pain and anger in Brad's face when he spoke of his father. "I see."

"Now that Gus is gone, nobody knows but you." He lifted a lock of her hair with the pistol. His face softened as he looked at her body. Her horror sharpened. "There's something so . . . intimate about that."

She shrank away from the hunger in his eyes. He stabbed the pistol barrel up under her chin. "Ah, ah, Ellen. Be good, now."

"Don't look at me like that." Her voice barely came out,

just a dry, scratchy wisp around the painful jab of cold metal. "You can't."

"Oh, but I could. No woman has ever known my secret." He thought for a moment. "At least not for very long," he amended. "Neither will you, I suppose, but I mean to enjoy it while it lasts."

She had to keep him talking, a frantic voice inside her warned. "What . . . what secrets?"

"The fire," he said dreamily. "Inside me. I knew I had to keep it secret." He held the gun up against his lips and giggled like a naughty little boy. "That's the trick, you see."

"Trick?" She would seize onto any part of his crazed meandering that might keep him talking. "What trick?"

"To creating the perfect conditions. So you can do anything you want. It was easy during the war, because there was violence and death everywhere. But even in normal civilian life, if you're clever, you can create the right conditions. If you're smart enough, powerful enough, rich enough. Careful enough. There's no end to how much you can indulge yourself. It's infinite, Ellen. Endless."

Ellen shook her head. "It's ended, Ray. Everyone knows now that it was you who burned the stables."

Annoyance flashed across his face. "Shame, about that. Scotty and Bebop's posthumous revenge. My own fault for using such idiots."

She swallowed as he stroked the gun barrel down the length of her throat. "So it was you who killed them?"

"Oh, I hardly count them," he said lightly. "No artistry there. That was just housecleaning. They had served their purpose, and it was time to eliminate them. Like I eliminated Gus."

That took her by surprise, though it shouldn't have. "Oh," she gasped. "Oh. Gus."

"Gus bothered me in Vietnam, you see." Ray's bedtime storytelling voice was back. "He was in the wrong place at the wrong time. Just like a Riley. I shot him then, but he didn't die. Stubborn bastard. But I got him in the end. Oh, I finally got him."

He started giggling. She shrank away from him. "Ray—"

"Didn't matter once we got home. No one believed him. How could they? A freak with a metal plate in his skull, ranting at a decorated officer. He ended up in the mental ward, where he belonged. Slave to his feelings." Ray shook his head. "I went to see him when he was locked up. Told him how I enjoyed burning his sister's house. With her in it." He was lost in blissful recollection for a moment, and then his eyes shifted back to her. "I think he really did start to go insane that day."

She was beyond surprise by now, but horror had no limit. "You did that?" she whispered. "Simon's mother? That was you?"

"I told Gus how it would be. That if he bothered me again, his nephew was next. And he knew by then that no one would ever believe him. Oh, yes. He learned."

Keep him talking, the voices inside her urged, but she was out of things to say. Her throat was frozen with grief and dread.

Ray caressed her jaw with the gun, a hideously sexual gesture. "I was so pleased when Brad picked you. You seemed perfect. So pretty and proper. My perfect daughter-in-law, just right for my perfect family." The gun barrel moved over her chest, and circled her nipple. "Then that Riley scum came back. Once he touched you, everything was ruined. He made you dirty. How could you let him do that?"

She could think of no reply that might not lead directly to a horrible death. She kept her eyes averted. She breathed in, and breathed out. As long as that was still happening, there was still hope.

Irrelevant thoughts raced through her mind. That if Simon hadn't come home, she might have sleepwalked right into Ray Mitchell's death machine, sickened on the hidden poison, and never even known why.

She was wide awake now. There was a chorus of loud voices inside her, screaming for her to come up with some valiant scheme to keep on living. "No one will believe that my death is a suicide or an accident," she said. "It's time to let me go. It's over, Ray."

His indulgent smile widened into a leer. "Oh, my dear, it's just beginning. I'm finally free. Masks off. No more pretending. I'm about to go on a rampage the likes of which you cannot imagine. And I'll start right here. Right now. With you." He gestured around the room with the lamp. "A dark, empty house, a beautiful young woman, a can of kerosene . . . and nothing to lose."

The twisted sexual energy he exuded was like poison gas. He used the barrel of the gun under her chin to pull her face closer to his.

She recoiled, and dove for the floor. She landed on her hands and knees. The pistol went off. The window exploded. She screamed, rolled and scrambled backwards in an awkward, crablike movement.

She stopped when he pointed the pistol at her face. He kicked her legs apart, panting, and held the kerosene lamp over her body.

"This must have been how he had you last night," he said. "There isn't even a bed in this place. Not so much as an old blanket. He had you on the floor, didn't he? You dirty, nasty girl."

Held at gunpoint was very bad, but flat on the floor at gunpoint was worse, if such things had degrees. She gathered all her nerve for one last-ditch scramble. If she could make her shaking limbs obey her.

"Mitchell. Over here." Simon's quiet voice came from the doorway.

It happened in fractions of a second. Ray's gun swung up to point at Simon. Rage powered her foot to slam up into Ray's groin. She used her other leg to kick her body around and roll away.

Ray screamed. The gun wavered and went off. Wood chips zinged. He swung it around at her again.

Thunk. The hilt of Simon's knife protruded from Ray's shoulder.

A red stain began to spread on Ray's dirty white dress shirt. His eyes went wide. The kerosene lamp fell from his hand and shattered at his feet. A soft *whump* as the flame found fuel and leaped up, crawling around the kerosene-soaked floor with hideous swiftness.

The flames crawled up Ray's pants. He screamed, dancing and beating at them with his hands.

Simon darted into the room. "Come on! Quick, quick, quick!"

She sprang to her feet, darted around the inferno and grabbed Simon's outstretched hand. He dragged her out of the room.

The screaming seemed barely human by then. They hunched over and raced down the stairs towards the kitchen. "There's a can of kerosene in there," she yelled. "It's going to blow—"

The explosion knocked them down, as if they'd both been slapped by a huge, hot hand. Ellen landed on top of him. Flames raced down the stairs. The whole house was illuminated, brighter with each second that passed. "Are you all right?" she shrieked. "Simon! Answer me!"

He stirred beneath her. "I'm great." He struggled to his feet and grabbed her hand again. "Come on, baby. Let's run like hell."

The place went up almost instantly. Fire roared out of every window. Heat blasted their backs as they ran across the meadow.

Ellen stumbled and fell. Simon followed her down.

She stared at the blazing house, and a terrible cry rose up, all the terror and rage that she had been forced to control. She put her hands to her face, stared at the hellish flames and screamed it all out.

Simon pulled her into his arms and pressed her face against his chest. "It's over," he kept saying breathlessly. "Done. All gone."

"How can that happen?" She struggled and flailed in his arms. "How can a person be so dead and foul inside? How can the universe let that happen? How is it possible?"

He held her tightly against his body. "I don't know," he said shakily. "I don't get it, either."

"I can't accept it!" she yelled. "I can't!"

"Nobody asked you to," Simon said. "Nobody cares what we think. It is as it is, and that's all."

His stark words made her think of his mother, and Ray's horrible revelation. Her body began to shake. "Simon? Your mother—"

"I know." His arms circled her. "Gus told me."

"Oh, God, I'm sorry." She threw her arms around his neck. They fell down into the grass together. "Oh, my poor baby. I'm so sorry."

His arms tightened. "I'm all right," he muttered. "Just keep hanging onto me like that, and I'll be all right."

"You couldn't pry me away. Not this time. No matter what you say. So don't even try."

"I won't," he said. "I'm done running. This is it. I'm all yours."

"You goddamn well better be. Oh, God, Simon. I can't believe it."

He pressed fervent kisses all over her face. "What can't you believe, sweetheart?"

"That I'm scolding you," she whispered. "After you just saved me."

He stroked her hair away from her brow and kissed it. "With a whole lot of help from that ferocious kick to the balls that you gave him. You are one bad-ass broad, sweetheart."

I don't feel bad-ass, I'm falling apart, she wanted to say, but it was too late, she was already lost, dissolving into a million shivering pieces. The only solid point in the universe was him.

He held her, rocking and crooning. She dimly noticed the flashing lights of the emergency vehicles when they arrived. At some point he carried her up to the house.

What followed was a series of disjointed images. Her mother looking blue around the lips, talking fast in a high-pitched voice. Lionel, pale and unusually quiet, tossing back whiskey. She couldn't make out what people were saying, but she couldn't close her eyes, either. Every time her eyelids fluttered shut, she saw flames leaping, she smelled kerosene, she heard that high, inhuman screaming.

A generous glass of whiskey softened the edges, but the only thing she dared to focus on was Simon. How beautiful he was, how brave and fine. The sound of his calm voice talking, explaining, was the thread that stitched the crazy quilt of her fragmented world together.

As she slid into unconsciousness, she clung to his image like a talisman to keep the flames away.

The waning moon was silvery bright, filling the valley with light. Simon cut the motor at the top of the Kent House driveway and coasted down the gentle curves. He parked the bike under the maple, hung the helmet on the handlebars, and pulled out the comb he'd bought at the gas station out of his pocket.

He ran it through his damp hair again, slicking it carefully back off his forehead. Damned if he'd propose marriage to the woman of his dreams with dumb-looking helmet hair plastered to his forehead.

He circled the lawn of Kent House, doing recon. Lights on in the parlor. Sure enough, Lionel and Muriel were still awake. He heard their voices floating out the French doors, and kept well out of range of the pool of light that spilled out.

A pall of acrid smoke hung heavy in the air. It was a

damn good thing that there had been so many rainstorms in the last few days, or the whole hillside might have gone up. Gus's old house was a blackened ruin, but he didn't mourn its loss. It had been steeped in misery. The fire had cleaned and purified it. The evil was gone. He was free.

He was still racked with fear and self-doubt, but it was different now. Hope bore him up, love drove him on.

He gathered up some acorns and circled the house until he stood under her window. He tossed the first one up against the glass.

One . . . two . . . three . . . maybe they'd given El too many shots of Glenlivet and she was out cold. Four . . . five . . . six . . . and this was the last one. If she didn't wake up for this, he would bite the bullet, go to the front door and deal with her mother.

He closed his eyes for a moment and called to her silently with all his mind and will. He tossed up the last acorn.

His heart leaped at the sound of the window sash being shoved up. She leaned out her window and smiled down at him. She looked tired and pinched and exquisitely beautiful. "Simon?"

"My God, you're beautiful in the moonlight," he said.

She laughed at him. "Big liar. I look like a hag from hell."

"You look gorgeous. Are you naked?"

She shoved the window open and framed herself so he could see the curves of her high breasts in the moonlight. "What are you doing down there?" she demanded. "Why aren't you up here with me?"

"I'm struggling with a dilemma," he told her. "I'm here to make a formal proposal of marriage." He dropped to his knees. "I mean to fall at your feet and beg you to be my bride, because there is nothing on earth more precious to me than you, Ellen Elizabeth Kent."

"Oh," she whispered.

"I want to do it right, see? A man can only propose to his own true love once. And I want to be swashbuckling and romantic, so at first I thought coming through the tree would be good, but then I got cold feet. I don't want to come across as sneaky. Like a thief in the night."

She giggled. "You don't. Relax. You're golden. My hero."

He pressed on. "So I decided to leave it up to you. Would you prefer if I climbed the tree and came in your window? Or would you rather I went through official channels and rang the front door?"

"At three o'clock in the morning?"

"Those guys never sleep," he said wryly. "Option number one has the advantage of simplicity. Option number two has the advantage of official sanction. I would be paying my dues, making a public statement. If you choose option two, I will grovel to your mother and let Lionel lecture me on how gentlemen behave, and only then, once I've proved my manhood, will I have earned the right to come up to your bedroom and lay my heart and fortune at your feet."

Her delighted laughter made his heart rise like a hot-air balloon. "You don't have to prove your manhood to me, Simon Riley. I know every last inch of it by heart. Get your butt up that tree, on the double. I don't want to hear one more second of your nonsense."

"Thank you, God," Simon said in heartfelt tones.

He leaped up into the tree and pulled himself from branch to branch until he swung himself into the dark opening of her window. He perched there, letting his eyes adjust to the room. The sweet odors of her soap, her candles, her lavender sheets, her flowers. Her lovely body.

He reached out blindly into the dark. She came into his arms, fitting herself against him. In that perfect sweetness, he was complete.

Ellen wrapped her arms around him. "Where the hell did you go?"

"I had to clean up," he said. "I couldn't propose to you all scuzzy and filthy. I checked into the motel on Hanson and scrubbed myself."

"That was so silly! You could have just stayed here and—"

"No, I could not," he said. "My dignity wouldn't allow it. I am now as clean as those cheap bars of hotel soap can make me, and I'm wearing the last clean clothes I have left in the world in your honor."

"I'm touched by all the trouble you've gone to, but I would prefer it if you just removed those clothes," she told him. "Immediately."

He hesitated, nuzzling her hair. "You know damn well I'll take advantage of any chance I get to be naked with you, angel, but you've had a really hellish night. Don't think you have to—"

"Please," she pleaded. "Come to bed with me. Remind me of everything in the world that's fine and beautiful and perfect. I need it."

"Oh, God, so do I," he muttered.

They came together in a sweet, clinging kiss that remained miraculously unbroken despite how they both struggled to get Simon's clothes off. He struggled with bootlaces while she attacked buttons, he wrenched open the belt buckle while she shoved his pants down.

They sprawled together across the bed, sighing at the velvet soft contact, the sweet, hot comfort of skin on skin.

He pushed her gently down against the pillows, and she lay back and let him lead. It was he who had come to her rescue, it was he who had put forth his formal pledge of love, and she sensed that he wanted to underscore his tender promises with his body.

He touched her everywhere, licking her with slow, lingering care, and covered her body with his own, letting her legs cradle him. "I love you, El," he said, between kisses. "I'll be the best husband I know how to be. I'll give you babies. I'll be a good father. I'll be true to you. I'll protect you from anything in my power. I'll stand by you through anything life throws at us. And, uh . . . not to guilt trip you, or anything, but I don't think I can make it without you."

She cupped his face. "Oh, Simon," she whispered. "My love."

"I saw it, in the fire," he confessed. "How the world would be without you. I just can't face it. I need you so much, El."

Ellen's heart was so full, she could find no words to reply.

Simon's arms tightened around her. "Uh, no pressure, but if you don't answer me quick, I'm going to totally lose it."

She had to laugh out the air in her lungs before she could draw in enough air to speak. "Yes," she gasped. "Yes, yes, yes. God, yes."

He entered her, pressing himself slowly, gently inside. She opened herself to him with perfect trust and shivering delight. No one led, no one followed. Their bodies surged and rocked in a dance of tenderness.

Lost in each other, but finally home.

Please turn the page for an exciting excerpt from
OUT OF CONTROL
Shannon McKenna's next Brava,
coming in April.

Chapter

1

San Cataldo, California

A poke in the eye, that's how it felt. That was what she got for coming home early from her conference. A brutal dose of reality.

Mag Callahan curled white-knuckled hands around the mug of lukewarm coffee that she kept forgetting to drink, and just kept staring, blank-eyed, at the Zip-Loc bag on her kitchen table that contained the evidence. She'd extracted it from her own unmade bed a half an hour before, with the help of a pair of tweezers.

Item #1: Black lace thong panties. She, Mag, favored pastels that weren't such a harsh contrast to her fair skin. Item #2: Three strands of very long, straight dark hair. She, Mag, had short, curly red hair.

Her eyes stung, and her mind reeled, fighting the unwanted information. Craig, her boyfriend, had been uncommunicative and paranoid lately, but she'd just chalked it up to that pesky Y chromosone, plus the stress of quitting his job and starting up his own studio. It never occurred to her that he would ever . . . dear God.

Her own house. Her own *bed*. That pig.

The blank shock began to tingle and go red around the edges as it transformed inevitably into fury. She'd been so nice to him. Letting him stay in her house rent-free while he bug-swept and remodeled his own place. Lending him money. Co-signing his business loans. She'd bent over backwards to be supportive, accommodating, womanly. Trying to lighten up on her standard ball-breaker routine, which consisted of scaring boyfriends into hiding with her strong opinions. She'd wanted so badly to make this work. She'd tried so hard, and this is what she got for her pains. Shafted. Again. God, it hurt.

She bumped the edge of the table as she got up, knocking over her coffee. She leaped back just in time to keep it from splattering over the cream linen outfit she'd changed into for her lunch date with Craig.

She'd come straight home from the conference this morning on purpose to pretty herself up for their date, having fooled herself into thinking that Craig was only twitchy because he was about to broach the subject of—drum roll, please—The Future of Their Relationship. She'd even gone so far as to fantasize a sappy Kodak moment; Craig, bashfully passing her a ring box over dessert. Herself, opening it. A gasp of happy awe. Violins swelling as she melted into tears. How stupid.

Fury roared up like gasoline dumped on a fire. She had to do something active, right now. Like blow up his car, maybe. Craig's favorite coffee mug was the first object to present itself, sitting smugly in the sink beside another dirty mug, from which the mystery tart had no doubt sipped her own coffee this morning. Mag flung them both at the wall across the room. Crash, tinkle. The noise relieved her feelings slightly, but this was her own house, and those were her own mugs.

She rummaged under the sink for a garbage bag, muttering under her breath. She was going to delete that lying bastard from her house.

She started with the spare room, which Craig had commandeered as his office. In went his laptop, modem, and mouse, his ergonomic keyboard. Mail, trade magazines, floppy disks and data storage CDs clattered in after it. A sealed box that she found in the back of one of the desk drawers hit the bottom of the bag with a rattling thud. So there. This room was hers once again. Onward.

She dragged the bag into the hall. It had been dumb to start with the heaviest stuff first, but it was too late now. Next stop, hall closet. Costly tailored suits, dress shirts, belts, ties, shoes and loafers. On to the bedroom, to the drawers she'd cleared out for his casual war. His hypoallergenic silicone pillow. His alarm clock. Shaving stuff, his special dental floss. Every item she tossed made her anger burn hotter. Scum.

That was it. Nothing left to dump. She knotted the top of the bag.

It was now too heavy to lift. She had to drag it, bumpity-thud out the door, over the deck, down the stairs, across the narrow, pebbly beach of Parson's Lake. The wooden passage-way that led to her floating dock wobbled perilously as she jerked the stone-heavy thing along.

She heaved it over the edge of the dock with a grunt. Glug, glug, some pitiful bubbles, and down it sank, out of sight. Craig could take a bracing November dip and do a salvage job if he so chose.

She could breathe a bit better now, but she knew from experience that the health benefits of childish, vindictive behavior were very short-term. She'd crash and burn again soon if she didn't stay moving.

Work was the only thing that could save her now. She grabbed her purse, jumped into the car and headed downtown to her office.

Dougie, her receptionist, looked up with startled eyes when she charged through the glass double doors of Callahan Web Weaving. "Wait. Hold on a second. She just walked in the door," he said into the phone. He pushed a button. "Mag?

What are you doing here? I thought you were coming in this afternoon, after you had lunch with—"

"Change of plans," she said crisply. "I have better things to do."

Dougie looked bewildered. "But Craig's on line two. He wants to know why you're late for your lunch date. Says he has to talk to you. Urgently. As soon as possible. A matter of life and death, he says."

Mag rolled her eyes as she marched into her office. "So what else is new, Dougie? Isn't everything that has to do with Craig's precious convenience a matter of life and death?"

Dougie followed her. "He, uh, sounds really flipped out, Mag."

Come to think of it, it would be more classy, dignified, and above all, final if she looked him in the eye while she dumped him. Plus, she could throw the panties bag right into his face if he had the gall to deny it. That would be satisfying. Closure, and all that good stuff.

She smiled reassuringly into Dougie's anxious eyes. "Tell Craig I'm on the way. And after this, don't accept any more calls from him. Don't even bother to take messages. For Craig Caruso, I am in a meeting, for the rest of eternity. Is that clear?"

Dougie blinked through his glasses, owl-like. "You OK, Mag?"

The smile on her face was a warlike mask. "Fine. I'm great, actually. This won't take long. I'm certainly not going to eat with him."

"Want me to order in lunch for you, then? Your usual?"

She hesitated, doubting she'd have much appetite, but poor Dougie was so anxious to help. "Sure, that would be nice." She patted him on the shoulder. "You're a sweetie-pie. I don't deserve you."

"I'll order carrot cake and a double skim latte, too. You're gonna need it," Dougie said, scurrying back to his beeping phone.

Mag checked the mirror inside her coat closet, freshened her lipstick and made sure her coppery red 'do was artfully mussed, not wisping dorkily, as it tended to do if she didn't gel the living bejesus out of it. One should try to look elegant when telling a parasitical user to go to hell and fry. She thought about mascara, and decided against it. She cried easily: when she was hurt, when she was pissed, and today she was both. Putting on mascara was like spitting in the face of the gods.

She slung her purse over her shoulder, intensely conscious of the automatic pistol that shared space with wallet, keys, and lipstick. A gift from Craig. He'd given it to her after she'd gotten mugged months ago. A pointless gift, since she had never been able to bring herself to load the thing and had no license to carry a concealed weapon. Craig had insisted that she keep it in her purse, along with a cartridge of ammunition. *Brrr.*

If she were a different woman, she'd make him regret that. She'd wave it around at him and scare him out of his wits. But that kind of tantrum wasn't her style. Neither were guns. She'd give it back to him today. It was illegal and scary, it made her purse too heavy, and today was all about streamlining, dumping excess baggage.

Emotional feng shui. Sploosh, straight into the lake.

By the time she got to her car, the unseasonably late autumn heat made sweat trickle between her shoulderblades. She felt rumpled, flushed and emotional. Frazzled Working Girl was not the look she wanted for this encounter. Indifferent Ice Queen was more like it. She cranked up the air conditioning to chill down to Ice Queen temperatures and pulled out into traffic, the density of which gave her way too much time to think about what a painful pattern this was in her love life.

Used and shafted by charming jerks. Over and over. She was almost thirty years old, for God's sake. She should be hitting her stride.

Maybe she should get her head shrunk. What a joy. Pick

out the most icky element of her personality, and pay some-one scads of money to help her dwell on it. Bleah. Introspection had never been her thing.

She parked her car outside the newly renovated old build-ing that housed Craig's new studio, and braced herself for the sight of Craig's assistant bouncing up to chirp a cheery greeting. Mandi was her name. Probably dotted the "i" with a heart. Nothing behind those big brown eyes but bubbles and foam. She had long dark hair, too. Fancy that.

There was no one to be seen in the studio. Odd. Maybe Craig and Mandi had been overcome with passion in the office in back. She set her teeth and marched through the place. Her heels clicked loudly on the tile. The silence made the sharp sounds echo and swell.

The door to Craig's office was ajar. She clicked her heels louder. *Go for it. Burn your bridges, Mag, it's what you're best at.* She slapped the door open, sucked in air and opened her mouth to—

She rocked back with a choked gasp.